Ex-Isle

DISCARD

ALSO BY PETER CLINES

Ex-Isle

A Novel

Peter Clines

B \ D \ W \ Y
Broadway Books
New York

Published in the United States by Broadway Books,
an imprint of the Crown Publishing Group,
a division of Penguin Random House LLC, New York.
www.crownpublishing.com

Broadway Books and its logo, B \ D \ W \ Y, are trademarks of
Penguin Random House LLC.

Library of Congress Cataloging-in-Publication Data
Clines, Peter, 1969-
Ex-isle / by Peter Clines. — First edition.
pages ; cm. — (Ex-Heroes ; book 5)
ISBN 978-0-553-41831-6 (softcover) — ISBN 978-0-553-41832-3 (ebook)
1. Zombies—Fiction. 2. Superheroes—Fiction. I. Title.
PS3603.L563E95 2016
813'.6—dc23
2015033148

ISBN 978-0-553-41831-6
eBook ISBN 978-0-553-41832-3

PRINTED IN THE UNITED STATES OF AMERICA

Title page illustration by STILLFX/Shutterstock.com
Cover illustration by Jonathan Bartlett
Series design by Christopher Brand

10 9 8 7 6 5 4 3 2 1

First Edition

Ex-Isle

A Quick Note about Time

THE WORLD ENDED during the summer of 2009.

Sorry you had to find out like this.

When *Ex-Heroes* was first published many years ago, I included enough details to make it pretty clear the story was set in what was then our present.

But, as you may have noticed, the zombie apocalypse didn't actually happen that summer. Which means that in more than a few ways, the characters of *Ex-Heroes* are trapped in the past. Things have progressed for us. For the people of the Mount, though . . . it all came to a halt that summer.

After all these books, the effects of my earlier decision have started to make themselves known in small ways. Barry often laments never knowing how *Lost* ended, but we all know because it ended in May of 2010. The survivors can see a Borders Books just outside the Big Wall at Hollywood and Vine, even though that Borders was shuttered (with so many others) back in April of 2011. There's a Walgreens there if you look today. In the world of *Ex-Heroes*, the United States never got out of Iraq, Scotland never held a vote for independence, and there were no *Hobbit* movies.

So when these oddities show up, please remember that their world hasn't moved forward, even if ours has.

Prologue
NOW

PRETTY MUCH EVERYTHING St. George could see was on fire at this point, including most of the zombies.

The fire had started a block south of the Big Wall about four hours earlier, just before sundown. Nobody knew how. The flames had crawled north across a dozen overgrown lawns that hadn't been watered in five years or rained on in five months. Then they'd climbed a few trees, and a light wind had pushed embers into the houses.

Now three city blocks of inferno lit up the night. The blaze reached for the Big Wall as it looked for more to consume, and the people of the Mount fought back as best they could. Half of them ferried buckets of water out to the flames or beat down the lawns with damp blankets. The other half—and St. George—pulled guard duty, keeping the firefighters safe from the exes.

The zombies—the ex-humans—had first appeared years ago. The undead had overrun cities, then countries, then whole continents. In the space of a year, the population of Earth dropped by more than ninety percent.

The living population, anyway.

Now millions of exes walked the streets of Los Angeles, and hundreds of them stumbled through the flames around the Mount. The *click-click-click* of their teeth meshed with the pop and crackle of burning wood. Sound and movement attracted them. Sound and movement and food.

The one St. George held by the throat pawed at him and clicked its teeth. It flailed at his face and scraped against the black leather of his biker jacket. The dead thing had a better chance of getting through the leather than through St. George's stone-like skin. Two of the ex's gaunt fingers hooked in his long hair but slid free as fast as they'd gotten tangled.

Yellow-orange flames raced across its body, burning away clothes and hair. It could've been a woman once, or a slim man with long hair. Too much of its body had burned for him to be sure. Ex-flesh didn't catch fire easily, dried out from years in the sun, but their hair and clothes could burn. Sometimes, when it did, what little fat they had left became fuel, just like a candle.

St. George flicked his wrist and the ex sailed across the street, its spine wrapping around a parking sign's squared-off steel pole.

Off to his left, two teams of people slapped at the fire with quilted blankets. Others kept the fabric soaked with water from buckets. They smothered the flames a few inches at a time. It was a slow, steady process, perfected after four or five similar fires over the years.

Two more exes lurched toward one of the firefighting teams, and a figure loomed out of the smoke to meet them. Captain John Carter Freedom, leader of the 456th Unbreakables super-soldier platoon, stood just shy of seven feet tall and almost half that wide. The flickering firelight gleamed across his dark scalp. He reached out and grabbed one of them with a gloved hand that covered the zombie's shoulder. A flex of his tree-trunk arm sent the dead woman sprawling. His massive fist came around and shattered the other ex's skull.

St. George grabbed a zombie and flung it back the way it had come. He tossed another one after it. The second one ended up draped in the branches of a burning tree, biting at the air.

A sound brushed against his ears. He'd almost missed it under the crackle of the burning lawns and bushes. He focused on a spot between his shoulder blades, felt an itch, and pushed himself up into the air. His boots went up a foot, then a yard, and then he was twenty feet over the pavement, looking out at the burning buildings and trees.

A mob of ex-humans stumbled and staggered up the street. At least another two hundred of them. Men and women and children, all reduced to dead things with endless appetites.

St. George had been expecting the sounds of the fire and shouting humans to attract the dead. There were probably similar groups closing in from the east and west. He'd expected them much sooner, truth be told.

He went higher. A few hundred feet up the smoke thinned out and he could see for a few miles in every direction.

The city of Los Angeles had been dark for almost five years now, even more so on moonless nights like this one. Downtown was a shadowy hand stretching up toward the starry sky. To the west he could see the black expanse of the Pacific.

The only real light came from below him. The Mount, formerly just a refortified film studio, had expanded out from the studio's original boundaries. Now it was a huge square that stretched over a good chunk of Hollywood. Surrounding it was the Big Wall, shining lights out into the surrounding streets.

The undead filled those streets. Hordes like concert crowds shuffled through the shadows. There were always a few hundred around the Wall, but now four or five times that were closing in, drawn by the flickering firelight and the noises that came with it.

St. George tapped his radio. "Captain? Company's coming. Time to go."

"Freedom to St. George. Copy that, sir. What direction?"

"All of them. Pull everyone back inside the Wall. We've got maybe five minutes."

"St. George," shouted a voice behind him. "Drop's ready."

He flew back to the triple-stacked cars of the Big Wall. People dashed back and forth across the series of platforms that topped the structure. A dozen of them prepped water drops for him—trash cans and tall recycling bins, all doubled up so they wouldn't burst when he lifted them. Usually rainwater filled them, but that went fast in a big fire like this one. The crew had hoses and filled the containers as fast as they could from the weak streams.

The rest of the Wall-walkers, armed with rifles and pistols, watched for exes. Many of them also carried baseball bats, golf clubs, and other blunt instruments. If an ex slipped past the firefighters, the guards made sure the dead didn't get any closer.

St. George dropped down next to a plastic trash barrel. A man with scruffy blond hair yanked his hose away and stuck it into the next container. "Should have another one ready in about two minutes," he told the superhero, gesturing at one of the other barrels.

St. George nodded and worked his fingers underneath the trash barrel. He grabbed the rim with his other hand and heaved. His feet lifted up off the Big Wall and he soared back to the flames, water sloshing out as he went.

A nearby lawn with a medium-sized apple tree burned. He swooped down through the air and shook water out of the barrel. It splattered through the leaves of the tree and smothered most of the fire. He made another pass and dumped the rest of his water across the tall grass. The lawn wasn't out, but it was enough for one of the firefighting teams to leap in with their blankets and pound out the last licks of flame.

A blackened, steaming ex lumbered toward the team. St. George dropped down and slammed it with the barrel. The impact knocked the dead thing back into a gaunt zombie in a charred business suit. Both of them tumbled to the ground.

He flew back to the Wall and swapped his water barrel for

a full one. He could empty all twelve faster than the teams could fill them back up, so he'd drop a few hundred gallons, then keep the exes away from the firefighters until the water team got three or four more refilled. Then the whole cycle would begin again.

He dumped the water across the fire line's right flank. Fifteen gallons crashed down onto an ex, a scrawny teenaged girl with a bloody, mangled shoulder, and slammed it to the ground. He emptied the next two barrels over the roof of one of the burning houses and heard the flames hiss as they fell back. Another fifty gallons of water spread across the house's yard. The last one he sloshed across the left flank, soaking a pair of burning grapefruit trees and the lawn behind them. The fire retreated for a moment, then lunged forward again.

Below him, he saw a pair of firefighters swing a wet blanket down on a patch of flames with a *thump*. Air and dirt blasted out from either side as the fabric struck the ground. They dragged the fabric back into the air and brought it down again. Their feet stomped out the last few licks of fire.

A gust of wind cleared the smoke and St. George saw a trio of exes heading toward the firefighters. The weathered thing in front wore denim shorts and a T-shirt blackened with old blood. He was pretty sure it had been a woman at some point.

When he could, he still tried to identify them. It was important to remember them as victims, not just as a threat. He knew it wasn't a popular view.

He dropped down to smash the exes with the water barrel. As he did, a slim form raced out from behind the fire line and tackled the dead woman, driving it back into the smoke and knocking down the pair of zombies behind it. The ex clawed at the air, unable to comprehend what was happening. The two figures stumbled back a dozen feet before plowing into a shrub. The attacker stepped back and left the ex tangled in the branches.

"Hey," yelled St. George. "You're not supposed to be out here."

The pale-skinned girl looked at him with chalk eyes. "You're not my dad," she called back with mock anger.

"I'm serious. There's a ton of smoke out here."

Madelyn Sorensen, the Corpse Girl, shrugged and looked around at the black-and-gray clouds. "It's not like I need to breathe or anything."

He landed next to her, stomping on a small tongue of flame as he did. "I'm not talking about breathing," he said. "I'm talking about you getting shot because someone thinks they saw an ex moving in the smoke."

Her lips pressed together. She glared at him.

The undead woman dragged itself out of the shrub. Its sightless gaze swiveled past Madelyn to lock onto St. George. Teeth clacked together four times before he slammed the heel of his palm against its forehead. Its skull caved in and the woman's body toppled back into the shrub.

"I'm not an ex," the Corpse Girl muttered.

He stepped past her to stomp on one of the fallen zombies. Its skull collapsed under his heel. "Everyone knows that. But right now there's a lot of noise and a lot of yelling and someone might take a shot before they realize it's you. Since you're not supposed to be out here."

"St. George," yelled a voice behind him. "One minute to barrels."

He glanced over his shoulder at the Big Wall, then back at the pale teenager. "Come on."

"I can help!"

He held out his hand. "Now, Madelyn. Or you can go explain to Captain Freedom why you're outside the Wall."

She sighed and wrapped her cold fingers around his wrist. He returned the grip and launched himself back into the air. She threw her other arm up and held his wrist with both hands.

They flew up to the wall of cars, and he let her drop onto the platform before he landed. Two of the crew members saw chalk skin and flinched back. Water from one of the hoses splashed over the plywood.

"Hey," St. George said. "We can't waste that."

"Right," said the man, with another glance at the Corpse Girl. He shoved the hose back in the barrel. "Sorry. Didn't realize it was her. You."

"Whatever," said Madelyn. She looked at St. George as he hefted the next barrel. "Can I at least help up here?"

St. George turned his head to the man with the hose.

"Yeah, sure," said the man. "We can use another body. Person. Sorry."

St. George nodded and pushed himself back into the air. He soared over the houses and soaked another rooftop on the far side of the fire. They still had a chance of containing it. Last year one had scorched its way through a large chunk of the Sunset Strip, almost sixty buildings, before burning itself out.

He circled back to the Big Wall and saw Freedom punch his way through a quartet of exes that threatened the re-treating firefighters. The giant officer turned, grabbed a pair of outstretched hands, and hurled another dead man back. A fifth stepped forward, and Freedom brought one of his huge fists down on its skull like a hammer. He crushed its skull and turned to a sixth.

St. George dropped the barrel off at the Wall and soared back to the center of the fire line. "Time to go," he said to Sally T. "How are we doing?"

The woman wore a yellow helmet with a red rag tied over her mouth and nose. She'd been a firefighter before the Zom-bocalypse and ended up in charge of the volunteer fire de-partment for the southern half of the Mount. Nobody knew what the T stood for, only that she insisted on it.

"It sucks," she said, raising her voice over the crackle of fire and teeth, "but I think we beat the worst of it." She pointed at a few houses. "We're going to lose those four, and all the trees around them. Don't waste any more water there. But other than that we're looking good."

Her eyes flitted past his shoulder and went wide. He turned and backhanded an ex, shattering its jaw and hurling it back. "What about the grove?"

She shook her head. "Not a chance."

"Dammit." He bit his lip. "What else can I do?"

Sally T shook her head. "Just keep doing what you're doing."

St. George nodded. "Get back to the Wall," he told her and leaped back into the air.

A handful of exes stumbled toward what was left of the fire line's left flank. One of them, a woman, had a burned scalp and wore a smoldering tweed jacket. Another one, he noted with a grim half-smile, had a fireman's coat and helmet. Its face was hidden behind a mask of grime-smeared glass.

He arced down and lashed out with his foot. The kick caught the dead fireman just under the edge of its helmet, lifted it off its feet, and slammed it into a phone pole. The others stopped their advance and turned to him. The click of their teeth was almost a hiss against the noise of the fire.

St. George landed between them and drove his fist into a bearded face coated with dried blood. The face collapsed, then the ex. Another punch put down the dead woman in the tweed coat. He drove his elbow into an ex's chest as it grabbed his arm, feeling the ribs splinter apart. The zombie wobbled for a moment and folded over on itself.

The last one got its mouth on his wrist. It bit down again and again. Each time knocked a few more teeth free of its withered gums when they failed to go through his stone-like skin. Or even scratch it.

He raised his arm and the ex rose up with it, still gnawing on his wrist. He brought his other hand around like an axe and smashed through the spine and the cords of muscle around it. The body dropped. The head managed one more bite before it slipped off his wrist and fell. It looked up at him from the ground, its jaws still gnashing away.

St. George looked around and spotted a trio of exes closing in on a pair of firefighters as they fell back toward the Big Wall. He grabbed the headless body at his feet, pulled back, and hurled it at the three dead people. It spun twice in the air and knocked them to the ground. One fell headfirst into a patch of fire, and the stench of burning hair washed across the street before being overwhelmed by the smoke.

He marched over to the fallen trio and twisted their skulls around until their necks snapped. The teeth kept clicking, but the bodies went limp. He wiped his hands on his jeans, heard a scream, and moved toward it.

Before St. George got there another figure leaped forward. Specialist Kurt Taylor, one of Freedom's men. The one with the shaved head and the mouth. He was another super-soldier from Project Krypton, but an earlier version, not even half as powerful as the captain.

A retreating firefighter had tripped over his equipment, and his two companions tried to untangle him before a pair of exes closed in on them. Taylor shoved both of the exes hard, and as he did something across the back of his hands gleamed in the flickering orange light. A vicious roundhouse punch exploded one zombie's skull. Taylor's other arm swung around, spraying teeth and bone from the other ex across the road.

He glanced back at St. George and grinned. Like most things Taylor did, it didn't seem very nice. He held up his hand and revealed the thick bands of metal across his fingers. "Fucking awesome or what?" he said. "Grade-A zombie dusters, that's what these are."

St. George bit back a frown at the man's glee. "Can't you hit them hard enough already?"

Taylor's face shifted, flitting between three or four emotions before St. George could identify them and then settling back into a sneer. "You can never hit those fuckers too hard."

To emphasize the point, he turned, batted aside the grasping hands of a dead Latina, and drove a punch into its exposed shoulder. The bones sagged and the arm flopped to its side. He crippled the other arm and threw an uppercut that sent a swarm of teeth into the air. His last punch slammed into the ex's forehead and caved in the skull.

Taylor lifted his brass-knuckled fists to the sky and howled. St. George sighed and watched the firefighters stumble away. "Make sure everyone's falling back," he told Taylor, then pushed himself back into the air.

He spotted a small pack of exes shambling toward a last group of firefighters and landed in front of them. He spread his arms wide and walked. A teenaged girl with a trio of arrows in her torso bumped into his shoulder, snapped her teeth at his face, and then staggered back as he kept walking forward. A man in a scorched Yummy Donuts uniform was next, then a brown and black figure that had been burned beyond any kind of identification. St. George kept walking and gathered an elderly woman with an empty eye socket, a half-charred little boy in a baseball shirt, and another blackened corpse. They all stumbled and tripped as he pushed them back, then collapsed in a heap on top of each other. He bent down and twisted their skulls around one by one, listening to the click of teeth and the crack of spinal bones.

Another call for a drop. He flew back to the Big Wall and grabbed a tall blue recycling bin swollen with over fifty gallons of water. He caught a glimpse of Madelyn switching her hose to a new barrel before he soared back into the smoke.

He remembered Sally T's instructions and poured his water over a burning grapefruit tree away from the burning homes. The branches spat and hissed and sputtered, but the flames vanished. So did some on the ground around the tree.

His next drop went onto the roof of one of the salvageable houses, and the third went down its chimney to soak the first floor. The next barrel traced a thick line across the fire's west flank and knocked down two exes, extinguishing one of them. He carried each of the last two barrels back over to the south side of the fire, soaking trees and rooftops and lawns.

A yell echoed behind him, the all-clear. Everyone was back inside the Wall with what sounded like zero casualties. St. George landed and stamped out a few small embers before they could grow on a dry patch of grass. He backhanded an ex as it reached for him. Its jaw crumbled against his knuckles, the skull collapsed, and the dead thing crumbled to the ground.

The flames didn't light up as much of the night as they had half an hour ago. The air didn't smell quite as smoky. He didn't know much about fighting fires, but it seemed like they might have this one under control. "Contained"—that's how Sally T would put it.

He hoped contained was going to be enough, but he was pretty sure it was too late.

St. George launched himself back into the air.

THEN

"IT WAS A disaster," George told me. "A complete disaster."

The fourth-floor room we stood in had once been an executive boardroom. I planned to use it as a base of operations. It was centrally located within the film studio, had an existing fiber-optic net within the walls, and had access to several of the physical resources I would need.

Ambient light from outside lit the room, although at seventeen minutes before sundown this created several shadows as well. A map of the film studio and a larger one of the surrounding area were spread out across the boardroom's oversized table, an ostentatious slab of marble. I also had blueprints and power schematics for several of the major buildings on the lot. I had been assigning new functions to them when George arrived to give a report on the day's rescue activities and began to pace along the opposite side of the table.

George had abandoned several elements of his uniform and taken to wearing a pair of cargo pants over the remaining bodysuit. I believe without the cape and mask, he felt a degree of self-consciousness wearing only such a tight article of clothing. He had ceased use of his chosen code name, the Mighty Dragon, and no longer made any effort to hide his civilian identity. The survivors of Los Angeles seemed to respect him even more for this gesture.

I have no plans to reveal my identity. Stealth is the only name I am known by within the Mount. I see no need for this to change.

The front of his bodysuit had been destroyed. Judging

from the heat and tearing damage at the edges of the area, I believed he had been hit with a 12-gauge at a distance of less than ten feet. He rubbed his exposed chest for the second time since entering my office. The skin was unmarked. Not even a bruise. The light amount of chest hair he had was unsinged.

George's tone and posture told me this was a personal crisis rather than one that required any action on my part. He needed to unburden himself of this supposed "disaster."

I had hoped to finish drawing up plans for a field hospital in one of the other office buildings and also a rudimentary power grid using the distribution systems left behind by various film productions. In the long term, however, it would be counterproductive to interrupt him.

He paced back and forth across from me. "We were going through Hancock Park, picking up survivors," he said. "We'd found three groups. Sixteen people altogether. And then Carter, one of the Marines, she spotted somebody watching us from a third-floor apartment.

"I jumped up to the balcony," said George. "Grabbed hold of the railing. This woman in a sundress was right there, inside the apartment. She looked like she hadn't eaten well in a while. Or showered much. She had a shotgun aimed right at me. I was still getting my balance on the edge, and she started ranting about thieves and rapists and murderers." He stopped to organize his thoughts.

I nodded once in understanding, accenting the movement enough that it would stand out in the low light beneath my hood. "We have encountered such attitudes from other survivors."

"She was the worst I've seen," he said. "She was almost screaming at me. I think she did it a lot, because her cat was barely reacting." He sighed. "I put my hands up, tried to calm her down, and she shot me. Knocked me away from the railing and I fell to the ground."

George paused and rubbed his chest again. "When I jumped back up," he said, "she was just lying there. Half the shotgun pellets had bounced back off my ribs. She'd been hit in the face and throat. I didn't even have time to pick her up and get her to the truck. She bled out on the floor of her apartment." He grabbed a handful of hair in each hand. "She never had a chance."

I allowed him thirty seconds of silence.

"From what you have said," I told him, "your mission was a near-perfect success. Sixteen survivors rescued and brought to the Mount without injuries."

"Someone died. Right in front of me. *Because* of me."

"Millions have died, George. We were not able to save them. In the days to come, there will be many more we will not be able to save."

His lips pressed into a thin line. "But that's the whole point of this. To save everyone we can."

"That is our stated goal, yes," I said, "but the reality is the ex-virus outbreak will continue to claim victims, either directly or indirectly."

"Then why are we even doing this? What's the point?"

"As you said, to save everyone we can. Did you rescue the cat?"

"What?"

For many years it bothered me when others could not follow or keep up with my thought processes. Now I accepted it. One of the rare lessons my father had taught me that did not involve violence. The majority of people do not think like us. "The woman had a cat," I explained to George. "Did you rescue it?"

He nodded. "Yeah, of course. I wasn't going to leave it there to starve."

"Good."

He stared at me. "Are you a cat person?"

George continues to probe for information about my true

identity. At first I mistook this for an indicator of romantic interest. However, while his physical attraction to me is clear, I have since realized these attempts represent an attempt to find common ground. George worries he cannot trust someone about whom he knows nothing or with whom he has little in common.

His tactics are, by traditional standards, somewhat clever. George is much smarter than even he believes. He does not ask where I lived in the city. He talks about nighttime noise levels and invites me to share my own recollections of such issues. He laments the lack of heavy clothing in his wardrobe and asks if I am prepared for a winter without heat— potentially a hint into my origins. He sometimes recalls favorite meals from establishments he frequented and asks if there are any regular dishes I miss, hoping I will name a restaurant near my former home. Rather than ask for facts he knows I will not provide, he seeks the pattern around the facts.

I have considered telling him he is wasting his time. His attempts are quite transparent, and I will not reveal information regarding my identity. It is also clear while he may not trust me to levels that satisfy him, he trusts me enough to carry out my instructions with a minimum of explanation or enticement.

"I see an unprecedented rodent problem in the near future," I told him, "with potential associated health and morale issues. Having cats within the walls of the Mount will decrease those factors and benefit the surviving population long-term."

He stopped most of his sigh.

I turned my attention back to the blueprints of the Zukor Building, located on the opposite side of the parking lot from our current location. It was central enough that it could work as a hospital. "Is there anything else?"

"I guess not."

"You should replace your uniform. Damaged like this, it creates an image of vulnerability you do not want to project at this time."

In my peripheral vision, he looked down at his exposed chest. "Yeah," he said. "Yeah, I should."

"If you have renounced your identity as the Dragon, it may be time to consider functionality over form. I suggest a more durable material. Perhaps leather or Kevlar."

"It'll probably deal with the draft, too."

I raised my head to look at his bare chest. "I was not aware you felt such minor differences in temperature."

"I don't," he said. "It was just a, an attempt at a joke. To lighten the mood."

His eyes stayed on the damaged uniform, but it was clear I was the focus of his attention. Six seconds passed. He waited for some final form of consolation or advice.

A number of ways I could bring the encounter to a close passed through my mind. I discounted several that would have an adverse effect on our dealings in the future. I also discarded several that would take too long.

I stood straight and turned to him. "Twenty-two days ago, on the roof of Hollywood and Highland, you told me you wished to be a symbol of hope. This is the challenge of hope versus fear, George. Fear is a simple, base emotion felt by every mammal, one that requires no rational thought, no logic. It is an easy thing to rule by fear."

He looked up. "I don't want us to be ruling by—"

"It is also," I continued, "an easy thing to be ruled by it. Making decisions based on fear requires no effort. In challenging times, many people prefer such a path. It is easier to be scared of a situation than to make the effort to understand it. Fear provides an excuse to avoid responsibility. Even before the ex-virus, there were many people throughout history who took advantage of this tendency."

His eyes probed my mask as he tried to guess my expression. "There's a lot to be scared of out there."

"There is much to be aware of and cautious of, yes," I said, "but this woman had given in to fear. She had no interest in being rescued. She had found what she thought was a safe, comfortable place to exist with her fear. You challenged that. You put her in a position of having a choice. Of being able to make decisions."

"But she died for nothing," he said. "Even if she thought I was there to rob her, she had a couple cans of cat food and some ramen. She would've made it another two weeks, tops, without us."

I lowered my head. The cloak shifted around me. "She died because she could not face the possibility of change," I told him. "In her mind, it made more sense to shoot her potential rescuer than to risk facing the world as it is without that fear. Had her attempted rescuer been anyone except you, she would have killed him or her, so it could be said you saved a life when this happened."

He sighed. "I guess that's something."

"It is. And every person who hears this story today will know it."

He straightened up and headed for the door. "Okay," he said. "I'm going to get some sleep so we can head out in the morn—"

"George."

He turned to look at me.

"You have given us a better path," I told him. "You can do what I cannot. What Gorgon cannot. You can inspire these people. You can show them hope is a real option. They do not need to live in fear in order to live."

TWO
NOW

ST. GEORGE HUNG in the air and looked down at the Mount.

That name meant a couple of things now. If you were outside the Big Wall, the Mount was everything inside it. If you were inside the Wall, the Mount was their original film studio-turned-fortress, located at the center of the more-or-less square area the citizens of Los Angeles now occupied.

Neither of these definitions took into account being three hundred feet over the ground. Granted, only he and Zzzap ever saw the Mount from this angle. And sometimes Stealth.

Outside the Big Wall, Los Angeles was a ghost town. An empty shell of a city. Buildings stood deserted, many with gaping windows. Cars sat in the road where they'd been abandoned. Tall grass covered La Brea, Sunset, Highland, Western, and Hollywood Boulevard—formerly some of the busiest streets in the area. A baker's dozen of small trees had sprouted along the Hollywood Walk of Fame. One had pushed its way up next to Godzilla's star, right by the Hard Rock Cafe, and stood over twelve feet tall. A long stretch of the Hollywood Freeway had turned into a small oasis, complete with grass, shrubs, and a rainwater pond. Nature had forced its way up through every crack and crevice.

And, of course, there were exes everywhere. Even with the hundreds—maybe even thousands—St. George had destroyed over the past five years, he knew the raw number of zombies hadn't changed much. They lurked in buildings, stumbled down streets, staggered along freeways. Sometimes alone, sometimes in packs, always hungry for the living.

But not inside the Big Wall. Inside, things were safe. Inside, hundreds of solar cells gleamed on rooftops, scavenged from all over the city. People lived more or less normal lives. They had jobs and families and even movies on the weekend.

Inside, you could almost forget the Mount was surrounded by thousands of mindless, merciless eating machines.

Although it seemed like everything was about hunger and eating these days.

He drifted down and south. A huge black scar marked three and a half blocks beyond the Wall. Two gutted houses had collapsed in on themselves. Two others still stood with charred walls and hollow windows. One had burned to the ground and left a brick chimney standing in the ashes, flanked by a few blackened boards.

In one sense, they'd been lucky. Dozens of overgrown lawns and under-watered hedges had survived the flames. If there'd been any wind last night, half the city could've gone up.

In another sense, the fire had really screwed them.

A little lower and he could see Billie Carter waiting for him on the Big Wall. She stood between the South Gate and the southwest tower, right in front of the burned area. Her head tilted up from her binoculars as he descended. "I'm double-checking just to be sure," she told him, "but it looks like we lost the whole grove and another twenty-three trees past that."

"Dammit," muttered St. George.

"Sorry."

"Are they definitely dead? Not just ... I don't know, scorched or something?"

She nodded. "All burned black and dead." She held out the binoculars. "Want to see? Half the grove is just ash."

He shook his head and pressed his lips into a flat line. The Larchmont area south of the Big Wall had been lots of high-end, suburban homes before the Zombocalypse. More than a few of them had fruit trees, either out front or hidden in their back lawns. Apples, grapefruits, lemons, even a set of twin fig trees. One spacious backyard had turned into a small grove of fourteen orange trees gathered around a koi pond. With the year-round growing season in Los Angeles, it had been one of the Mount's few dependable sources of food.

Had been now being the key phrase.

"Dammit," St. George said again. "This does not help things."

Billie's stomach grumbled. "No kidding."

He managed a brief smile. "We've got to get Eden going now. Right now."

"It's not ready," said Billie. "I was talking with Al the other day. They've got the fences extended, but that's it."

"I know," he said. "I've been up there moving a couple dozen cars around for them. But we don't have a choice."

"Yeah, everyone's still whining about only getting two meals a day."

"Still better than no meals a day," said St. George, "and that's where we'll be in a month or two if Eden isn't up and running."

"Speaking of which . . ."

"Yeah?"

"I think there need to be more scavengers up at Eden."

"So you've said a couple times now."

"They've got twelve, but think how many more houses they could be going through if we sent up a full team of twenty. Or both teams. They could be pulling in three or four times more supplies than we've been getting here in Hollywood. And we need that after this." She gestured out at the blackened buildings.

"I know," he said, "but Eden's only got space and resources for so many people. More scavengers mean less people actually working up there."

Billie's jaw shifted back and forth as she ground her teeth. "They'd be working."

"You know what I mean. Right now the priority has to be getting Eden up and running. It's a continuous source of food."

"Or," she said, "we could finally hit downtown."

They both looked to the east. The distant buildings gleamed in the sunlight. Canyons of steel and concrete choked with dead vehicles and undead people.

The scavengers had made one attempt to conquer downtown, almost four years ago. It ended in near-disaster as almost a thousand exes had surrounded and immobilized their truck. St. George had been forced to airlift the scavengers away one by one—a brutally long process in the days before he'd mastered flight. Billie had been the second-to-last person out. The truck was still down there, another dead thing on 3rd Street.

"I know the idea of working a garden doesn't thrill you," he said, shaking his head, "but we both know it's a better option than downtown."

Billie gave him a tight grin. Her jaw worked back and forth again. St. George wondered how busy she kept the last two dentists in Los Angeles. He'd never met either of them himself. Not professionally, anyway. His nigh-invulnerability extended to his teeth.

"I'd still like to give it a try someday," she said.

He bit back a grin of his own. Only a Marine would be excited about leading a mission into hell. "If we don't all starve in the next few months," he said, "we'll talk about it."

Billie perked up. "I'll hold you to that," she said.

"I've got to go check in with Danielle and then Freedom." He waved his hand at the blackened streets. "If you spot anything positive out there, let me know."

"I'm positive I saw a couple crispy exes staggering around."

St. George gave her a loose salute and pushed himself back

up into the air. He spun twice, got his bearings, and let his flight become a slow arc to the north. His gaze drifted west as he did. The air quality in LA was really amazing these days. No haze, no smog. He could see for miles.

Zzzap had been gone for two days now. For the past few months they'd been trying to reestablish contact with the rest of the world. Before civilization had taken its last wheezing step and collapsed, there'd been stories about other safe zones. Pockets of survivors were scattered throughout Europe and Africa, one or two in South America, and a large group in Japan. That's where he was now.

Zzzap could make it around the world in twelve hours. Less if he went suborbital. And in his energy form he could see almost all types of electrical activity, provided it wasn't shielded somehow. It made him the perfect person to search for other groups and serve as an impromptu ambassador.

It was strange not having him around, though. Even expanded out to fill a square mile, the Mount was still a small place. Over the past few years, St. George had grown used to seeing people every day.

He turned his head and mind back to his destination. He shot higher into the air, looped around in a wide arc, and plummeted back toward the ground. The wind dragged his hair back and his collar snapped like a whip.

A year earlier, a mind-controlling villain had trapped St. George and the other heroes in a sort of group hallucination—a waking nightmare where most of their powers were gone and the Mount had fallen. He hadn't been able to breathe fire. Or fly.

The not-flying had bothered him the most. To the best of his knowledge, only five or six superheroes in the world had ever been able to fly. Really fly, not just jump or glide.

Somehow, he'd almost been taking it for granted.

In the months since escaping the dream world, St. George

found himself enjoying flights much more. Taking joy in the fact he could soar through the air on nothing more than willpower. He did loops and barrel rolls and once or twice used the excuse of maneuvering exercises to pretend he was dodging missiles and streams of bullets.

The children of the Mount loved it.

He looped around the studio water tower, back past the Roddenberry Building, and then dropped to the ground in front of a large building with a hangar-sized door.

For the past few years Danielle Morris had lived and worked here, in what had once been an old scene shop, back when the Mount was in the business of sitcoms and *Star Trek* shows. She'd blocked off a small section with curtains where she kept what amounted to a sparse studio apartment. The rest of the warehouse-sized space was her workshop, an area devoted to the care and maintenance of her greatest creation, the Cerberus Battle Armor System.

In the months since St. George had been forced to destroy the battlesuit, the workshop had been all about building a new one. Danielle had salvaged motors, wiring, subprocessors, and other components from the original Cerberus battlesuit. What she couldn't salvage, she'd earmarked for raw materials. She worked all the time and rarely left the workshop. In fact, St. George couldn't remember seeing her outside since then.

Several tables in the big space had been pushed together. Various parts sat in a rough outline matching the battlesuit. On reflection, he thought it looked like an autopsy in progress.

Danielle hid behind a welding mask and heavy gloves. Sparks cracked and leaped around her hands while she worked on the battlesuit's torso. The welding torch moved to a new spot, and the sparks began again.

Two tables over, Thomas Gibbs worked on a laptop

plugged into one of the huge mechanical hands. His hair had grown out into a mess of brown curls. Gibbs was an Air Force lieutenant who'd trained to pilot the Cerberus armor back when he was at Project Krypton. He'd been helping Danielle with the Mark II suit. His head came up and gave St. George a nod, but their eyes never met. The lieutenant's knuckles rapped hard on the table three times.

Danielle looked up from her welding, then saw St. George framed in the door. She pushed her mask up and revealed her freckled cheeks and wisps of red hair. "What's up?"

"Just checking in."

She gestured at the framework in front of her with a gloved hand. "You want a progress report?"

"No," he said. "I meant in the sense of just saying hi."

"Oh." She looked down at the steel ribs and back up at St. George. Then she reached back and twisted the knobs on the welding tanks. "Hi."

"Haven't talked to you in a couple of days."

She shrugged. "You've been busy up at Eden pushing cars around."

"Yeah, sorry. You doing okay?"

Danielle pulled the welding mask off, and a messy ponytail fell behind her shoulders. "I'll feel better once it's together." She tried to pull her arms across her chest and fumbled with the bulky mask. She shifted it in her hands, then set it down on top of the torso.

They looked at each other.

"So," said St. George, "what've you been up to?"

She waved a hand at the skeletal battlesuit again. "Work."

"Nothing else?"

"Not really."

"Seen any movies?"

She shook her head. "No. Barry's been gone all the time, flying around the world."

"Ahhhh." A moment passed between them, and he nodded at the metal ribs. "So, when do you think you're going to have it up and running?"

Danielle's shoulders relaxed a bit. "All the core elements are functioning now," she said, her voice a little bolder. "We assembled the frame and did a test last week. I just walked around the shop. The balance isn't quite right because there's nothing on it, but it worked. I'm hoping to have the outer shell and the armor plating done in the next six weeks or so."

"Sooner the better," said St. George. "We're going to have to get Eden up and running a lot sooner than we thought. We'll need you."

She frowned. "How much sooner?"

"Two or three days. Friday at the latest."

Gibbs snorted but still didn't look up.

Danielle stared at him. Her shoulders hunched back up. "Two or three days? I thought I had another two months."

"The fire wiped out pretty much all the trees in Larchmont," he said. "We've gone from being really tight on food to officially not having enough food. We need to have people in Eden now."

She looked at the torso. "Well," she said, "it all depends on Barry."

St. George glanced up at the banks of lights, then down at some of the cables stretched across the floor. "You don't have enough power?"

"Not enough heat. He's a walking forge when he's Zzzap. Well, a floating one."

"Score another point for superpowers," said St. George. He looked around the workshop. "Speaking of which, where's Cesar?"

Danielle shrugged. "He's out at the scavenger warehouse getting us some supplies."

"And lunch," said Gibbs without looking up from his computer. "Assuming there's still food."

"You might want to savor it when he gets back," said St. George, "just in case."

Cesar Mendoza had been a member of the South Seventeens gang who'd taken refuge in the Mount years ago with his family. At the time he'd been a scrawny young man barely out of his teens and always wearing a pair of driving gloves. He'd held off revealing his superhuman abilities for almost a year after joining the Mount. Being able to merge with vehicles and control them had seemed like an all-but-worthless ability in post-apocalypse Los Angeles. Then Cesar realized he could possess the Cerberus armor and use it better than any pilot. Danielle had grudgingly accepted him onto her team.

Lieutenant Gibbs walked over with his laptop. A low *whisssk*, like a steel brush on oily stone, whispered up from the floor with every other step. "Still can't keep power steady to the left hand," he said to Danielle.

"A short?"

"Maybe." He rattled off a bunch of technical terms St. George didn't understand. Danielle pointed at the screen and fired back with a few terms of her own. The air between them became a swarm of electronic- and engineering-speak.

Then the swarm scattered, Gibbs nodded, and he walked away with his whispery steps. St. George glanced down. He tried not to stare, but he felt a twinge whenever he saw the man's foot.

The lieutenant had been the last person to wear the original Cerberus armor. His mind had been under someone else's control and he'd attacked St. George, damaging a dozen buildings across the Mount in the process. And then Zzzap had blasted off one of the battlesuit's feet and a good part of the calf. Gibbs's own foot had been incinerated in the process, cauterized right through the ankle. Doc Connolly had to remove what was left and an inch of the leg itself to make a clean stump.

Gibbs had hobbled around the Mount with a crutch for three months and made a point of avoiding all the heroes. It took that long for Danielle to burn through most of her anger and resentment at the loss of the battlesuit.

She built him a new foot as a peace offering. It was purely mechanical, a steampunk thing made of steel and brass and a collection of gears Cesar had found for her. The joints worked off pressure and counterweight and movement. Gibbs could walk again with a faint limp, and they'd never spoken of his part in the armor's destruction.

St. George looked away from the foot and found Danielle watching him. "It wasn't your fault," she told him.

"I know."

"No, you don't," she said, "but maybe someday you'll listen to one of us."

He coughed. "So, going good, overall?"

She shook her head, then nodded. "Yeah. The original Cerberus was a prototype suit. It was made for easy use and assembly in demonstrations, not so much active duty. There's about a dozen things we would've done differently, and I'm trying to implement as many of them as possible."

"Like?"

"The Mark Two's going to be about fifteen percent stronger, if my numbers are right. Grip strength is up almost twenty." She tapped the torso section in front of her. "I've increased the range of motion in the wrists, shoulders, and hips, too."

St. George couldn't see the changes, but he nodded. He saw a component he recognized, one of the rotating arm mounts she'd built out at Project Krypton, and pointed at it. "Still using those?"

Danielle's mouth curled into a tight smile. "So," she said, "problem. At this point, both of the armor's M2s are ruined.

We've got replacement barrels, but one of the guns would need its threads recut to get the barrel on, and the bolt group's ruined on the other one. We've got one replacement, but they've got it mounted on the East Gate watchtower."

"And there's only six hundred rounds left for it anyway," added Gibbs.

St. George remembered the days of cheering when they'd find a box of shotgun shells. "Isn't that a lot?"

"For a pistol or a rifle it's not bad," Danielle said, "but for Ma Deuce it's about a minute of firing time. Cerberus needs a new ranged weapon."

"Okay."

She waved him around to one of the worktables. One of the arms was there, held up in brackets. A few cables ran from the shoulder joint across the table. "Thing is, we're not swimming in any type of ammunition. So I've tried to come up with something else. I played with a few railgun models for a while, but every shot would eat up at least sixteen percent of the armor's battery life to get anything to an even halfway decent velocity."

"I'll take your word for it," said St. George.

Danielle shrugged off her flannel shirt to reveal the black spandex bodysuit studded with metal contacts. It had been years since St. George had seen her without it. It wouldn't surprise him if she slept in it. He wasn't sure if she had more than one or if she rinsed it every other night.

She settled in next to the table and slid her right arm into the framework. It blended in with the metal and wires. "Then it struck me I was going about this all wrong," she said. "I kept trying to solve it in a high-tech way, and that means precision ammunition or lots of power. What if I did something low-tech instead?"

She nodded over at Gibbs, and he tapped a few keys on the laptop. Several elements in the framework arm lit up. Tiny sparks danced at all the contact points along the bodysuit's sleeve.

The battlesuit arm lifted its forearm out of the brackets. Danielle looked lopsided with the one massive arm. She flexed the fingers a few times and relaxed. Without the insulation and armor muffling it, the hum of the joints seemed closer to a squeal.

She shot a grin at St. George, then nodded across the room. "See that sheet of plywood?"

At the far end of the workshop, about twenty yards away, the oversized panel was propped up with some of the wooden jacks that had once held scenery in place. SW PLAT 2 had been stenciled on it. At least a dozen ragged holes had been punched in the target, each one the size of a golf ball.

Danielle turned her attention back to the battlesuit's dissected arm. Servos hissed as she wrapped the steel fingers into a ball. The fist pulled back to her shoulder, like the first step in a salute, and something clacked inside the arm. St. George ran his eyes across the different struts and cables, but couldn't spot the source of the sound.

The arm straightened out with a clicking, ratcheting noise. The clicks became twangs and then pings as it slowed to a stop. The sounds of tension. Danielle adjusted the arm, aiming it at the plywood. "I think that's good," she said to Gibbs.

"Three," he said, "two, one." He tapped a button on the laptop, something clicked in the battlesuit's arm, and St. George heard a quick noise like a guitar string being plucked and muffled.

Something smashed into SW PLAT 2 with the sound of metal on concrete. The target rocked on its stands and then came to rest. A fresh hole had appeared at shoulder height.

Danielle's lips formed a tight grin.

"Nice shot," said Gibbs.

St. George walked toward the plywood. "So what the heck is that?"

"I wanted to call it a slingshot," she said, "but Gibbs pointed out it's a lot closer to a repeating crossbow."

"A cross-shot?"

"Yeah," said Danielle, shaking her head, "I'm not calling it that."

"Sling bow?"

"Sounds like an indie film," Gibbs said.

St. George reached the target and poked a finger through the hole.

"By my math," she said, "it hits about four hundred and forty miles per hour. That's double what an arrow can do from a compound bow but about half the velocity of your average pistol round. And it tumbles a lot, which is okay at close range but sucks as it gets farther out. It's got a range of about thirty yards before the aim turns to crap."

"That's not bad."

"It's not great, either." Danielle tapped her forehead. "The whole reason the bullet in the head works with exes is because the hydrostatic shock from a rifle round turns the brain to jelly. A pistol round bounces around inside the skull two or three times."

"And turns the brain to jelly," added Gibbs.

"Don't some people survive getting shot in the head, though?"

Danielle nodded. "And so do exes, every now and then. Or they keep moving, anyway. But head shots are still the best bet, so that's what I'm basing this around. And right now, this isn't fast or powerful enough to take care of that." She crossed her arms again. "I just need to figure out something that'll go in a streamlined magazine, be light enough to give us decent range, but still strong enough to punch through a skull."

St. George shrugged. "What about nails? Like a super nail gun or something."

"Sounds good on the surface," Gibbs said, "but how many stories have you heard about someone who survived with a nail in their head?"

St. George nodded. "Ahhh. Anyway, I need to go talk with Freedom, and I should let you get back to wo—"

"Hey," called a voice. "St. George. How you doing, man?"

He turned. "Hey, Cesar." The young man had filled out in the arms and chest, but St. George still thought of him as a kid. Probably because of the wispy beard and mustache Cesar kept trying to grow.

He still wore his driving gloves. They hid a series of long scars stretching across the palms of both hands. One time, while "driving" a getaway car, he'd hit a spike strip. The car's tires had been ripped to shreds, and when Cesar phased out of the vehicle he discovered his hands and feet had been slashed, too. It'd been a lesson not to be too reckless with his powers.

Cesar set a canvas bag on the counter. "We got lunch," he said. "You want some? There's plenty. I can share."

Gibbs pulled at the lip of the bag. "What'd you get for our last meal?"

"Our what? Stir fry."

"Again?"

Cesar shook his head. "Bro, there's three people in the whole Mount who make food to go. You want something else, open your own taco stand or something."

"I've got to get going," said St. George. He pushed himself off the ground and drifted backward through the door. "I'll stop by when I get back. We'll . . . have lunch and hang out for a while or something."

Danielle tugged her welding gloves back on. "Sure," she said with a nod. "Lunch."

"I want to hang out and have lunch," said Cesar.

Danielle waved the welding torch at him.

St. George spun in the air and sailed up into the sky. He rose above the buildings, turned once to get his bearings, and headed north toward the Corner. The sun was already low in the west. The day was already gone and he'd barely done anything.

Just as he remembered it was still morning, the sun roared toward him out of the west and came to a halt in the sky. It was shaped like a man. The brilliant silhouette crackled as it hung in the air in front of him.

George!

"Hey," he said. "I wasn't sure when you were due back."

The wraith shook his head and pointed behind himself. *You're never going to guess what I found back there.*

"In Santa Monica?"

Out in the Pacific. I mean, we're superheroes in the middle of a zombie apocalypse and this is still really frakkin' cool.

THREE

NOW

"IT'S AN ISLAND," said Barry. "A man-made island. Right around here." He spun his finger in a circle somewhere in the mid-Pacific.

Captain Freedom peered down at the map spread across the desk. St. George leaned in and almost bumped heads with the mayor. "Sorry," he said.

"My fault," said Richard. He was a short man with a beard he tried to keep neat and professional, but it kept getting away from him. He shuffled his feet a bit. Even after all his time running the Mount, even here in his own office, he was still timid around the heroes. Especially Stealth, who stood on the other side of the table, surrounded by her cloak.

Of course, most people were timid around Stealth. She still insisted on wearing her full uniform. Even people who didn't know what she was capable of found the black, eyeless mask unnerving.

It also didn't help that it had been her office for many years. Blinds had kept it shrouded in perpetual gloom, but now it was bright and well lit. The marble slab serving as the mayor's desk had been her war table. Richard's assistant, Todd, had even found some potted plants and a few generic paintings to give it some life.

The room was very different now . . . but to St. George, it still felt like her room.

Barry's wheelchair had been pushed back into the corner to make more space around the table. He balanced on the edge of the desk and shoveled food into his mouth. His bowl held scrambled eggs, half a dozen random vegetables, and a good-sized helping of the "goat cheese" that came out of the Corner. Everyone just called it goat cheese rather than wondering where it might've really come from.

St. George looked at his friend. Barry still got double rations, but it wasn't enough. Zzzap burned up more than he took in each day. Not by much, but the cumulative effect was starting to show. He'd always been thin, but recently his appearance leaned toward gaunt, and his dark skin looked ashy. Barry caught his eye, winked, and scraped up another spoonful of egg and veggies.

"Are you certain?" asked Stealth.

Barry looked at her blank mask. "There's a man-made island out there? Yeah, of course."

"Of the location."

"Oh." He swallowed another mouthful of food. "Pretty sure, yeah. I mean, there aren't any landmarks. I'm going off magnetic flux lines in the atmosphere. It's maybe seventeen or eighteen hundred miles from here, south-southwest. I saw the magnetic signature on the water from a few miles away and doubled back to check it out."

Richard looked up from the map. "Magnetic signature?"

Barry's bald head went up and down. "It's a huge chunk of metal, so it makes ripples in the Earth's magnetic field. Nothing huge. It stood out because it was in the middle of the ocean on top of the water."

St. George drummed his fingers on the edge of the map. "What's it like, this island? Is it a lot of boats or rafts or what?"

Barry set down his bowl, swept up a legal pad and a pen, and began to sketch quick outlines. "Boats," he said. "It's kind of like *Waterworld*. But, y'know, believable. Or maybe the Drexel colony."

"The Drexel what?" asked St. George.

"Yeah," Barry said. "When I was six I saw *The Empire Strikes*

Back. That's what turned me into a real sci-fi nut. My cousin Randy, he gave me this big pile of *Star Wars* comics he'd kinda grown out of and didn't want anymore. A bunch of the old Marvel ones. I don't think he had any idea what they were worth. I mean, I didn't either, but I was six."

Stealth flexed her fingers. "Is there a point to this story?"

He nodded again, with even more enthusiasm. "In one of the early story arcs Luke ends up on this planet, Drexel, that's all water. But there are a bunch of old wooden ships that've been lashed together to make a big floating island, and the colonists who live there are in this ongoing war with people who ride sea dragons. And Luke has to figure out—"

"Sea dragons?" Richard interrupted.

"Yeah."

"In *Star Wars* stories?"

Barry smiled. "I know, cool, right?"

"If the planet was all water," asked St. George, "where'd the wooden ships come from?"

"Huh." Barry's smile faltered. His pen tapped against the notepad. "Y'know, I never thought about that as a kid. It wouldn't be cost-effective to bring them there from another planet, would it?"

"If we could return to the matter at hand," said Stealth. "The layout of this island?"

"Right." Barry scratched at his diagram again with the pen. "There's a cruise ship here in the center," he said, tapping at the sketches. "Like the mountain in the middle of Skull Island. Then there's an oil tanker and a freighter on either side of it, both facing the other way. The freighter has a bunch of shipping containers, but it looked like they've all been emptied out." He circled part of his diagram, looked at them, and shrugged.

"How large are the ships?"

He closed his eyes. "I'd put the cruise ship around . . . nine hundred feet, maybe? The tanker and the freighter were both longer, but they sat a lot lower in the water."

Stealth's mask shifted beneath her hood.

"Thoughts?" asked St. George.

"Possibly a Panamax tanker, if Barry's size estimate is correct. Although it would be unusual for one to be so far out in the Pacific."

She said nothing else. Everyone's attention drifted back to Barry. He finished some new additions to the diagram and sat back up on the desk's corner. St. George offered an arm for balance, but Barry waved it away and leaned into the sketch again.

"Okay," he said, pointing with the pen, "if I remember right, here and here are fishing boats. Or maybe some kind of oceanographic research. Greenpeace or something. Definitely some kind of business-work boat. These three are yachts. Really big, expensive-looking things. And then there's a half dozen or so little boats around the edges. Smaller fishing boats, things like that. I think one of them might've been a tugboat."

St. George glanced at him. "Out in the middle of the ocean?"

Barry shrugged. "It could've been a banana boat for all I know. I'm just saying what it looked like. And over here"—he tapped one side of the sketch—"was one of those boats where it's two narrow hulls with a platform between them."

"A catamaran," said Stealth. "How are they all connected?"

"Ropes. Chains in a few places. There's something between them, keeping the boats from hitting each other too hard. Maybe tires?"

A frown crossed Captain Freedom's face. "Tires?"

Barry shrugged. "A bunch of round, nonconductive, and slightly magnetic objects, two or three degrees warmer than the water." He tapped his temple by his eyes. "They looked like tires to me."

"Where would they get tires in the middle of the ocean?"

"Automobile tires are manufactured worldwide," Stealth said. "It is not difficult to believe a container ship would have at least one load of custom tires onboard."

Richard tugged his tie straight. "People?"

Barry plucked a mushroom out of his bowl and swallowed it. "Not sure. A couple hundred? Six, maybe seven hundred, tops. Some of them were down belowdecks, and all the metal and water kind of screws with my vision."

"Jesus," said St. George. "Six hundred people just sitting out there."

"If infected crew or passengers were contained," Stealth said, "the survivors would be in an extremely safe position. Provided they could balance resources."

"It looks like the freighter deck was turned into a garden," said Barry. He used the pen to point at the diagram. "From about here to here." He drew a dotted rectangle inside the ship's outline. "Some of the tanker, too."

"A lot bigger than what we started out with," St. George said, "and we had five times more people."

"A garden with soil?" asked Stealth. "It is not a hydroponics farm?"

"Nope," Barry said. "It looks like they just spread about two feet of dirt across the deck and went at it. I think I saw potatoes and something green. Maybe cucumbers. Or carrots. I didn't get close enough to be sure."

St. George looked at Stealth. He knew the shifting surface of her mask well enough to know she was staring at the sketch. "Something wrong with that?"

"As the captain stated, they are in the middle of the ocean," she said. "Assuming this was a modern container ship in 2009 with standard deck size, where did these people get over fifty-seven thousand cubic feet of soil?"

"Maybe it was in the storage containers, too?" suggested Richard.

"It is unlikely a merchant paid to ship high volumes of soil from Asia to North America," she said.

"Maybe they stopped at an island?" St. George said.

"The configuration Barry describes would not be mobile."

"The individual ships would be, though," said Freedom. "They could've sent someone off to get dirt."

Stealth's head shifted inside her hood. "Based on these ship descriptions, that would require multiple trips. Such a project would require a great deal of fuel and a sizable work-force."

"They've got people," said St. George.

"And an oil tanker," added Richard.

Barry shook his head. "I'm not sure raw crude would work as fuel, even in a diesel engine. I think it'd need some refining."

"Which would require more work and resources," said Stealth. "Were you lost?"

"Say what?" Barry asked.

She pushed the diagram aside and drew a line across the map with her finger. "A return flight from Hokkaido should not have taken you anywhere near this area. How did you end up there?"

"Oh," said Barry. "Well, I was flying back and I realized I'd never seen Easter Island. You know, with the big stone heads."

"They are called *moai*," she said.

"Right. So I headed down that way and looked around, but I couldn't find it. So I headed back up to come home and that's when I saw Waterworld."

Stealth didn't respond. Her head bowed to the map and diagram again. She crossed her arms.

"Any sign of exes?" asked St. George.

Barry shook his head. "Couldn't see anything. Like I said,

it's tough seeing all the way into the ships, but the decks didn't seem to have any defenses set up, and most of the hatches were open."

"So the island's clean?"

"As near as I could tell. Also worth mentioning I didn't see any electricity. No engines, no generators—they're just drifting out there."

"How did they react to you?" Stealth asked.

"Actually," said Barry, "they didn't. I didn't see anyone looking right at me. It almost felt like a couple of them were trying not to look at me."

"Too bright?" asked St. George.

Barry shrugged again. "Beats me."

"Odd," said Freedom.

"I know, right?"

They all looked at the map and the diagram.

"So," said Richard, "the big question. What now?" He looked at St. George.

St. George nodded. "We should head out there," he said. "Offer assistance or a safe port, I guess. Whatever they might need."

Freedom cleared his throat. "Should we do this right now? We're tight on resources as is, and if we need to accelerate the Eden project we're going to need to focus our efforts there."

"If we don't do it soon," said Barry, "there's a chance we might not be able to find them again. Not for a while, anyway. The whole thing's drifting in the currents out there. A month from now it could be almost anywhere in the Pacific."

"It's just like contacting Japan," said St. George. "We need to let them know they're not alone. Give them some hope."

"A noble sentiment," said Stealth, "but also our only possible offer at this time. We have no access to any form of watercraft. For the moment, our ability to offer aid is limited."

"I can get to a boat with no problem," St. George pointed out.

"But for a crew and a truck with supplies," she said, "it would take the better part of two days. That is time and resources we currently do not have." She waved a hand at the map. "This should be treated like any of our other attempts to make contact with survivors. First we must ascertain if this group is in need of help and if it is willing to accept it."

"I can fly back out there and talk to them," said Barry.

"If you'll forgive me for saying," Richard said, "when you're all light and electricity you can be a bit hard to understand. No offense."

Barry smirked. "None taken."

"It's not that far offshore," said St. George. "I mean, it's closer than Hawaii. We could both fly out there. Seeing another physical person could be a good thing."

"I can go physical," Barry said.

"You can go naked and vulnerable," Freedom said.

"Hey, some people like that."

"Richard's right," St. George said. "It's better if you don't make contact alone. This could be a real scary moment for some people if they've gotten used to their world. I could bring a backpack, maybe offer them a few goodwill tokens, that sort of thing. There's got to be something useful we've got extras of." He glanced at the huge captain. "I could bring one of Freedom's beacons so Barry can find them again later."

"It would take you almost two days to cover such a distance," said Stealth.

"I could do it."

"Where would you sleep? You would be in the middle of the ocean, hundreds of miles from shore."

"I could . . . I could bring a raft or something."

Her face shifted beneath her mask. St. George recognized the movements of her lips and cheekbones. "The more important issue," she said, "is Eden. After last night's fire, it must be our priority."

"Agreed," said Richard. He looked up at Freedom. "How secure is it at this point, Captain? Can we start sending people up there?"

The giant tipped his head once. "The main building is secure, sir, and the existing fence line there is intact. St. George has helped us expand and reinforce several key sections, but there's still a few areas that aren't as solid as I'd like. The watchtowers and gates still need some work, too. Overall, though, I think it could be occupied without compromising anyone inside."

"There is another issue," said Stealth. She turned to St. George. "You and Zzzap are the only two capable of rapid travel between the Mount and Eden. If both of you go to this island, we will have no emergency response team."

"We could send extra guards up there," St. George said.

The cloaked woman bowed her head beneath her hood. "Extra guards means less personnel working in Eden itself."

"Only for a week or so," said Barry.

Richard rubbed his temple. "I'm not sure we can spare a week of manpower with the current state of our food supply." He looked at Stealth. "Without a summer harvest from the trees we only have enough left for, what, two months?"

"Forty-three days," she said, "if we continue at our current level of rationing."

"We could swap out the assigned guards for my soldiers," said Freedom. "Each one of the Unbreakables is worth at least three regular guards. That effectively triples the manpower up there without using any extra resources."

Stealth's expression shifted beneath her mask, and St. George felt his own mouth tighten. The super-soldiers from Project Krypton had become a standard part of the Big Wall's defense forces. They were a big part of why the Big Wall had never failed.

Freedom acknowledged the looks with a deliberate nod. "First Sergeant Kennedy's been considering something along these lines anyway. She wanted to take a fire team up there and put them through their paces. Some of them have been getting a little . . . lax."

St. George thought of Taylor gleefully punching exes with his brass knuckles and thought "lax" was a polite way of putting it.

"It's still not much up there for defense, though," said Richard, "especially if the fences aren't one hundred percent yet."

"What about Cerberus?" asked Freedom. "How much longer until Dr. Morris has it rebuilt?"

St. George shook his head. "I just talked to her about it this morning. She's still at least six weeks away from having it finished. The basic framework's done, but it doesn't even have any armor or weapons yet."

"So right now it's a high-tech vulnerability suit," Barry said.

"Pretty much, yeah."

Richard sighed. "Perhaps we should put off going out to this island. Just until we can get Eden established and Cerberus up and running."

"We'll lose it," said Barry.

"But you'd be able to find it again eventually," said Freedom.

Barry shrugged. "Yeah. I could track some of the currents and stuff but . . . well, we are talking about the Pacific Ocean. It took me the better part of the day to find Hawaii once, and I knew where to look for it. And it was glowing."

Stealth crossed her arms beneath her cloak. "There may," she said, "be another option open to us."

FOUR

NOW

"NO," SAID DANIELLE. "No, absolutely not. No."

Stealth crossed her arms. "It is the best solution to our problem."

"No, it's a crap solution." The redhead gestured at the frame stretched out across three worktables in front of them. "There's no armor at all, not even dust shields. No padding or supports, either. Assuming whoever was in it didn't get bitten by the first thing they ran into, an hour in this would rip them up."

"Danielle . . ." started St. George.

She pulled up her sleeve and pointed at a line of tight stitches in the contact suit, then at a thin scab along her thumb. "See that? I cut myself last week just doing a few test shots with the auto-crossbow. Cut my thumb putting my arm in and then sliced the suit while I was cocking it. There's a hundred points like that all over the superstructure." She reached out and tapped one of the support struts on the arm. It rang.

"We are not discussing someone wearing the battlesuit, though," said Stealth. She gestured over at Cesar. "We are discussing someone being in it."

Cesar bounced on his toes. He tried to keep his face blank. Everyone saw the smile creeping up across his tight lips.

St. George nodded. "It won't matter that there's rough edges or no armor because he'll just *be* the battlesuit. Right?"

A barely restrained nod from Cesar.

Danielle shook her head again. "Nothing's protected. If the suit's walking around like this it'll be getting dust and grit into everything. It'd be like driving a car without the air filter."

St. George glanced at the bare struts of the torso, then back at Danielle. "We're talking about a week, tops."

"George, doing it for a day could ruin some of the components. Do you think I have Cesar sweep in here all the time to keep him busy?"

"Yeah," said Cesar. His smile cracked. "Wait, you mean that was important?"

Her fingers tightened into fists. "And you want to send him up there in charge of the battlesuit?"

"Eden is our highest priority," said Stealth, "and you have yet to offer an alternative solution."

"Just let me finish the armor. Five weeks. Four if Barry sticks around. Then you can all go off to this boat-island place."

"We might not be able to find it in four or five weeks," St. George said. Danielle put her hands on the table and lowered her head. Her ponytail slipped over her shoulder and hung against her cheek. She muttered something under her breath.

"What was that?"

She straightened up and threw her hair back over her shoulder with a toss of her head. "I'll go with the suit. With Cesar. We'll be together up in Eden." His smile returned, and she shot it down with a look. "That way I can keep working on it and do maintenance."

St. George wrinkled his brow. "How much can you really do in a week?"

"Depends on how much he damages it in a week," she said, jerking her head at Cesar.

"I'm serious," said the hero.

"So am I," she said. "I can do some work. Enough. We'll come out ahead."

"No," said Stealth, "we would not. Eden has been designed and balanced. Additional personnel will put a strain on space and resources."

"What resources? I eat two meals a day. I sleep on the floor half the time."

Stealth gestured at the skeletal framework. "Having Cerberus on site will strain the available power. A large part of your workshop would have to be relocated as well, which would mean reallocation of more vehicles and fuel."

"I don't need much," said Danielle. "I wouldn't be able to finish the work there, but I could take everything I'd need for the next week's schedule in . . ." She glanced around the workshop. "I could fit most of my tools and the material I'd need in there," she said, gesturing at a red tool cabinet. "Hell, I can fit two changes of clothes in there, too. I won't take up any room at all."

The hooded woman shook her head.

"What?"

Stealth looked at St. George. "We are wasting time. Cesar should assume the role of Cerberus at Eden while you and Zzz—"

"HE'S NOT CERBERUS! I'M CERBERUS!"

Cesar and St. George flinched. Danielle's shout echoed in the big room. She glared at the hooded woman.

"Of course," said Stealth. "I misspoke. Forgive me."

A set of quick, *whisk*ing steps approached. Gibbs appeared in the workshop's big door. His limping run lost momentum and became a staggering halt when he saw who was gathered there. "Is everything okay? It sounded like shouting?"

Cesar gave two quick shakes of his head.

Danielle reached over to grab St. George by the arm. She dragged him a few yards away from the table. "Don't do this," she whispered. "You can't take it away from me."

"We're not taking it away from you. We're just—"

"It's my suit!"

"I know," he said. "It's just . . ."

"Just what?"

St. George glanced over at the hooded woman. "She's try-ing to be nice," he murmured.

"Nice?"

"She's giving you an out. A reason not to go."

"It's my suit. I go where Cerberus goes."

"I know that," said St. George. "I remember. But Eden . . ." He looked back at the battlesuit. Twin threads of smoke trailed from his nose.

Danielle stared at him. "What?"

"Eden isn't like the Mount. It's like things were in the be-ginning. Nothing but chain-link and some plywood around the whole thing. It's very open. It's very exposed. Most people are living out of tents because there's only one real building."

Her shoulders hunched. She forced them back down, but he saw it. "I'll be okay," she said.

"Will you?"

"I just said—"

"You've gotten worse," said St. George. He looked her in the eyes when he said it. "I'm sorry, but we both know it. You used to be able to force your way through it, but since Smith messed with our heads you've pretty much been trapped in here, haven't you?"

She snorted and waved his words away. "No. No, it's not that bad."

"You don't even go near the doors if you can avoid it," said St. George. "Cesar and Gibbs bring you food and supplies. You wash your clothes in the sink." He glanced back over at Stealth. "You know she keeps track of all this stuff."

Danielle's eyes widened a bit. "What's she told you?"

"Enough."

"Like what?"

He looked over at the open doorway. "Have you even seen an ex since we woke up?"

Her shoulders relaxed a bit. "Since this morning?"

"You know what I mean. Since I destroyed Cerberus."

She bit her lip but didn't look away.

"You're going to be out in the open, you're going to be surrounded, and you're not going to have the armor," said St. George. "There's nowhere in Eden you can go and not hear them. There aren't many places you can go and not *see* them."

"I'll be okay," said Danielle.

"You'll have to be," he said. "Once you're up there, that's pretty much it. They can't send the truck back just for you. I won't be here to give you a lift. You'll be stuck there for three or four days, at least."

"I'll be okay," she repeated. She took a deep breath. "I'll be fine."

"Are you sure?"

"Yeah."

He nodded. "Okay, then. Let's go tell them you're going."

She took another breath. "Thank you."

"Nothing to thank me for. It's your suit, right?"

They walked back to the others. Stealth stared at them from inside her hood. Cesar tried to hide a hopeful smile.

"Danielle should go," St. George said. "She's right, it's dumb to send Cesar out there without someone who can troubleshoot the suit. If something went wrong on day one, it'd make all this pointless."

Stealth studied his face, then bowed her head. "Very well," she said. "If you feel this is the correct course of action."

"It is," said Danielle. "It'll be fine. I'll be fine."

"If they're both going," said Gibbs from across the room, "I might as well go, too." A few *whisk*ing steps carried him over to the table. "I won't have anything to do here without Dr. Morris or the battlesuit, and if Cerberus is going to be a key part of Eden's defenses you'll want a full crew behind it."

Danielle nodded. "Yeah," she said. "And we'll be able to get more done if we can split maintenance and actual work between us."

St. George glanced at Stealth. She made no move to respond. "I can't promise anything," he said. "It's kind of tight up there. It's going to take some work to make extra people fit."

"If it helps," said Gibbs, "I could pull a few shifts on guard duty." He waved his hand toward the prosthetic foot. "I can't do the half marathon anymore, but I can still walk a patrol and pull a trigger."

"We'll see," said St. George. "Let me talk to Captain Freedom and some of the Eden people. It might not be great, but I bet we can work something out."

"This is going to be awesome," said Cesar. He bounced on his heels again. His eyes went from Danielle to Gibbs and back. "Freakin'-A."

"Freakin'?" St. George raised an eyebrow.

"Hey, I got a little niece, I gotta set a good example, right? That's what superheroes do?" His eyes went wide. "Damn. I need to tell my sister I can't babysit next week."

FIVE

NOW

ST. GEORGE PUSHED off the floor and sailed up to the next landing of the stairwell. The fire door there was propped open with a cinder block. At some point in the past, one of the other residents had spray-painted it grass green.

Like most of the living quarters in the Mount, his home had started out as something else—in this case, a large office for one of the sub-companies of the film studio. Their publicity department, judging from the packages of postcards and mini-posters he'd found in the closets.

When they'd first moved into the Mount, every room in every building had been converted and occupied. They'd needed all the living space they could get. With the closets emptied, the desks and filing cabinets cleaned out, and a few extra pipes run, most of the offices served as passable apartments.

Once the Big Wall went up, though, people moved back out into the city. After almost three years behind the studio walls, some folks couldn't resist the idea of windows and trees and across-the-street neighbors. And with the depleted population, there were houses and luxury apartments for anyone who wanted them.

The Zombocalypse had really turned Los Angeles into a buyer's market.

St. George hadn't seen a point in moving. His office-apartment was more than twice the size of the little studio he'd had before the dead started to walk, and he still had more space than he needed. Now he had the floor to himself, and shared the building with two other singles and a couple.

Plus, he'd come to see the Mount as his home. He'd managed to rescue a few things from his old studio and added a few more since then. It was roomy, it was his, and he couldn't picture himself living anywhere else.

He fished the lone key from his pocket and opened the door.

The light was on. The one by the couch in the living room. He'd found it in the back warehouse of a Big Lots store two years back or so. The tall torch could blast light against the ceiling, but it also had a small reading lamp that branched from its trunk. The light sent a wide shadow from the overstuffed chair to his feet.

He hadn't left it on when he left this morning.

"I'm home," he said to the air.

"Did they agree to your terms?"

The kitchen had looked empty when he stepped in, but Stealth stood there now. Her mask was gone, her black hair pulled back tight against her head. Her dark skin gleamed in the soft light. She'd traded her body armor and cloak for a pair of dark slacks and a red Henley.

For *his* red Henley, St. George noted with a small degree of pleasure. It was two sizes too large for her. She made it look fashionable and sexy and elegant.

"God, you're beautiful."

"That is not an answer."

"It's still the truth."

Her mouth made the ever-so-faint curve he'd come to recognize as her smile. "Did they agree?"

"Yes," he said. He slipped out of the biker jacket and hung it near the door. "Les wasn't happy, but he understands the situation. He'd rather have one less farmer for a week than have everyone up there feel like they've been left to fend for themselves."

"I believe he is now asking people to refer to him as Lester."

"Right. Force of habit."

Les Briggs had managed a community garden on the edge of Koreatown before the ex-virus swept across the city. He'd been one of the guiding forces behind the garden at the Mount. Stealth had known what staples they needed, but Les had known what they could grow in their half acre of scavenged potting soil and how they needed to grow it. When Eden had been proposed, he was the first choice to lead it. He'd been up there a dozen times already and spent the night for half of them.

And he'd insisted people start calling him Lester if he was going to be in charge. It was an odd quirk, and it worried St. George a bit. It wouldn't be the first time responsibility changed someone.

"Anyway, he's going to bump one of his people and they're going to give Danielle the big room in the main building for now. He says they can work around her for a week without too much trouble." St. George set his heel on the floor and pried his boot off. "To be honest, I think he just wants to show off Eden to someone new."

"Danielle will refuse such an offer."

"Yeah, I know. But I wasn't going to tell him that. I'm still not sure how many people know about her . . . issues." He set his toes against the heel of the second boot and worked it off his foot.

"She kept it hidden because of her ability to move about as Cerberus. However, since the destruction of the battlesuit, I believe nineteen people have formed suspicions about her lack of visibility."

He joined her in the kitchen. She'd been cutting vegetables for a salad. "Exactly nineteen?"

Stealth nodded. "Cesar and Lieutenant Gibbs each realized within four weeks and have helped keep her secret. Mayor Linhart contacted me seven weeks ago expressing his own worries. Gayle—"

"I believe you." He leaned down and kissed her on the cheek. She turned her head and their lips met.

She looked up into his eyes. "How did Billie Carter respond to the requests?"

It took St. George a moment to find his footing in the conversation again. "Not bad, all things considered. She'd wanted more scavengers up there, so asking her to lose one so Gibbs could go didn't exactly thrill her. But she gets it, too. She pulled the guy with the mohawk and the beads under his skin."

"Benjamin Kim."

"Yeah."

"This arrangement bothers you?"

He shrugged and plucked a slice of hard-boiled egg from the salad. "It's a little weird to have most of the Unbreakables heading up there. They've made the Big Wall a lot more secure."

"I am sure Captain Freedom and I can manage for one week with three hundred and twenty-four regular guards."

St. George pushed the egg into his mouth. "We have that many now?"

"Not counting the twenty-five now assigned to Eden, yes."

"What if something bigger happens?"

Stealth tilted the salad bowl and split it between two plates. "There has been no sign of Legion since the destruction of Cairax Murrain."

"Doesn't mean he's gone."

"It does not," she agreed, "but this absence has now been three times longer than any other. We know his abilities allowed his consciousness to travel as far as Yuma. Perhaps he has gone farther."

"Maybe. It just feels weird that we haven't seen anything from him. I mean, not a thing."

"Your concern for our enemy is touching, even if it is unwarranted." She gifted him with another tight smile and picked up the plates. "The glasses, please."

"Of course."

They walked to the table. He raised his glass. "Thanks for making dinner."

She bowed her head. "It may be our last night together for several days. I knew you would want it to be memorable."

He leaned in and kissed her again. "You know who surprised me with all this? Cesar."

Her fork pinned a tomato to the plate. "In what way?"

He shrugged. "I figured he'd look at this as his big chance to go solo, that he wouldn't want Danielle looking over his shoulder. But he looked really happy that they're all going."

Stealth raised her fork. "I believe his joy comes from the hope of another sexual encounter once they are somewhat isolated."

"Really?" St. George swallowed a mouthful of water. "With who?"

"With Danielle, of course."

"What?" He blinked. "Wait . . . *another* encounter?"

"There were at least two, but no more than four. Danielle has since ended the arrangement. I do not believe there was anything romantic between them, although I believe there was a risk of Cesar becoming infatuated with her had it continued."

"Are you spying on them?"

Her eyebrows shifted as she stared at him. "I do not spy on anyone, George. I observe and deduct."

"But you're sure they're sleeping together?"

She set her fork down. "One observation was during my night patrol of the Mount three months ago. I heard a cry and investigated."

"And it was . . . Danielle?"

"It was Cesar. I believe that first encounter was brought

on by her own frustrations with her condition and by three bottles of ale. I do not know what instigated the other encounters, but I would presume a degree of familiarity was a factor."

St. George loaded his fork with salad. "Okay," he said. He set the fork back down on his plate.

She looked at him. "I did not think this knowledge would bother you so much."

He shook his head. "It's not that. I mean, it's a little that. She's, what, ten or fifteen years older than him?"

"Thirteen. Only two years more than the difference between Gorgon and Banzai."

"Fair enough," he conceded. "But, no, I was wondering if this is such a good idea after all. I mean, do we want to risk any . . . complications up there."

"There will be none," Stealth said. She picked up her own fork. "There is also little chance of Barry learning about it."

St. George coughed. The temperature in his mouth shot up and wilted a piece of lettuce on his tongue. He swallowed it anyway. "You know about that?"

"As I said, I observe and deduct."

"Wow."

She raised an eyebrow. "This surprises you?"

"No," he said, "it's not that."

"Then what?"

"Have we become a couple that talks about their friends' relationships over dinner?"

Her mouth formed another tight smile as she sipped a bit of water.

"Well," he said, "in the interest of fairness, then, I guess I should throw my own grenade on the table. Something I'd like to bounce off you, anyway."

"Please do."

"I've been thinking about it, and when Barry and I head out to this boat-island, Madelyn should come with us."

Stealth impaled two spinach leaves and a small piece of egg yolk. She looked at him as she raised the food to her mouth.

"I've got a couple of good reasons," said St. George. "She barely ever gets out because people still don't feel comfortable around her. She deserves a chance to be outside and feel like she's contributing."

The fork speared another leaf and a tomato wedge.

"It gives us a third set of eyes out there. And people tend to disregard her, either for her age or because, well, they're not used to an ex who can think. So they might be a lot more honest around her without thinking about it."

"The Corpse Girl is not an ex-human."

"Everyone here knows that," said St. George, "but no one out there does."

Madelyn's father, Emil Sorensen, had been the mind behind Project Krypton's super-soldiers. But St. George and Stealth had learned he'd also treated his daughter with experimental nanotechnology to cure a childhood ailment. It had cured her disease and made her the picture of health. After she was killed and mutilated by exes, the nanotech had rebuilt a complete copy of her body. The reanimated corpse of a teenage girl.

Stealth set the fork down and picked up her glass. She sipped some water and looked at him over the rim. "It will be awkward to carry both Madelyn and whatever supplies you plan to take as a goodwill gesture."

He shook his head. "I can just get a safety harness or something to clip her to my back, and that leaves my hands free."

"You have never carried a large amount of weight while flying for a significant amount of time."

"She's not exactly heavy. She's, what, maybe a hundred pounds?"

Stealth nodded once, picked her fork back up, and turned

her attention back to her plate. She ate another two mouthfuls of salad in her efficient manner before she looked up at him again. She blinked twice, her eyelids sliding down and up across her pupils. "Are you awaiting some word of approval from me, George?"

"Kind of, yeah."

"Your reasoning is sound. If you need approval from me, you have it."

He smiled. "Really?"

"Of course."

"I have to admit, I was a little worried about what you'd think since it's such a last-minute idea."

Stealth lifted her napkin and dabbed at her lips. She pushed her chair away from the table, stood up, and walked into the bedroom. She returned with a square of folded black material that looked like rubber. "Madelyn will need this."

She held it out to him and he stood to take it. "What is it?"

"An insulated wet suit. There is a good chance your journey will involve cold and possible immersion."

St. George shook it out. It was a narrow shadow with white accent lines down the front that gave it a high-tech look. "Should I even ask when you got this?"

"I located it for her before I came to make dinner," said Stealth. "It should fit perfectly."

"WATCH IT," GIBBS called out to the people in *Mean Green*. "If Dr. Morris sees you moving the components like that she'll tear you a new one."

Taylor and Hector de la Vega muttered something in the back of the truck. They lifted the exoskeleton's leg again, gentler than before, and worked the padded blanket around the mechanical limb. Hector strapped it against the tool chest while Taylor hopped down onto the liftgate to help Cesar and Gus Hancock carry the other leg out of Danielle's workshop.

St. George tilted his head at the two soldiers carrying the leg. "Why are you having them carry them out like that?"

Gibbs glanced at him. At his lapels. They'd been standing together for twenty minutes. Gibbs had managed to avoid eye contact the whole time. "Like what, sir?"

"All loose. Danielle has a bunch of custom cases and forms all lined with foam, doesn't she?"

"She did," said the lieutenant. "Once we started building the Mark Two, they were all useless. These components are all a little bigger, and they connect in different places. The old forms were too custom to hold them."

"Ahhhh," said St. George.

"She cut up one of them to make a new pillow, I think."

"Sounds like her."

Taylor and Hancock heaved the leg up onto the truck's liftgate. It rang with the dull peal of metal on metal. Cesar's face scrunched up. The two soldiers both smirked, then glanced over at Gibbs.

"Real funny," he said.

"Sorry," said Taylor. After a moment he added, "Sir."

"Get it strapped down and I might forget to have First Sergeant Kennedy drive her foot up your ass."

Taylor's lip curled. He huffed in a breath.

"Unless you want me to drive *my* foot up your ass," Gibbs said. He took a step forward. His steel toes scraped the pavement, and the mechanical ankle *whisk*ed as it adjusted. "Because her foot is going to hurt a lot less than mine, believe me."

Taylor glared at the lieutenant. Then he turned away and lifted the exoskeleton leg up onto the truck bed. Hancock kept quiet and followed the other man's lead.

The truck's door opened and Mike Truman, another one of the Unbreakables, hopped out. "*Big Red*'s calling from the East Gate," he said. "They want to know how much longer."

St. George looked up at the sky. It was past noon, almost one. About six hours of daylight left, and the trip out to Eden could take five if too many exes clogged the road. "Maybe you should have Cerberus assembled and ready, just in case," he said to Gibbs.

The lieutenant bit back a sigh and shook his head. "It'd take us over an hour to get it unloaded and assembled."

"I could help."

"I figured you would. That's why I said an hour." Gibbs glanced into the truck, where Hector levered another ratchet strap back and forth. "That's the last piece. Just let us grab our bags and I think we're ready to go."

A few nods passed back and forth between the group. Cesar hopped off the back of the truck and dashed back into the workshop. Truman headed back to the cab. "Let me know when it's all good to go," he called up to Hector.

"Dr. Morris," shouted Gibbs. "Train's leaving, ma'am."

Cesar came back with a safety-orange backpack slung

over his shoulder. "She's coming," he said. He looked at Gibbs. "She just needed some last-minute stuff, y'know?"

Gibbs dipped his chin in understanding. St. George counted off four Mississippis and wondered if Danielle was going to need help stepping outside. Then he saw movement inside and relaxed.

"Sorry," she called out as she shuffled forward. "Just locking up a few last things." She stopped at the oversized doorway and set her duffel bag down. Her fingers flexed inside work gloves, she turned to the door, and then looked down at her bag again.

The collar of her contact suit peeked out from under a threadbare flannel shirt, covered by a battered hoodie. Her Army Combat Uniform jacket rode on top of all of it. She was thin enough that it didn't make her look too bulky, but her hunched-up shoulders didn't help.

"I got the door, boss," said Cesar. He hopped down, walked past her, and got the big door rolling on its track. She stood in the way for a few moments, then took a cautious step out into the sunlight.

St. George stepped forward. "You want a hand with that bag?"

They locked eyes. Her pupils were wide and her nostrils flared in and out with rapid breaths. He thought she was going to bolt. He could picture her pushing past Cesar and running back inside.

Then her eyes hardened. "I'm fine," she said. "It's just some clothes and my laptop."

She stood there and her fingers flexed again. She bent down and grabbed the bag, then looked up at the sky. "Wow," she said just a little too loud, "feels like ages since I got out."

The big door closed behind her. Cesar took a few extra seconds with the chain and the padlock. Danielle took another deep breath, raised her foot, and took a step toward the truck. Then she took a second. And, after a brief pause, a third.

St. George bent and scooped up his own luggage, a bright red gym bag with a heavy shoulder strap. He straightened the pad at the top of the strap before he slung it over his shoulder. He made a point of not looking at Danielle while he did.

When he turned back, she was at the liftgate, all but gritting her teeth. It had taken her a minute to cover the five yards between the workshop and *Mean Green*. She met his eyes again and gave him a tiny nod.

Truman reached an arm out of the driver's side window and banged on the door. "Come on," he shouted. "I don't want to be driving in the dark."

Cesar walked past her and jumped back up into the truck. Gibbs stepped onto the liftgate with a clang of steel on steel as his foot hit. They both reached their hands down for her at the same time.

Danielle glared at them and hopped into the truck bed on her own. She stood there for a second, as if she were close to losing her balance. Then she adjusted her bag on her shoulder and turned to St. George. "You out of here?"

He nodded and tugged on the strap of his own bag. "I'm meeting Barry and Madelyn down at the southwest tower. We're taking off from there."

"Okay," she said. She took another step into the back of the truck. Her shoulders relaxed a little more once the wooden sides were around her. "Have fun out there on Fantasy Island. Guess I'll see you when you get back."

"You will." He pushed off the ground and rose up until he was looking down at the truck. "Cesar."

The young man looked up. "Yeah?"

"Don't get too comfortable. You're getting one week with the armor. That's it."

The other people in the truck bed chuckled. Cesar's face

ran through a few expressions—confusion, sadness, understanding, excitement. "Yeah, we'll see. You're all going to be so impressed when you see how good I can—"

Danielle smacked him on the shoulder. "I'm standing right next to you, jackass."

Taylor barked out a laugh.

Cesar's face dropped again. "Sorry."

Hector pushed a button, and the liftgate rose up with a whine of hydraulics. Gibbs moved to check the strapped-down components. Taylor and Gus stood in the front of the bed and looked over the cab as *Mean Green* rumbled into motion.

St. George gave Danielle a last wave and soared higher into the sky. He was a little over a hundred feet up when he saw the gleaming wraith hanging there. "Hey," he said. "I thought we were meeting over at the tower."

Zzzap turned his head from the departing truck. *Oh, yeah,* he said. *I was just heading over that way and saw you. Figured I'd wait for you.*

"You didn't want to say good-bye to Danielle?"

Nah. He spun in the air and darted south. St. George had to lunge after him to keep up. *They were all ready to go and I didn't want to delay them any more. Besides, it's a week, right?*

"Right. Maybe less, depending on when we get back."

Yeah. Nothing's going to happen. His head turned to the bag slung over St. George's shoulder. *Did you remember my stuff?*

"Yeah, it's all in here."

Even the extra socks?

"I packed everything you put out."

Just making sure. I don't want to get halfway there and have to turn around. What about the snacks?

"I've got about two dozen of those oatmeal-fruit bars for you and three bags of jerky you can fight Maddy for."

That stuff they make in the Corner?

"Yeah."

The wraith shuddered. *Y'know, it smells good but I'm always wondering what that stuff's made of. Does it bother you they just call it "jerky"?*

"Stealth says it's not human. I try not to think about it past that."

Oh, jeez, said Zzzap. *I never even thought of that. I was just thinking rats or possums or something.*

"I'm pretty sure it's chicken."

And you know what chicken jerky tastes like? Soylent jerky.

"Barry?"

Yeah?

"She's going to be fine."

What? Oh, yeah, I know.

"Eden's got good fences, the main building's practically a bunker, and with the scavengers there's going to be almost forty guards. And Cesar's going to be in Cerberus." St. George regretted his choice of words as soon as they slipped from his mouth.

Yeah, I know, said the gleaming wraith. *Just a little worried. It's been years since we all split up this much.*

"True."

And last time we did, I ended up stuck in a reactor core.

"But they did give you bacon first."

True. I guess it wasn't all bad, when you put it like that.

They soared down through the air to the southwest corner of the Big Wall. A large guard post stood at the corner, almost twenty feet up and sixteen feet square. Low, wooden walls ran around it, and half of it had a roof. There were four guards on duty. They stood as far as possible from the fifth person in the tower and tried to make it look casual.

She just looked too much like an ex for some people to be comfortable.

Madelyn looked just as excited as Cesar had. A pair of tinted goggles hid her eyes. She wore a pair of cargo pants and her battered denim jacket over the wet suit Stealth had found for her. The suit's white slashes and accents matched the Corpse Girl's skin.

She waved when she saw them. "Is this cool or what?" she called up to them. "I've got a uniform and we're going on a mission!"

"Yep," said St. George. He nodded at Makana and the other guards before looking back to her. "You bring everything?"

She held up her backpack. "Two changes of clothes. Toothbrush. Two journals and three pens double-bagged in Ziplocs. Four bottles of water. Three bags of chicken jerky."

St. George glanced up at Zzzap. "See? She knows it's chicken."

Yeah, but she also thinks it's still 2009. No offense.

"None taken, jerk," Madelyn said.

His electric laugh buzzed in the air.

She turned to St. George. "So how are we doing this?"

St. George pulled a bundle of yellow straps and buckles from his bag. Then he pulled out a smaller one with thinner, black straps and handed it to her. "Five-point harness for me, three-point for you. Like a tandem skydiver."

She unrolled the harness and twisted it back and forth. "I'm going to hang off your chest for the whole trip?"

He shook his head. "Piggyback. Leaves my hands free, keeps you kind of sheltered if something happens."

Her eyebrows went up. "So you want me to . . . ride you?"

The electric laugh buzzed in the air again. Makana and one of the other guards snickered. A murmur of "necrophilia" echoed from the farthest pair.

St. George shook his head. "Don't even go there." He glanced over at Makana. "You know how these things go on, right?"

The dreadlocked man nodded. "It's not hard." He took the yellow harness and spread it out over the floor of the tower. "Haven't put one on in years, but it's like riding a bike."

When was the last time you rode a bike?

Makana grinned up at the wraith.

He guided St. George into the harness and pulled the different straps over his shoulders and around his waist. He cinched straps down tight and pulled another one through a buckle on the hero's chest. The fit was a bit awkward over St. George's biker jacket.

He watched Makana's hands move back and forth. "Is it going to be this much work to take it on and off every time?"

"Nah," said Makana. "Most of this is sizing it to you. You can get out of it by undoing this and wiggling it a bit." He tapped the chest-buckle. "It'll be loose if you wear it without the jacket, though. Not as safe if you fall."

"I'm not worried about falling," said St. George. He glanced at Madelyn. "Not me, anyway."

Makana finished adjusting one of the lower straps and turned around. He didn't move toward Madelyn. "Stand up straight," he said.

"I am standing straight."

"Chin up."

Zzzap had floated a few yards back up into the air. He glanced down at Makana. *What are you, the posture police?*

The dreadlocked man inched forward, his eyes on Madelyn's face.

"Oh, for God's sake," she said. "It's not like I'm going to bite you or something."

"Yeah, well . . . just don't try anything," he said.

"You should be so lucky." She pushed her chin up and rolled her eyes at St. George.

"Give it a rest," he told her. He looked at the dreadlocked man. "You're not scared of a teenage girl, are you?"

Makana took in a breath to reply, but thought better of it. He shuffled forward and took the black harness Madelyn held out to him.

She crossed her arms and glared up at a cloud. Makana

had her step into the harness and tightened it around her thighs and waist. He touched her as little as possible. When he was done, she made a point of smiling at him without showing any teeth. "Thank you."

Trucks are pulling out, Zzzap called down to them. He'd drifted up and now hung almost twenty feet above the tower. *They just went through the East Gate. Looks like there weren't any problems.*

"Good to hear," said St. George.

Madelyn slung her backpack over her shoulders. "So are we ready to go now?"

St. George slid a piece of paper from his jacket. "We need to make one stop, down in Marina Del Rey."

x x x

"And there they go," said Cesar.

St. George and Zzzap shot across the sky. Everyone in the truck watched them fly away. The heroes shrunk to black and white dots in the sky, and then they were gone behind a building.

The convoy of trucks rumbled on down the street. They could drive at almost thirty miles an hour for this stretch. All the roads around the Mount had been cleared out when they built the Big Wall.

Danielle pulled her arms a little closer to her body. Sitting in the center of the truck didn't provide the most gentle ride, but it felt less exposed. The people standing along the sides of the truck and hanging on the rails almost blocked her entire view.

She recognized some of them. Two or three in particular. Just before they'd gone through the gate, Gibbs had looked around their truck, too, and decided to ride in the other truck with the Unbreakables.

Not a surprise, all things considered.

Cesar had stayed with her, of course. She had to talk to

him about it. Again. He was getting a little too puppy dog-gish. Someone was going to notice.

Stealth had probably already figured things out. Which meant there was a good chance St. George knew. And maybe Barry, too.

She shook the thoughts from her head and went back to studying the other people in the truck.

Hector leaned against the side of the truck and spoke with a younger woman. Danielle was pretty sure her name was Desi. A young man with a shaved head and a messy goatee stood on Desi's other side, trying not to look angry or jealous and doing a poor job at both.

One of the old drivers, Harry the Hook, was by the lift-gate controls. He swung at something as they drove along, and she saw his spear shake with an impact. "Points," he crowed.

"You get points for celebrities," said Al. The brown-skinned man tugged the brim of his hat down a little more against the flow of air.

"It was," said Harry.

Paul and another scavenger, a broad-shouldered woman named Keri, both snorted.

"It was," Harry repeated.

"Who was it, then?" asked Paul.

"I don't know. Some guy I'd seen in a couple things."

Al shook his head. "Some guy?"

"Yeah, it was some guy. You'd've known him. It counts."

"If you have to say it counts," said the woman, "it doesn't count."

"Says who?"

"Says everyone," Danielle chimed in.

Harry shot her an angry look. He'd never been fond of the heroes, and actively disliked them since one had broken his nose a few years back. He muttered something under his breath and turned back to the street.

Mean Green slowed as it rounded a corner. Danielle heard the clicking of teeth, and she tried not to look at the pale, outstretched hands she could see through the slats that made up the truck's sides. Spears descended to push and prod the undead away. Then they were heading north on Highland Avenue, accelerating to catch up with *Big Red*.

"Hey, speakin' of not counting," said the not-angry-or-jealous man, "how long's everyone think we're going to last out there?"

Half the eyes in the truck fell on him. "What the hell's that supposed to mean?" asked Al.

The young man shrugged. "I'm bettin' we last two weeks before the fences fall or something and we all get eaten."

"Javi," sighed Desi, "give it a rest."

"I'm just saying it, Des. We're all thinkin' it."

Danielle scowled at Javi, and found scowling took her mind off being out in the open bed of the truck. "Please," she said, "tell us what we're all thinking."

Javi shrugged. "They're gettin' rid of us. Sending us off to fend on our own."

"You're going to work the garden," said Al. "We're going to search all the houses up there."

The younger man blew air out of his lips. "That's what they're telling us, but I'm not stupid like you."

Paul's face hardened. "What was that?"

"It's not a garden, man. It's a big prison camp. Like, back when England shipped all their criminals to Austria."

Hector rolled his eyes. More than a few people smirked. "Australia, you idiot," said Keri. "Not Austria."

"Yeah, whatever," said Javi. "Point is, they're shipping all of us off. Buncha prisoners, couple of guards. We work 'til we all get killed by zombies. I give us two weeks, tops."

"You're an idiot, bro," said Cesar.

"What, you think you're one of the Superfriends now?" Javi smirked at him. "D'you forget you used to be one of the

Seventeens, little man? Because I betcha none of them did."
He waved his hand at the scavengers next to Cesar, then
pointed it at Danielle. "She didn't. That's why she's here,
right? 'Cause she doesn't trust you with her toys?"

"No," said Danielle and Cesar at the same time.

"Why do you think I'm here?" asked Javi. "Me or Desi or
Hector or any of us? More'n half of us used to be in the Seventeens, and we all got volunteered."

A low murmur traveled through the back of *Mean Green*.
Looks went back and forth as they all counted up the faces
around them. Eight of the fifteen people in the truck bed
had been members of the South Seventeens gang.

"Maybe you just don't have any skills past using a shovel,"
said Al, "and they finally decided to make you earn your
keep."

Javi smirked. "Yeah, if that helps you sleep for a few more
nights, old man."

Harry the Hook shook his head and swung his spear as
they drove past another ex. Desi and Hector edged away
from Javi and grumbled to each other. The broad-shouldered
woman, Keri, whispered something in Paul's ear. Neither of
them looked happy. Even Cesar looked a little grim.

Danielle looked around. Right now, St. George would
crack a joke or say something uplifting to boost the mood.
Freedom or First Sergeant Kennedy would just yell at them
to shape up and shut their mouths.

But St. George was somewhere out over the Pacific by now.
Kennedy was up ahead in *Big Red*. Captain Freedom was back
at the Mount, probably patrolling the Corner.

Danielle took in a deep breath and forced her arms down
to her sides. She let the air out and tried to relax her shoulders. She pushed her chin up.

"Eden's important," she said. "Right now it's probably the
most important thing we've got going. We can't keep scavenging the city for cans of soup." She took another breath

and fought the urge to cross her arms. "This garden's going to keep all of us alive. Everyone's depending on us to make it work." She looked Javi in the eye. "We're all important."

Javi chuckled and shook his head. "Oh, yeah," he said. "We're all important and it's not a fucking prison work camp. That's why it's all Seventeens and screw-up soldiers, right? Is that why she's coming, too? 'Cause she's important?"

He waved his hand at the woman crouched in the opposite corner of the truck bed. The one no one had looked at, but they'd all kept an eye on. The one Gibbs had seen just before he announced he'd be riding in *Big Red*.

The Asian woman in drab sweats scowled at Javi and tried to sink deeper into the corner between the toolbox and the side of the truck, away from everyone's stares. Half of them tried to look her in the eyes. The other half looked at her throat, at the square of red scars. It had only been three months since Doc Connolly cut out the woman's vocal cords.

Christian Smith dismissed the other people in the truck with a wave of her mangled, three-fingered hand. The ring and middle finger were gone, removed all the way down to the palm. It had turned her left hand into a claw.

She saved one last glare for Danielle. The redhead wasn't surprised. She'd been the one who shot the fingers off. Christian walked with a limp now, too. Connolly had fixed the kneecap as best she could, but the bullet had done a lot of damage.

Danielle hoped it hurt a lot.

Christian turned to stare out at the road. She'd chopped her black hair into a short, masculine style. With her different clothes and posture, she didn't look anything like the councilwoman who'd been part of the Mount since the beginning.

Which made sense, because she really wasn't anymore.

"Yeah," said Danielle, "even her."

SEVEN

NOW

MADELYN LEANED IN close to St. George's ear. "You know what's awesome about having my memory reset all the time?"

He twisted his head around. She wasn't far away, but they were moving fast enough that she was a little hard to hear. "What?"

"By tomorrow I'll have forgotten this whole boring trip!"

He laughed. It shook him enough that she clenched the straps of his harness even tighter and flattened herself against his back. Her head pressed down between his shoulder blades. She'd kept it there for most of the flight so far.

They'd been flying for almost seven hours, skimming along about sixty or seventy feet above the ocean. Nothing but sky and water for most of it. The air was cool and wet and salty.

In all fairness, St. George didn't think the trip had been all boring. Three things had broken the monotony. Maybe an hour of excitement spread out over all their flight time.

They'd come across the first one about two hundred miles past the island of Catalina (now the home of about three hundred exes and twice as many bison), barely an hour out into the ocean. The sun-bleached sailboat's lines were brittle and its sail tattered. They'd found no bodies and no exes. A few old cans sat in the small pantry, two bottles of water in the mini-fridge. The drawers near the bed held clothes for a man and a woman.

The second had come two hours and three hundred miles later. A quartet of humpback whales had churned through the sea below them. St. George, Madelyn, and Zzzap had paused to watch for a few minutes before the massive creatures dove beneath the surface and vanished.

The third had been almost three hours ago. The large yacht rode low in the water and leaned to one side. There'd been nine bodies. Three of them were still moving around. One had been an older man with a thick beard and a dark polo shirt. The two others had been younger women, a blonde and a brunette. The blonde wore a swimsuit covered with old blood splatters. The brunette ex just had bikini bottoms, but was painted with gore from its chin to its stomach.

St. George had put down the man and the topless woman. The ex in the gory one-piece followed them back out onto the deck, its teeth clicking the whole time. He'd tossed it out over the water. It sank beneath the waves and vanished.

"Do you think sharks eat exes?" Madelyn had asked. "Or do the exes eat them?"

"The ex-virus doesn't affect animals," St. George reminded her.

Still, said Zzzap, *zombie sharks. Got to admit, that'd be kind of cool, in a really horrific way.*

They'd had a quick snack on the tilted deck before taking off again.

On St. George's left, the sun crept closer to the horizon. Moving west had slowed it down a bit, just enough to notice, but they had maybe an hour of daylight left. He looked down at the boxy white case hanging from his left hand. It was the size of a large cooler and weighed a little less than Madelyn. They'd found it in Marina Del Rey on their second try.

To his right, the light shifted as Zzzap raced back to them. He'd been flitting ahead and back since they'd left the yacht. *Still on track,* he said. *It's about another eight hundred miles that way. Give or take.*

St. George slowed down and felt Madelyn shift on his back. "We're not going to make eight hundred miles before it gets dark," he said. "You want to go a little farther or call it a night?"

Doesn't matter to me either way.

"Is there anything neat up ahead?" asked Madelyn. "Another boat? Desert island? More whales?"

I think I might've seen a dolphin.

She shook her head. "I say we call it a night."

"Okay, then," said St. George. He slowed to a stop in midair. "Making camp."

He shifted and felt Madelyn pull on the harness straps. The red gym bag swung back and forth between them. He hefted the white case.

It's silly, said Zzzap, *but I've kind of always wanted to see one of these things in action.*

"Me, too," said Madelyn. She was leaning forward, trying to see over St. George's shoulder.

"On three, then?" he asked.

They counted together. The white pack plummeted through the air. It hit the surface and vanished beneath a swell. A few seconds later the raft exploded up out of the waves, spraying water in every direction.

The life raft was a bright orange hexagon about ten feet across. A canopy stretched over it on inflatable arms and created a small tent. It trembled on the waves while a last few wrinkles stretched tight, and then it was still.

Okay, said Zzzap, *that was pretty damned cool.*

"Hella cool," said Madelyn.

They sank down until they were a few feet away. Zzzap kept a safe distance. Madelyn shifted on St. George's back, and he heard her fumbling with her harness. She slid off his back, down his arm, and caught herself on his hand. She dangled for a moment while he carried her over the raft's entrance. He let go and she dropped a few feet onto the raft. She wobbled and fell forward into the tent.

"It's like a bounce house in here," she called out to them.

St. George unslung the red gym bag and let it hang from his hand. "Incoming," he said, and swung it into the raft.

"Got it!"

He turned to Zzzap. "You ready?"

The brilliant wraith nodded. He lowered himself to a foot above the surface, and the water began to steam below him. *First time for everything,* he said.

He pulled his arms and legs in close to his body, and his light dimmed. The air around him settled and then made a quick, dry woofing sound as it was shoved out of the way.

Barry cannonballed into the ocean. He came up a moment later, shook the water from his eyes, and looked up. "Oh, it's great," he said. "You should try this. It feels like the warm spot in a pool, but in a good way."

"I'll pass, but thanks."

Barry stretched up a thin hand, and St. George grabbed it. He dragged his friend through the water to the raft. Madelyn was waiting for them. "Robe or sweatpants?" she asked.

"Sweats," said Barry.

She pulled a roll of black fabric from the gym bag and placed it near the entrance. Then she crawled to the far side of the tent and faced the wall. "Okay," she called out, "my innocent eyes are averted."

St. George heaved Barry's naked form out of the water and into the raft. "It's for your own safety," said Barry. "Seeing me naked could ruin you for all other men."

"Too late," she sang at the orange wall.

Barry rocked back and forth on the floor and wrestled himself into the sweatpants. "All clear," he said. "Thanks for the moment of almost-privacy."

St. George leaned in through the entrance. "No problem," he said. "Hang on for a second."

He put his hands against one of the inflatable supports

and pressed. The raft turned in the water as he drifted in the air. He rotated it a third of the way around, then stepped inside.

"What was that about?" asked Madelyn.

He waved his hand out the entrance. "Sunset view."

She crawled over on her knees, and Barry shifted himself over on his hands. "Nice," he said. He reached into the gym bag and dragged out a thick cranberry robe. He wrapped it around himself and tugged at the lapels. "It's very Hef, don't you think?"

"Did Hef end up in a lot of lifeboats?"

"No idea." Barry reached into the bag again and pulled out a Ziploc full of jerky.

"Dibs," said Madelyn.

"Actually," said Barry, tossing the dried meat to the Corpse Girl, "did anyone ever check out the Playboy Mansion? It's in LA, right?"

"Yeah," said St. George. "But I don't know where. I'm pretty sure I've never been there, though."

"It's got the big pool. The Grotto. And a lot of zombie Playmates. You'd know."

"Y'know what," said Madelyn, tearing off a chunk of jerky, "you two guys just go right along talking about the Playboy Mansion in front of the teenage girl. There's nothing skeevy about it at all."

Barry laughed, and St. George blushed a little.

"Why'd you drop into the water?" she asked Barry. "Isn't that kind of dangerous for you with, y'know, your legs?"

"Well, if I tried to drop into the raft I'd either burn a hole through the roof or bounce off."

She smirked. "I mean, why not change in the water?"

He shook his head. "Not a good idea. Water and the energy form don't mix."

"Electricity and water?"

"More like the emergency cooling system in a reactor," he

said. "They'd douse the core with water if it was overheating. Same thing with the energy form. If I'm in the water, I'll just bleed energy like mad. And the energy is me, soooo . . ." He shrugged.

"Gotcha."

They ate a dinner of jerky and soybeans, sipping water while they watched the sun vanish over the horizon. Madelyn chewed on one last piece of dried meat while she unzipped her backpack and pulled out the bag with her journals and pens. "Okay," she said, pushing her goggles up onto her forehead, "time to write down the day."

The biggest downside to Madelyn's condition was her near-inability to form memories past the moment of her death. Every time she fell asleep, her brain reset itself and she forgot the previous day. The only way she'd found to learn new things was to keep a detailed journal and reread it each morning. It could take her four or five days of repetition before a name would stick with her, even longer for other facts.

St. George pointed at a bundle on one of the tent's supports. "I think there's a flashlight in the emergency kit."

"Don't need it, but thanks." Madelyn thumbed through the journal, her chalk-white eyes darting back and forth across different pages. She flipped a few more over and began scribbling.

St. George settled against one of the thick inflated tubes. The raft didn't rock on the waves, but every now and then a little tremor shook the outer walls. "So, did they see you when you went back to the island?"

"The Others?" Barry shrugged. He pulled a third oatmeal bar from the bag. "I don't know. I don't think so."

"The Others?"

"He's talking about *Lost* again," said Madelyn without looking up from her journal.

Barry tapped his nose and smiled at her. "I don't think I got any closer than a mile," he told St. George, "and I was there for ten or fifteen seconds both times. But the sun was on the other side, and this last time it was pretty dark behind me. If they happened to be looking that way, I would've been tough to miss." He bit off a mouthful of oats and fruit. "You really worried about the element of surprise?"

This time St. George shrugged. "It's always tough to tell how people are going to react, y'know?"

"I'm surprised Stealth hasn't written up some first-contact rules for us."

"She tried, way back when, but even she admitted there were too many variables."

Barry smiled. "So how are we playing it tomorrow? Riding on your rep?"

"Maybe. Winging it, I guess."

"The usual, then."

"Yeah."

The sunset faded, and the inside of the tent went from dim to dark. The raft thrummed like a drum as waves tapped it.

The scratching of Madelyn's pen stopped. "Okay," she said, "now I need some light."

St. George rooted around in the emergency kit and came up with the flashlight. "I thought you didn't want to remember the day?" he said with a yawn.

She smiled. "It'd be nice, but it's always better to remember something than nothing."

"Maybe," said Barry. "There's a bunch of stuff I'd like to forget. *The Phantom Menace*. The last two seasons of *Heroes*. Spider-Man trading his life with Mary Jane to Mephisto to bring Aunt May back. Pretty much all of—"

"You wouldn't," she said. Her smile faded. "It sucks."

"Sorry," Barry said. "I didn't mean anything."

She switched on the flashlight and balanced it on her shoulder so it lit up the journal. Her face vanished in the shadows. St. George tried to get a sense of her expression behind the light. "You okay?"

"Yeah," she said. "It's a little bright, that's all." The pen went up and tapped her temple, then went back to the page. "Eyes are always dilated now, remember?"

"I meant you. Are you okay?"

She kept writing. Then she shrugged. "I worry I'm going to forget something important," she said. She kept scribbling. "That I don't have enough . . . y'know, enough memory space in my brain."

"That's why you write everything down, right?"

"Yeah, but I mean . . . past that. I've got the facts, but sometimes I lose the actual memories."

Barry pushed himself up against the raft's wall. "What do you mean?"

Madelyn finished another line in the journal and ended it with an emphatic jab of the pen. "I had this friend in high school, Janice. She had a pair of retro rocker jeans she wore that had about two dozen rips and tears in them. Showed a ton of skin."

St. George had a sip of water. "And . . . ?"

"And that's it," said Madelyn. "That's all I know about her. It's the only thing in my journals. I don't know if she was just a friend or my best friend or maybe 'friend' is code for frenemy or my secret lesbian girlfriend or . . . or what. I don't know if we had classes together or went to the same school or even what she looked like."

She bent her head back to the journal. The pen scratched at the pages again.

"It might not mean anything," said Barry. "I don't remember half the people I went to high school with. Heck, I couldn't tell you the names of half the people I used to work wi—"

"I can't remember my mom."

The ocean lapped against the sides of the raft. It was a gentle drumbeat. The sound made the thick tubes tremble.

"Not at all?" asked St. George.

She set the pen down on the journal. It rolled into the groove between the pages. "I mean, I know she existed. I know she and I were heading to meet my dad at Krypton when I was killed. But past that . . ."

The three of them listened to the ocean for another minute.

"When Smith did his thing," said Madelyn, "when he . . . she . . . put us in the dream, I think it erased a lot of stuff in my head to make room for all the fake memories. I remember my dad in the dream better than I remember him in real life." She picked the pen back up and tapped it on the page again. "And then I realized one day my mom hadn't been in the dream. The idea of her was there, I'd talk about her, but I never actually saw her or heard her. And I hadn't noticed because I couldn't remember her in real life, either."

"I'm so sorry," Barry murmured.

She shook her head. "No, it's okay," she said. "I mean, it's not okay, but it's not like it makes me upset or anything. I mean, it does kind of abstractly, like the way you get upset about people dying in stupid wars and stuff, but I can't get upset about it because, well, I don't remember her." She shrugged. "I don't know, now I just worry I'm going to . . ."

St. George looked at her. "Going to what?"

She stared at the journal for a moment. Then the flashlight tilted and she slumped back against the wall of the tent. It gave under her weight, tilting her enough that she slid down to the floor.

"Maddy?" He picked up the flashlight and spun it around.

The Corpse Girl's eyes were half-open. She looked relaxed. He lifted her hand and it was limp.

"Whoa," said Barry. "Is that how she falls asleep?"

"Yeah. Haven't seen it happen in a while. I forgot how sudden it is."

"No irony there."

St. George snorted.

"Jesus, that's awful. About her mom."

"Yeah. Just in case we all needed another reason to be pissed at Smith."

"Either of them," Barry said.

EIGHT

NOW

IT CROSSED DANIELLE'S mind that Lester Briggs could've been a very successful criminal before the Zombocalypse. No one would be able to describe him. He'd raised "average" to an art form.

Lester stood just under six feet tall. His brown hair needed a cut, but wasn't long enough to be shaggy. Nor was it thick. His eyes were brown, too, his skin tanned but not dark, his nose large but not to the point it drew the eye. There was muscle in his arms and chest, but not enough to make anything fit him tightly. Even his facial hair rode the fine line between stubble and a full beard.

What he lacked in appearance, he made up for in enthusiasm. He insisted on giving them a tour of Eden the morning after they arrived. Danielle hadn't wanted to leave the safety of the main building—the architectural love child resulting from a three-way between a community center, a freeway rest stop, and a storage shed—but Gibbs had pointed out she needed to know the garden's layout on the off chance anything happened.

The lieutenant had bowed out of the tour himself, though, claiming his mechanical foot wasn't good on uneven ground for long walks. Danielle thought it was more that he didn't want to waste time with Lester's overexcited spiel about the garden. She glanced back at Gibbs and the building as the overly average man led her and Cesar away. First Sergeant Kennedy joined them as they headed down the first of the long, narrow aisles.

Eden had been a large community garden at one point, one of over fifty scattered across Los Angeles. There'd been individual plots filled by individual tastes. Now, though, it was wall-to-wall plants. More than a few sprawled into the aisles. Some of them were almost six or seven feet tall, and the group walked past a monstrous clump of cacti that stood well over ten. As the four of them made their way down the overgrown path, Danielle caught glimpses of an old lawn chair, some sun-weathered tools, and what looked like a birdbath half hidden in the weeds and vines.

Danielle's shoulders relaxed a bit inside her ACU jacket, and she wasn't sure why. She was outside, and she'd never been much of a nature person even before her phobias had kicked into high gear. They'd been walking for almost two minutes when she realized the thick plant life muffled the *click-click-click* of distant teeth.

"We're lucky," Lester said, half turning to them as he walked down the path. "So many things were already thriving when we got here. A lot has died off, and some things have gone wild, but there's still plenty of variety up here for us to get started with." He pointed at a plot filled with sprawling vines as they walked along. "That's all one squash plant. There's four or five more of them in this row. They're monsters. They grow like mad, and each one'll put out a couple dozen squash each season. We should have about a hundred pounds worth ready to send back to the Mount by the end of the week. There's a few hundred soybean plants the next row over. They reseeded themselves and just took over four or five plots."

"Oh, yay," sighed Cesar. "More soybeans."

Danielle reached out to smack him in the back of the head. Force of habit. But a flicker of movement caught her eye. Something gray two aisles over, hidden by a cluster of tall sunflowers.

The chatter of teeth seemed closer. Her sides tensed as her arms pulled in. She staggered to a halt.

Kennedy almost bumped into her. The first sergeant set a hand on Danielle's shoulder. "Sorry," she said. "Not any room to pass."

The gray thing was gone. The sound of teeth was a faint echo. Two people in bright colors walked down another aisle, carrying garden tools and talking.

"Yeah, sorry," said Danielle. She crossed her arms and grabbed her elbows. Her back was sweating. A cold sweat. She could feel it beading up.

A few quick steps and she caught up with the two men.

Lester hadn't even noticed she'd fallen behind. He pointed at green beans and peas to be harvested, turned a corner, and pointed out more changes they were going to make. "Garlic's like a weed up here," he told them. "There's some of it growing in pretty much every plot."

"Too bad there wasn't a vampire apocalypse," said Cesar.

Lester grinned. "While you're here," he said to Danielle, "there's a couple of rototillers I'd love to have you take a look at. It'd speed things up a lot if we could get them running again."

Most of the plants were low to the ground. The overgrowth wrapped around fence posts and grew between slats and chicken wire. It was like wading through a wide, waist-deep pool of leaves and twisting vines and stems. A shredded shade umbrella hung like a tattered flag. Danielle took a deep breath. Her fingers bit into her arms.

Kennedy pointed at a thick patch of sprawling plants, one of the tallest things in the row. Their leaves looked like swollen ferns, and spiky purple flowers topped tall stalks. "What are those?"

"Artichokes," said Lester with a smile.

"Really?"

He nodded. "The big flowers? That's what happens to

the part you eat if it isn't harvested. Watch out for that," he called to Cesar. "It's a snare trap."

The young man leaned away from the curved branch. "A what?"

"Believe it or not, we've got a rabbit problem," Lester explained. He waved at the surrounding greenery. "Five years alone in here with all this let their population boom. There's a couple hundred, at least. They were everywhere when we first showed up. There's some cats and a fair amount of rats, too, but the rabbits are out of control. We've got snares set all through the garden."

Kennedy's mouth twitched. "A few people told me they had stew up here," she said. "I thought they were joking."

"It's delicious," said Lester. "And we've got sweet potatoes, carrots, lots of spices. I think it's going to be a big draw to get people up here to work."

"You're killing bunny rabbits?" asked Cesar.

Lester looked at him and blinked twice. "Well, yes," said the average man. "They're a danger to the crops and a good source of meat, so it's a win-win."

"That's messed up, bro. You know how much my niece would love to see a bunny?"

"Bunny rabbits?" echoed Kennedy.

Cesar shrugged.

"Believe me," Lester said, "there's no danger of us getting them all."

Behind them, something rustled. Unsteady movement in one of the plots. Danielle turned, looked past Kennedy, and saw leaves moving. The teeth were near, the clicking was so close, and she was in the open.

Kennedy saw her staring and glanced back. "Something wrong?"

Danielle blinked. Two drops of cold sweat ran down her back. Another one ran between her breasts down to her stomach. "Are we . . ." She took another breath and turned around, forcing her hands down. "Are you sure it's safe to be out like this?"

It was Lester's turn to blink. "Pretty sure, yes."

She grabbed the side of her pants and squeezed. "The whole place has been cleared? All the exes cleaned out?"

His face lit up again. "You don't know?"

"Know what?"

"The story about this place? God, I thought everyone knew."

She looked at Cesar. He shrugged. Kennedy stared back at the artichokes.

Lester slipped past them and waved for them to follow. They retreated a few paces and turned down a different path through the garden. He glanced back and kept waving, an overeager tour guide.

"This place should've been dust years ago," he explained. "That was our first big surprise—how much of the garden had lasted. This side of the hills, all of the valley, it's a desert. The only reason it was ever green was because of us. With no people, you'd expect everything up here to dry out in a few months, tops."

"Automatic sprinklers?" asked Kennedy.

Lester shook his head. "No. Even if they were, they would've stopped when the utilities shut down. Now we've got the well Zzzap drilled for us, but before that he was doing it all with solar stills and irrigation."

"He?" asked Danielle.

"We don't know his name," said Lester. "We've just been calling him the Gardener."

"The Gardener," echoed Kennedy.

Cesar gave Danielle a gentle elbow. "And you said the Driver was a dumb name?"

"It is a dumb name."

"As near as we can tell," Lester said, guiding them into a cross-aisle, "when the exes first started showing up and everyone made a run for it, this guy came here. And he just ... took care of the place. Watering, weeding, keeping the fences up, and cleaning it out. That's why it's all in such great shape."

They stepped out of the aisle onto a strip of sun-faded pavement. The far side of it was a chain-link fence. Behind that was a tall wooden one, a classic American picket fence, right down to the white paint and beveled tops. Someone's backyard butted up against the community garden.

Next to the fence was a pile of eight or nine bodies. They were dried out and shriveled, almost skeletons. In several places the skin had crumbled to show pale bone. None of them moved.

Danielle sucked in a sharp breath.

"There's three more piles like this one around the garden," said Lester. "Check this out." He reached out and pushed at the closest body with his boot, tilting the head. The neck creaked as it twisted.

A razor-straight gash ran right above the dead man's brow. It stretched across the entire forehead, almost temple to temple. The papery skin around the wound trembled, as if there was nothing underneath to support it.

"What is that?" asked Kennedy. She stepped past Danielle to examine the bodies. "An axe wound?"

"That's what we thought at first, too," said Lester, "but then a few weeks ago we found the Gardener while we were sweeping for exes."

The answer leaped to Danielle's tongue. "It's a hoe."

Cesar looked at her. "What?"

"A garden hoe," said Danielle. The mechanics of it unfolded in her mind. "I mean it's an axe with the blade mounted crosswise instead of in line with the haft. It'd lose a bit of force, but with a long handle giving you leverage it could still do some serious damage."

Lester smiled and nodded. "Yeah, the Gardener figured

that out, too. Like I said, about forty bodies around the perimeter, and we've found a few places where it looks like he dumped them over the fence while he could."

"So where is the great Gardener?" asked Kennedy.

Lester walked back toward the aisles and pointed. "About three rows over. We walked real close to him when we first came down that way."

"He's dead?" Cesar asked.

Lester nodded. "Looks like he sat down in a nice chair, finished off a bottle of scotch, and put a bullet in his head. Right through the roof of the mouth. No chance of coming back. He had the hoe with him."

Kennedy gave a slow nod of approval.

Danielle felt the sweat running again, but forced her hands to stay at her sides. "Any idea why?"

"We'll never know," Lester said. "Not for sure. My guess though . . ." He held up his hands and hooked the fingers into claws. "My mother had rheumatoid arthritis. His hands are twisted up the same way, especially the left one. It might just be a rigor mortis thing, but he was pretty old from the look of his hair. I think he realized he was running out of time, might've been in a lot of pain, and just . . ."

"Bang, thud," said Cesar.

"Yeah. He's still in his chair. Been there for about two years, I'd guess. He's covered in bean plants. They just climbed all over him."

"And you left him there?" asked Kennedy.

Lester shrugged his not-that-muscular shoulders. "He loved this place. He's not coming back. It just felt right to leave him in his spot, like a memorial. You want to see him?"

"No thanks," said Danielle.

Cesar looked at his boss. "Yeah," he said. "Let's get this finished up, bro. We need to go get Cerberus put together."

"Right, of course," Lester said. "Sorry. Let's swing back this way, and that'll bring us around to the main building."

He led them deeper into the garden. They walked past a trio of people harvesting green squashes and one person digging a trench. The narrow path led them between a plot filled with cornstalks and another that looked like grape-vines.

Danielle registered the chattering just as they stepped out of the tall corn.

Another section of faded pavement stretched in front of them, part of the same service road circling the garden. A chain-link fence stood on the far side of the pavement. It was four feet tall and lined with 55-gallon drums. A single strand of barbed wire twisted along the top.

Past it was a wall of exes. At least a hundred of them stretched along the length of the fence. Dead men and women, young and old, some covered with gore and some with just a single obvious wound. Many of them had dried out after years of exposure, but a few still had curves. The lasting effects of a very healthy life or a surgically-enhanced one.

The four humans stepped into the open, and the undead turned chalky eyes on them. The dead pushed at the fence, shifting as they milled and shoved. It flexed and straight-ened, flexed and straightened, squeaking every time. It was just high enough that the exes' grasping hands ended up pressed back against their bodies. The *click-click-click* of their teeth rattled across the road.

Danielle staggered back. Her heart tried to pound its way out of her sweat-slicked chest. She couldn't get any air into her lungs. The ACU jacket seemed to tighten around her.

Kennedy caught her before she fell. "Easy," said the first sergeant.

"That's the freeway up there," said Lester, pointing up the ridge behind the exes. "A lot of these guys fall down the embankment and get stuck in the ditch. The Gardener re-inforced the fence with those barrels, but it's pretty solid on its own. And they can't get any numbers or leverage on it because of the uneven ground back there."

Danielle sucked in a breath. There was too much space. Nothing but open space between her and the exes.

Kennedy grabbed Danielle's left hand and held it tight. "It's okay," she whispered. "They can't get past the fence."

Lester walked away down the road, gesturing at the mass of zombies. Cesar followed him. "We'll have to clean them all out at some point," continued Lester, "but for now there aren't enough to pose a worry for us. We've planned to make this a regular part of all patrols for now."

Danielle grabbed Kennedy's arm. The first sergeant had muscles like rock. She closed her eyes and pulled in another breath, and then another one.

"It's okay," Kennedy said again. "You're okay."

Cesar glanced back and saw Danielle curled over next to the first sergeant. He cleared his throat, breaking Lester's monologue. "You know what, bro," he said, "can we just cut this short and go straight back? I think we've all seen enough."

Danielle forced herself up, lifting her head and straightening her back. She ignored her pounding heart, her sweaty skin, the tremble that swelled in her chest, and pushed her arms down. She fought her screaming instincts and turned her back on the dozens and dozens of exes past the fence line. Two jerking steps had her back between the corn and the grapes. Three more was far enough to muffle the sound of clicking teeth.

Kennedy walked next to her. The first sergeant half carried her through the cornstalks and back into the open area. The bright purple artichokes were on her left now, and there was the ruined umbrella. Kennedy had a good sense of direction.

"Sorry," Lester called out from the other side of the corn. "I get carried away when I talk about the garden. I didn't mean to take up so much of your time."

Cesar fell in behind them, between Danielle and Lester. They marched back through the overgrown garden. The main building stood a hundred yards away, just visible over the tall plants.

The sounds of teeth and squealing chain-link faded behind them. The pressure on her side faded, and Danielle realized her arm was no longer crushed against her. It wasn't moving away from her body, fear still held it rigid. Kennedy still held her other hand.

The big patch of sunflowers stood next to the path ahead. Past that, the fifteen-foot swath of peas and beans Lester had pointed out during the walk. They were already halfway to the main building. Halfway back to Cerberus.

Two people worked in a plot the next row over. One of them, a black man with a fuzzy scalp, leaned on the long handle of some garden tool. His smug expression dropped as the quartet moved out from behind the patch of sunflowers and into view. The other worker also had a near-shaved head, an older white man with a heavy brow and a torn earlobe. He was kicking at something on the ground, half-hidden by the overgrowth between them. A large bag or sack or . . .

Dim recognition flickered in Danielle's mind. The two men were soldiers from Project Krypton. Not Unbreakables, but some of the civilians who'd been recruited into the base's ranks.

And she recognized what the man was kicking.

"Hey!"

The leaning man stepped back and tried to look busy. Earlobe looked up, angry at the interruption. The look slipped when it landed on the quartet. It fled when he saw Kennedy.

The first sergeant was a few beats behind Danielle. "Privates," she bellowed. "What the hell are you doing?"

Fuzzy took a few steps away, tensing to run. Earlobe looked frozen between fight or flight. He glanced at the shape on the ground.

Kennedy let go of Danielle's hand, took a few running steps, and leaped into the air. She sailed over the patch of vegetables and landed between the two men and the thing they'd been attacking. "I said what the hell are you doing, soldier?" she bellowed again.

The two men froze, stunned by her shock-and-awe display of power.

Danielle lunged into motion. They were just people. She could deal with people, even people in wide-open spaces. She took a few quick steps to a cross-path that let her cut across to the other aisle. Cesar's loping footsteps followed her.

When she realized how much she'd been acting on instinct, she paused. The pressure of the open spaces pushed down on her. She looked at the figure on the ground, shoved back the thoughts she'd had, and took a breath to steady herself. "You okay?" she asked.

Christian Smith uncurled from the fetal position she'd been wrapped in and crawled away. She grabbed a fence post and dragged herself to her feet. Cesar tried to help her up, but she smacked his hands away and hissed at him. It was a soft sound with no bite behind it.

"I apologize, ma'am," said Kennedy. "These—"

It earned her another weak hiss of air. Smith's lips fired off a flurry of silent curses and insults. Danielle wasn't a good lip-reader, but most of the words were short and to the point. Kennedy stayed just as silent throughout it.

When Smith was done with the first sergeant, she turned and launched another volley at Danielle. A few moments in she coughed, a jarringly loud sound, winced, and grabbed at her side with her claw-hand. She wound up her silent speech by giving Danielle the finger. Then she limped off toward the main building.

Danielle had known John Smith, the man who'd somehow copied his consciousness into Christian's body, erasing her mind in the process. Danielle had dated him. Slept with him. Lived with him.

She recognized the eyes in Christian's face. They were a different shape and color, but still . . . they were John Smith's eyes.

"I'll make sure these two know not to try something like that again," Kennedy said.

"Fuck that," said Earlobe. "You know who she is."

Kennedy whipped a finger into the man's face. "Private, did I give you permission to speak?" she barked.

He stiffened. "No, First Sergeant," he said.

But his eyes followed Smith up the path as he spoke.

ST. GEORGE WOKE up to the pounding sound of drums.

Madelyn scooted on her knees to the front of the raft and thumped on the inflated tubes there, too. She threw open the flaps of the tent and let in the morning sunshine. "We're out in the ocean," she called over her shoulder. "I think this is a lifeboat."

He stretched. "Is it?"

She leaned out and splashed at the water, then squinted up at the sky. "Were we in a shipwreck or was it just a really wild party?"

"D'you remember anything?"

She dropped back inside the tent and blinked a few times. She crawled back to her bag and journals. Her eyes closed and her brow furrowed. "Flying with you and Zzzap," she said. "A big fire." She shook her head and opened her eyes. "That's it."

"The fire was a couple of days ago."

"Oh."

"Quiet," muttered Barry without opening his eyes. "Some of us are still using the waterbed to sleep."

St. George prodded him. "Come on. We've still got a lot of flying to do today."

"I don't," Barry said, throwing a robe-wrapped arm across his face. "I can be there in less than an hour. Why can't I sleep in?"

"Get up."

"But mommmmmmmmm . . ."

Madelyn chewed on another strip of jerky while she read

through the journal pages. "We're going to an island made up of boats?"

St. George bit off a chunk of an oatmeal bar and nodded.

She skimmed through a few more pages. When she was done, she closed the notebook and picked up the other one. It was smaller and more dog-eared. She opened it to the first page and began reading.

Barry wolfed down his third oatmeal bar, reached over, and pulled a piece of jerky from the Ziploc next to Madelyn. She slapped his hand. He smiled and waved the strip of dried meat at her.

They finished breakfast while Madelyn refreshed her memories. Then she and St. George pulled their harnesses back on while Barry worked himself out of the robe. Madelyn turned her back while she repacked the bags.

Barry crawled to the tent entrance and wiggled out of his sweatpants. "Whoa," he said. "Sea air's a little brisk in the morning."

St. George lifted his friend by the armpits and held him out over the water. "You ready?"

He nodded. "Frak, yeah. Throw me before I freeze."

St. George bent his arms and hurled Barry up into the air. The black man soared into the morning sky, flailed a bit as he began to arc back down toward the water, and then exploded in a blast of light. A wave of heat rippled out through the air and over the life raft.

That's better, said Zzzap. *Good night's sleep, some food. I don't know about you guys, but I'm ready to go explore a mysterious man-made island.*

St. George slung the red gym bag over his shoulder. Madelyn ate one last piece of jerky and shoved the Ziploc into a thigh pocket. She glanced around the tent. "So we're just going to leave this out here? Seems kind of . . . I don't know, wasteful."

The batteries in the flashlight sparkle, said Zzzap, pointing at where his eyes would be. *It'll drift, yeah, but I should be able to spot it on the way back.*

St. George crouched in the entrance in front of Madelyn. "Seatbelts on."

She wound the strap through his harness and grabbed his shoulders. "Ready."

"Then here we go." He focused on the spot between his shoulder blades, just above where the D-ring sat, and launched himself into the air. Madelyn hollered as they shot up sixty, eighty, a hundred feet into the air and then leveled off.

Okay, said Zzzap. He pointed west and a bit south. *That way.*

x x x

It was late afternoon when Zzzap came rushing back from his latest scout-ahead and gave them a thumbs-up. They slowed to talk. *About another sixty miles,* said the gleaming wraith.

"Just over the horizon?" asked Madelyn.

Maybe another twenty minutes, half an hour. He looked at St. George. *Pretty sure they saw me this time.*

"How sure?"

Ummm, well they were pointing and shouting and waving things.

St. George nodded. "Okay, then." He leaned forward and pushed through the air again.

Twenty-five minutes later the first shapes appeared on the horizon. They slowed to a halt in the air. He glanced at Zzzap. "That it?"

Yep. Any further ideas on how you want to do this?

St. George looked at the form in the distance. It was a blocky bulge sticking out of the sea. "Let's not go too crazy," he said. "Maybe once around the whole thing, figure out a place to land, and see what they say. Sound good?"

Works for me.

"And me," said Madelyn.

He glanced back at her. "If anything goes bad, just stay low, okay?"

"Bad like people shooting at us?"

"That was what I was going for, yeah."

They headed forward again. The shape on the horizon looked like a real island for a few minutes as it grew in size and detail. Then the lines and angles of it became clear. When they were still about two miles away, St. George pushed himself higher into the air, almost two hundred feet up. He wanted a good view of everything.

There were about a dozen ships. Like Barry had said, the core was a trio of large ones. St. George tried to work up from the smaller boats on the edge to estimate size, and decided the tanker and cargo ship were each somewhere around twelve hundred feet long. The ship between them was a few hundred feet shorter, but loomed over the others.

The center one was a multidecked cruise ship, the kind Carnival or Disney sailed. There'd been a logo on one of the cruise ship's big smokestacks, some kind of fish, but it had weathered away and left a blue blur. A thick carpet of dark green covered the top decks.

A cargo ship rested against the cruise ship on the side facing them. Two long staircases reached down from the cruise ship. Stacks of steel containers spotted its deck, and a dense garden covered the rest, just as Barry had said. At least two dozen people worked the plants and soil.

"The other side's the oil tanker, right?" asked St. George.

Yeah. And there's also a big stone foot with four toes.

"A what?"

"He's doing the *Lost* thing again," said Madelyn.

Come on, he said. *How often am I going to get to make crazy island references?*

They swung to the right and circled around. There was a large yacht alongside the front of the cargo ship, and an industrial-looking fishing boat with a pair of cranes crossed in front of both of them. Boarding planks and ropes stretched between the ships, and across to a larger but less elegant yacht alongside the fishing boat that extended across the cruise ship's bow.

People on the deck of the cargo ship pointed. The wind caught shouts and cries and carried fragments of them up to the heroes. More figures appeared at the railings of the cruise ship, and some ran out of the yachts.

I see guns, said Zzzap. *Shotguns. A few pistols.*

"Yeah, I see them too," said St. George. They swung around the front of the ships and headed behind the island. Many of the people scrambled along to keep them in sight. "Looks like some people have weapons. Two or three on one guy, nothing on the people around them."

"Maybe they don't have any exes to deal with," said Madelyn. "Not everybody at the Mount carries a gun."

Fair point.

On the far side of the cruise ship was the oil tanker. It faced the opposite direction from the cruise ship, so its tall bridge and towers blocked their view of its deck. The heroes sailed around and saw the long expanse stretching out alongside the cruise ship. More people were here tending to another long garden spread out across the deck. St. George noticed a raised slab at the far end of the tanker. A bright white-and-yellow target spread across the slab, and it took him a moment to recognize it as a helipad.

Small ships ran along the side of the tanker. A yacht-sized boat. The tugboat Barry had mentioned. Another fishing boat. They were connected by planks and walkways at odd angles.

"I don't mean to sound all bitchy," said Madelyn, "but this place is kind of a dump, isn't it?"

Once she said it, more of the little details leaped out at him. Ropes and chains ran back and forth between the vessels like a dyslexic spiderweb. Blankets and sheets hung from railings on all the ships, making small lean-tos and tents. Alongside the elegant gangways from the cruise ship, there were extension ladders braced between the different vessels.

About two hundred people watched them from the assorted decks. St. George saw male and female faces. Most of them looked thin, but none of them seemed unhealthy.

He looked over at Zzzap. "You see anything we should know about before we land?"

The gleaming wraith shook his head. *Kind of a big lack of stuff. The only major heat sources look like campfires. No electrical currents here at all. No batteries. No radio signals. No solar cells anywhere, unless they're covered.* He shrugged. *There might just be a lot of stuff belowdecks. All the layers of metal make it tough to see.*

Madelyn craned her neck as they flew. "If they've got campfires, what are they burning for firewood?"

"Seaweed, I think," said St. George. "Or kelp, maybe? They're drying a bunch of it on a couple of the ships."

I've always wondered, said Zzzap, *is there a difference between kelp and seaweed?*

"I don't know, to be honest."

"Kelp's a type of seaweed," said Madelyn. "Didn't you guys ever take a biology class?"

You can remember that but not why you woke up in a life raft?

She shrugged.

St. George nodded. "Okay, then. Where do we land?"

"I think there was a helipad back on the oil tanker," said Madelyn. "It had more seaweed on it, but I think that's what it was."

They continued around the cluster of ships and swooped down toward the helipad. St. George's boots hit the slab. Madelyn unhooked herself and bounced on the tarmac. "Oh, wow," she said. She took a few stiff steps and shook her legs out. "Oh, solid ground feels good." She reached back and pulled one foot up toward her shoulder blades. One of her joints popped.

St. George sniffed the air. "Is it just me, or does it smell . . . bad?"

The wraith waved a hand at his head. *I can't smell anything.*

Madelyn sucked in a deep breath through her nostrils. "I smell . . . something," she said. "My nose doesn't always work that great anymore. Sorry."

Hey, people coming, said Zzzap. He floated a few feet higher into the air. *Looks like . . . well, everybody.*

"Anybody with weapons?"

A couple of them. Maybe half a dozen?

Madelyn went to push her goggles up onto her forehead, but St. George waved her to stop. "Hold off showing them your eyes for now," he said. "Let's get a better feel for everyone here first."

She gave him a quick salute. "Yes, sir."

"Don't joke around too much," he told her. "You can be friendly, but remember we don't know how long these people have been cut off out here. We might be the first strangers they've seen in years."

"Okay," she said. "Sorry." She prodded one of the seaweed piles with her boot.

"Don't be. I'd just love to do one of these that doesn't involve gunfire."

This is going to be it, Zzzap said. *Did you see how excited all those people were to see us? There's no way this could go wrong.*

"Did you actually just say that out loud?"

Yeah, but I just said it to be funny, so we're safe. Don't worry.

They heard the clang of feet on metal stairs, and people came streaming up either side of the pad. They hung back as more bodies spilled onto the tarmac. Their clothes weren't ragged, but were very well worn.

They were all lean. St. George remembered that lack of

body fat from the first year of the Mount. Enough food to survive, but nobody worried about gaining weight.

The crowd and the heroes exchanged glances.

"Hi," called out St. George. He raised a hand to the dozens of people looking at him.

Then a handful of them marched forward. A tall, heavily built black man with a thick beard. A big, square-shouldered woman with short, dark hair. A bald man with a biker beard and nicks and scabs across his scalp. A wiry woman with strawberry blond hair and leathery skin.

The two men and the leather-skinned woman swung shotguns up to cover the heroes. The dark-haired woman pulled a pair of pistols. More weapons appeared back in the crowd.

"Dammit," St. George muttered.

Wow. Okay, I guess I shouldn't've said anything.

DANIELLE CHECKED THE bolts for a third time. "Okay," she said, "I think it's ready."

They'd put the exoskeleton together in the small court-yard of the main building. A dusty soda machine that had long since been emptied stood off to the side, next to a wall-mounted first aid kit that had been refilled with some basics. Danielle had wanted to do the initial start-up inside, but Cesar and Gibbs both pointed out the room had standard-sized doors.

The Cerberus Mark II battlesuit stood almost nine feet tall. Without the armor plates, it reminded Danielle of an old man or woman, a bony thing robbed of its vitality. It was a gaunt framework of exposed wiring and components. At more than a few points it was possible to see straight through it, past cables and pistons and load-bearing struts to the sunlit walls of the courtyard. A few wire loops sagged out around the forearms and calves, and Gibbs tucked them back in, making sure they weren't endangered by gears or hinges. He held out his hand, and Cesar put a roll of electri-cal tape in it.

Danielle looked up at the battlesuit's head. The helmet had been finished, but still lacked an armored faceplate. Two large round lenses dominated the gaping hole. The speakers were a set of blocks at the bottom of the opening.

Cerberus hadn't been whole for almost a year. She hadn't been strong for a year. A year of being weak and defenseless.

A clang from outside made her tense up. Voices laughed

and mocked each other. The Unbreakables had a bunch of barbells, dumbbells, and a bench outside, under the big canopy just outside the courtyard. At least three of them were there working out at any given time. Danielle wasn't sure where the weights had come from, although she was going to be pissed if she found out later she'd only been allowed one tool chest because they'd brought gym equipment from the Mount.

She walked around and checked the rear camera. It had its raised protective ring, but not the housing that blocked rain and larger objects. The leg joints were exposed, too. Cerberus had always been a "face front" machine, but in this state a six-year-old with a sharp stick could cripple it from behind. She reached down and brushed some imaginary dust from the right knee.

Gibbs watched her move around the titan while he taped an errant bundle of cables in place inside the thigh. "You sure?"

Danielle glanced at Cesar, then took in a slow breath. She looked the battlesuit in its eyes. "Yeah. Let's bring it online."

Cesar rubbed his hands together. Gibbs followed a line of cables back to the laptop on a courtyard picnic table. He flicked at the track pad a few times, tapped a few keys, and hit ENTER.

A tremor washed over the exoskeleton as dozens of servomotors and gyros powered up. Tiny lights flickered throughout the battlesuit. The gray circles of the lenses lit up, then surged to full brilliance.

Cesar shrugged his sweatshirt up and pulled it over his head. Underneath was a tight spandex shirt, the type of thing worn by cyclists. Two different shades of green swooshed back and forth across his chest. He tossed the sweatshirt on the picnic table bench and peeled off his driving gloves. His scars were bright pink against his palms.

Danielle looked at the shirt. "What's with the green?"

"You like it?" He flexed his arms, then set his fists against his hips. "I'm thinking this could be my uniform, y'know?"

"Your uniform?" echoed Gibbs.

"You know, bro, like, my costume. My super-suit. If I'm stepping up like this, I got to look the part, right? Green for go, like driving. Get it?"

"You know," Gibbs said with a smile, "thanks for the reminder. Every now and then I forget how young and stupid you are."

Danielle coughed. "You don't think all the green's maybe a little . . . tacky?"

Cesar looked at her. "What's tacky about green?"

"About green? Nothing." Danielle pushed her chin up, but still stood two inches shorter than him. "About gang colors? I think there's still some people who might have a problem with that."

"Been years since the Seventeens went down," said Cesar. He reached up and touched his sleeve. Danielle and Gibbs had both seen the tattoo there. Cesar didn't show it off, but he also never went out of his way to hide it. "Can't keep judging people off the past. Or 'cause they're wearing a color."

Danielle shook her head. "Seeing green still makes a lot of people nervous."

"It's a color. That's all." He smiled. "I'm takin' it back. From here on in, people see green they're going to think of the Driver."

"Oh, Jesus," muttered Gibbs. He turned his attention back to the laptop.

Danielle smiled. "Please just stop talking and get in the suit."

Cesar winked at her, and her stomach flopped. She couldn't keep being friendly with him. She had to keep a good, professional distance.

He stepped forward and set both of his scarred hands

against the battlesuit's chest. Static electricity sparked between his fingers and the metal, and the sparks grew into long arcs that twisted up his arm and around the exoskeleton. There was a flash of light, a tiny thunderclap, and Cesar vanished.

Cerberus jerked up. "Ow!" wailed the speakers. The battlesuit hopped on one leg as the hands reached down to grab its shin. "Owww! Left foot, left foot!"

"Watch the leg!" snapped Danielle. "Let go. And stop moving."

The skeletal titan straightened up and lowered the leg. Metal toes tapped on the concrete again and again. "Oh, jeeeez, that hurts," said the battlesuit. "Something down in the foot. I think it's some kind of . . . crystal? Feels like I got a splinter in my toe."

"One of the piezoelectric sensors," muttered Danielle. She glanced over at Gibbs. "Take fourteen through twenty-six off-line, all the evens."

Gibbs's fingers danced on the keyboard, and Cerberus sighed. "Ahhhh," said the exoskeleton. "Thanks, bro."

"Bring 'em up one at a time," she said.

The keyboard clicked and clicked and clicked and Cesar yelped.

"Flag it," she said. "I think we've got two spares up here, right?"

"Yep," said Gibbs as he scribbled on a notepad.

She looked the exoskeleton in the eyes. "Anything else?"

The metal toes hinged up and down. The fingers flexed. The whir of the servos seemed loud without the armor muffling it. "Think we're good," said the battlesuit.

She waved at his arm. "Up." The power cable was still plugged into the exoskeleton's hip. She gave it a firm twist and unhooked it. The glowing lenses flickered for an instant, and the battlesuit gave her a thumbs-up.

While the teams had been setting the garden up, they'd

stripped dozens of solar panels from nearby homes. The roof of the main building was covered with them, as was part of the outside canopy, the greenhouse, and the big steel storage shed. Cerberus would be sucking up four-fifths of Eden's electricity every day. Not great, but it was only for a week.

The battlesuit took a few steps. Its toes chimed on the concrete. Then it took a few more, ducked its head through the door, and stepped out beneath the canopy. Danielle and Gibbs followed.

The canopy had been a shade area once, forty-odd yards of netting spread between six steel poles, where gardeners met to trade cuttings and seedlings and composting tips. Now a baker's dozen of crates were stored between the storage shed and the weather-beaten greenhouse. A weapons rack had been set up to hold a squad's worth of rifles. The canopy area looked like any one of half a dozen military depots seen on the news or in movies. Back when there were news programs and movies.

A weight bench sat just past the crates with a stack of iron plates. The Unbreakables stopped their workout to look at Cerberus as it stepped out under the canopy. Kennedy stood nearby with a set of huge dumbbells. Sergeant Johnson let the barbell clang down against the rests and grinned up at the exoskeleton. Truman gave a thumbs-up. "Good to see that up and moving again," he said.

Cerberus managed a loose salute that got a few smirks. The battlesuit took a few more steps, its half-armored head brushing against the canopy, and then it was out in the sunlight. The brightness turned cables into curved lines, supports into thin shadows.

Once again, it struck Danielle how many places she could see through the titan.

She took a few steps of her own but stopped at the edge of the building. Any farther and she'd see the chain-link fence off to her left. Bad enough she could hear it from here. The sound of clicking teeth was much clearer outside, like a swarm of enamel crickets. She could see the fence in front of her, too, another long section backed by wooden planks. If she stared at it for a few seconds, she could see flickers of movement between the boards.

She focused on the battlesuit. "Okay," she said. "Don't get cocky. You're strong, but you're not as solid as you're used to being."

"Feels solid," said the exoskeleton.

"You're not going to fall apart, but be careful if you run into something or try to hit it with your arm instead of your fist. Just remember, everything's exposed."

The battlesuit nodded. "Anything else?"

"Keep an eye on the power levels. You should get a little more battery life because you're not carrying around all the armor, but you don't want to get stuck somewhere."

"Got it."

"I'll go with him over to the fence line," said Gibbs. "We'll get in a long walk before dark, see if I spot anything in the stride once he gets moving."

Danielle nodded. "Good. Let me know."

He glanced up at the lenses. "Here we go. Don't screw up."

"Hey, don't worry about me, bro."

They walked off together. Gibbs had to take long, limping steps to keep up with the exoskeleton. His mechanical foot scraped in the gravel, its gears *whisk*ing as it moved. He was never going to wear the Cerberus suit again. His foot was the wrong shape, and its materials wouldn't react with the sensors the same way. At best, the battlesuit would have a severe limp when he wore it. At worst . . .

A hand touched Danielle's shoulder, and she bit back a scream. The muscles there knotted up. Her arms tensed.

"Looks like a dinosaur," said Kennedy.

"Sorry?"

"The foot you built him. It looks kind of like a dinosaur, doesn't it? Long toes in the front, short one in the back."

Danielle turned. "It's close to the skeletal structure of a human foot. You're just not used to seeing it without skin."

"I still think it looks like a dinosaur."

"A big T. rex fan?"

Kennedy shrugged.

The sound of teeth seemed louder, somehow. Danielle's fingers curled into fists, and she forced them flat against her sides again. "Was there something I could do for you, First Sergeant?"

Cerberus and Gibbs reached the far access road and headed for the southern fence line. Johnson and Truman traded positions and went back to pumping iron. Johnson muttered encouragement while he spotted.

Kennedy put her hands behind the small of her back and turned away from the soldiers. "I was wondering if we needed to talk about what happened this morning?"

"What about it?"

"Is there anything . . . I should know?"

Danielle looked past the first sergeant, at the crates, at the exercising soldiers, at the garden plots on the far side of the main building. A half dozen people plucked small shapes off plants and tossed them in buckets. Another trio crouched and tugged at weeds. One of the weeders reached back to throw a clump of dirt and grass into a wheelbarrow, and she recognized Javi the loudmouth.

She glanced up at Kennedy, then toward the corner of the building that blocked her view of the fence line. "It was nothing," she said. "Just a little panic attack. It's been a while since I was outside in an area this big, you know?"

Kennedy's mouth pulled to one side, as if words had tried to pass her lips and she'd yanked them back. "It seemed like a little more," she said after a moment.

"It wasn't."

Kennedy let her own gaze drift. Truman puffed out his fifteenth rep and let the barbell clang back onto the holders. He hung his arms at the sides while Johnson added two more Frisbee-sized plates to the bar.

"My second tour in Iraq," said the first sergeant, "I set off a booby trap. We were clearing a building, I opened a door, and it pulled the pin on a grenade."

Danielle's brows went up. She glanced at the first sergeant's face, then down her body.

Kennedy shook her head. "I was lucky. Not all the Al Qaeda guys over there were tactical masterminds. We all heard the pin drop, realized what it was, and had a three-count to scatter. They hadn't planned for that. I wasn't on top of it when it went off, but I still got thrown and caught some shrapnel in the side." She ran her hand down her body. "Thirteen scars. Two that look like spider bites up to one on my hip about as long as a pen. That was the serious one. Chipped the bone. Took twenty stitches to close it up."

"You're lucky," Danielle said. Her fingers started to curl and she forced them flat again.

Kennedy's mouth tugged into a tight, brief smile. "I ended up in the hospital for a week. But as soon as I was up and moving around, I realized I couldn't get near a closed door without the hair going up on the back of my neck. And if I had to open one . . ." She shook her head. "I'd get cold sweats and my heart would start pounding. I knew it was stupid. I knew nobody'd booby-trapped the bathrooms. But there were so many times I came close to pissing my pants because I couldn't open the door."

Truman puffed away under the barbell again.

"Anyway," said Kennedy, "one of the doctors noticed and they signed me up for ten sessions with a shrink. We just sat in his office and talked for fifty minutes a day. About my dad and why I signed up and movies I liked. All sorts of random crap. And on the second-to-last day we ended up talking about baseball and I said something about three strikes and you're out. And then he mentioned the old story about not lighting three people on the same match."

"Snipers," nodded Danielle. "Ready, aim, fire."

"Right. Anyway, we're going on about trouble always coming in threes, and then it hit me. That was the second time I'd walked away from an explosion, a really bad one this time. Part of me was convinced that I'd used up all my luck."

"Kind of makes sense."

"Yeah. And realizing that . . . I mean, the only thing I ever wanted was to be a soldier. It's a family thing. And now it took me an hour to get out of the cafeteria if someone let the door close. I just saw my whole future collapsing. I figured I was going to get drummed out with PTSD or something.

"I told the shrink and he smiled. Said it was a common thing. Happened to a lot of soldiers after a near-miss. He was impressed I'd made it through two before needing to talk to someone."

Danielle leaned in a little. "So what did he do?"

Kennedy looked her in the eyes. "Nothing. He could give me some guidelines, some exercises, but it was all up to me. He couldn't make me better, only I could. And just knowing that . . . it was just what I needed to hear, the way I needed to hear it."

The air slipped out of Danielle's lungs. "And it worked?"

Kennedy shrugged. "I'm still in the Army," she said, "and I'm not wearing a diaper."

"Good for you."

Kennedy looked over at the soldiers on the weight bench. "My point is, you can get past things like this. I don't know what happened to you—I don't know how bad it was—but from what I've seen I think you're tough enough to get past just about anything. So if it'll help you out, if you ever just need to . . . to talk to someone about it, or about anything . . . well, I know what it's like."

Danielle pursed her lips and nodded twice. "Thanks," she said. "I'll keep it in mind."

"Good."

Truman and Johnson had traded positions again. Something about his form—about both of their forms—nagged at Danielle, but she couldn't put a finger on it. She watched Johnson's arms flex for a moment.

Then she took a few steps away from the corner of the building, toward the courtyard entrance. She glanced back over her shoulder. "You sure you're not wearing a diaper?"

Another tight smile crossed Kennedy's face. "You can check if you want."

"I'll take your word for it."

THE BIG WOMAN aimed one pistol at St. George and one at Madelyn. "Who are you?" she asked. "Where did you come from?"

"Hey," said St. George, "let's take it easy."

"Answer the question," growled the black man with the beard. He had his shotgun trained on the hero, but from his angle it would be easy for him to shift to Madelyn. He glanced up at Zzzap.

"We're friends," said St. George. "I'm hoping we're all friends here."

The woman looked over the barrel of her pistol at St. George. She was an inch shorter than him. "Where did you come from?"

"Any chance we could talk about this without guns pointed at us?"

"No," she said. "Answer the question."

Want me to take them out? Zzzap hung in the air behind St. George and Madelyn. The bald man with the biker beard and the leather-skinned woman had their shotguns trained on him.

St. George glanced up at the gleaming wraith. "Hang on."

The big woman glanced up at Zzzap, then back to St. George. "Were those words? What did he say?"

"He's hard to understand until you get used to him," said Madelyn.

"Shut up," snapped the woman. She glared at St. George. "What did he say?"

St. George took in a slow breath. It hissed out of his nostrils as dark smoke. "He wanted to know if he should take out your weapons. I told him to hang on."

A murmur swept through the crowd as the trails of smoke curled up into the air and were broken apart by sea breezes.

Zzzap waved his hand and twiddled his fingers. The bald man's shotgun trembled. Farther back in the crowd a few people raised hoes and narrow shovels. One woman even had a pitchfork.

The big woman raised her pistol so it was aimed right between his eyes. "Where," she said, "did you come from?"

He raised his arm and pointed east. "My friend saw your ships out here the other day. We flew out to say hello and see if you needed any help."

The leather-skinned woman blinked. "You have a plane?"

St. George smiled. "No."

"Helicopter?"

"Shut up, Alice," said the square-shouldered woman. "How did you fly out here?"

"We flew," said Madelyn. She tipped her head back at Zzzap. "Just like he's flying right now."

The gleaming wraith waved again.

"I told you to shut up," said the woman.

"Okay," said St. George, "I think it's time to calm down and stop being rude."

"In case you didn't notice," said the woman, "we have the guns. That means we're in charge unless you feel like getting shot."

Zzzap chuckled. Madelyn smirked.

"What's your name?" asked St. George.

"I ask the questions," said the woman. "That's how this works. I ask, you answer."

"I'm just trying to be friendly."

"Eliza," said the bald man with the biker beard.

The woman—Eliza—gritted her teeth.

"Eliza," St. George said. "Pleased to meet you. Short for anything?"

"None of your business."

He nodded once. "Eliza, most people these days call me St. George." He looked past her to the crowd. "I'm guessing some of you may have heard of me as the Mighty Dragon."

Another murmur went through the crowd, this one closer to a rumble.

Eliza set her jaw. "Nice try," she said. "Now who are you and how did you get here?"

"I told you," said St. George. "I'm the Mighty Dragon, and we flew out here to see if you needed any help."

"They flew," said Madelyn. "I just sort of piggybacked."

"You are too young to be the Dragon," said someone in the crowd, a Middle Eastern–looking man with one of the narrow shovels. He was just holding it at his side, though, not up like a weapon.

Zzzap looked down at St. George. *You do look good for your age.*

"You're not helping."

Sorry.

St. George looked at Eliza. He took in a slow breath and let it mix in the back of his throat. The flames crawled up out of his mouth and rolled over his face to dance in the air.

Her eyes went wide. The bald man's jaw hung open. A few gasps came from the crowd.

St. George focused on the spot between his shoulder blades and rose three feet into the air. Eliza swung the pistol up to keep him in her sights. He managed to hang there for a few seconds before his lungs emptied out and the flames flickered away. Then he took a deep breath, tilted his head back, and shot a cone of fire into the sky.

People shouted. A few screamed. The bald man's shotgun sagged to point at the helipad.

St. George sank down and landed in front of Eliza. "The

Mighty Dragon," he said. "Really. Or you can go with St. George. I'll answer to either of them."

The pistol relaxed a little. "We'll see," she said. She looked at the others. "Who are these?"

St. George tossed a glance over his shoulder. "The glowing guy is Zzzap. I think you've seen him a few times in the past couple of days. You've probably heard of him, too."

Hey, everyone, said the wraith. *Nice man-made island.*

Alice, the leather-skinned woman, snorted.

"And this is Madelyn," said St. George, "who sometimes goes by Corpse Girl."

The black man with the shotgun frowned. Eliza's brow furrowed. "Why?"

"Y'know," murmured Madelyn, "I'm really not sure this is such a good idea."

St. George looked at her. "Go ahead. It'll be okay."

"You sure?"

He took a small side-step and moved closer to her. "Yeah."

She sighed, shrugged, and pushed her goggles up onto her forehead. It pulled her hair back from her face, and her white skin gleamed in the sun. She squinted and blinked against the brightness, but managed to get her eyes open. They were dry and chalky after most of a day with no eye drops.

"Zombie!" bellowed the black man. His shotgun shifted from St. George to Madelyn. St. George stepped to block it. "Out of the way!"

The cry echoed through the crowd. People panicked and surged away. They clogged the stairs, and some jumped off the helipad down to the deck. A few stepped forward with their farming tools raised.

One, he couldn't help but notice, was the woman with the pitchfork.

Alice swung her shotgun between Zzzap and the dead girl. The bald man took a few steps back. Eliza had both pistols on St. George, one lower than the other.

Madelyn sighed.

"Calm down," said St. George. "She hasn't attacked anyone. She's not doing anything."

"Move out of the way," said Eliza. "She's infected. She has to be put down."

"I'm not infected," said Madelyn. "I'm just dead."

St. George smiled. "She talks a lot for an ex, doesn't she?"

"Hey!"

"Mister," said the black man, "this is your last chance. Move away." He pushed past Eliza and lowered his shotgun toward the Corpse Girl.

George . . . ?

"I've got it." St. George reached out and wrapped his fingers around the weapon's muzzle. His palm blocked the barrel. "Again," he said, "I think you just need to stop for a minute, calm down, and consider what's going on here."

The man stared at St. George with cold eyes. "You do not want to be playing this game with me, mister."

"I'm not wor—"

The roar of the shotgun echoed across the helipad, and then the open space swallowed up the sound. The blast knocked St. George's hand away from the barrel. More people shrieked. Madelyn was one of them.

St. George glared at the man. Then he held up his hand. Smoke curled off the cuff of his leather jacket. He opened his fingers and let the buckshot clatter and ping down onto the deck. "I'm fine with it if you want to keep playing this game," he said, "but I think my turn's going to go very differently than yours."

About twenty people were left up on the helipad. They stared at St. George with wide eyes and open mouths. The Middle Eastern man with the shovel studied the hero's face.

"You rock," said Madelyn.

Sure, sighed Zzzap, *take all the cool moments for yourself. I'll just hang back here with the power of a star and make sure you're well-lit.*

"We've been polite," St. George told Eliza, "but I think at this point either we start talking, we start fighting, or we leave. Your choice."

She didn't take her eyes off St. George, but she holstered one of the pistols she'd been pointing at him and made a point of fastening the strap over it. Then she raised her hand. "Everyone stand down for the moment."

"For the moment?" Madelyn raised an eyebrow.

Eliza turned her head, still keeping her eyes on St. George. "Steve," she told the black man, "stand down."

Steve still had his shotgun up. His wide eyes flitted back and forth between the barrel, St. George's hand, and the pellets being pushed along the helipad by the breeze. He looked at Eliza and lowered his weapon.

She turned her full attention back to the heroes. "We'll talk more once you've cleared inspection and we've established who you are."

"I told you who we are," said St. George. "The Mighty Dragon. Zzzap. Corpse Girl."

"So you say."

Madelyn shook her head. "You're telling me you never heard of the Mighty Dragon?"

"Of course I have." Eliza tipped the pistol aimed at St. George. "Doesn't mean I believe you're him."

"Who else could I be?"

"I don't know," she said, "but you'll understand if I don't believe you're the Mighty Dragon."

"No," he said, "not really."

She took a step back and murmured some quick commands to the bald man with the biker beard. He glanced at the heroes, nodded, and jogged away. His feet clanged down the helipad stairs and he was gone.

I think this was a Twilight Zone *episode,* Zzzap said. *One day you wake up and nobody knows who you are.*

"They know who I am," said St. George, "they just don't believe I'm me."

"Is that a line from a song?" Madelyn asked. "It should be if it isn't."

Eliza stepped back to them. "Here's how it works," she said. "You get a full exam to make sure you're not infected. We hold you in quarantine overnight. If you pass, tomorrow we'll talk." She stared at Madelyn.

"I'm not an ex," said the Corpse Girl. "I'm just like all of you, I'm just . . . dead. It's my superpower."

"Not much of a superpower," said Eliza.

Madelyn smiled. "It all depends on what you do with it."

Do you have a big problem with the ex-virus out here? asked Zzzap.

The square-shouldered woman furrowed her brow at the wraith, and he repeated himself. She shook her head. "It was bad at first, on different ships. We lost a lot of people. Once we all came together, we got strict about who could come aboard. We haven't had someone turn in almost ten months."

Steve stared at St. George. "Why do you call yourself the Mighty Dragon?"

He shrugged. "It seemed to make sense. I could breathe fire and sort of fly."

"No, I mean, why didn't you pick your own name? It's disrespectful."

"What is?"

"Using his name," said the big man. "A lot of people looked up to him."

"It's my name," St. George said. "I made it up."

Steve grunted.

Eliza gestured at the red gym bag with her pistol. "What's in there?"

"Some supplies for the trip," said St. George. "Food, water, some clothes. There's a bag with about a thousand vitamin C tablets. We thought you might be suffering from scurvy out here and figured they'd make a nice gift."

"Where'd you get those?" Eliza asked.

We make them, said Zzzap. *It's a little time-consuming, but it's pretty easy once you've got everything set up.*

"Where the hell are you people from?" asked Alice. "I mean, how'd you dodge everything and end up with all this stuff?"

"It took a lot of time," said St. George. "For a long while we were struggling and scraping by. But we managed to get a lot of survivors together and we're doing . . . okay. Not great, but okay."

"And where is this?"

Hollywood, said Zzzap.

Steve looked at the wraith. "What was that?"

"We're in Los Angeles," said St. George. "If you know the city, our main complex is near Hollywood, heading toward downtown."

Eliza's lips flattened out. Steve lifted his shotgun and held it across his chest. Alice's face came close to a snarl.

St. George looked at each of them. "What?"

"It isn't that bad," said Madelyn. "I always heard bad things about LA, too, but it's nice. The Mount is huge. There's tons of room, and you can just walk around without worrying about exes."

Alice brought her shotgun around. It wasn't pointed at the Corpse Girl, but it wasn't far off, either. "Is that supposed to be funny?"

"No."

Whatshisname is back, said Zzzap.

The bald man with the biker beard came up the steps to the helipad. He took a few deep breaths and nodded. "Rooms are ready. Thirteen, fourteen, sixteen."

Eliza nodded. "Last chance for you and your people to get lost," she told St. George. "Our home, our rules. Everyone gets checked. No exceptions."

He looked at his friends. "I think we're all okay with that, yeah?"

Madelyn shrugged. Zzzap nodded.

"Okay, then." Eliza holstered her other pistol, but the shotguns and spears stayed up. "Follow me." She scooped up the red bag and headed for the stairwell. Steve, Alice, and the others stepped aside and gestured for the heroes to follow her.

"Welcome to Lemuria," said the Middle Eastern man as they walked past him. His flat tone made it less a greeting and more a statement. He didn't meet their eyes.

Lemuria? Zzzap glanced back at the man.

"It was a made-up continent," Alice said as they walked down the steps. "Some guy made it up back in the 1800s to explain where lemurs came from."

"That's stupid," said Madelyn.

No, actually, that's pretty much the truth, said the wraith. He drifted down from the helipad and followed alongside the dead teenager. *I was just expecting you would've gone with Atlantis or Lost Island or something.*

"We're not in the Atlantic," said Alice.

They walked along one of the gardens. People stared. Most of them were adults, but there were a few teenagers.

The garden was a raised bed, about twenty feet wide and a hundred long. There was another one a few yards past it. There were lots of plants growing that St. George recognized, but none he could name. The soil was dark and wet. Thin streams of brown water leaked out from the edges. He wrinkled his nose.

"Whoa," Madelyn whispered. "Even I can smell that. Kinda like a sewer." Her nostrils flared and her lips tightened up.

No, I get that, Zzzap said to Alice, drowning out the Corpse Girl. *Lemuria's just a little more obscure than most people would've chosen. You have my geeky approval, believe me.*

"We don't need your approval," said Steve.

I'm just saying—

"If you don't want to tell us the truth, just keep your mouth shut," the big man said. "Got it?"

"What's the problem here?" asked St. George. "Why is it so hard for you to believe we are who we say we are?"

"Because you're lying," Eliza said over her shoulder.

"But he's not," said Madelyn. "He's the Mighty Dragon. He used to be, anyway."

Steve turned and glared at them. "The Mighty Dragon's dead," he snapped. "Everyone knows that."

St. George stopped walking. "What?"

"He's dead," growled Steve. "He died when they nuked Los Angeles to contain the virus."

THEN

I THINK I saw Kathy earlier. Way up on Western, past the freeway. It was just a thin figure in white, standing in the middle of the road about a mile and a half away.

It could've been a zombie altar boy, I guess. Anybody in a white outfit. There's probably a few hundred people in white staggering around Los Angeles right now. It might've just been light gray that looked white because of the distance. The odds of it being my dead girlfriend are pretty slim.

Some people think I've got all kinds of eye powers. Telescopic sight. X-Ray vision. But the goggles don't make my eyes better, they just keep everyone else safe. Truth is, I'm not much better off than anyone else when it comes to seeing things at a distance.

I'm pretty sure it was her.

I wanted to quit being Gorgon after she died. I just wanted to curl up in my apartment for a month. Or punch something. Punching won out.

One good thing about the zombie apocalypse—there's lots of stuff to punch. Idiot gangbangers. Looters. Hysterical people. And zombies.

Lots of zombies.

Stealth had me on escort duty. Getting some of the better-armed groups into her film studio fortress. The ones who can travel on their own without too much help.

Today's group was twenty-three people. Two extended families out of Hancock Park area and four loners we'd picked up on the way. Mostly adults. A few kids. One baby keeping its trap shut. A few old people. One woman was in a wheelchair. I figured she was a goner. Her grandson pushed her, never fell behind once. He had Grandma's chair leaning back in a wheelie the whole way. They'd been hiding out six blocks away from the studio, so the decision was we could make it on foot safer and faster than driving a truck with a loud engine. I'd taken a quick hit off the group, enough to get me up to tier-two strength so I could deal with any problems that showed up.

We passed Wilton, worked the whole group around an abandoned SUV, and I saw the corner of the studio half a block up ahead. I also saw about half a dozen exes between us and that corner. With the thirty or so dead people trailing us since we passed Western, that added up to some of my group dead if I didn't take care of things.

One thing Kathy and I learned fast. Standing still is how they get you. Except for the Mighty Dragon, everyone who's tried to stand their ground against these things has been overwhelmed and died. Everyone. Police, soldiers, stupid punks with guns. Hell, they even took down Blockbuster. Eight feet tall, seven feet wide, and it just didn't matter when there's one of you and a hundred of them.

I heard the Dragon had to break his neck.

I was still at a solid tier two, and seeing Kathy earlier made me want to break something. I headed for the closest ex. There were four more behind it and a fifth a little farther back. The *click-click-click* of their teeth was a Geiger counter telling us we were close to something dangerous.

The ex saw me coming. It had been a woman, maybe in her forties when she was killed. Dark hair, sharp chin, messy bite in the left shoulder. It started to raise its arms, but I smacked them back down and grabbed its head in both hands. One sharp twist up and back snapped its neck. It went limp and dropped. The jaw kept snapping open and closed. Even if you take the head clean off, they won't stop biting until the brain's destroyed.

I tossed the head, raised my arm, and pointed out the fallen ex to my group. Didn't want anyone getting too close to those teeth. I've heard some people call them anklebiters when they're down but still active.

My arm came down and broke the wrist of the next ex before it could grab at me. I would've broken both of them, but its other arm ended at the elbow. Looked like it had been chewed or twisted off. Maybe both. No question how that guy bought it. A solid backhand spun its head to the side as its teeth scraped against the outside of my gloves. I put one hand on its jaw, one on its shoulder, and twisted it around even farther until I felt cartilage tear and heard bones snap. It fell, and I kicked it in the head as I walked past.

Two down and I'd already bled off some strength. Not much, but I could feel it. I'd have to put the rest of them down before I ran out of power.

I don't like fighting like this. I got spoiled, being able to drain strength from people. Exes don't have any life to drain. It's like trying to fight a punching bag, and I didn't adapt fast enough. That's why Kathy had to fight them alone so many times.

That's why she died.

Guilt's a great motivator. Who would've suspected?

A dead man reached for me. I kicked its legs out from under it and stomped on its head. The skull cracked on the second stomp, and its teeth stopped moving. I grabbed the next one by the arm, spun it around, and slammed it head-first into a phone pole. Its face caved in with a crunch, and I let it drop in a pile.

I heard a guy gasp behind me. They'd all stopped to stare. Seeing four exes put down in a minute can be pretty brutal. I didn't care if they were shocked as long as they were alive. "Come on," I said. "No stopping, remember?"

One of the loners we'd picked up—Ivan? Ilya? Something

Russian-sounding—was watching the rear. He had a pistol, a rifle slung over his shoulder, and an aluminum baseball bat. In the past four blocks he'd put down two exes that got too close, and he'd been smart and used the bat every time. No extra noise to draw in more of them.

He'd have to put down more soon if we didn't get moving. More likely he'd get killed and all these people would panic. The ones with guns would start shooting and attract more exes. And then we'd all die.

Just like she died.

I took a few steps back and grabbed one of the guys by the collar. He tried to flinch away, his eyes locked on the stains and bits of gore on my gloves. "Move," I hissed at him. "Do you want your family to get eaten?"

I dragged him forward a few feet and shoved him toward the film studio. He took the hint. So did the rest of them.

I marched past the guy and drove my fist into a dead woman's face. I aimed low and shattered the jaw. The ex staggered back and gave me time to move in and twist its head around. Neck broken, body dead, mouth flapping back and forth on broken bones.

I waved at the families. "Come on," I said. "Move!"

We ran past the intersection. There were a few scattered exes here, but when they're alone they're easy to dodge. A dead kid with no lower jaw and an AC/DC shirt headed toward us, stumbled off the curb, and fell facedown in the street. A female ex in a blazer and slacks limped forward, but we were past it before it could shuffle more than a few feet.

We passed Bronson, the blocked gate, and the entrance was coming up. There were a dozen or so exes past that, maybe twenty, but they were pretty far back. Exes weren't fast. We could get in the gate before they reached us.

Provided we got past the next three. They were all together. A small pack. There was a dead woman with a torn shirt. A dead police officer with one arm ripped up so much it couldn't even raise it. The third looked like it had been dragged facedown for a few blocks, or maybe burned. It had a few long black hairs and wide shoulders.

I grabbed one of the dead woman's outstretched arms, pulled her close so I could put a hand on her shoulder, and spun around. She whirled into the air, and I slammed her into the cop. The impact dropped them both in a heap in the middle of the road. Not down for good, but it'd take them a few minutes to get untangled and back to their feet.

And that was the last of my strength. Back to normal human levels. No better than any of the civilians following me. And I didn't even have a fucking baseball bat.

The faceless zombie lumbered at me. I kicked it hard in the gut. Lots of soft tissue to absorb a blow, but it's a hinge point. Bodies fold there.

Faceoff staggered back, but it didn't fall.

Dammit.

"Go," I yelled over my shoulder. I pointed past Faceoff to the studio's big main entrance. "I'll keep it busy. Get to the gate!"

In the back of the group, I got a quick glimpse of Ilya urging them on. The big group of exes behind them was getting closer. I could hear chattering teeth. Lots of them.

Then Faceoff bit my arm.

It's not a big deal. I've been bitten two or three times. They can't make it through the leather sleeves on my duster. In a way, it's a good thing. Once an ex has a mouthful of people, it'll stop fighting.

It hurts like all hell, though. Especially when they start gnawing. For someone who looked like they'd been dead for at least a month, Faceoff still had some pretty impressive jaw muscles.

I let the zombie chew on my sleeve while the rest of them ran past me. Even the kid pushing Grandma in her wheelchair. I was going to have some serious bruises on my arm when this was done.

Ilya stopped for a second and raised his bat, but I waved him on. They needed someone watching their back. Depending on how this went, it might not be me.

The sound of teeth got louder behind me. Got closer. I wasn't going to have a lot of time.

Once they were a few yards away, I punched Faceoff in the forehead. It didn't flinch, so I punched it a second time. And a third. On the fourth I felt something crack under the mess of its face.

For a few seconds it felt like it was looking at me. Its eyes kind of flickered, like it knew who I was and what I was doing. What would happen if it didn't respond. It was just a second, but man . . . I could feel hate in that look. Like it knew me.

Then the moment passed and I hit it again. This time the punch knocked it off my arm. One of its front teeth popped out, tumbled over my sleeve, and bounced off my chest.

The teeth-clicking was loud behind me. Less than twenty feet away loud. I didn't have much time.

I slammed my fist into the lack-of-face again and felt its nose collapse. The impact knocked it back again and let me kick its legs out from under it. I left it there and ran to catch up with the group. I didn't waste time looking behind me. They weren't close enough to bite, so they weren't close enough to matter.

I caught up to the group just before the gate. The exes farther down the street had seen them coming and staggered forward. Three of the men had stopped to shoot at them. I grabbed two of them and shoved them toward the gate. "Idiots," I shouted. "Just—"

The third one spun around with his pistol up. One of the dads, Jorge, I think. His eyes were scared. Somewhere on our little jaunt he'd snapped. Maybe right here.

No time to deal with panic. My goggles snapped open as soon as I saw his eyes. Just for two seconds. I felt the strength pour into me as it leeched out of him. Not much, but it was something.

The pistol dropped and he stumbled. A lot of people have told me seeing my eyes is like getting hit in the back of the head with a baseball bat. It makes dealing with people very easy. Living people, anyway.

"Help him inside," I told the other two. "Now."

They looked at him, then at me. One of them glanced back at the mob of exes. There was a walking corpse with a Nike logo on its shirt about twenty feet from us.

"Now!"

The two men grabbed their friend and ran for the gate. The guards inside had opened it about five feet, and the big robot, Cerberus, stood out in front. There were half a dozen exes flopped around its feet. One or two of them were still snapping their jaws. The robot had two more, one in each hand. She threw one at the approaching mob, then the other.

I stepped forward, grabbed the Nike lady by the shoulders, and hurled it back at the crowd. Three of the exes went down in a heap. And that was pretty much it for my borrowed strength.

The entrance to the studio is this big cobblestone driveway up through a double arch. Very old-California, old-Hollywood classy. The wheelchair was stuck in the ruts. Six blocks the kid makes it pushing Grandma and the chair gets stuck fifteen feet from the gate. Almost everyone else was inside. The two guys dragged Jorge right past Grandma and her wheelchair without stopping. The kid couldn't get her free and another quartet of exes was closing in, with a lot more behind them.

I flicked open my goggles and drained Grandma until she passed out. It gave me the boost I needed. A good tier two.

I threw her over my shoulder with one hand and flung the wheelchair at the exes with the other. When the kid tried to say something I grabbed him by the collar and dragged him to the gate.

Cerberus smacked away two last dead people, stepped through, and the gate clanged shut behind her. A pipe slammed down into a set of brackets they'd welded across the entrance. About twenty seconds later the clicking got louder and the arms started reaching through the bars to claw at the air. Some of them had expensive watches or rubber bracelets or rings. A few of them were missing fingers or whole hands.

The family surged forward and caught Grandma as I set her down. I know enough Spanish to know they were worried she was dead, but she started moving and mumbling while they talked. They shot me some angry looks I ignored. Another plus of wearing the goggles.

Then the guards closed in and started moving them toward quarantine and screening. A couple of the people freaked out a bit, but they all knew it was coming. I'd explained it to them before we'd left their safe house, and the bilingual folks had translated for the three or four of them who were bad with English.

It's a smart procedure. The guards walk them about a block down one of the studio roads to the quarantine building. Gives them time to see who's limping, favoring arms, or just acting funny. It's a way to spot people with bites they're keeping quiet about. They all know they're going to be found out eventually, but they still hope for the best.

Quarantine's a big movie theater at the far end of the studio lot. It can hold a couple hundred people, but I don't think there's more than fifty or sixty in there at a time. Everyone stays there until they get checked out. It sounds like a recipe for disaster, I know, locking a bunch of untested people in a room together, but it isn't. Unlike the movies, exes don't re-animate in seconds. No one falls down dead and then jumps up as a zombie thirty seconds later. It takes a couple of hours for the ex-virus to get someone back on their feet.

Counting these people, I've helped get almost two hundred people inside so far. Two hundred people saved in less than a week.

It's been seven weeks since she died. Since Regenerator screwed up and didn't save her. He said we had more time, she'd be fine for another day or so, he needed to focus on more serious cases. Then she started convulsing. And bleeding out.

By the time someone found him she was already dead. There was nothing he could do. He put his hand on my shoulder and told me how sorry he was.

I think if the Dragon hadn't shown up, I might've killed him. Or I would've found out just how fast he can heal. How many times can you crush someone's hand in five minutes?

When I found out he'd been bitten, I almost laughed. Four weeks to the day after Kathy died. Irony. It'll get you every fucking time.

The robot walked over to stand near me. I know it's armor, not a robot, but I can't help it. First impressions and all that crap.

"Close one," said Cerberus. The words had a sharp, harsh edge. I think she had something set in the speakers so she'd sound tougher.

"Shouldn't've been," I muttered. "If they'd just kept moving it wouldn't've been a problem."

"Come on," she said. "Let's get you cleared."

"Yeah, sure."

Every time I come back in, I have to go through a full exam. That's the big procedure right now. It's why all the people I brought back are in quarantine. One by one they're brought out, taken somewhere secure, and stripped naked. Every inch of you gets checked for cuts, scrapes, stabs, bites—anything that means you could be infected. They even look at your tongue. I know Stealth wanted to shave people's scalps, but the Dragon thought that'd be pushing it.

Plus, head wounds bleed like mad. You can't hide one. Even an old one's going to have a big scab, and if it's older than that . . . well, it'd be clear you're infected.

We walked down the road to one of the four white pop-up tents that had been set up near the quarantine building. Two for men, two for women. The guards were leading a teenage girl with messy brown hair into the farthest tent while we approached. She hadn't been in my group.

Cerberus stopped a few yards away from the tent and let me walk in on my own. One of the few privileges of being a superhero. I can cut in line for the naked test.

An older guy with a beard was waiting in the tent. He'd checked me four or five times before. I think his name started with a J. I didn't pay a lot of attention to introductions these days. He had two folding tables on either side of him.

Two guards with rifles flanked the tent's entrance. One of them wore a camo jacket with a Marine badge on the shoulder. I knew there were a couple real Marines here, but there were also people floating around who'd found or looted military clothes. This guy's posture didn't scream military.

Some people freaked out during the test. That's why there were armed guards. A few of them had reason to freak out. I'd never asked what happened when they found somebody with a bite. To be honest, I didn't care.

The bearded guy smiled at me. "Y'all want to admit anything up front, save us some time?"

I shook my head and pulled my gloves off. They had some slime and a bit of blood on them. I dropped them on the left-hand table. Questionable material. No one was sure how the ex-virus spread, so anything questionable got doused in disinfectants, washed, and doused again. I'd get them back just in time to head back out again.

I shrugged out of my duster and draped it over the table on the right. Then I unbuckled my body armor and pulled it over my head. Arm guards were next, then my utility belt, and my shirt. All piled on the right.

"Goggles," said the guard in the Marine jacket.

I stopped unbuttoning my jeans and looked at him. "What?"

"Take your goggles off," he said.

Nobody else said anything. I felt my mouth twist. "Are you new here or just fucking stupid? The goggles don't come off."

His jaw tensed up. He started to raise his rifle, but the other guard pushed it back down. "Sorry, Gorgon. He's new *and* stupid."

I shook my head and let my jeans drop. I was a boxers man for years, but over the past few weeks I'd switched to briefs, just to speed this whole process up and spare myself a little dignity. They hide a lot less.

"Got a big bruise there," said the smart guard. He gestured with his chin at my forearm. His hands stayed on his rifle.

"Ex tried to bite me through my jacket," I said.

"It break the skin?" asked the bearded man.

I shook my head. "Didn't even scrape the sleeve."

He nodded, glanced over at the duster, and then studied the bruise from a few angles. "Hold your arm out," he said after a minute, flicking his fingers at it.

I did. He peered at it some more, then nodded. "Looks okay," he said. He twirled his fingers and I turned around. He started high, and I heard his boots creak as he crouched to look at my thighs and calves. A lot of people get bitten on their calves. Anklebiters.

"Step your feet out a bit."

I moved each foot out eight or nine inches. Another minute passed.

He tapped my shoulder and I faced front again. "All looks good to me," he said. He glanced back at the guards. "Y'all see anything?"

The smart guard shook his head. The idiot seethed for a few seconds and then shook his head, too. "Nothing," he muttered.

"Good to go," the bearded guy told me.

I got dressed. Everything but my gloves. I knew the drill, and so did the bearded guy. Last thing was my duster. I swung it around and let it settle on my shoulders. I looked at the idiot and thought about opening the goggles for a few seconds. Instead I just walked outside.

Cerberus was waiting for me. Could've been a statue. Didn't look like she'd moved an inch. "All good?"

I didn't answer. She tried to talk to me a lot. It struck me I had no idea what the woman inside the armor looked like. I'd never met her face-to-face. I didn't want to meet anyone. Especially not any women.

We walked back toward the main gate. There was a cafeteria on the other side of the lot where they had some basics. Canned soup. Oatmeal. They were trying to go through all the stuff in the freezer before it went bad. There might even be some meat. I could get some dinner, grab a few hours of sleep somewhere, and be back outside at sunrise.

Cerberus was talking about defenses. Walls, gates. I didn't pay much attention. None of this stuff involved me. I just wanted to be alone.

I think there's a good chance that one day I'll head out and not come back. I don't know where I'd go. Maybe I'd try to find Kathy. Whatever was left of her. Maybe I'd just go back to my apartment and curl up. One or two people had told me it'd pass. I'd get over it.

They were idiots.

I didn't have any reason to stay here. The Dragon and Stealth and robot-lady could handle all this without me. I wasn't needed here. I just wanted to—

"Stop pushing me, asshole," someone shouted.

A new group was heading down the cobblestone street toward us. Maybe a dozen people. Not sure who brought them in. I didn't see the Dragon or Stealth anywhere.

There was a big guy in a gym-gray T-shirt and jeans off to one side of the group. He had a shaved head and a face full of stubbly whiskers. His body was thick. Not muscular or fat, but that solid midpoint.

One of the guards was saying something and pointing toward us. Toward quarantine. The guy shook his head. The people around him looked nervous, and he wasn't helping.

"No," shouted the guy. "I'm not going to no death panels! Let me out of here."

The guard tried to calm him, but out of nowhere the guy threw a wild punch. The guard stumbled back. People screamed. The guy ran.

After being on edge and alone for a few months, some people couldn't deal with the idea of being safe or being told what to do. Sometimes they freaked out. A few of the freak-outs were small, but most were like this guy—loud and convinced they could do something about it.

I had a bit of extra strength left from Grandma. Enough I could take a few leaping strides and get ahead of the guy. He looked at me, raised his fists, and I opened the goggles wide.

He stood there for a moment. Then his legs wobbled and he sagged. He dropped to his knees in front of me, still trapped by my eyes. I held him in my stare. Strength was just pouring out of him into me. His eyes were watering, and he started to shake.

I heard something heavy walk up behind me. "I think you got him," said Cerberus.

The goggles snapped shut. Death-panels guy toppled over. From the way my skin was tingling, he'd be waking up in an hour or so with a serious headache.

The guards came and dragged him toward quarantine. Being unconscious didn't get you out of an exam, and this guy had just gotten bumped to the front of the line.

"Stupid," I said. "They should've been expecting something like that."

"Probably," said Cerberus. "What do you want? Most of these guys aren't trained military or police." The big helmet head moved side to side. "Hell, we're lucky when we can find a mall security guard."

"Well, they better find someone to put in charge. Things are going to get ugly in here fast if it keeps going like this."

I watched them haul him into the same tent I'd been in a few minutes ago. When he woke up he was either going to be naked or his underwear'd be sitting funny. Either way, he'd probably keep his head down for a while.

I decided to be in the area when he woke up. Just in case.

For now, I turned and headed for the cafeteria.

THIRTEEN

NOW

"**ERRRRRR** ... Nobody nuked Los Angeles," St. George said.

"Yeah, they did," said Steve.

"No, they didn't. And I'm not dead."

"The Dragon is," the tall man with the shotgun said.

"He's not," said Madelyn. "I'd know, believe me."

So would I, said Zzzap.

"Are you stupid or something," asked Alice, "or is this part of some plan?"

"Okay, hang on," said St. George. He came to a halt near the end of the muddy garden. Alice almost bumped into him. "You think someone dropped a nuclear bomb on LA?"

"They didn't drop it," said the bald man with the biker beard. "I heard they drove them in on trucks."

"Them?" Madelyn echoed. "More than one?"

"No," Steve told the bald man, "they dropped it."

St. George waved his hand. "Not the point."

"Point is, don't act like idiots," said Steve. He made a little move-along gesture with his shotgun. "It doesn't help your case."

I'm a part-time idiot, Zzzap said, *although I'm considering taking the leap to full-time. Maybe you could explain it to me?*

The bald man chuckled.

Steve took a breath. His fingers squeezed the barrel of the shotgun. "This isn't funny," he said. "At all."

"We just . . ." St. George glanced at the others. "We're all a little confused here."

"Hey," shouted Eliza. She was a dozen yards ahead, already at the top of the long walkway. "Move it. Now."

They started moving again.

St. George took a quick step to be a little closer to Steve. In the corner of his eye he saw Madelyn do the same, staying near him. "So," he said to the tall man, "they dropped a nuclear bomb on Los Angeles."

Steve looked down at the hero and shook his head. "You're a piece of work."

"Just trying to get some answers."

They reached the bottom of the walkway. The sides were tight canvas, not as white when seen up close. The floor of it was scuffed down to bare metal in most places. The wheels on the end slid back half an inch as the deck shifted beneath them.

Steve waved St. George up the ramp, then Madelyn. He followed behind them. Zzzap floated through the air alongside the walkway. St. George glanced back and saw the bald man frowning at the glowing wraith.

The ramp ended at a doorway in the cruise ship's hull. A stairwell on the other side led them up to the main deck. Zzzap floated up the side of the ship and met them there. Eliza shot a look at St. George, another one at Steve, and then started off across the open space. The tall man nodded for St. George and Madelyn to follow her.

Big plastic drums stood along the railings. Two long strings of colored flags had been converted into clotheslines. There were tables and chairs cluttering every space, and even a few beds.

And no people at all.

"Where is everyone?" asked Madelyn. "I saw a lot more people when we were looking for a place to land."

"They're safe," said the bald man.

"Safe from what?"

"From you," said Alice.

"I'm not an ex," Madelyn said with a sigh. "Talking's the big clue."

"We'll see," said the leather-skinned woman.

Something else didn't look right, but St. George couldn't put his finger on it. He'd never been on a cruise ship. Never even visited the *Queen Mary* down in Long Beach, just an hour south of LA back when traffic had been an issue. His total experience could be summed up with a few *Love Boat* reruns when he was little and the occasional Disney cruise ad.

But something wasn't right here.

He cleared his throat and looked up at the tall man. "The bomb?" he asked again.

"You don't quit, do you?"

"I'm just trying to find out how I died."

Steve snorted and shook his head. "Telling you now, there are people here who'll smack the shit out of you for talk like that."

"Not you, though?"

"Not until the boss tells me to."

St. George glanced ahead at Eliza. "Until then . . . why don't you tell me what happened? Why do you think they nuked Los Angeles?"

"Because it's all gone."

"The city?"

"All the cities." he said. "Los Angeles. San Diego. San Francisco. Seattle. New York. Boston. Houston. Dallas. Every major population center. All gone. It was the only way to contain the virus."

"Of course they didn't drop one on Washington," said Alice. "Fucking politicians, always covering their own asses before anyone else's."

"Look," said St. George, "I don't know where you got all this but . . . Los Angeles is fine." He glanced up at Zzzap. "I think all those cities are fine. Relatively speaking."

The wraith nodded. *I was just in San Diego about a week ago, and New York last month. There's a pretty good-sized group of survivors in Queens.*

"Don't joke about shit like that, man," said the bald man. "My brother and his family were in Queens."

I'm not joking. There's almost three thousand people living in the Queens Center Mall.

They headed up a broad staircase. Laundry dried on the railings. There was a diagram of the ship sealed behind a scratched Plexiglas plate. The small YOU ARE HERE star stood out in the bottom corner. They reached a new deck, and Eliza continued up onto another set of stairs. On the next level they headed down a long walkway that stretched along one side of the ship.

"When do you think this happened?" St. George asked the tall man. "Or, when did it happen, I guess. The bombings?"

Steve glared at St. George. He opened his mouth, his lips pulled back, and then he just shook his head. He turned away from the hero and stomped down the walkway, pulling ahead of the group. He muttered something to Eliza, and she glanced back at the heroes.

St. George turned, but the bald man and Alice had dropped back a few paces.

Guess no one wants to talk about it. Zzzap floated alongside them just outside the walkway.

"Nobody got nuked, right?" asked Madelyn in a lower voice. "That's not just you being nice to them."

St. George shook his head. "The only thing I know about is one bomb that went off in Hawaii long after everything fell apart. About four months after we got everyone into the Mount."

Christmas Eve, added Zzzap.

"Stealth thought it was some survivor messing around with a submarine at Pearl Harbor," said St. George, "that they set off a missile or something like that."

It took out the harbor, the airport, and half of Honolulu, said Zzzap. *The other half burned. Well, about half of the whole island burned, really.*

Madelyn's eyes went wide. "How many people were there?"

The wraith let out a buzzing sigh. *A few hundred,* he said. *Hawaii didn't do so well when the Zombocalypse hit. There weren't a lot of survivors.*

The Corpse Girl mulled on this as they walked. "But no one ever did it deliberately? Nuke somewhere?"

"I never heard of it happening," St. George said. "Stealth told me once it was a fallback plan, using nukes to sterilize the cities, but the virus was everywhere before they decided to do it. The bombs wouldn't've made a difference. Never heard of any being dropped anywhere else, either."

A lot of people in the military kept expecting North Korea or China to do it, said Zzzap. *Either nuke themselves or nuke someone else. But they never did.*

"Are you sure?" Madelyn asked.

Yeah. Even with a small explosion like the one on Honolulu, I'd still be seeing radiation flares from something like that today. Never seen anything.

"Do you think they saw it?" St. George looked up at the glowing figure. "Maybe they saw the Honolulu nuke go off, or the aftermath of it, and just figured it happened everywhere?"

Maybe? It's closer than the mainland. Timeline doesn't seem right, though.

Eliza led the group a third of the way down the length of the cruise ship, where they came to a pair of wide double doors. They'd probably looked glamorous at one point, but now the glass was smudged and the handles were tarnished. She pulled one side open and revealed a dark hallway. It ran the width of the ship, and at the far end sunlight shined through a grubby window.

Ummmmm, said Zzzap, *hang on.* He waved a hand up and down his brilliant silhouette. *I don't do well in small, enclosed spaces.*

Eliza turned back to look at him. "Can you ... turn it off?"

Zzzap turned his head to St. George. *What do you think?*

The hero took in a breath and let it curl out through his nose as streamers of smoke. "Can we trust you?" he asked Eliza.

"What's that supposed to mean?"

"We're here as friends," said St. George, "but so far you haven't been too friendly back. Pretty much aggressive and unhelpful. So can we trust you, or are things only getting worse from here?"

Eliza stared back at him. Her eyes flitted up to look at the curls of smoke as they thinned out in the air. "Once you've been cleared and quarantined," she said, "and we've cleared up who you are—"

"We've told you who we are," said Madelyn.

"—and what you are," Eliza continued with a glance at the Corpse Girl, "I don't think we'll have any more issues."

St. George looked at Barry. The wraith shrugged. *Would you ladies mind turning around?*

The broad-shouldered woman frowned. "Why?"

Because I'm about to suffer a slight case of nudity and I wouldn't want you to get exposed to it.

Alice snorted and half turned her head. Zzzap turned his head to Eliza. She set her hands on her hips, just above her pistols. "I said you could trust us," she told him. "I didn't say we trusted you yet."

Can I at least trust you to give me my robe out of the bag?

The gleaming wraith slid into the narrow walkway. He sank low to the deck and spread his arms to catch himself. Steam crawled out of the deck boards. His brilliant form dimmed, the faint hiss of heat and static faded, and the air was shoved out of the way. Barry fell out of the air and landed on the hardwood with a *thunk* and a yelp.

"Dammit," he muttered, rubbing his elbow. "Funny bone."

"Looked like you whacked your knee pretty hard," said the bald man.

"Yeah, but I can't feel my knee," Barry said.

"You numb?" asked Eliza.

Barry nodded. "For about thirty years now." A few minutes later he was wrapped in his robe, and St. George carried him into the hallway.

The group moved to a crossing hallway. This one was lit by a few random open doors. Barry glanced up at one of the light fixtures.

Eliza walked a few yards down the dark hall to the first open doorway. The next pair were another twenty feet down the hall. "One for each of you," she said.

St. George glanced into one of the rooms and saw two men with guns. A plaque near the door read MOTHER OF PEARL and right below it, in smaller numbers, 13. "The exam?"

She nodded. "Should take ten or fifteen minutes if you all cooperate."

Madelyn crossed her arms. "What are you looking for?"

Eliza looked down at the dead girl. "Signs of infection."

"Like being dead and still moving?"

St. George stepped next to the Corpse Girl. "Madelyn's dead," he said, "but she's not an ex."

"So you keep saying," said Steve. His fingers stretched on the pump of his shotgun like someone playing the frets of a guitar.

Eliza held out a hand. "Steve," she said, "you take the handicapped guy. Sand Dollar." She turned to Alice. "Take the . . . the dead girl over to Jewel Box. Look for signs of bites, cuts, anything that could mean infection."

"I don't have any," said Madelyn.

Eliza turned her gaze to St. George, but kept talking to

Alice. "If you find anything, if she attacks you . . . you know what to do."

"You people are dense," said the Corpse Girl.

"We're submitting to your exam on good faith," said St. George. He let more smoke curl out of his mouth. "Don't make us regret it." He cleared his throat and let a few sparks of flame tumble from his mouth.

The bald man stared at the licks of fire. So did Alice.

"Okay," said Eliza, "everyone's clear, then."

Steve stepped forward and held out his arms. St. George locked eyes with the man, then set Barry into the other man's embrace. "Good?"

"I'm good," said Barry.

"I have him," said Steve. The tall man's eyes relaxed a little as he shifted his arms under Barry's weight. "You're heavier than you look."

"You're the first person to say that in a couple of months," Barry said. He glanced back at St. George and threw a two-fingered salute from his temple. "See you on the other side, Ray."

Madelyn smiled. Alice gestured with her head, and they walked down to the open door across from Barry's. Madelyn looked back, gave St. George a confident nod, then vanished inside. The door closed behind her with a click that echoed in the hallway.

Eliza pointed at the entrance next to them. "This one's you," she said.

St. George walked into the room. Two big picture windows in the far wall showed the sea outside and the orange light of the setting sun. He couldn't see any closets or anything that looked like a bathroom. Nothing but bare walls and the kind of over-patterned carpet only hotels and casinos could get away with. And apparently cruise ships. He guessed Mother of Pearl had been a room for conferences or events.

The two men he'd glimpsed earlier watched him. Each one wore a sidearm. The scruffy Asian man on the left had tattooed arms and a sidearm in a clip-on holster. The one on the right was a rail-thin white man with dense brown dreadlocks and a shotgun. They waved him into the center of the room.

"I'm going to go check in with Maleko," Eliza said to the bald man with the biker beard. "You got this?"

"Yeah."

She closed the door.

St. George stood there. The three other men stared at him. "I'm guessing you haven't had a lot of visitors?"

"Strip," said the bald man.

"What's your name, anyway?"

"What's it to you?"

St. George unbuckled the safety harness. "Just trying to be friendly, remember?"

The man looked him in the eye. "Devon," he said. "I'm Devon."

St. George rolled his shoulders and let the webbing straps fall off him. His tendons popped as he did it. He looked over at the other two men. "And you guys?"

The Asian man muttered something in a language St. George didn't understand. The other man shifted his shotgun so the barrel was pointed more at the hero than away from him. "My name is get your damned clothes on the floor before I blow your head off."

The hero glanced back at Devon. "You want to tell him how useless that thing is, or should I?"

"He blocked Steve's shotgun," the bald man told the others. "With his hand."

"What do you mean?"

"I mean, he caught it. The buckshot."

"Bullshit," said the dreadlocked man.

"Swear to God," said Devon. "He did it right there in front

of me. Steve tried to shoot the zombie girl they brought with—"

"She's not a zombie," said St. George. He unzipped his biker jacket and set it on the floor. "She's just . . . dead."

"He's bulletproof," said Devon, "he breathes fire, and he flew out here with the others."

"Bullshit," the dreadlocked man said again, but he looked at the hero with a critical eye.

"Swear to God," Devon said again.

St. George crouched to untie his boots. "It's true," he said.

"So, you're . . . what?" said Dreadlock. "A Mighty Dragon knockoff or something?"

St. George pulled off one of his boots and looked back at Devon. "Actually," he said, "I am the Mighty Dragon. But most people just call me St. George these days."

Dreadlock's jaw tightened. His eyebrows knotted. "Bullshit."

"I am."

The shotgun shifted again, moving even closer to St. George.

He sighed and pulled off his other boot. His utility belt came off next, and then he slid off his pants. He added them to the pile.

"That supposed to be some sort of super-suit?" asked Devon.

St. George looked down at himself. "It's a wet suit," he said. "I flew two thousand miles across the ocean to get here."

"Flew," muttered Dreadlock. The Asian man smirked and added a few syllables. Dreadlock responded in the same language and they both chuckled.

St. George reached behind his back, and after two tries he grabbed the thin strap on the wet suit's zipper. It slid down with a low razzing noise. He pulled it away from his neck and enjoyed the cool air that rolled down his chest.

The three men shuffled their feet as he peeled off the wet suit. He had a pair of damp boxers on underneath, and a faint chill swirled around them as they hit the air. He kicked the neoprene suit off his legs and stretched his arms out wide.

The Asian man stepped forward. He leaned in close to St. George and focused on the thin flesh of his hand and wrist. The intense gaze worked its way up his arm to his shoulder. The Asian man kept one hand near his holster the whole time.

After ten minutes of poring over St. George's skin, the man barked out a few sharp syllables. "Boxers," said Dreadlock. "Lose 'em."

"Seriously?"

Devon shifted behind him. "Lots of people into weird stuff before the zombies showed up. We don't know you. Who knows what you're into."

Dreadlock's hands twitched on the shotgun. "There some reason you don't want to take them off?"

"Aside from being naked?"

"What are you hiding?"

"Nothing."

"Everything off," he said. "That's the rules."

St. George looked over his shoulder at the bald man. "You saw me catch a handful of buckshot with my bare hand but you still think something might've bitten me and broke the skin?"

Devon shook his head. "No exceptions, man."

x x x

Madelyn stood in the center of the room and stared down at the pile of clothes. Jacket, shorts, sneakers, wet suit. She was glad she'd worn a sports bra and boxer briefs under the wet suit. It was uncomfortable enough standing in front of the male guard. It would've been worse in regular underwear.

The room was cool. It was probably cold. She couldn't tell. She wondered if most people would be cold standing there in their underwear. She couldn't remember enough about her life before to be sure.

The woman, Alice, had a pistol one of the other guards had handed her. She pointed it in Madelyn's face while she examined every inch of skin. She stayed a few feet away. The pistol wavered a bit, but stayed more or less on Madelyn's head.

She'd never been shot in the head. If she had, she didn't remember it. She wasn't sure if it would hurt her or not. It would probably put her down, but for how long?

Alice batted Madelyn's left arm up. She grabbed the wrist and twisted the arm back and forth. She pinched the flesh once or twice at a few points. It wasn't hard enough to be malicious or soft enough to be concerned. Then she did the same with the other arm. She pried Madelyn's fingers wide apart and examined the skin between them.

"I don't see any bites on it," said Alice. She gave a quick glance over her shoulder to one of the two guards. Both of them had rifles aimed at Madelyn. One of them, the female guard, didn't look much older than her.

"Because I haven't been bitten," Madelyn said.

"Jesus, it almost sounds like it's alive," the younger guard mumbled. She had dirty blond hair like St. George and a sharp chin.

"It might be one of those automatic things," said the man. He had a thick, cowboy-type mustache that spilled over the edges of his mouth. "Maybe enough of its brain's still active and it's just spitting out words."

"You're talking about yourself," said Alice.

Madelyn snickered and smiled. As soon as her lips pulled away from teeth, Alice stepped back. Three weapons rose to point at the Corpse Girl.

"Hey," said Madelyn, "just laughing. You made a funny."

"Mouth shut," the cowboy said.

She thought about banging her teeth together, just to see if he flinched, but he looked a little too trigger-happy as it was.

The pistol went back up to Madelyn's head. "Foot up."

"What?"

"Lift your left foot."

Madelyn brought her knee up and wobbled. Alice yanked the foot up and twisted it side to side. The Corpse Girl flailed at the air, reached for Alice's shoulder, and the shotguns loomed in her face.

"Gimme a break," she said. "She's pulling on my foot."

"Don't," said the female guard, "move."

Madelyn looked down at the leathery woman. The eyes looking over the pistol were cold. They could've been staring at a paper target or an old can or an ex-human, just something that needed to be shot.

She sighed and straightened up. Her arms went out for balance, and she tried to focus all her weight onto her other leg. "You people are jerks."

"And stop looking at me," said the cowboy. "Your eyes give me the creeps."

Madelyn made a mental note to never blink when she looked at the cowboy-mustached man. She repeated the note silently to herself three times.

Alice bent the foot in different directions. She checked between toes, squeezed the calf, examined the knee. Then she made a few quick gestures and Madelyn switched feet, holding the other one out. More twisting, more prodding.

"Take the rest of it off," said the leathery woman.

"What?"

"The rest of the clothes. Off."

Madelyn looked at the guards on either side of her. "But he . . . I mean, shouldn't this be a girls-only thing?"

Alice glared at her. "You hiding something?"

The sports bra and boxer briefs suddenly didn't feel like enough clothing. "I just . . . do I really need to take everything off?"

"Why not?"

"I just . . ." She looked over at the jerk cowboy, and then back at Alice. She leaned forward and the other woman leaned back, but didn't shift her feet. "I've never been naked before," said Madelyn. "With a guy. In the same room."

The leather-skinned woman rocked back on her heels and gazed at the dead teen. "Now," she said. "Or we put you down."

Madelyn stood there. She looked at Alice. She looked at the man with the cowboy mustache. She looked at the girl with the dirty blond hair. They all had flat expressions. None of them were looking at a teenage girl. They were all looking at an it. At a thing.

She sighed, pressed her lips together, and pulled her sports bra up. Her hair snagged, and for a moment she was caught in a tangle of arms and spandex wrapped around her head. She wiggled free and dropped the bra on the pile of clothes. She hooked her thumbs in the waistband of the boxer briefs and pushed them down until they dropped to her ankles.

Alice gestured for her to lift her arms again. Madelyn raised them out to her sides. She waited what felt like a cool and confident amount of time while the other woman examined her, then glanced at the cowboy.

He smirked. Madelyn stared at him, not blinking, until the smirk faded. At least she didn't have to be the only uncomfortable one in the room.

"I can't find a bite anywhere," Alice said.

"I told you," said Madelyn, "I haven't been bitten. Exes can't even see me."

The leathery woman walked around to face her. "What's that supposed to mean?"

"Can I put my clothes back on?"

"Answer the question."

Madelyn shifted her thighs, put one arm across her boobs, and waved the other one up and down herself, at all her pale skin. "They don't see me as food because I'm like this. They just don't notice me. Like, aggressively don't notice me."

"Because you're one of them," said the younger woman.

"I'm not an ex," said Madelyn.

"But you're dead."

She took in a breath. "I'm dead, yeah," she said, "but I'm not an ex."

Alice still had her pistol up. "So what are you?"

"I'm kind of naked. Could I please put my clothes back on?"

"After you answer the question." The leathery woman reached out with her foot and swept the pile of clothes away from the Corpse Girl. "If you're not an ex, what are you?"

Madelyn watched the clothes retreat. Her other hand drifted down to settle between her legs and cover herself as best she could. "Nobody knows," she said. "My dad was a scientist and I think he did something to me, but . . . I don't know. I don't remember."

"Oh, real convenient," said the cowboy.

"Not really, no."

Alice frowned. "Did something to you how?"

"I don't know," said Madelyn. "When I was little he'd give me shots sometimes, or things in IV bags. I was sick when I was a kid. I think whatever he did then made me like this after I died."

They looked at her again, their eyes going up and down her body.

"How did you die?" asked the young woman.

Madelyn bit her lip. "Ahh," she said. "Well, I don't really remember it. I have memory problems sometimes. There's a lot of stuff I've forgotten."

"So you don't know how you died?" Alice's brow knotted up.

Madelyn looked at the pile of clothes. "Could I just put my underwear back on, at least? The exam's done, right?"

"How'd you die?" asked the cowboy.

She sighed and looked down at the floor. "I think I got torn apart by a bunch of exes."

"So you *have* been bitten," said Alice.

x x x

Barry pushed himself over and back up into a sitting position. He tensed his abs to hold himself in place and dragged the robe over himself. "Everybody convinced I don't have the mark of the beast or anything like that?" he asked, bracing his arms on the floor. "Or do I need to flop around like a fish for another ten minutes?"

"We have to be sure," said Steve. There were two other men with shotguns. They'd relaxed a bit when it became clear Barry couldn't walk, but they hadn't lowered their weapons. "I needed to make sure you weren't faking."

"Faking what?"

"This." He waved his hand at Barry sprawled on the floor. "It might be a trick."

Barry glared up at Steve. The other man looked six feet over him from his current position. "Yeah, I'm tricking you into putting me in a very vulnerable position. Damn, I'm clever." He shook his head. "What's next? You want to drown me in the pool and make sure I'm not a witch? Or just see if I weigh as much as a duck?"

Steve let the barrel of his own shotgun drift down to the floor. "When was the last time you had contact with the ex?"

"What ex?"

"The dead girl you brought with you."

"It's Corpse Girl," said Barry. "Like Steamboy, but with

more death. I think she copyrighted it, so be careful about using it too much."

"Answer the question."

"What are you asking? 'Contact' is pretty vague. Are we talking about the Sagan book or the movie with Jodie Foster or *First Contact* when the Borg travel—"

Steve tapped his boot against Barry's foot. A little harder than a tap, but not a kick. "When was the last time you touched it?"

Barry raised an eyebrow and looked from his foot up to Steve's face. "We have to work on your people skills."

"Answer the question."

He sighed. "I think we might've brushed feet while we were sleeping last night, but it's hard for me to be sure." He waved at his legs.

"You *slept* with it?" spat one of the guards. He had the dark, flaking skin of someone who lived in an ongoing cycle of sunburns and peeling.

Barry twisted around to look at the man. "First off," he said, "she's a she, not an it. And yes, all of us slept together in the same life raft."

"I'd never close my eyes around one of those things," muttered the other guard. There was a thin gap between each of his teeth, as if they'd been spaced out.

"So, hey," said Barry, "fascinating as all this narrow-mindedness is to listen to, how about we shake things up with a little quid pro quo, Clarice?"

Steve looked down at him. "What?"

"While we were walking up here, you were talking about the bombs going off. When did that happen?"

The tall man's jaw tensed up.

"Hey," said Barry, "I'm flopping on the floor. You can at least answer one or two easy questions, right?"

Steve's fingers flexed on his shotgun and Barry tensed. He found the switch in the back of his mind, the one that turned him back into Zzzap, and put a little bit of mental pressure against it. The change took less than a second, but it didn't hurt to be ready.

Then the tall man's grip shifted. "About four and a half years ago," he said. "Right after things got bad."

"What day?"

"We don't know for sure. We were all out here, at sea. One day the Internet crapped out, and then all the broadcasting stopped. And then . . ." He tapped his fingers on the shotgun. "We think they dropped the bombs in July or August."

"August of . . . 2009?" asked Barry.

Steve's jaw shifted again and he nodded.

"Typical government morons," said the gap-toothed guard. "Too late to do any good."

Barry nodded without hearing the man. "So," he said, "you saw the flash or what?"

Steve shook his head. "Not from out here. We got it all from witnesses. Los Angeles was just a crater. Most of the West Coast was gone. Most of Honolulu, too. The whole island of Oahu."

"Yeah," said Barry, "I've seen Honolulu, too."

The sunburned guard looked down his peeling nose at Barry. "How d'you know about Honolulu but not know about everything else? Where've you been all this time?"

"I have been," said Barry, "in Japan."

The men paused and looked at each other. "Japan's still there?" Steve asked. "I heard Tokyo got hit, too."

Barry shook his head. "Nope. Must've been a translation problem. They're fine."

The man's eyes opened a little wider. "Really?"

Barry nodded. "All the experience they had dealing with giant monsters, you think they couldn't deal with a zombie uprising?"

Peel frowned. "Giant monsters aren't real."

"A couple of years ago we would've said zombies aren't

real," said Barry. "Let's not say anything that'll make us all look stupid later, right?"

Peel nodded awkwardly.

"Remember the super-samurai? Most of them survived and they've got a safe zone set up, and, hey, speaking of which, are we pretty much done here? I'd love to get back with my friends."

"In a couple of minutes," said Steve. "What about your buddy? Why's he keep saying he's the Mighty Dragon?"

"Why do you keep saying he's not the Mighty Dragon?"

"Because the Dragon died in LA," said Peel.

"How do you know that? You don't even know when the bombs went off, but you know he was there?"

"Yeah."

"But you're not questioning me about not being there."

"You're not saying you're the Mighty Dragon."

"Okay, yeah, but . . ." Barry stopped, shifted his weight onto one hand, and rubbed his temple. "Hey, is there any chance you've got a wheelchair stashed here somewhere? Or just a chair-chair? It's kind of a pain to keep holding myself up like this."

"In a minute," said Steve. "We'll get you back to your friends, you can all rest for the night, and tomorrow morning we'll all talk with the boss."

"Why not tonight?"

"Quarantine," the tall man said. "Just want to make sure you're all clean before we let you out and about."

"Isn't that what this whole strip search was about?"

"Just a follow-up thing. You can get infected other ways, too."

Barry looked at him. "It's Madelyn, isn't it? You're just waiting to see if she attacks somebody or something."

Steve shrugged. "You brought an ex on board. We've got to keep everyone safe."

"She's not an ex. She's just a teenage girl. Sort of."

"She's dead, right?"

"Well, yeah. But not that way."

"If she's dead," said Steve, "she's an ex."

Barry leaned forward and crossed his arms. "I've got to be honest," he said, "I'm sensing some serious trust issues from you guys."

FOURTEEN

NOW

THE SUN CAME up over the freeway and flooded the armor's optic systems. Cesar shook his head until the whited-out view readjusted. Color flowed back into the world, and he saw the garden, the fences, and the exes out on the street.

"You okay?" asked Gibbs. The hisses and whirrs of his foot blended in with the sounds of the titan as they walked the fence. It was only Cesar's second time out in the battle-suit, and they were still checking a few things.

"Sunlight made the lenses flare up," Cesar said. "Just took a minute to adjust."

Gibbs frowned. "That shouldn't be happening."

"Might just be me, y'know. I get all the input direct."

Gibbs pulled his clipboard out from under his arm and made a note as they walked.

The community garden had been two big areas on opposite sides of a residential street, each one surrounded by a low chain-link fence. Those fences had been connected and reinforced with vehicles, like the Mount. Granted, Eden's wall contained a much higher class of car, overall. And a lot fewer of them.

It was still a bit of a work in progress. Lots of vehicles could be found in the suburban residential area—mostly SUVs and sports cars—but they hadn't had as much time to gather them and get them into place. Unlike the Mount, the cars weren't stacked, and in most places it was just a single car parked against the fence. There were still long stretches with nothing but chain-link, posts, and some plywood to block the view.

One such place was the Hot Zone, the twenty-foot-wide walkway between the two gardens. When the people of the Mount first started working on Eden, they'd extended the fence across the road. St. George had found extra material around some nearby houses and driven new posts into the pavement. It was where they'd set up their gates for the trucks, and where the vehicles were parked.

The gates and necessary open space also made it the least reinforced part of the fence line.

Cesar and Gibbs walked past one of the Hot Zone's simple guard stations. The blueprints showed a squat tower, but for now it was two folding chairs on a stack of wooden pallets, just high enough to see over the car that reinforced that length of fence. A man and woman sat and watched the exes thump against the vehicle. They each gave the armor a nod. "Good to have you out here, Cerberus," said the man.

Cesar raised an arm and gave them a confident salute. They both smiled before turning back to the undead.

The exoskeleton and the lieutenant walked out of the Hot Zone and continued along the fence line. Cesar looked at some of the exes straining against the fence. There hadn't been many when they'd arrived a few days earlier, but all the activity in the garden had attracted them. He winked, or thought of winking, and the armor's targeting system came up with sixty-three targets. One shy of hitting its max. Dozens and dozens of red crosshairs filled his view. He swept them away with another thought.

Instead, he looked at the faces. St. George did that. He tried to remember these were people once, not just teeth-clacking zombies. So Cesar wanted to do the same.

There was a dead woman in a floppy straw hat that was close to falling off its head. A gaunt man in a black suit and tie had withered away to skin and bones. A kid about Cesar's age was missing its entire right arm at the shoulder. A couple of zombie kids got jostled at hip-height, their faces pressed into the fence. One little boy gnashed his teeth on the chain-link.

One—it might've been a flat-chested woman or a slim man—had a chunk missing from its head, including one eye. Cesar could actually see inside its skull. However much of an ex's brain needed to be destroyed to drop it, this one was just a few points above that.

The blood on all of them was thick and dry, like layers of old paint.

"Huh," said Gibbs.

"What?"

"They're following you." He gestured at the exes as their skulls turned after the battlesuit. "They're watching you."

"Yeah, man," said Cesar. "That's what they do. You new here?"

The lieutenant snorted. "You're in the suit. Why are they still going after you?"

"'Cause it's what they do. That's why Danielle's so . . ." He dropped the volume of the speakers. "That's why she wants to get back in here, bro. So she'll feel safe when they go after her."

"Right," said Gibbs. "Except she'll be in the armor. Wearing it. Meat in a can."

"Bro . . ."

He shrugged it off. "It makes sense they'd go after her. Why are they going after you?"

"What do you mean?"

Gibbs reached up between the struts and put his hand inside the skeletal titan, right where the pilot's stomach would be. "There's nothing in the suit right now," he said.

The battlesuit took a step back. "That's weird, bro. Don't reach inside without asking or saying something first."

"My point is, you don't have a body like this. There's no meat for them to go after. So why are they following you? What do they see?"

"I dunno. I thought about it for a while, the first couple times I saw it. I think it's 'cause the suit's me when I'm in it."

"What?"

The battlesuit held out a hand and flexed the fingers. "This is me right now. So they see the suit as alive cause it's me. It's, like, living metal or something."

Gibbs scowled up at the exoskeleton. "That doesn't make sense."

"It kinda makes sense," said Cesar. The steel hand flipped over, and one finger bent down to tap the palm. "Y'know, that's how my hands got all cut up. Was in a car, the wheels got shredded on a spike strip, and then my hands and feet were all shredded when I got out."

"You've got scars on your feet, too?"

"Yup."

"Still doesn't make any sense. Exes don't see any more than we do. They don't see 'life.'"

"Just the way it is, bro."

The lieutenant shook his head. They walked across a small lawn spread between the main building and the fence. The toes on Gibbs's mechanical foot sank into the grass, and his limp grew. Cesar slowed down a bit for him.

The battlesuit registered movement on top of the building. It was one of the Unbreakables in the little watchtower-slash-sniper nest they'd built up there between the solar panels. Cesar zoomed in, and the figure leaped from thirty feet away to five. Sergeant Johnson could see almost two-thirds of the fence line from there. His elbow brushed the basketball-sized warning bell they'd hung up there as his binoculars scanned back and forth. The big lenses held on the exoskeleton for a moment, then continued on to check the people working in the gardens.

Cesar and Gibbs headed for a concrete path that cut through the lawn and down through more garden plots. It led to the parking lot, and on the far side of the parking lot was the service road that looped around the northern fence, the one along the freeway. And that would bring them back to the Hot Zone.

Cesar sighed. It came out as a buzz of radio static. The lieutenant glanced at him. "Something wrong?"

"Bro," said the titan, "this whole patrol thing is boring as hell."

"Welcome to the military," Gibbs said.

"I'm not in the military, man. I'm a superhero."

Gibbs snorted.

Something moved in one of the garden plots, and the suit systems highlighted it. Cesar used the digital zoom again. It was a woman with a good butt and nice hips, working alone in one of the plots, crouched over to pull weeds. She looked a bit older, but still in good shape. He'd been feeling kind of sophisticated lately, checking out some of the older ladies in their thirties and forties, and congratulated himself on being so mature just as the figure shifted and he saw the claw-hand and realized he was checking out Christian Smith. He shuddered, and the battlesuit reacted with a tremble that made some of the servos whine.

"What's wrong?" asked Gibbs.

"Umm, nothing." He unzoomed his view. The armor took a few more steps.

"Jesus, kid," said the lieutenant, limping alongside him. "You don't even have a face right now and you'd suck at poker."

"Hey, you know what," Cesar said. "I think I'm good now. You want to head back to the workshop and I'll see you once morning patrol's done?"

Gibbs shook his head. "I was going to walk with you at least to the other side of the parking lot." He paused in his step to lift the mechanical foot. "I need all the exercise I can get. This thing lets me walk, but I can't run anymore since I lost . . ."

His voice trailed off as his eyes found Smith. His free hand squeezed into a fist. Then he let it go and flexed his fingers.

Cesar looked down at him. "You cool, man?"

"Yeah." The lieutenant stepped forward. "Yeah, I'm fine." His metal toes came down on the concrete path with the sound of a steel rake.

Smith leaped up and slashed the air with something. She held the small shovel like a knife in her good hand. She glared at Gibbs, then up at the battlesuit.

A purple-red bruise covered one side of her face. Cesar had seen bruises like that on his aunt growing up. When he'd joined the Seventeens, he'd seen them on one or two girls who hung out with some of the wilder, more violent gang-bangers. He'd stood up to one of the guys about it once. And gotten smacked down.

That was back before he was a superhero, though.

He took a step toward Smith. The battlesuit's broad toes sank into the dark soil. Gibbs muttered something about cleaning.

The Asian woman took a step back. She glanced to either side, checking for paths away from the titan. A collection of syllables formed and died on her lips.

Cesar cleared his throat, and a raspy squawk came out of the speakers. Smith flinched back. "Are you okay, ma'am?" the battlesuit asked. "Or sir?"

Smith looked up at Cesar and rattled off another string of silent words.

"Ummmmm . . . I didn't catch any of that. Maybe yes or no?"

The Asian woman scowled, shook her head, and gave him the finger with her mangled hand.

"Do you want to tell me who hit you?"

She turned back to her weeding. Her shoulders went up as she took in a breath. Then the trowel went back into the ground and she tried to work out all the roots of a weed the size of a small bush.

"I want to help," said Cesar. "People shouldn't be beating you up."

"Just let it go," murmured Gibbs.

The exoskeleton turned, and the lenses focused on him.

The lieutenant shrugged. "She doesn't want to make a thing out of it. And it's not like she doesn't deserve it."

"Hey," said Cesar, "nobody deserves to get beat like that."

Gibbs smirked. "Weren't you in a gang? Did you just hug people back then?" He walked away, his metal toes rasping on the concrete.

Smith looked over her shoulder at the lieutenant for a minute. Her eyes slid down to look at the steampunk foot as he walked past. Her shoulders slumped.

"If they do this again," said Cesar, "let me know."

She waved him away and turned back to the weeds.

He caught up with Gibbs a few yards down the path. "You should leave that alone," said the lieutenant.

"Bro," said Cesar. "If someone's beating her, we gotta do somethin' about it, y'know?"

"No, we don't."

"Yeah, we do."

"No," said Gibbs. He glared up at the titan. "Our mission here is to keep Eden safe. Patrol the fences. Keep the exes out. Don't let yourself get distracted by unimportant things. That's how you get everyone killed."

He turned and stalked away.

"Are you the one who did it?"

The metal foot rang against the concrete. Gibbs turned around. "What?"

Cesar closed the distance between them in two large strides. He knocked the suit's volume down a few notches. "Did you hit her?"

"No, of course not."

"Did you?"

Gibbs blew some air out of his nose. His shoulders relaxed. "No," he said. "I didn't hit him. Her. Whatever."

The exoskeleton stared at him, then dipped its head. "Okay."

"You think I would?"

The battlesuit shrugged. "Before he died, my old man, he always said when something bad happened, you either got to move past it or do something about it. You're pissed at Smith. She . . . *he* got you all messed up in the head. Risked people's lives. Lost your foot. Got the suit wrecked. And you ain't movin' past it, bro."

"Yeah I have."

The titan shrugged again. "Doesn't look like it, man. Or sound like it."

Gibbs turned around and headed down the path. Cesar followed him.

Near the edge of the parking lot, a handful of people worked their way through the dense weeds. Lester walked from person to person, pointing out useful plants they should leave in the ground. He looked up at the exoskeleton and smiled as Cesar approached.

The battlesuit systems zoomed in on different faces. Cesar recognized some of the former Seventeens among the workers. Javi had taken off his shirt to show off the array of tattoos spread over his lean arms and shoulders. Desi was wearing a tank top about two sizes too small for her. And in the back was Rafael, an old guy covered with tattoos that had blurred with age.

Gibbs stepped around an oversized wheelbarrow filled with stalks and leaves. It and another one, mostly empty, blocked half the path. Cesar bumped a leg on the full one as he walked past.

Desi tossed a double-handful of greenery into the mostly empty wheelbarrow and checked out the battlesuit. "That you in there, Cesar?"

"Yeah," he said. The skeletal titan turned back to look at her and seemed to push its chest out. "But, y'know, when I'm in the suit you're supposed to call me Cerberus. Or the Driver."

Gibbs glanced back and shook his head.

"Oh, yeah?" she said with a grin. She walked over and looked up at him. "What are you driving these days?"

"I . . . well, the suit," he said. "I mean, I'm walking, but I'm still driving it, y'know?"

She gazed at him for a minute, then shook her head and cackled.

"No, I am."

"No point tryin' to get on his good side, Desi," Javi called out. Across the garden plot, he stood up straight and pointed at the battlesuit. "He's a fucking super-sellout. Either gonna work you to death or let the zombies eat you."

"Give it a rest, Javier," said Lester.

"You know it's true. None of them care what happens to us. We're all—"

"Shut up, Javi," Desi spat at him.

Tattooed Rafael glared at her, at Lester, then up at the battlesuit.

"Sorry," she said to Cesar. "He's kind of a paranoid jerk."

"Yeah, I noticed."

"Cesar," shouted Gibbs. He was at the end of the path, by the old parking lot. "Come on."

Cesar looked down at Desi. She winked and walked back into the plot. Javi glared at the exoskeleton, then reached down and ripped a big handful of tall greens out of the ground.

Gibbs shook his head as the battlesuit approached. "We've

got to come up with some other name when it's you in there, kid."

"What do you mean?"

"It just doesn't feel right, you calling yourself Cerberus," the lieutenant said. "She's Cerberus."

Cesar nodded. "Yeah, that's what she says, too."

"She's right."

"You can just call me the Driver."

Gibbs looked up at the titan. "Look, we've all been meaning to tell you . . . that name sucks."

"What?"

"The Driver. Seriously. What were you, twelve when you came up with that?"

"Sixteen."

Gibbs shook his head.

"It's cool."

"Cesar, I know you don't want to listen to me, but please believe me when I tell you that name is not cool."

He thought about it. "What about Cesarus? Y'know, it's me, but it's also—"

"No. Even worse. Hang on." Gibbs crouched near the exoskeleton. "It looks like you've got something stuck in the knee joint."

Cesar bent over to look. "I don't feel anything."

"Give me a minute. Straighten the leg out."

Cesar stood up tall and looked out across the parking lot. Diagonal slots for two dozen cars decorated the pavement. The large swinging gate had been chained shut and blocked with a pair of dumpsters on the inside and two minivans on the outside. Two small pillars marked the pedestrian entrance, a steel gate in the middle of the expanse of chainlink. According to the battlesuit, there were forty-two exes lined up against the length of fence, another sixteen within ten feet of it.

Far across the pavement, Hector used his hand to sweep another wheelbarrow clean of weeds and dirt. Like most of the scavengers, he was working in the garden until everything was set for their first run into the nearby homes. He tossed a last handful of greenery on the compost pile, flicked some sweat off his forehead, and stretched his arms up high over his head. He had a collection of gang tattoos on his arms, too, much more impressive than Cesar's or Javi's.

He grabbed the handles of the wheelbarrow and started pushing it across the parking lot. The exes along the fence followed him, shifting and bumping into each other as they moved. A dead man and woman both wore black-and-purple LA Kings jerseys. One had a ragged hole in the side of its neck, the other's shoulder was a mess of sun-baked meat. Past them was a massive ex. It had been a huge woman when it was alive, in height and weight. Death and years in the sun hadn't shrunk it much.

A teenage girl with dark hair and dried blood around its mouth stood near the steel gate. At first glance, Cesar thought the dead girl looked a lot like Madelyn. But its eyes were the wrong shape, and its skin was a yellow ivory while Madelyn's was chalk white. And the ex was flat-chested, but he'd learned that might just mean it had dried out a lot.

Two of the super-soldiers kept an easy watch farther down the fence line, on the other side of the dumpsters. Wilson still wore his full uniform, while Franklin had stripped down to a sand-colored T-shirt. The latter grunted out push-ups while the former egged him on. The suit's directional microphones heard Wilson chanting "Fifteen . . . Sixteen . . . Seventeen . . ."

Hector was halfway across the lot with his wheelbarrow. The exes had stumbled and rolled and shifted along the fence. The huge dead woman staggered back, then lunged forward and slammed into the gate. Kind-of-Madelyn was crushed between the ex's bulk and the steel bars.

The microphones picked up a squeak of metal on metal that drowned out the constant clicking of teeth for a second. A sharp bang. A quick scrape.

The gate swung open.

The kind-of-Madelyn ex was pushed forward and fell beneath the massive dead woman. A withered, sexless figure dressed in rags lurched behind them. The battlesuit's targeting systems picked out seven more forcing their way through the gate. Two other zombies staggered in on either side of the obese one. The three of them stumbled forward and wedged themselves between the gate's pillars for a moment.

Hector looked up at the sound of metal on metal. He saw the exes as they fumbled through the gate. He dropped the handles of the wheelbarrow.

Cesar lunged forward.

Gibbs yelled something.

Wilson and Franklin looked up from their exercises.

Even without all of its armor, the exoskeleton weighed enough to take chunks out of the pavement as Cesar raced for the gate. He passed Hector, grabbed the withered ex reaching for the man, and hurled it over the fence. A second ex staggered past him, and he brought a steel-and-carbon fist down on its skull. He grabbed the limp form by the neck and flung it back the way it came.

"The gate," shouted someone. It sounded like Gibbs. "Close the gate!"

In the distance, the warning bell rang.

Cesar lashed out an arm and closed a fist on an ex's shoulder. He swung it around and used it to knock a dead woman over backward. Both of them fell, and he slammed down two punches that struck bone and went through to connect with the pavement.

Proximity warnings flashed in his eyes, and the huge dead woman slammed into him. The ex had to weigh three hundred pounds, easy. The impact forced one of the titan's legs back. Broken teeth snapped shut again and again inside the sagging face. Cesar could see strands of hair and flakes of blood between the teeth.

He set his hands on the ex's shoulders—strong, mechanical hands—aimed, and heaved. The dead thing sailed back and knocked over five-six-seven other dead people as it flew through the open gate. The battlesuit's targeting system highlighted each one.

Cesar stomped forward and drove his fist into another ex. The dead man in the Kings jersey. The punch blasted through the corpse and left it impaled on the exoskeleton's arm. The *click-click-click* of the zombie's teeth didn't falter. It flailed at the battlesuit's head, its fingers filling the field of view. He grabbed it with his free hand and pried it off. It dropped to the ground and twisted back and forth.

The exes forced their way through the gate, jamming themselves in the opening again and slowing down the flow of their numbers. Only a handful had made it through.

Cesar reached out with both hands, fingers spread wide. He struck one ex in the chest, another in the shoulder, and caught a third between them. Servos spun, pistons thrust, and he shoved the undead back between the two pillars. Four or five more went back with them. One stumbled, tipped over, and landed on top of the obese woman.

The exoskeleton reached out and grabbed the gate with gore-soaked fingers. Cesar swung it toward himself and then pushed it shut. Two or three exes pressed against it, but the suit overpowered them with minimal effort and power drain. One last dead person, a man with blood-streaked sideburns, tried to stumble through the shrinking opening. The battlesuit's servos whined once and crushed the man's arms between the gate and the latch.

Cesar shifted his feet. He set two steel toes against the base of the gate and locked the joints. "I got it," he called back.

The targeting system lit up something in the rear cameras. The kind-of-Madelyn. It was inside the gate.

The dead thing staggered after Hector, its arms raised and teeth chattering, but Franklin was between them. The soldier darted in, slapped the dead girl's hands down, and then leaped back out. The ex's head swung to follow him, and it turned away from Hector. Its arms came back up as Franklin jumped in to tease it again.

Wilson lunged in from the side and grabbed the dead girl by one arm. The ex twisted around, and Franklin grabbed the other arm. They dragged it back to the fence line. The ex rolled its head from side to side, gnashing its teeth at them. They were yellowed, and the front two were cracked and splintered. Another way it didn't look like Madelyn.

The super-soldiers reached the fence next to Cesar, counted to three, and threw the ex over it. The kind-of-Madelyn sailed up over the chain-link, over the undead, and crashed down onto the pavement. It twitched a few times, then rolled over and struggled back to its feet. One side of its body sagged where it had struck the street.

"We're clear," Wilson called out. Gibbs limped forward. A few people appeared on the path behind him. Smith. Desi. Javi.

"WHAT THE FUCK?" bellowed Hector. He glared at the two soldiers, at Gibbs, up at Cesar, at anyone he could blame for his close call.

"You okay?" asked Franklin. "Did it get you?"

"No, it didn't get near me," said Hector. "What the hell were you waiting for? Why didn't you punch its head off?"

"You're fine," said Wilson. "That's all that matters."

"No it isn't all that fucking matters," said Hector. "I wanna know how the fuck it got in here!" His finger stabbed through the air toward the exoskeleton. Past it, to the gate. "What the fuck was that? All this time something just had to lean on the fucking thing to open it?"

Steel scraped on pavement as Gibbs walked up to stand near the exoskeleton. "About four hundred pounds had to throw itself against the gate all at once. It was a cheap latch that just got overlooked in the rush to get things set up here." The lieutenant tapped the gate, and the exes on the other side of the steel mesh flailed at his knuckles.

He walked back to Hector. "We stopped it, nobody got hurt. Like Wilson said, that's the important thing."

Hector shook his head and stalked back to his wheelbarrow. "Fuck all you guys." He pushed it across the pavement toward the crowd of gardeners at the edge of the parking lot.

"Cesar," called Gibbs, "is the gate secure?"

"Yeah," said the exoskeleton.

The lieutenant looked at the two soldiers. "Go down to the scrap pile by the back fence and find something to brace this with. Some cinder blocks or long boards or something."

The two men glanced at each other, then nodded. "Yes, sir" echoed across the lot.

"Man," said Cesar after the soldiers jogged away, "so this thing's just barely been held shut all this time?"

"Looks like it."

"That's crazy, man." The battlesuit shook its head. "Lucky we were here. Lucky those guys were here, too."

"Yeah." Gibbs stared after the soldiers. "I think we were lucky."

FIFTEEN

NOW

ST. GEORGE PACED in the small room. "How late do you think it is?"

"It's been about an hour since they brought us breakfast." Barry sat on the edge of the couch. He'd asked again for a wheelchair, but hadn't seen one yet.

Breakfast had been a salty stew of fish, potatoes, and a few green bits he couldn't identify. Madelyn had picked all the fish out of her bowl and eaten it plain. She'd given Barry the rest of it.

It was a nice little suite. St. George guessed it wasn't the best on the ship, but he was pretty sure it was better than average. It felt like a high-end room in a midrange hotel. There were two separate bedrooms, a couch, some chairs, and a small dining room table bolted to the floor. He'd slept on the couch and given Barry and Madelyn the beds. Barry got to sleep so rarely it seemed rude not to give him the best accommodations, and it only seemed right to give Madelyn some privacy.

All things considered, it was one of the nicest rooms he'd spent time in over the past few years.

St. George glanced over at her. The Corpse Girl sat in a large, comfy chair reading her journal entries from last night. The square-shouldered woman, Eliza, had brought the journals and clothes to their room, but nothing else from the red gym bag.

Except for her chalk eyes flitting back and forth, she was motionless. No rise and fall of her chest, no flexing stiff limbs. She hadn't looked happy when the three of them had been brought back together the night before. After assuring him they hadn't hurt her, she'd brushed off his questions about her examination to write in her journals. He wasn't sure if she'd ever slept. She'd been awake and reading when he woke up. And still not in a mood to talk.

"So," said Barry, "how much longer you want to wait?"

St. George paused and tapped his fingers against his thigh. "I don't know," he said. "I want to help. I don't like giving up on anybody . . . but these people are wearing on my patience."

"They're seriously paranoid," agreed Barry, "but I think it goes with this deluded view of the world they've got."

"I know we've all probably thought about it," said St. George, glancing at Madelyn, "but maybe . . . could this be a mind-control thing?"

Her chalk eyes paused in their back-and-forth.

"Agent Smith? The real Smith?" Barry shook his head. "I don't know. I mean, it's possible, I guess. He made all of us believe a bunch of stuff, but this doesn't seem like his style."

"How so?"

"First, let me point out I've always wanted to say that about a super-nemesis, so let's remember today for that." He paused for laughter, sighed, and continued. "Second, it just doesn't feel like his kind of gig. Not to be harsh but . . . well, these people don't have a lot to offer."

"Not that we know of," said St. George.

"Oh, sure, there's always a chance the cargo ship had the Ark of the Covenant down in the hold or something. But, realistically, does it look like these people have anything Smith would want? That'd make it worth his time to come out here?"

St. George shrugged, then shook his head.

"And, seriously," said Barry, "how lame does your theory have to be if I'm the one offering the realistic view?"

Madelyn snorted out a laugh. She still didn't look up from her journal, but the corners of her mouth twitched a bit.

"It's aliiiive," moaned Barry. "Allliiiive!"

"Shut up," she said. She closed the journal. "He could just be doing it to mess with people. That *is* his style."

Barry bit his lip. "I don't think it is," he said, his voice a bit lower. "I don't think he minds messing with people, but it never seems to be his end goal."

Madelyn patted the cover of the journal three times. Then she reached for the big Ziploc and sealed the book back inside. "Okay, then," she said. "Maybe a meteor?"

St. George looked at her. "What?"

"A meteor. Sometimes they blow up in the atmosphere. Depending on how big it was and where it came down, they might think it was a nuke."

Barry pursed his lips. "Not a bad idea."

"Wouldn't we have seen something like that, too, though?" St. George mused. "I mean, if it was big enough for them to think it was a nuke, you'd think we'd see it. Maybe hear it."

"We didn't hear Honolulu," Barry said.

"We're almost two thousand miles away," said the Corpse Girl. "It could've hit the water five hundred miles from here and still be a thousand miles from us."

"It's also possible," said Barry, "they all just got drunk and fell asleep watching disaster movies."

"What?"

"Y'know, just before their ships lost power. And then in the morning they had to sort out what really happened and just made some bad decisions. Now you've got a bunch of people saying, 'Oh, we saw LA get nuked,' and really they just passed out watching a bad Sci-Fi Channel movie or something."

Madelyn blew a raspberry at him. "So," she said, "my meteor theory is still the best we've got?"

"Yeah," said St. George. "But Barry has a point. I'd understand Honolulu, but they told us some people had seen Los Angeles destroyed."

"Sooooo," said Barry, "my theory is back on top." He returned her raspberry.

"Okay," she said, "you can stop trying to cheer me up."

"It's not always about you, y'know."

"Actually, I've got a question," she said, looking at St. George. "Did anyone say what they did with their exes?"

"What do you mean?"

"Well, all these boats, there must've been somebody with the ex-virus, right? Probably a couple somebodies. Are people turning and getting . . . I don't know, tossed overboard? Or maybe . . ."

"Maybe what?"

"Maybe put in their gardens?"

"Ewwww," said Barry.

St. George tapped his knee. "Do exes work as . . . well, fertilizer? How's that work with all their diseases and everything?"

Barry shrugged. So did Madelyn.

Two quick raps sounded on the door before it opened. Eliza pushed it wide and stepped in. She had on a weathered bomber jacket and a different shirt, but the same threadbare and stained jeans. "Morning," she said. "Hope everyone's decent."

Madelyn scowled.

"So what's going on?" asked St. George. "Have we passed your quarantine?"

She nodded.

"Can we talk, then?"

Another nod. "I'm here to bring you to Maleko, our leader. He's going to help us figure out who you are."

Barry sighed. "Still this?"

She studied his face. "Yeah," she said. "Still this."

St. George managed to keep from frowning. "Is he going to be a little more open-minded about who we are than you?"

Eliza turned her gaze to him. "What do you think?"

"I'm starting to think you're all a bunch of jerks," muttered Madelyn.

Eliza ignored her. "Ready to go?" She gestured at the door.

Barry cleared his throat. "Don't suppose you've found a wheelchair for me?"

The woman's head shifted side to side. "No. Couldn't find one."

"Ship this big, all these passengers on board, they didn't have a wheelchair in case someone broke a leg on the waterslide or something?"

"Maybe they did. A lot of things have been moved and repurposed. It could be on any of the ships. It might've gone overboard in the early days while people were still freaking out a bit." She shrugged and raised her hand to the door again.

Barry sighed. "You mind lugging me around again?" he asked St. George. "Just 'til we get outside?"

"Actually, we're going to be inside for most of the walk to Maleko," said Eliza. "You probably shouldn't . . . light up."

Barry snorted as St. George lifted him.

A small crowd waited for them in the hall. Big Steve from the day before. Bald and bearded Devon. Sun-leathered Alice. The two men from St. George's examination. A new man with a thick mustache. All of them were armed.

Madelyn focused on the mustached man. "You must be the cowboy," she said.

"Cowboy?" St. George looked at the man.

"It's nothing," she said. "He's nothing."

The cowboy smirked at her.

She glared back at him and shifted her weight so she leaned closer to St. George.

"You okay?"

"Great," said the Corpse Girl.

The group moved down the dark hall. Light came from an occasional open door. One larger room had skylights. It had been a ballroom once, but now it was piled high with open suitcases and travel bags. All of them were empty. They exited the far side, turned a corner, and headed up a staircase.

Barry leaned his head in closer to St. George. "Did you notice her face when she was talking about her boss?" he asked.

St. George gave a slight nod. "Like she was watching for a reaction."

"You ever heard that name before?"

"Nope. Was it Japanese?"

Barry shook his head. "Don't think so, unless I'm picturing it wrong in my head."

"What are you two talking about?" demanded Steve. His voice echoed in the hallway.

"Just wondering about breakfast," Barry answered, just as loud. "Where'd you get all the seeds for those gardens of yours?"

"The *Queen*," said Devon. His head tipped up, indicating the ship they were on. "There were some vegetables in the galleys that survived long enough to get in pots. There were even some seed packs down in the daycare area. Y'know, little kids can plant a bean while mom and dad get drunk in the sun, that sort of thing."

The mustached cowboy and one of the others chuckled. It wasn't a happy sound.

"What did you do for soil?" asked St. George. "Did one of the other ships have it?"

"There were a bunch of potted plants on board," Devon said. "Ferns and crap. We used them for compost, all the dirt went to growing stuff. Then we added in a lot of . . . fertilizer."

"Like what?" Barry asked.

"Leftover fish parts. Some seaweed." Devon looked ahead. "Other stuff."

Madelyn's brows went up. "Other stuff like what?"

Devon didn't say anything.

The dreadlocked man from St. George's examination cleared his throat. "The Chinese call it 'night soil,'" he said. "It's a pretty classic fertilizing techni—"

"Oh, for fuck's sake," said the cowboy. "It's shit, okay? We all have to shit in buckets so nothing goes to waste."

"Shut up, Mitchel," said Steve.

"It's what it is. Why's everybody got to pussyfoot around it?"

"I said shut up, Mitchel," Steve repeated.

"But you couldn't've had enough with just that," said Barry. "Not even if everyone got a hundred bowls of Super-Colon-Blow cereal. You've got a couple of good-sized garden patches there."

"We dredge some stuff up from the bottom, too," said Devon. "Mix it in with everything to make better dirt."

Madelyn looked at the man. "From the bottom of the ocean? That's, like, a mile down. How are you getting anything from down there?"

"Quiet," called Eliza.

She stood before a big set of double doors. They were imitation stained glass, like a church window, making the image of a leaping dolphin with a crown instead of a religious figure. St. George was pretty sure it was the same logo he'd seen half-obliterated on the ship's smokestacks, just done in color. On the other side was bright light and movement.

There were no voices. Not even the low murmur of conversation. Just the dim sound of breezes and a few flags.

"Maleko's going to talk with you," she said. "Show a little respect." She looked St. George in the eye as she said the name, then shook her head.

"Is he the king or something?" asked Madelyn.

"He saved every one of us by bringing the ships together," she said. "We'd all be dead without him."

Barry raised an eyebrow. "Live together, die alone?"

Eliza nodded. "Exactly."

"Told you this was a mysterious island," he said to St. George and Madelyn. "I bet there's a pirate ship filled with dynamite around here somewhere."

Madelyn laughed.

"What the hell are you talking about?" growled the cowboy.

"That show," said Devon. "The big one, right before everything fell apart. *Lost.*"

Barry gave the bald man a thumbs-up.

Devon managed a weak smile. "No one likes talking about that too much out here. Sore subject."

"Ahhh," said Barry. "Sorry."

Eliza snapped her fingers three times. "Everyone had their fun?"

She rapped on the glass, and the doors pulled open. Sunlight blasted into the halls. St. George and Barry squinted. Madelyn winced and fumbled for her goggles. The air swirling in was warm and fresh with hints of salt.

St. George blinked a few times and glanced at the guards near them. They'd had their heads turned when the doors opened. They'd been ready. Expecting it.

The group moved out into the open.

It was a big space, somewhere between a huge courtyard and a small arena. A walkway circled it up above. There was a pool at the far end. It wasn't hard to believe it had once had dozens of sun chairs or some kind of sea-themed aerobics or yoga classes. Maybe all that and more.

Men, women, and children surrounded them. At least two hundred people. Just as many watched from the walkway above. Their clothes were faded and patched. Most of their hair was long and uneven.

The people above looked back at him with nervous eyes.

The Middle Eastern man they'd seen on the helipad stood just off to one side. He glanced away when St. George looked at him. Devon took a few steps back and settled near the man. He leaned his head back, and they exchanged a few words.

A few pillars of wood helped form a small gazebo-type structure in front of the pool, and beneath it was a large chair on a low platform of wood and steel. St. George recognized it as staging, the kind of riser used for presentations in small venues. It took him a moment to figure out the chair, but he was willing to bet there wasn't a space on the cruise ship's bridge for the captain to sit. Not anymore, at least.

The man next to the chair had his back to them. He stood five foot ten at the most, not much taller than Madelyn, and had long black hair like her, too. His thick ponytail was bound with a half dozen strings down its length. He wore two or three layers, but all the sleeves had been torn off. St. George wasn't sure if the man's skin was very tanned or naturally dark. A curling tattoo wrapped around the man's right bicep, an intricate array of bold lines and triangles.

He had solid arms, St. George noticed. Not huge, but not thin. A worker, not a gym rat.

Eliza walked across the open space. A single folding chair sat out in front of the crude throne. She stepped around it and took up a position near one of the gazebo posts facing the heroes. Steve moved to stand across from her. The other guards faded back into the crowd like Devon had.

Barry craned his neck to look around. "Anyone else getting a vibe that's less *First Contact* and more *Thunderdome*?"

"I think I am," said Madelyn, "and I'm not even sure what you're talking about."

"I'm getting some kind of vibe," said St. George. He looked around the crowd again. Something was off. He tried to look at the crowd the way Stealth would. She'd've already picked out the nagging element and deduced what it meant. He looked at the sunburned men and women, the wide-eyed children.

The children.

He looked up at the walkway, then around the courtyard again. "All the children are down here with us," he murmured.

Barry looked around. "Yeah," he said. "Almost a third of the people down here are kids."

"Why?" said Madelyn. "If they don't trust us, why are they letting us near their kids?"

St. George looked back at the throne. The man had turned around. Their eyes met.

The man looked Polynesian, or maybe Asian. He had large eyes, a small nose, and a stern mouth framed by a square jaw. The ponytail pulled every strand of hair away from his face.

His clothes hung on him. The threadbare pants and silk shirt were at least two sizes too big for him. Maybe three. A leather vest that could've fit Captain Freedom draped over the man's shoulders, reaching halfway down his thighs. All the loops of extra fabric made St. George think of the baggy ren faire clothes he'd seen sometimes on the college campus he used to work at, back in the days before the ex-virus.

The man was barefoot on the wooden deck. His feet were smooth. Not the feet of someone who went barefoot a lot of the time.

He held out a hand toward the chair. "For your friend," he said.

St. George stepped forward. Madelyn fell in next to him. "Thanks," said Barry. He shifted in St. George's arms and tried to straighten up a bit.

"Of course," said the man. "We're not savages." He had a confident, strong voice. One used in front of crowds a lot. This crowd, at least.

St. George settled Barry into the chair. Madelyn tapped his side. When he turned around, the man stood just a few yards away.

"So," the man said, projecting the word, "my lieutenant says you claim to be the Mighty Dragon." He glanced at Eliza.

A low murmur passed through the crowd.

"That's right," said St. George. "And I'm guessing you're Maleko?"

The murmur became a low rumble.

The man—Maleko—nodded once. "I am," he said. He studied St. George's face the same way Eliza had, but he played his expressions big, like a stage actor. Or someone working a crowd. "Could you offer us some sort of proof of your claim?"

St. George focused on the spot between his shoulder blades and pushed himself up into the air. He went up until he was level with the walkway, then shot fifty feet higher and drifted back down. The rumble of the crowd became gasps and whispers. "Him" carried up to St. George again and again.

As he sank past the walkway, he took in a breath, let it tickle the back of his throat, and let flames drift out of his mouth again. He looked up and puffed out the last of it as a small fireball. Shrieks and cries echoed up to him.

His boots hit the deck next to Barry's chair. A few children were sobbing. The adults were wide-eyed. Maleko glared at St. George with a stone face.

"Sorry," said St. George. "The kids back home get a kick out of seeing me do that." He turned to the crowd. "I didn't mean to scare anyone."

Adults were whispering. The murmuring had started back up. Some of the kids calmed down, but most of them were still crying.

Where were their parents? Why were all the kids standing alone? Why wasn't anyone holding them or wiping noses?

Maleko took a breath. His face softened. "And back home," he asked, "is where?"

St. George glanced down at Barry, then back up to the Polynesian man. "We're from Los Angeles," he said. "There's a few thousand survivors there. We've made a large safe zone we call the Mount."

Maleko didn't smile, but he looked satisfied with the answer. Content. The murmur climbed back up to a rumble.

Courtyard seemed like an all-too-appropriate term for the space they were in.

"I'm telling the truth," he said, raising his own voice to the crowd. "I've heard what you think happened, that there were bombs, but it isn't true. We're from Los Angeles. The Mount is right in the middle of Hollywood."

"And we show movies on Friday nights," said Barry. "Kids get in free, but the popcorn still costs way too much."

"How can you sit there and make jokes about it?" snarled Eliza from her post. "Do you know how many people died in the bombings?"

"I'm going to go with 'What is none, Alex,'" said Barry, "since they didn't drop any bombs."

Eliza sucked in a breath, but Maleko raised a hand to cut her off. He walked back to his big chair and picked something up. "This was in your bag," he said. He held the desert-tan box up for the crowd to see. "Care to tell everyone what it is?"

St. George sighed. "It's a radio beacon. There should've been a solar charger with it."

"There was," nodded Maleko. "Very small. Not much bigger than a pack of cigarettes. Easy to hide, I'm sure."

Another uneasy rumble pushed and shoved its way through the crowd.

"More like very light," Madelyn said. "We couldn't carry a ton of stuff with us out here."

Maleko didn't look at her. He lowered the beacon so it was between him and St. George. "What were you going to do with it?"

"We were going to give it to you," said the hero. He looked up at the crowd. "To all of you here, so we'd be able to find you again."

"So you'd know where we were," Maleko said. "So it could lead people to us."

The people around them muttered and whispered. Some of them pointed.

"Oh, frak me," Barry muttered. He looked up at St. George. "I'm all for helping out, but how much more of this are we going to sit through?"

St. George cleared his throat, and a wisp of smoke drifted between his lips. "I don't know what's going on here," he said. "I don't know why you all feel threatened, why you're insisting I'm dead. But we're just here to offer our help. To let you know you're not alone."

Some of the muttering died, but not all of it.

Maleko's eyes never left St. George's. "I'd be inclined to believe you," he said in a stage whisper that carried across the crowd. "If anyone could've survived the blast which incinerated Los Angeles, it would've been my friend. But even he couldn't."

"Your friend . . . ?"

Now the tattooed man did smile. A tight curve of his lips that didn't reach his eyes. "The Mighty Dragon."

Madelyn and Barry looked between the two men.

"Ummmm . . . ," said St. George. "Do I know you?"

The man turned to the crowd. "Your little flight was very impressive," he said before looking back at the heroes, "but you missed one important detail. The Mighty Dragon couldn't fly. He could only jump and glide through the air."

The low rumble wasn't low anymore. The crowd looked between the two men. Their suspicious eyes lingered on St. George.

"I've had a lot of time to practice," said St. George. "I got better. I can fly. I'm stronger. I'm—"

"You're a fake!" Maleko spun and jabbed a finger at him. "An imposter. The Dragon is dead. He died a hero, trying to save people 'til the very end."

"I'm not an imposter."

"Seriously," said Madelyn. "How many flying guys do you know?"

"The guy in Iraq," said Eliza. "Marduk. He could fly and breathe fire, just like you're doing."

"No offense to anyone here," said St. George, glancing at the Middle Eastern man, "but do I look like I'm from Iraq?"

"Not every terrorist is from Iraq," said Steve.

St. George stared at the big man. "What?"

Barry shook his head in amazement. "Now we're terrorists?"

Steve shrugged. "You said it, not me."

"Liar!" the call came out of the crowd. The faces were angry now.

"Really not liking this," murmured the Corpse Girl.

"Same here," said Barry. He shifted to the edge of his chair, ready to launch himself off.

"We're not lying," St. George said to the crowd. "I am the Mighty Dragon. This is Zzzap. We came here from Los Angeles."

"You are not," said Maleko. His voice echoed in the ship's courtyard. "And you did not. You made a mistake by saying you were from Los Angeles when we all know Los Angeles is gone. You made a mistake by flying in front of all these people when we know the Mighty Dragon can only glide. And you made a mistake by claiming that name, because if you were really him . . . you'd know who I was."

St. George stared at the man. "I've never seen you before in my life."

"See?" roared Maleko. "He admits it." He turned to glare at St. George. His nostrils flared with three quick breaths.

"Who the hell are you?"

Maleko's jaw trembled. He took in three more short breaths. The muscles in his arms and neck tensed. He inhaled three more times, his face darkened as if he was holding his breath for too long, and he closed his eyes.

St. George realized the man hadn't let any air out yet.

Veins bulged on Maleko's arms and chest and neck and face, like a bodybuilder at the peak of his workout.

Madelyn leaned forward. "Is he . . . is he having a seizure?"

St. George glanced at the crowd. They'd calmed down. Most of them looked relieved. A few, like Steve and Alice, looked excited. Eliza tilted her head down and crossed her arms.

Dark bruises burst across Maleko's skin. The flesh under his eyebrows puffed up. Hives broke out across his bare shoulders, flowed together, and bubbled up even more.

He opened his eyes. They were all black. Black and oily. He bared jagged teeth in a snarl.

St. George and Madelyn both took a step back. "Oh, frak," said Barry, hopping in his chair. "He's a Zoanoid!"

Maleko grew.

He threw his head back, and by the time his ponytail settled he was a foot taller. His chest swelled inside the baggy clothes until the silk shirt was tight at the seams. The cord he'd been using as a belt snapped, and then the ragged slacks were tight, too. His arms and neck thickened under the bulging veins.

His hands spread wide. The palms widened, and the fingers shrank to little stubs with one knuckle. Then the hands flexed again, and St. George realized the palm hadn't grown at all.

The fingers were webbed.

He glanced down and saw Maleko's toes had stretched out. Just enough that the webbing there was apparent. The toenails curled into short claws.

The growths on his shoulders rippled and continued to swell. The bruised skin paled, but to a glossy blue-gray, not the golden brown it had been. His shoulders lost even more color and hardened until they were like bone.

Or shell.

"Whoa," said Madelyn. "Nautilus."

Maleko twisted his head in a slow circle until his neck popped. His black eyes gazed down at St. George, shaded by a Neanderthal brow. "Your pet ex knows who I am," he said. His voice rumbled in his chest.

"Hey," she snapped, "don't be a jerk."

"We thought you didn't make it," said Barry. "I flew out to Hawaii twice, but we never saw any sign of you."

"Still keeping up this game?" Maleko—Nautilus—lifted one hand and made a fist. With the webbed fingers, it looked like a boxing glove. "I'll give you one chance to come clean. Tell me who you are and you won't be harmed."

"I've told you who I am," said St. George. "I've told you. I told your guards. I've told everyone here." He waved his hand at the crowd. "My name is George Bailey. Most people have been calling me St. George. And for about two years before the ex-virus appeared, I was known as the Mighty Dragon."

Nautilus hit him.

It was a powerful backhand, one that would've shattered the jaw of a normal person, if not killed them outright. St. George had been expecting it, though, and he wasn't a normal person. It knocked him back toward the stained glass doors, but he managed to focus on gravity and made it more of an upright flight than a tumble.

A blinding flash, a hiss of air, and the crowd's screams told him Barry had changed into Zzzap. The light shifted as his friend darted up, away from the people and into a better position. *Okay,* he called out, *let's all stay calm.*

St. George leaped back, fists up, and came to a jerking halt.

Nautilus held Madelyn up in the air with both hands. One was wrapped around the back of her neck. The fingertips of the other hand sunk into her thigh. He kept her between himself and Zzzap like a living shield.

Madelyn's goggles sat crooked on her forehead, pushing her hair in random directions. She was squinting against the sun, but her chalk eyes were plain to see, and more than a few people in the crowd were pointing at her. She twisted her hands back to claw at the arm holding her neck, and her free leg kicked back at his chest.

"Put her down," said St. George. "I don't know what the hell your problem is, but it's with me, not her."

"You disgust me," said Nautilus.

He took a few steps back and shook Madelyn for emphasis. When her head stopped moving her eyes went from St. George up to Zzzap and back. "Kick his ass," she wheezed. She didn't need to breathe, but she still needed air to talk. "Don't worry about . . ."

Her lips twisted up in frustration as she ran out of words.

"Let her go," said St. George.

"The Mighty Dragon was one of the greatest men I'd ever known," said Nautilus. "When the dead rose, he fought to save human lives. Not to protect these things." He glared at St. George. "He knew how to deal with ex-humans."

Nautilus flexed his shoulders and tore her apart.

Madelyn's neck stretched, snapped, and her head swung around. Her arms flailed. Her hips cracked. The wet suit pulled tight and burst as her stomach ripped open. Gray intestines spilled out onto the deck, and lumps of meat and muscle fell after them.

Nautilus let the two halves drop just as St. George slammed into him.

The punches echoed across the small courtyard, the sound of a sledgehammer hitting a punching bag. The sledge struck three more times, driving the blue-gray giant back with each blow. St. George leaped into the air, bringing his knee up to smash the other man's jaw—

There were kids behind him. If Nautilus went down he'd crash right on top of a little girl and boy. St. George hesitated and the other man grabbed his leg.

The world spun and the deck rushed up to strike St. George in the face. Two of the planks cracked. He pushed himself up and Nautilus yanked on the leg, swinging him up, around, and back into the deck. Another plank split. One more heave and he was in the air, spinning. The crowd whizzed by, the captain's chair, a quick glimpse of Madelyn's arm, and then wind ripped at St. George's hair as he flew away.

He focused and came to a stop in midair. The ship was off to the side and a bit below him. He looked back and forth, spotted the open area of the courtyard, and then saw the figure growing in his vision.

Nautilus slammed into him. One thick arm wrapped around St. George's back, squeezing his ribs. The other one came down again and again, driving punches into his face. They wrestled in the air before St. George realized the ship's hull was next to them. Nautilus twisted around, and the Pacific Ocean crashed into St. George's back.

Much like he'd heard, hitting the water from a great height was like hitting pavement or concrete.

The waves closed over him, and the sound of wind vanished. Nautilus grabbed the lapels of St. George's biker jacket and dragged him through the water. The cold pressed in on him. The sunlight dimmed.

They were going deeper.

St. George threw a punch that churned the water around them. It bounced off one of the other man's armored shoulders. He lashed out again, connected, and the hand holding his jacket let go.

Nautilus slipped back through the water. He glared at the hero. Then his legs kicked twice, and he vanished in a whirl of bubbles.

St. George thrashed in the water, trying to get his bearings. The same dim blue-green stretched in every direction. There were no shafts of sunlight or a mirror-like surface.

Bubbles. Follow the bubbles. Bubbles go up.

He tried to relax and his lungs gave him a burning reminder he needed to get back to the surface. A few precious grams of silver air flew from his lips. They went off to the side of his mouth and raced away to his left.

Left was up.

He twisted himself around and swept his arms through the water. A few strong strokes carried him up enough that he saw daylight in the distance.

Something huge and dark loomed off to the side. St. George watched the gigantic chisel-shapes grow in his vision and realized he was seeing the underside of the ships. Three long wedges surrounded by smaller ones.

A long shape drifted beneath them, dwarfed by the monstrous hulls. It was hard to see in the shadows, but it looked like a whale. It didn't seem to be moving, and he wondered if it was dead or—

Nautilus came rushing at him like a torpedo. He caught a glimpse of the shark grin before the boxing-glove fists slammed into his gut and the last of his air erupted from his mouth. The cloud of silver bubbles flew away and Nautilus grabbed his collar and dragged him in the other direction.

The tightness in St. George's chest crawled up into his throat, pushed at his jaw, clawed at his throat. He grabbed the merman's wrist, flung him away, but Nautilus spun around and came at him again. St. George batted away a punch, took another one in the jaw, and took in a sharp breath through his nose without thinking.

Water gushed through his sinuses and clogged his throat. He tried to cough it out, and more poured past his teeth and down his throat. He coughed again, choked, spat, and the ocean filled his mouth, his nostrils, his lungs, his chest.

Nautilus released him and he drifted away. He thrashed in the dim light. He needed to find the surface. He needed to follow the bubbles.

There weren't any more bubbles.

In the back of his throat, the burning itch of flames was smothered and went out.

The water dimmed. He was sinking deeper. He had to move in the other direction. He . . .

He realized the darkness wasn't the water.

His jacket pulled tight under his arms as the ocean went black around him.

The Honeymoon Is Over

THEN

"LIZA," SHOUTS STEVE.

I turn, hear a few more yells, and see one of the new arrivals just over a yard away from me. He's crossed a third of the *Pacific Eagle*'s deck in just a few seconds. He's lucky no one's shot him. There are lots of itchy trigger fingers here.

It's the big guy from the end of the line. One of the eight people we found adrift on what looks like a Discovery Channel research ship. All Asian, except one of the women who looks like she may have mixed ancestry. She and one other woman speak some English. They say they ran out of fuel seventeen months ago, started drifting, and have been living off fish, kelp, and distilled seawater.

I'd pegged the big guy as the twitchiest of them. When he hadn't tried anything after fifteen minutes or said anything all through the speech, I figured he'd wised up and gotten his nerves under control. I'm usually good at reading people, but it's not the first time I've been wrong. Over the past three years since Lemuria came together, I've guessed wrong a few times. Some people I thought were clean had hidden bites. A few I thought were safe and sane—as sane as Mitchel, at least—turned out to be complete head cases.

I've survived all of them. Mostly because I don't care if they kill me or not. Not being scared if you'll die lets you be a lot gutsier as a fighter.

I haven't been scared for a while now.

My left hand goes up to warn the big guy, to hold him off, even as the fingers of my right hand flick the strap on my holster. He doesn't seem to notice either. I hear shouts and late warnings. He slams into me and takes us both down to the deck.

Just before we land I crack my forehead against his. It's not a great head butt. Too much of it gets spread between us. But it keeps me from slamming the back of my head on the deck and it catches him off guard.

He's big, but not as heavy as he looks. Who is these days? He has a beard and breath that smells like the worst parts of the ocean and the tiny scabs of early scurvy across his scalp.

I hear footsteps. Steve yelling commands. People are coming to drag the big guy off me. He's not doing much past shouting and keeping me pinned. I don't think he thought it through past "knock down the woman in charge."

If Maleko was here, if he was Nautilus, the big guy would be sailing through the air right now. He'd hit the water a hundred or so feet away from Lemuria. Probably break an arm on impact. And then he'd drown. Slowly. Painfully.

The pistol settles in my right hand. If I shoot him at this range, I'll be covered in his blood. And we don't know if he's infected or not yet. If any got in my mouth or eyes or if I've scraped an elbow on the deck . . .

Everyone else realizes this, too. It's why they haven't shot him yet.

I keep my finger off the trigger, stretch my arm up around his back, and let the pistol's barrel crack against the back of the guy's skull. He jerks his head back and it lets me get back under his arm and smash him across the jaw with the pistol.

He's twisting off me, trying to get away, but I follow him. I spin the pistol in my hand and swing my arm. He rolls over, brings his own arm up, and the butt of the .45 catches him right below the wrist, right on the bone. He howls. The pain's sharp and fresh and he thinks it's broken.

The fight's over, but there needs to be an example.

I stand back up and bring the butt down hard on his shoulder blade. The same side as the hurt wrist. He howls.

Like the wrist, it isn't broken, but he's going to feel that for a couple of days. I kick him in the ribs, just for good measure.

"He was stupid," I tell his shipmates, raising my voice so it's almost a shout. "And he just made all your lives worse. Now we can't trust any of you." I wave my free hand at Steve. "Get them all cleared and then quarantine them. Be thorough."

He nods.

"And for Christ's sake," I tell him, "don't call me Liza."

"Sorry," he says. His mouth twitches into that almost-smile he does sometimes.

I wave him away. He turns back to the new arrivals. Steve and I have worked together for two and a half years now. If I trusted anyone here on Lemuria, it would be him and Maleko.

But I don't trust anyone.

The new arrivals file past me, flanked by Steve, Devon, Alice, and a few other faces I don't recognize. Because I'm looking at the woman at the front of the line. Forty, weathered, black hair with a single thin line of gray.

The woman wears a frayed red T-shirt, almost pink it's so faded, with a stylized black mask across the chest. I'm pretty sure it's the superhero from Los Angeles, the Mighty Dragon. The one Nautilus is always talking about. The one John was so sure would fix everything.

I've never been a superhero fan. Not as a kid. Not as an adult. Even when real superheroes started showing up across the world. Stealth. The Dragon. Midknight. The super-samurai in Japan. Some people never get into sports or game shows, no matter what amazing thing's going on. I never got into superheroes.

John was into all that stuff. He believed in heroes. Comic books. Movies. All the real ones. He kept saying they'd save us. They'd save the world.

He's been dead for almost three years now.

I stop at the base of the ramp and look up at the *Queen*'s logo. More than half of it has been scraped away. Some by time and the elements. Most of it by time and me. Back when I cared, I spent the better part of eight months chipping at it with knives and deck tools. I didn't want a reminder looming over me.

It was supposed to be a three-week cruise with two stops in Mexico, but the *Queen* never actually docked in Mexico. Medical scares kept us out in the harbor. A week later they announced our return to California was going to be delayed. The crew smiled a lot and tried to act like it was no big deal.

Two days after that, the first infected people showed up. A couple who'd spent half the cruise in their stateroom. They'd told everyone it was the flu. It turned out their flu was the ex-virus people had been talking about. All the rumors we'd joked about with strangers over dinner were true. The ex-virus turned people into actual, walking-dead zombies.

The infected couple bit five people before security contained them all.

A couple days later there was a second outbreak. Eight people that time.

The crew stopped smiling. We still didn't head for shore. At the start of the fifth week, a helicopter with the cruise line logo made the first supply drop. Four big pallets. The helicopter didn't actually land, it just lowered them with a winch one by one. Mostly food, but there were some medical supplies in there, too. It reminded me of news footage of third world countries getting relief supplies after a natural disaster.

Two weeks after that was the next outbreak. Twenty-two dead. The captain said we had to dump the bodies overboard. There was no room left in the ship's morgue. I remember a lot of people being shocked at the idea of dumping bodies, and exchanging a look with John that said we were both surprised a cruise ship had a morgue.

The day after the bodies went into the ocean, a bunch of people banded together and took three of the lifeboats. The next day four more were gone. By the end of the week all of them had vanished.

I think it was early July when we got the last drop. A Navy helicopter this time. Only three pallets, but we were feeding a lot less people at that point.

Has it only been three years? It feels like twice that. Sometimes I can barely remember my life before this.

I stop looking at what's left of the *Queen*'s logo. Maleko is going to want to hear about this new ship. He doesn't like to be kept waiting.

I walk up the gangplank, feel it tremble with each step. A crowd of people mill about the top, aboard the *Queen*, and they draw back a bit when they see me coming toward them. They're all nervous around me. Many of them are openly scared.

They should be scared. They know I make the tough calls. I do the things that need to be done to keep Lemuria safe.

"New arrivals," I bark at them. "Watch yourselves."

They flinch and nod.

It's exhausting. They just don't get it. If there was another way that would keep us safe, I'd do it. I don't like having to be like this.

Sometimes, though, they disgust me. So many of them won't do anything to protect themselves. They aren't willing to take action. They think it's somebody else's problem. A few of them have even suggested it's not a problem at all. That in "the big picture" we're pretty safe and should stop assuming the worst is going to happen.

The worst isn't going to happen. The worst already happened. My job now is making sure the next worst thing doesn't happen, whatever it might be.

I walk through the ship. Up stairs. Down halls. Over the

past three-plus years, I've come to know the *Queen* better than the old two-bedroom John and I shared just off Fremont Street.

I push open the doors and walk out into the courtyard. I remember being here by the pool as a passenger. Sitting by the pool in the shade and ordering big rum drinks we really couldn't afford but it was our honeymoon. The deck chairs and umbrellas are gone now, of course, scavenged for firewood and fabric.

Maleko sits in his chair under the gazebo. A bar stood under it once, where they made those big rum drinks, but that got smashed too. I recognize his pose, the casual way he looks off to the side. Walking up here has been a waste of my time. I could've been helping to process the new arrivals or their ship.

But he's the boss. With him, we have order and security. That matters more than any inconvenience I have to deal with.

He looks human right now. He knows I prefer talking to him this way. He's a good-looking man, if you don't think about the monster under his skin. Merman. Atlantean. Were-shark. Landshark. A lot of names people used when they thought he couldn't hear them.

Then everyone learned that Nautilus could hear everything.

"Eliza," he says.

"Maleko."

"Any trouble?"

He still doesn't look at me. I've never asked what he did before this, when he wasn't being a superhero. It feels like he spent a lot of time reading life-coach books about "how to be executive" and that sort of thing.

"Nothing out of the ordinary," I say. "Most of them are a little stunned. They're headed to their exams now."

"No signs of infection?"

"Nothing obvious."

"No resistance?"

"Nothing out of the ordinary."

He nods once. "Do you think they are who they say they are?"

Two and a half years ago, a group of pirates attacked us. They had a drifting yacht and they called out to us about starving families and sick children. The guns came out when they docked. They killed six people before we fought back. Three more before Nautilus showed up and they tried to shoot him, too. He's just flesh and bone, but it's really dense flesh. The bullets barely slowed him down. He punched one hard enough to crush his rib cage. Threw four of them almost half a mile out to sea, one after another. The others surrendered, but we sent them away anyway. We'd never be able to trust them.

We learned our lesson the hard way. The world was different. The rules were different. Don't believe what anyone says. Trusting gets people killed. You can't build real security on trust and beliefs. You build it on what you *know*.

"None of them have weapons," I tell him. "No other signs of life from their ship, but we won't know for sure until we search it."

"When do you want to go?"

"As soon as possible," I say. I step under the gazebo into the shade and lean up against one of the posts. "Their boat has solar cells."

His brows go up. "Are you sure?"

"It's only half a mile out. They're pretty clear." I know how he'll react to the next words. "Lots of people saw them. Not sure how many realized what they are."

He raises a hand to rub the bridge of his nose. "Damn."

I nod. "Yeah."

He finally turns to look at me. "Did they say anything about them?"

"The solar cells?"

"The new arrivals. Did they mention having power to anyone?"

"Yeah. Sounds like they were just using it for their galley. Refrigeration and distilling water."

"Nothing else?"

"That's all they said."

"But they must have a radio."

I shrug.

He shifts in the chair and rubs his nose again. He sighs. "People will want to sweep every channel and set up shifts to monitor it," he says. "We all know it's pointless, but they'll do it anyway. Human nature."

"Probably, yeah."

Now he drums his fingers on the arm of the chair. It's an old routine. He goes through it every time. He worries that he'll seem heartless, so he has planned responses he falls back on, even when it's just the two of us.

He stops drumming, takes in a breath, and holds it. For a moment I think he's going to change. Then he lets the breath out between his teeth. "We're getting close to harvest time with the potatoes, aren't we? I'm not sure we can afford to have people distracted right now." He stares at me, waiting for me to say it. He never likes to be the one to suggest things.

I know what happens when people aren't paying attention. When they aren't doing their job. That's how John died. He was bitten because somebody slacked off in those early days of helicopter drops. Someone didn't do their job.

And then I—

I made it safe for everyone. That's what I do now. That's my job.

"The sun's already on the way down," I say. "We'll tell everyone we're searching the boat first thing in the morning.

Tonight you can slip over there, do a quick search, and disable the radio somehow."

He thinks about it and nods. "Maybe we'll get lucky," he says. "Maybe it will already be broken."

"Maybe," I say.

"I know how troubling it is to do this again," he says. "How wrong it feels. But I believe you're right. It's what we need to do."

John knew what needed to be done. He died saving me. He died so I could live. So I could make sure everyone lives.

So I could make sure he stayed dead.

Maleko and I talk for a few more minutes. The usual stuff. He congratulates me on being so brave, like he always does. I tell him I'm not brave, like I always do. He gives me one of his tight smiles. I wonder if he had braces when he was little.

I head back down to the *Pacific Eagle*. People will be staring out at the new ship, wondering if it's got some magic button on it that we can push and it'll fix the world. They don't want to admit the world's broken forever and they just need to deal with it.

I wasn't lying to Maleko. I'm not brave. I'm just not scared.

John and I saw this Affleck movie once, *Devil-man* or something like that. One of the superhero movies he always wanted to watch. He liked it, but he said lots of people online liked to shout about how awful it was. It wasn't a horrible movie, but I don't remember much about it. A blind superhero just didn't make a lot of sense to me.

One of the things I do remember was a bit with a priest. Devil-man was in the confessional—not in costume, just as Affleck—and he tells the priest he's not afraid of dying. And the priest tells him that a man without fear is a man without hope.

It's a catchy line. And it's true. I'm not brave. I just haven't been scared since I gave up hoping things would get better.

SEVENTEEN

NOW

HIS OWN COUGHING woke him up. There was saltwater in his mouth, scratching at his tongue. He spit it out, coughed up more, and spit that out, too.

St. George opened his eyes enough to wonder where he was. Somewhere dark. His clothes were damp, and the cold reached through his wet suit. He blinked a few times, salt stung his eyes, and he blinked a few more. He reached up to rub them, and something tugged at his wrists.

"Owwww," said Barry from behind him. "Watch it. You almost dislocated both my arms."

"You're okay?"

"I was going to ask you the same thing. They squeezed a lot of water out of you, and you've been out cold since then."

"How long?"

"About twelve hours, I think. I nodded off for a while, and you were still out when I woke up. The sun went down about an hour, hour and a half ago."

St. George looked around and tried to blink more water from his vision. He thought they were under the wooden gazebo in the cruise ship's courtyard. His eyes cleared a little more and he saw the slats were much closer. And made of metal.

The cage had been bolted together out of railings and a few long strips of steel. It sat a few yards from a two-high stack of storage containers. Half a dozen low bonfires lit up all of the metal deck he could see. In the flickering light he saw the outline of plants twenty or thirty feet away, and his nose caught the strong smell of . . . what had they called it? Night soil.

He moved his arms again. He and Barry were hand-cuffed back to back, wrist to wrist. Shackles connected his feet.

"Madelyn," he said.

"Yeah," said Barry. "Still dead."

St. George closed his eyes and took a few slow breaths. He felt a faint tingle at the back of his throat. The faint ember of a fire, weak but growing.

"How'd they get you?"

Barry sighed. "The whole thing was a trap, George. All the little kids there at that gathering? Human shields."

"Yeah. Yeah, I think I realized that a minute into beating the crap out of him."

"If this is what happens when you beat the crap out of someone, I think you need to get some pointers from your girlfriend."

"Not in the mood, Barry."

"Yeah, sorry. Anyway, I couldn't fire any bursts without hurting a kid or blowing a hole straight through the ship. Then Nautilus came back with you half dead, put one of his funky Deep One hands over your nose and mouth, and said he'd smother you if I didn't turn human. Soooo . . . yeah, not a lot of options."

"Why haven't you changed back to the energy form?"

"Ummmm . . . You might not have noticed but we're all in kind of close proximity here."

"Yeah?"

"George, when I change everything around me tends to get incinerated by the radiation surge. The air all around the energy form hits six hundred degrees before I get it under control. It only takes a second, but still . . ."

"So? You know it wouldn't hurt me. Might've woken me up sooner."

"No, you're missing the . . . Can you look over your shoulder without giving me a concussion or something?"

St. George shuffled on his butt and twisted his head around.

A little girl with curly hair and hazel eyes stared back at him. In the dim light, her skin was a few shades darker than Barry's. "H'lo," she said.

The hero looked at her for a minute. His eyes flitted down, saw her ragged clothes and the shackle chaining her to his friend, then looked back to her face. "Hi," he said.

"George," said Barry, "this is Kaitlyn. She's three and a half and she's been hearing all about you while you were asleep."

She nodded once and continued to stare at him.

There was another child, a little boy, shackled to the other leg. He was curled up alongside Barry's calf with his eyes closed, his head just below the knee. The boy's nostrils trembled as he slept.

"That's Colin. He's four and he's never read a comic book in his life. I was getting him caught up on Batman until he passed out. It's been a long day for them."

The chains were maybe twelve inches long. Even if they hadn't been in a cage, the kids couldn't get far away from Barry. Not far enough to be safe.

"Okay," St. George said. He stretched his legs, rolled his ankles, and then snapped the shackles with a quick flex of his hips. "Give me a minute and I'll have us out of here."

"Stop!"

"What?"

"You need to get caught up before you do anything, okay?"

"I think I've got the general idea."

"No, believe me, you don't. These people have gone full Murderworld on us, okay." He said it in a calm, almost amused voice. St. George realized it was for Kaitlyn's benefit.

He took a breath and felt the fire smolder a little more in his throat. "Okay," he said. "What's going on?"

Barry tipped his head toward one of the small bonfires.

"If you look around," he said, "you should be able to spot a couple guards watching us. I saw whatshername, Alice, out there for a while before it got dark, and then one of the guys who was there when I was getting my 'inspected by' seal of approval."

St. George glimpsed some faces in the flickering light. "Yeah," he said. "I see one of the guys from my inspection. And that guy with the big mustache who kept staring at Madelyn. Mitchell?"

"Mitchel Kirby with one *l*," sighed Barry.

"What?"

"Better not to ask. He's a talker. So, I can't break out without giving Kaitlyn and Colin an extreme sunburn. If you break out, or they think you're trying to break out, they start shouting an alarm."

"And Nautilus comes back? I wasn't ready for him, but I can—"

"No, George. The alarm goes off and three cages of kids get dumped in the ocean."

"What?" St. George twisted his head around again. Kaitlyn blinked at him.

"Yeah, I know," said Barry. "Serious Marina del Lex–level supervillain stuff. Three cages, four kids in each cage all around the island. I can't catch any of them in the energy form, and . . . well, you're not fast enough. Even if we knew right where they were, you might be able to get one of them. Not all three."

"How do you know all this?"

"They explained it all to me," Barry said. "Nautilus and his sidekick-girlfriend, Eliza. They took great pains to explain it all to me."

St. George looked at the shackle cuffs on his ankles and the broken chain hanging down to the deck. "You believe them?"

"I wasn't sure at first. They used the kids at the meeting as shields, yeah, but this hostages-in-cages thing is a whole new level of messed up. But while I was waiting for you to wake up I've been talking with Kaitlyn and Colin. And I think I'm a believer now."

"H'lo," she said again. This time she raised her hand and flapped her fingers. The boy wheezed once at the mention of his name, then slipped back to sleep.

"Hi," said St. George again.

"Kaitlyn's a little shy at first," Barry said, "but once she gets to know you she tells lots of great stories. Right?"

The girl nodded, giggled, and then yawned.

"You want to go to sleep?" he asked her. "You've been real good keeping me company while George was asleep. He can talk with me now. We'll keep quiet."

"'Kay," she said. She rolled over and put her head against Barry's other calf. "G'night, Barry. G'night, Sajorj."

"Sleep tight," said Barry.

She yawned again and her eyes fluttered.

He tipped his head back so it was brushing St. George's. "So, here's what I've put together from what the kids told me, kind of aging some of it up a bit so it makes sense," he said. "Nautilus is a full-on hero to these people. Pretty much everyone out here believes the reason they're all alive is because of him. He helped put the boats together into this island, he finds other boats for them to salvage, fishes with them, takes care of any exes, all that sort of stuff. And he tells lots of stories about back before the ex-virus, when he was a full-time superhero with his best friend, the Mighty Dragon."

"What?"

"Yeah. You're kind of a local legend by association, if that makes sense. There are stories about you two fighting mobsters, robots, sea monsters, saving the world."

St. George turned his head. "Sea monsters?"

"Yep. So says the gospel according to Kaitlyn."

"But I've never even met the guy until today."

"No one seems to care," Barry said. "It's like he's pulling a Jonathan and editing himself into all of your life and history."

"A who?"

"Jonathan, on *Buffy the Vampire Slayer*. They did an episode where he cast a spell that made him the most important person in town, so he became the main character of the show. They even redid the opening credits so it was all—"

"Barry."

"Sorry. I just thought you'd remember that one. I mean they fully committed to—"

"Barry!"

"Right, sorry. Anyway, Nautilus's told everyone he's best buddies with the Mighty Dragon, and now everyone's so deep in the fandom they kind of gloss over some of the more . . . well, evil stuff he's doing. He says something's for the greater good, so they all go along with it."

St. George turned again so he could see his friend in the corner of his eye. "Yeah, but this? This has to be too much."

"You think they had cages for a dozen kids just sitting around?" Barry shook his head. "From what Kaitlyn and Colin told me, this is standard procedure whenever a new ship shows up. They've both been in the cage at some point before, him twice, her once. Any newcomers give in because nobody's going to risk getting a bunch of kids hurt. Then they become part of the community, drink the Nautilus-flavored Kool-Aid, and everybody's happy."

"Jesus," muttered St. George. "How does he get anyone to go along with it? Parents let him do this to their kids? Hell, why don't we hear all the kids crying right now?"

"The kids don't think there's anything weird about it," Barry said. "This is all normal for them. They think it's a game. It's what they grew up with. Figure any kid under the age of ten has spent at least half his life out here." He gestured at the two children curled up against him. "Heck, these two have never even seen dry land. They were born out here."

"So you think this is some kind of cult?"

"For some of the adults, yeah, but I think the kids just don't know any better."

St. George looked across the nighttime deck. Two of the guards were talking in low tones. He thought one of them, Mitchel with one *l* of the cowboy mustache, might be staring at the cage, but he couldn't be sure.

Then Mitchel set off memories of Madelyn glaring at the man, and then the image of her being torn in half. The look of terror on her face. Her limbs sagging as her spine came apart. The sound of wet meat hitting the ship's deck.

He shook the thoughts from his mind. "And all this stuff about being dead? And Los Angeles being destroyed?"

"Yeah, I heard some of those stories, too. Translating from little kid, it seems like most of these ships decided to stay at sea when the ex-virus broke out. A couple of them formed a little fleet. They got food drops from helicopters for a while, but then those stopped."

"When was this?"

"She's three and a half, George."

"Right. Sorry."

"Anyway, they were starving, and when people died they started turning into exes anyway. Not clear how the virus got out here. And that's about when Nautilus showed up and told them that they'd nuked all the big cities to stop the spread of the virus. They had to stay out here until all the radiation cleared. When fuel started running low he helped them push the ships together like this."

"He pushed the ships together? By himself?"

"According to Kaitlyn, he's the strongest man in the world when he's in the water. What do you think?"

"He's no lightweight." St. George rolled his stomach muscles, then shifted his jaw back and forth. "So nobody saw or heard the nukes? He just showed up and told them it happened and they all believed him?"

"Well," Barry pointed out, "there was Hawaii. And it was the CDC's fallback plan, right? And a plot point in at least a dozen movies. Is it really hard to believe they'd believe it?"

"I guess not."

They sat in the cage.

Barry lowered his voice a little more. "Did you ever hear anything about him being all, y'know, delusional? 'Cause everything I'm seeing and hearing says Nautilus let his Aquaman syndrome drift all the way over into a full-on Napoleon complex, if you know what I'm saying."

St. George shook his head. "I knew of him, but I'd never met him or even seen any interviews or anything. What about you?"

"I've been trying to think about it," Barry said, "but all I remember is making a joke with someone. Banzai, maybe. I wasn't sure if he took his name from the submarine, the shell, or the gym equipment. Banzai'd seen a picture of him online, and she said it might've been all three."

St. George managed a grim smile.

"Honestly," said Barry, "if Madelyn hadn't recognized him, I'm not sure I would've."

The smile faded.

Barry moved his own head, careful not to shift the two children. "You okay?"

A thin wisp of smoke came out between St. George's lips. "Madelyn."

"Ahhhhh." A few moments of silence passed between them. "Did you ever tell her?"

"About what?"

"Her condition. That she's not a zombie, she's an android made out of a big pile of nanites trying to copy a dead girl."

St. George snorted and felt the chemical scratch in the back of his throat. "There was never a good time," he said.

"Half the Mount's scared of her. Every day she'd wake up with her memories messed up. How do you add on to that with 'by the way, you're not even a real person, you're just a robot'?"

"Hey," Barry said, "machines need love, too."

"D'you remember how many times Freedom had to tell her about her parents being dead? What was the final count? Four times? Five?"

"Something like that, yeah. Yeah, I think so."

"I just . . . if I had to tell her she wasn't even human anymore, I wanted it to be at a good point for her. When she'd have time to process it."

"So to speak."

"Yeah," said St. George. "So to speak."

"You do realize you're still talking about 'her' parents, right? You know she's still a person. In all the ways that matter."

"Yeah. I wish a lot of other people had realized it."

"Still, you should tell her soon. She's going to figure it out sooner or later. Or figure out she's a hell of a lot more than a random dead girl, at least."

St. George tilted his head to his friend. "What do you mean, tell her soon?"

Barry turned his head, too, so they were eye to eye. "Oh, frak me," he said. "I thought we were on the same page here, George."

"What?"

Barry chuckled. "You're such a lovable idiot sometimes. You never got around to reading *Swamp Thing*, did you?"

"What's your point?"

"Think about it."

"About what?"

"She's already dead," Barry said. "Remember? And even if she wasn't, you can't kill an android by tearing her in half."

EIGHTEEN

NOW

"OKAY," SHOUTED AL. The brown-skinned scavenger banged on the side of *Mean Green* with his fist until they all stopped talking. The movement made his chain mail rattle. The other scavengers switched back to leathers in the cooler months, but Al wore the chain mail year-round. "We're heading out. Everybody shut up and pay attention."

"Sir yes sir," shouted Taylor from the truck's liftgate.

"Just told you to shut up, not shout," Al said with a glare.

Taylor grinned and looked around at the other people in the Hot Zone. The scavengers weren't smiling. Neither was Gus Hancock. The battlesuit didn't even have a mouth, just speakers. Pierce just glared at him.

"Just trying to lighten the fucking mood," Taylor muttered.

Everyone shifted their attention back to Al, and he tugged the brim of his hat down. He'd been one of the scavengers since the early days of the Mount, and Eden was his first command position. He wasn't a tall man, but he was lean and well-muscled, the kind of build that came from a life of physical labor. Iron gray streaks ran through his black hair, and his eyes were dark circles on either side of his hawk nose.

"So we're all on the same page," he said, "we're going to go fast out of the gate as soon as it's wide enough. Cesar here cleans up any exes, makes sure the gates are closed, and then he joins us in the back."

"Can't you just keep up?" asked one of the scavengers, the big woman named Keri.

Cesar shook his head. "Running uses too much power. We'd get there and the suit'd stop dead."

A couple people nodded their understanding.

"Anyway," said Al with a glare at Keri, "Cesar gets in the back, we go slow for a few blocks, try to draw some of them away from the fence."

He jerked his thumb at the dozens of exes pressed against the western wall of the Hot Zone. Their fingers stretched through the fence to grasp at the air. Some tore their lips on the chain-link. They stared at the crowd of scavengers with dead eyes. Their chattering teeth echoed in the air.

"We're going to start about six blocks down and work our way back. We'll go over the rules again there, and then you all split into your teams. Try to keep it as quiet as we can— let's not attract a ton of exes. Everyone got it?"

The crowd gave off a collection of nods and murmured confirmations.

Danielle watched them from the gate at the north end of the Hot Zone. They'd set up the rectangular area to function as a four-way airlock. Gates on each end shut it off from the two sides of the garden. Then the gates on either side could open, depending on if a truck was heading back to the Mount or out to scavenge Encino for supplies.

Cold sweat burned her eyes, and she forced a hand up to wipe it away. Not even noon, the air already bordered on hot, and she had four layers of clothing wrapped around her. Almost all the clothes she had up at Eden. A few of the guards and scavengers had given her odd looks, but none of them had said anything.

With the width of the gate and the cars parked on the other side of the chain-link, the closest ex was almost fifteen feet away from her. It stood in the road that led back to the Mount. A dead man, short but with a lot of muscle that had withered away over the years. Dried clumps of gore decorated a tight beard, trimmed close to the jaw. Its clothes were casual, but blood spotted the T-shirt and jeans, and one of the blazer's cuffs was torn and frayed. Something brown with age was smeared along the lapels, just below the beard.

The ex stared at her over a car and through the fence. Its dry chalky eyes never blinked, even as each snap of its jaw made the bearded skull tremble. Its fingers reached across the car's roof and flailed a good two feet from the fence.

She wondered if there was something behind the eyes. Was it a mindless ex, or was there real hatred or anger? Legion, maybe, lurking and watching her and waiting for a chance to get some stupid revenge.

She took a breath and ignored the dead man. And the thunder in her chest. She forced herself to stand there with her arms tight across her chest and watch the scavengers leave.

Al yelled out another command, and the last few people climbed into *Mean Green*. Gibbs gave the battlesuit a thump on its skeletal arm, traded a few quiet words with Cesar, and limped back toward Danielle. His toes *clink*ed on the pavement. "Didn't think you'd still be here," he said to her.

"What's that supposed to mean?"

"Just that. I didn't think you'd still be here. Figured you'd've headed back to the building by now."

"I'm fine."

Gibbs pushed his lips into a line and nodded once.

She made a point of turning her head to stare back at the dead man. Its teeth clicked together and metal glinted in its mouth. One of its front teeth was gone. An implant had broken off and left a thin pin of surgical steel in its place.

The northern garden and the interior gates of the Hot Zone closed behind him. Another layer of chain-link between her and the bearded ex. A guard stepped past Danielle and Gibbs to wrap a chain around the two fence posts. She looped it three times and then spun a quick-link shut on the two ends before running back to her post.

The battlesuit walked to the front of *Mean Green* and

slipped in so it stood between the truck and the seam where the two gates met. It flexed its fingers. The exes reached for the exoskeleton through the chain-link.

The truck's engine revved.

The latch clicked.

One shove from the battlesuit swung the gates open and knocked a dozen of the undead back. Two right in front managed to stay on their feet. The exoskeleton slammed a fist into each of them and sent them flying. It walked forward and backhanded two more zombies. Then it moved to the side and the truck rolled out, plowing down the exes still in front of the gate. Their bones crunched and snapped beneath the tires.

Ropes and pulleys closed the gates behind them. One ex stumbled inside the Hot Zone, a gaunt and gory teenager with an iPod earbud in its remaining ear. A guard knocked it down with a pole, and another smashed the dead thing three times in the back of the head with the stock of her rifle.

Mean Green rumbled forward a few more yards until the liftgate was close to the exoskeleton. A minute later the battlesuit was in the back and the truck was rolling down the street. They drove four blocks from Eden, a parade of exes trailing behind them, before *Mean Green* accelerated a bit. The truck turned a corner and vanished. The sound of its engine faded a minute later.

A deep breath rushed out of Danielle's nose. She took a few steps back from the gate. The bearded ex had wandered off, lured away by the sounds and activity of the scavengers, even though it was on the other side of the Hot Zone.

Gibbs rolled his shoulders. "Want to go back and work on the crossbow?"

She sucked in another breath. "No," she said. She took a few more steps away from the gate. "No, I'm going to go for a little walk."

"What?"

Danielle pushed her arms down to her sides. "A walk. Just . . ." She forced an arm back up and waved at the garden. "Just around the garden. Get another look at the place."

He looked at her. "You don't have to do this."

She clenched her jaw.

"You don't have to pretend. I know what's going on."

She turned from the gate and walked away from him. It didn't take him much effort to catch up, even with his mechanical foot. "I'm just going to walk around the garden," she said. "Alone."

"I don't think that's a good idea."

"Why not?"

He sighed. "Let's just go back to the—"

"No!" She glared at him and jerked her head at the utility road that ran around the garden. "I'm going for a walk. I'll be back in half an hour or so."

"You don't have to."

"Of course I do," she snapped. "You think I enjoy being like this?"

Gibbs shook his head. "No, of course not. I just don't think—"

Danielle waved her arm at the building to cut him off. Anger made the movement easier. "I'm never going to get better if I spend every minute inside hiding. I've got to face this someday, so let me go for a damned walk on my own!"

She took a few ragged breaths while he stared at her.

"Okay," he said. He didn't look her in the eye. He swung his chin in a way that wasn't quite shaking his head.

"I have to do this," she said again.

"I get it," he said. "I don't agree with doing it right now, but I get it." He turned away and walked across the lawn toward the building.

Danielle watched him go.

Then she took another breath, turned north, and started walking.

Not so much a walk as a shuffle. Her limbs refused to make big movements that would open them up and expose them. Her eyes kept darting to the small group of plots to her right, nestled against the lawn and the building. It was overgrown with corn and sunflowers and what looked like grapevines. They swayed back and forth in the breeze.

Was there a breeze?

The cold sweat washed over her again. Then the breeze hit it. She took another breath and another determined step.

The left side of the utility road was a wall of fences. Chain-link backed by wooden fencing. Literally, the backs of fences, put up by long-dead homeowners who hadn't wanted to look out at a community garden.

Some of them were still back there, stumbling in their backyards. Danielle could hear teeth chattering. Twice she'd glimpsed a shadow of movement between the wooden slats. Both times it had made her freeze up. She'd had to count off five slow breaths before she could move again.

In the five minutes since Gibbs had walked off, she'd barely gone forty feet.

Danielle wondered if the guards back at the gate were watching her. They were supposed to be watching the fence lines and the street, but she was standing by one of the fences. She was thirty yards from the Hot Zone. Someone must've noticed her.

Something thudded against the far side of the wooden fence hard enough that the chain-link rustled for an instant. It got her moving—a wide, serpentine movement that wove back and forth from fence to garden plot, but it was movement.

She sucked in air. Her breathing couldn't keep up with the thunder of her heart. Both sounds echoed in her ears. White spots appeared in the air in front of her.

No, she told herself. They're not in the air, they're just in your vision, and you are *not* passing out.

Danielle lifted her head. She shoved her hands down and grabbed her pant legs to help hide the tremors in her arms. Even through four layers of clothes, people would be able to see it.

Another breath.

Up ahead was a clean spot. No leaves or dirt on the narrow strip of pavement. The pile of bodies had been here, the one Les . . . *Lester* had shown off the other day. The exes that had been killed by the Gardener. Cesar had mentioned something about all the bodies being moved. Part of the general cleanup of the garden. Lester had most of the people harvesting all the existing food, but some just weeded and cleaned out all the crap.

She shuffled past the clean spot. Up ahead stood an old storage shack. Past that, an open space, a wide spot in the utility road that marked the corner of the garden. She'd covered one short side of the garden. Maybe a sixth of the distance in just ten minutes.

The *click-click-click* of teeth bounced off the wooden fence and the edge of the shack. Once Danielle passed the small structure, she'd see the northern fence. The one with the ditch full of exes that had paralyzed her during Lester's tour.

But they'll be farther away, she told herself. *Much farther, and I know they're there. No one's springing them on me.*

Another minute of hesitant steps got her to the shack. Then she moved her foot forward, shifted her weight, and an ex came into view, pressed up against the fence. The dead woman wore some kind of police uniform, but it was tan instead of dark blue. The light uniform contrasted the huge spill of dried, black blood that covered the ex's shoulder and spilled onto its chest.

Her next step revealed a dead man and something so withered Danielle wasn't sure what it had been when it was alive. The chattering grew in the air around her. A dead woman with a shredded shirt pawed at the chain-link fence. So did a tall man with dark skin. A small ex sprawled against the fence, pushed flat by the bodies behind it.

Every inch of movement showed her more of the dead. She could see ten, then twenty, then at least thirty. Each step was smaller than the last, but there were so many against the fence, all tumbled down from the freeway and attracted to the sounds of living people. A tall cluster of cactus, just a dozen feet ahead, and a thick patch of cornstalks were the only things blocking her view, and once she went past them she'd see all of the exes. The whole north side of the garden.

Danielle's shirt tightened on her. Her shirt, her bra, her hoodie ... all so tight she could barely breathe. The ACU jacket was a weight on her chest, straining her lungs and her heart and crushing her arm and—Christ, she thought, I'm having a heart attack.

No. No, I'm not. It's just another damned panic attack. That's all. There's nothing wrong.

She forced her eyes open and her arms away from her body. Air flooded into her lungs. Sweat coated her body and soaked her clothes.

Her eyes went to the fence line. The solid fence line. Even more 55-gallon drums had been added along the length, and a few planks of wood. It wasn't much, but it was still better than just the chain-link.

I should've been helping with this, she thought. I'm a god-damned engineer and I'm sitting inside while they've been trying to build a better barricade.

And the shack was behind her.

None of the zombies noticed her. Their chalk eyes aimed past the cactus and corn at something she couldn't see. They bit at the air and strained against the fence.

The panic creeped back up her body. It crawled over her stomach and across her back and set prickly fingers on her chest and shoulders. The sweat made her clothes clingy and tight.

An image slid through her brain. Some of the Unbreakables—maybe Taylor and Hancock, of course it would be them—finding her curled up on the utility road. Shaking in a little fetal ball. No one would be able to depend on her again after that. No way they'd let her near the battlesuit.

She had to go back to the main building. But if she went back, she'd never get past this. But if she went any closer to the exes, she'd break down and never get in the suit again. But if she . . .

"No," she said. She clenched her jaw. For a moment, her anger contributed to the panic loop. Then it punched through. Danielle took eight strong steps, right up alongside the cactus, before her breath caught again.

So many exes. A hundred along the back fence, easy. Maybe two. Past the chain-link was nothing but dull skin and pale eyes and so many teeth, shaking the air with the ongoing barrage of clicking.

Somebody else watched the exes, too. A tanned, bald man with work gloves and no shirt. He stood a few feet from one of the fence poles, between two of the big barrels. The dead tried to push fingers and lips and teeth through to reach him. One tall woman with no scalp had an arm over the fence and across the barbed wire. The dead thing swung its hand back and forth, grasping for the man even as it ripped its own limb apart on the steel barbs.

The chain-link swelled and squeaked. For every one of the zombies that managed to push hard, another stumbled and dropped back down into the ditch between the fence and the freeway. A constant cycle of exes, never getting enough traction to actually knock the fence down.

The man reached out and rocked one of the barrels just as she registered the tattoos across his arms and shoulders. He tugged on the drum, and it tipped up into his hands before he let it drop.

"Hey!"

Her shout echoed across the garden. The man spun around and took a few steps away, a movement too smooth to be the first time he'd done it. Almost a dozen undead skulls swung in her direction, but her anger and amazement at the man—at *Javi*—let her ignore them.

"What the hell are you doing?" she yelled at him. She took a few more adrenaline fueled steps before the exes began to shut her down. They were so close. Some of them turned their focus on her.

Javi's brows narrowed. "What's it to you?"

"Are you messing with the fence?"

"No."

"What the hell were you doing?"

"Nothin'," he snapped back. "I was just checking it out."

She looked at the 55-gallon drum. As far as she could tell from fifteen feet away, he hadn't moved it. It had dropped right back down in the same position.

Don't look at the exes, she told herself as the swinging hand brushed through the top of her field of vision. Just don't look at them. Stay angry at him.

"This is the only thing keeping us alive," she said. "If they get through, pretty much everyone in here is going to die."

"Yeah," he said. "And we both know who will and who won't, right?"

Her anger tripped over its own feet. "What?"

Javi kicked the barrel. The echo rattled inside of it and blended into the chatter of teeth. "This is all fucking crap," he said. "Empty barrels. Old wood. Tryin' to dress it up and make it look like you people give a flying fuck about any of us. This goes down, you'll be safe inside and all of us will be out workin' massa's fields."

"What are you . . . ? Are you still thinking that? What the hell's wrong with you?"

"Nothin's wrong," he said. "I'm just not as dumb as all the rest of these sheeple. I know where things stand."

"I'm not sure you know where you're standing now," snapped Danielle. She needed her anger back. Needed it strong. Her right knee trembled inside her pant leg.

Where were the patrols? Supposedly guards and super-soldiers did regular laps around the garden. Why was she dealing with this idiot?

"You're supposed to be some awesome robot-mechanic," he said. "Funny they don't got you helping to make the fence safer. Funny you aren't askin' to do it."

Her anger stumbled again. The tremor had reached her hips. "I wanted to," she said. She pressed her hands against her sides and set her jaw. "I've just been busy with Cerberus."

Javi shook his head and dismissed her with a wave. He turned and headed back toward the garden plots. "When it all comes down," he said over his shoulder, "I'm gonna fight. Don't think I won't."

Danielle waited until there was almost thirty feet between them. Then she spun and lurched back up the utility road. She couldn't run, but her frantic steps carried her away from the exes, past the cactus, past the shed. The sound of teeth faded to its usual dull clatter. Her breath whooped in and out. The sweat stained through her hoodie and made her ACU jacket damp.

She wanted to scream.

NINETEEN

NOW

"GAAAAAHHHHHHHHHH ..."

Madelyn wasn't sure why she was screaming. She didn't remember having a bad dream. She hadn't had a bad dream in years.

She hadn't had any dreams in years.

At least it hadn't been a loud scream. Just one of the muffled ones, where you stop yourself as soon as it starts. Not quite as embarrassing.

The room was dark and big. Pitch dark if *she* couldn't see anything. Echoes and acoustics told her the size. A gymnasium, maybe?

Where was she?

She'd woken up in her room yesterday ... no. Wait. Yesterday she was on a boat? An inner tube? An orange inner tube?

A raft.

She'd been on a life raft with Mom and they were going to see Dad. No, dammit. St. George. She'd been with St. George and ... and ... and ... St. George and Barry! Zzzap!

She needed her journals. Where were they?

Where was she?

Madelyn sat up. Well, tried to. Her head and shoulders went up about three inches and then flopped back down. The move made her dizzy. Her arms felt funny, like they were sitting on her shoulders the wrong way.

She reached up to touch her forehead and poked herself in the cheek. Her arms weren't where they were supposed to be. Or her head wasn't.

She took a breath to calm herself and realized she couldn't

breathe. Not that she needed the air, it was just a habit she still had. But she couldn't get her lungs to fill up.

She tried to take another calming breath, then mocked herself for being stupid. The mocking was good. She could still embarrass herself out of panicking.

Her hands came up again. Her neck was sore. She found two weird lumps on the side of her throat. The word *vertebrae* floated up from the random stew of memory fragments at the bottom of her consciousness.

Okay. Her neck was broken. That was new. She hadn't broken a bone since coming back from the dead. Not that she could remember, anyway.

But her body always repaired itself. Cuts, burns, even her hair grew back. The main doctor at the Mount, Connolly, said it wasn't "healing," but she never wanted to explain the difference. Madelyn wondered if the woman had explained it a dozen times and just gotten frustrated.

If her body was repairing itself now, it would probably go faster with all the parts in the right place.

It took her a few minutes to get her hands in position. One on her jaw, one on the back of her head. She decided to count to five. Then she changed her mind and decided to count to three. And then, before she could lose her nerve, she just twisted her skull hard to the right.

There were two loud pops and a sharp pain—sharper than she'd felt in ages. Her spine thumped together, and her head slipped down an inch or so. Enough to make her vision shift. Another random memory. Someone lifting a stack of red poker chips an inch or so off the table and dropping them one after another. *Click-click-click-click.* Her head and neck did that.

Madelyn flexed her head left and right. No soreness. No stiffness. She could still move her fingers and arms. Couldn't feel her toes, though.

The *click-click-click* of poker chips was still echoing in her mind. And just as she realized it wasn't in her mind, she registered the sounds that had let her judge the size of the room. She mentally kicked herself over the rookie mistake. What kind of superhero woke up surrounded by exes—even in a dark room—and didn't notice?

She tried to sit up again and flopped back down. Her core muscles were weak. Probably why she was having trouble getting air in her lungs, too. She wiggled her elbows around and levered herself up onto her arms.

Her eyes strained against the blackness, but there was nothing. Not even hints of movement. Just the echoing sound of teeth on teeth. There had to be at least a hundred of them, maybe more, but none were close enough to stand out from the echoes.

She reached down and felt something rubbery brush her fingertips. She traced the edge of it back and forth. Her wet suit had been ripped almost clean in half. The frayed edge had curled up and was showing off her abs to . . . well, anyone who could see in the dark. She shifted her weight onto one arm, then reached out to push the flap of wet suit down flat.

It didn't hit her stomach. The flap went down lower and lower. It hit the lumpy surface she was laying on.

She felt around the ragged edge of rubbery material. Her fingers touched one of her floating ribs, then felt the loose flesh a few inches lower down. She curled her hand around under the arc of skin and found . . . nothing. Something dripped on the inside of her knuckle, and she realized her hand was inside her own rib cage. And there was nothing in there with it.

She wheezed out a silent cry. No wonder she was having trouble breathing.

"Okay," she mouthed after she calmed down, "this is different."

She racked her brain and tried to remember what had happened to her.

Back when she'd died, when the exes had killed her and her mom, they'd torn her apart. John—Captain Freedom—he'd tried to skirt around it, but one of the other Unbreakables had told her the whole story. She'd been in a dozen pieces, at least, and after the exes were done all those pieces hadn't added up to one teenaged girl.

But she'd healed from it. Whatever treatment or chemical or miracle cure her dad had given her, it had been enough to put her back together. To let all those pieces grow back together.

All she needed to do was find the other pieces.

She swallowed and reached as far past her ribs as she could. There was no sign of her . . . of the rest of her. She stretched her fingertips and found scraps that were too dry or too soft, but nothing that was her. And she felt confident she'd know her own legs if she felt them.

Her head wobbled. She had a quick mental image of her spine coming apart and her head falling off, then recognized it as the usual twinge of dizziness before she fell asleep. Not surprising. She hadn't had much food, and being torn in half probably burned up a lot of calo—

"Dammit!" she mouthed. She didn't have her journals. She didn't have anything to write with, or any time to write even if she did. She was going to have to go through all this again when she—

x x x

Madelyn woke up screaming. Or she would've if there'd been any air in her lungs. She wasn't sure why she was screaming. She didn't remember having a bad dream. It had been years since she'd had any dreams.

She blinked twice, an old habit from being alive, and looked around.

The only lights were high above. It looked like sunlight seeping in through cracks. More than enough for her to see by.

There were a lot of exes. At least fifty she could see from her low angle, but probably more. Most of them were just swaying back and forth—that weird lack of activity they fell into when they hadn't seen anything move in a while. Maybe a third of them were staggering around. The chamber was big enough that the closest ones were a couple of yards away. The sound of teeth echoed off the metal walls.

Solid metal walls. Big sheets of metal. Definitely a chamber of some kind, not a room. She couldn't remember seeing anything like that anywhere in the Mount.

Where the hell was she?

How had she ended up here? She'd woken up in her room yesterday . . . no. Yesterday she was on a small boat? An orange inner tube? A life raft. She'd been on a life raft with Mom and they were going to . . . no, dammit. She'd been with St. George and . . . and . . . and Barry! St. George and Zzzap.

Where were her journals?

Madelyn tried to sit up, got her head a few inches off the ground, and dropped right back down. Her abdominal muscles felt super-weak. She shifted from side to side and walked herself up onto her elbows.

She was on top of a pile of bodies. Almost on top. It looked like she'd landed hard and slid off to the side. A few streaks and stains decorated the nearby wall all the way up to where a few bright shafts of sunlight shone through cracks.

Many of the corpses were withered skeletons. A few still had meat on them. One or two moved their jaws back and forth. They didn't even have enough strength to click their teeth together. A lot of them seemed to be wearing black coveralls, or maybe they were dark blue. A few of them had name tags and patches, but the light wasn't good enough to read them, even for her. A few yards away, a little lower down the pile from her, she saw a pair of legs. A long coil of intestines spooled out of the legs and twisted back and forth across the pile. It was the bottom half of a small person, still pretty fresh. Whoever it was couldn't've been much bigger than her. In fact, they'd been wearing boots and cargo shorts like hers, and the black tights might be part of a wet suit, but it was hard to tell from way over . . .

Madelyn screamed, but there wasn't any air in her lungs, so it just ended up being a wide mouth and some frantic arm movements. She looked down at her body. Someone had ripped her wet suit, and one stretched-out, frayed flap had curled up and blocked her view of her legs. She shifted her weight onto one arm, then reached out to push the flap down. It didn't hit her stomach.

She looked over at the legs, at least ten feet away. Her eyes traced the line of intestines, but the tangle confused her. She tried to take a breath to calm herself and wondered if her lungs were still inside her ribs. Were they somewhere else in the pile?

What the hell had happened to her?

Going off the stains on the wall, it looked like someone had tossed her—or parts of her—down onto the pile. It looked like a lot of bodies got tossed down here. If they didn't break anything in the fall, some of them got back up. She was lucky she hadn't broken her neck. Or her skull.

She looked over at the legs again.

Her body always repaired itself. Burns. Cuts. Even her hair grew back. Doctor Connolly at the Mount said it wasn't "healing," but never wanted to explain the difference. Madelyn wondered if the woman had already explained it to her a dozen times and finally just gotten frustrated.

Whatever drug or treatment or miracle cure her dad had given her, it let her fix her injuries. Repair every injury she could remember getting, and probably a bunch she couldn't remember. And it made sense things would repair faster if they were all in the same place.

She lowered one elbow, then twisted her other shoulder hard enough to lift herself a little bit and get her hand down. Her arm straightened out, her body tipped up, teetered, and then flopped over on the pile. She slid a few feet and almost tipped again, but she grabbed a handful of Hawaiian shirt on one body and stopped herself.

A sensation twitched in the back of her brain and carried down to her tongue. She was hungry. Starving.

Could you be hungry without a stomach? Or intestines? A Dad question. He knew all those answers.

She shook it off, pushed herself up onto her hands, and started to crawl toward the legs. There was just enough torso below her ribs to drag across the pile and make her into a rough tripod. She was pretty sure the scratch-thump-scratch-thump as she moved was the broken end of her spine bumping against things. It was good she didn't feel a lot of pain.

Her slide had taken her a little farther from the legs, so her crawl was uphill and across uneven ground. Twice the pile shifted beneath her hands and sent her sprawling. She stopped herself from tumbling and hand-walked across the rest of the bodies.

Madelyn slipped one last time and flopped down with her head on her own thigh. Weird on so many levels. She grabbed her legs and threw one arm over her lap. Her fingers tugged at the buttons on the cargo shorts. She wasn't used to undoing them from this angle. A memory floated up from the soup at the bottom of her mind. Out in the desert, going through the pockets of dried-out bodies in a car. Buttons had slowed things down then, too. Velcro would've been much smarter. Mental note for her next mission.

She was on a mission. A mission with St. George and Zzzap. That's where she was. A mission and something had gone wrong. If she'd been on a life raft yesterday, she probably wasn't at the Mount. Maybe a boat? The hold of a big ship?

"Crap," she muttered. The word didn't make any sound, but she heard her dry lips brush against each other, and it was better than nothing. She'd been digging at the wrong pocket. Again, not used to it from this angle. Her hands made their way over to the other thigh pocket, the one pretty much in her armpit. She pushed her fingers into the pocket and found the folded-up plastic bag she'd put there when she was in the life raft. Four good-sized pieces of chicken jerky. Her mouth couldn't get wet, but her tongue twitched again. She fumbled with the seal, yanked out the smallest piece, and crammed the whole thing in her mouth. Her jaws chomped it to a meaty pulp while she tore another piece in two with her fingers.

A thought hit her just before she shoved the next piece between her lips. Most of her digestive system was scattered across the pile. She didn't even know if her stomach was still in her rib cage, and shuddered at the thought of reaching in to check. The jerky might be going to waste, falling out of her throat and into an empty body cavity.

Madelyn sighed and swallowed the meat in her mouth. The rest went back in the bag. After a moment's thought, she unzipped the top of her wet suit and stuffed the bag between her boobs. If she fell asleep she might forget it in a pocket, but she'd notice it there pretty quick.

She pushed herself back up onto her hands and crawled over her legs. She turned herself around so she was facing the open wound of her waist. She could see her hips and the other half of her spine and something that might've been . . . her uterus, maybe? Gallbladder? Something smooth and slick and gray. She didn't want to think about it too much, and she hadn't done well in biology, anyway. One of the few sore points with her dad.

She reached out and wrapped her fingers around her intestines, half expecting to feel a squeeze in her belly. It was like holding a soft, limp garden hose. She could feel a few small lumps through the flesh and wondered what she'd eaten. Her eyes closed, and she tried to take a calming breath.

Still no lungs. Or lung muscles. Dammit.

It made sense to have all the parts in the same place.

She pulled, and the length of intestine slithered across the pile toward her. Her hands stretched out, grabbed, and pulled again. One of the loops straightened out. Another tug made a section higher up the pile shift a bit. She realized she could go faster if she pulled hand over hand. Smaller movements, but faster. She had to stop at one point when a loop of intestine got caught on a body. Four hard shakes got it loose.

Her guts slipped over the corpses as she dragged them home. A few moments later the end popped up over the far side of the pile, a lopsided bean about the size of a softball. She was pretty sure it was her stomach. It bounced and twisted across the bodies as she pulled it close.

A quick wave of dizziness ran through her head and down her arms. A minute or two at best before she passed out. No journals, either. She was going to have to figure out most of this again when she woke up.

She turned around again and then lowered herself onto one elbow. It put her at a good angle to flip herself over without sliding down the pile. She wiggled on her shoulders, reached down to grab at the hem of her cargo shorts, and tugged the two halves of her body together. Then she reached out and scooped the yards of intestine toward her. She shoved the stomach up into her body cavity and piled the rest below her ribs.

"I'm on a mission," she said, mouthing each word. "I'm on a mission and my body's repairing itself. I'm on a mission and my body's repairing itself. I'm on a mission and my body's repair—"

x x x

Madelyn woke up screaming. Or she would've if there'd been any air in her lungs. She wasn't sure why she was screaming.

She didn't remember having a bad dream. She hadn't had a bad dream in years.

She hadn't had *any* dreams in years.

Her body tingled, like the pins and needles after a leg or hand fell asleep. But it was everywhere. Like her whole body had fallen asleep.

Which, granted, it did sometimes. But it never felt like this when she woke up. Not that she could remember, anyway.

And, wow, was she hungry. Starving hungry. Hadn't eaten in days hungry.

The only lights were high above. It looked like sunlight seeping in through cracks. More than enough for her to see by. She sucked in a deep breath and sat up.

Her chest crinkled as she did. Madelyn pulled the zipper down on her wet suit and found a bag of chicken jerky wedged in her sports bra. She had no idea how it had gotten there, but she was glad to see it. She shook the bag out and looked around.

There were a lot of exes. At least sixty or seventy exes she could see, but probably more. It was a big crowd. Most of them just swayed back and forth—that weird thing they did when they hadn't seen anything move in a while. Maybe a third of them staggered around. The closest ones were a couple of yards away. It was a big room. The sound of all their teeth echoed off the metal walls.

Solid metal walls. Big sheets of metal. She couldn't remember seeing anything like that anywhere in the Mount.

"Ewwwwww."

And she was sitting on a pile of dead bodies. A couple still had some meat to them, but most of them were just withered skeletons. A few moved their mouths open and shut, but didn't have the strength for actual teeth-clicking. Some were dressed like tourists, but a lot of them were wearing dark jumpsuits.

Madelyn pushed herself up onto her feet. A few quick

steps carried her down off the pile of limbs and torsos without tripping. Her boots hit the floor and she wobbled. Her core muscles felt loose, almost rubbery.

She wiggled her toes and felt them flex inside her boots. She could feel the thin spot in one of her socks. A few threads stretched back and forth across her big toe and caught on the nail. She'd meant to cut her nails before the mission, but she'd found some black nail polish and done her toes two days before and didn't want to waste it.

Where the heck was she? She'd woken up in her room yester . . . no. On a small boat? An orange inner tube? A life raft. She'd been on a life raft with Mom and they were going to . . . no, dammit. She'd been with St. George and . . . and . . . and Barry! St. George and Zzzap.

She was on a mission. She'd been hurt. Her body was repairing itself.

Her wet suit was ripped apart just above her waist, all the way around. Stretch lines wrinkled the material, like it had been pulled tight before tearing. The zipper was snapped in the middle, and the splayed-open ends showed off gaps from missing teeth. Her bare stomach looked fine, though, and aside from the tingling she couldn't feel any other injuries or . . .

Madelyn shifted her hips, leaned back a bit, and looked at her stomach again in the light.

The skin across her belly reminded her of fast food wrappers, all slick and see-through. She could see dark veins and strands of muscle going back and forth. Her belly button was a little knot of cloudy gray.

She turned her hips a little more and pulled up the ragged edge of the wet suit. There were a bunch of holes in her side. Oval ones, maybe two or three inches long and half that wide. The gray muscles underneath flexed and relaxed as her hips moved.

"Huh," she said. "This is new."

TWENTY

NOW

"COMPANY'S COMING," SAID Barry.

Five people walked across the deck. Three adults and two children. When they got closer to the cage, St. George saw one of them was Eliza. One of the others was the dread-locked man from his examination.

The boy was eight or nine with a red baseball cap. He could've been a younger version of Devon, just without the wiry biker beard. The little girl had brown hair and Asian features. St. George was pretty sure she'd been in the court-yard when they'd had their meeting with Nautilus. She wore a baggy dress, and it took him a moment to recognize it as a modified T-shirt.

Eliza looked over her shoulder into the distance, then at St. George. "Did your friend explain to you how things work?"

"About the other kids in cages?" He glared at her. "Yeah, he did."

"Do you believe him?"

"From what I've seen so far, I don't have a real problem believing you'd do it."

"Good enough." She took a few steps to her right and stood where they could both turn their heads and see her. "We're going to open the cage. If you try anything, there are still guards watching. They'll signal the drop."

"Why are you opening the cage?" asked St. George.

"We're going to let the kids trade places." She looked at Barry. "We're going to do one at a time, so there's always going to be someone cuffed to you. Clear?"

"Crystal," he said.

"Why even risk it by trading them out?" asked St. George.

She raised an eyebrow at him. "We're not going to leave them in there with you twenty-four-seven. They're going to go home to their families and play with their friends."

"Well, yeah," Barry said. "I mean, keeping someone locked up in a cage all day would be cruel and barbaric."

"Cute."

"I'm just glad someone's thinking of the children first."

"Keep this simple," she said, "and you get breakfast."

The dreadlocked man stepped forward and spun the dial on a padlock. It opened with a clunk. He unwrapped a length of chain, stepped back, and pulled a big panel of the cage open with him.

Eliza stepped inside and crouched by Colin. She unlocked him and shifted his manacle onto the little girl in the T-shirt dress. Then the broad-shouldered woman took Kaitlyn out and put in the boy St. George already thought of as Little Devon. The boy whimpered as the shackle ratcheted shut on his wrist.

"Hey," said Eliza, taking his chin. "Be brave. Your dad's proud of you."

The boy stuck out his chin and nodded.

Colin yawned. Kaitlyn waved from outside the cage. "Bye, Barry."

"Bye," he said. He waved back and managed a tight smile. "You be good. Learn some more stories for me."

The dreadlocked guard frowned. "Don't talk to her."

"Hey," said Barry, "she talked to me first."

Dreadlock opened his hands and let the cage door fall back into place. It crashed shut, and the echo rang across the deck. He wrapped the chain around its bars and slammed the lock shut.

"Wow," said St. George, "you're so brave when it comes to prisoners and children."

The man took a step forward, but Eliza stopped him with a raised hand. She set it down gently onto the little girl's shoulder. "Kaitlyn," she said, "you can't forget, these are bad men."

"Not Barry. He's funny."

"They're liars."

Kaitlyn's eyes got wide.

"So, about breakfast," said Barry. "Whenever I'm being held captive by a bunch of nutjobs, I like to go with French toast, scrambled eggs, and bacon. If you've got cream for the coffee, that'd be fant—"

"You'll get some food once we've checked the kids and made sure nothing's happened to them."

St. George cleared his throat. "You mean like someone leaving them outside in a cage overnight?"

The woman grunted and guided the kids away. The guards followed her. Kaitlyn snuck a last glance at Barry, then looked away.

"You didn't write my order down," Barry called after them. "Are you sure you're going to remember it?"

The girl played with her end of the shackle. Little Devon scowled at Barry. He scooted across the cage until the chain was tight between them. Then he shooed the girl back until her chain was tight, too.

An hour later, the sunburned guard with the peeling nose showed up carrying a tray of bowls. A holster rode on his hip. He handed two of them through the cage to the kids, then slid two more a little closer to St. George and Barry. The bowls held more stew, but it was closer to soup than the stuff they'd had the day before.

"Dammit," said Barry, glaring at the bowls.

Peel looked up. "What?"

"This isn't what I ordered. I told her to write it down."

St. George smirked. The little girl giggled. Even Peel's lips curled up a bit.

"The service here has really gone downhill."

The guard pulled a canteen off his shoulder and twisted the strap around a crossbar so it hung inside the cage.

"How are we supposed to eat?" asked St. George. He shook one wrist and jingled the cuff binding his arm to Barry's.

"Sorry, man," said the sunburned man. He didn't meet St. George's eyes. "It sucks, but I've got my orders."

St. George sighed. "We'll figure something out."

The guard walked a few yards away and sat down on a hatch with his back to them.

After a few tries they figured out how to take turns lifting the bowls, twisting their arms and leaning to the side. Barry slurped his bowl empty on his third turn. St. George sipped his. Little Devon pulled down the canteen and passed it back and forth with the girl. After his third sip, he grudgingly held it out for Barry, tilting it so the chained man could swallow a few mouthfuls.

"Thanks," said Barry.

Little Devon glowered at him.

"How you doing?" asked St. George.

"Locked in a cage," Barry said. "You?"

"Kind of the same. I meant calorie-wise. Are you doing okay?" He twisted around toward his friend.

Barry shrugged. "Been worse. Could be better."

St. George set his bowl on the floor and slid it behind him, toward his friend. "Here. You can have the rest. I'm not hungry."

"Why? Was yours worse than mine?"

"Once we get out of here, I can't have you weak. You need it."

The sun crept higher and forced the shadows back into hiding. A few more people appeared, most of them wearing broad hats and carrying farm tools. They stared at the prisoners in the cage until one of the guards—cowboy Mitchel with one *l*—yelled at them to get to work. Some of them crouched and worked the soil with their hands. Others pushed at the sides of the raised beds with their tools. A few had watering cans they moved back and forth between the plants while they snuck looks at the superheroes.

"Hey," said St. George.

Peel looked over.

"Can I ask you a question?"

The sunburned guard glanced at Mitchel farther down the deck. "I'm just supposed to feed you and get the bowls back when you're done."

"So they said you couldn't talk to us?"

"What's your question?"

St. George tried to nod his head toward the farmers. "Devon told us you got seeds from the cruise ship. Where'd you get all the farm stuff?"

"Huh?"

"Pitchforks. Hoes. Rakes. That's not stuff you find on a boat."

The corners of Peel's mouth twitched again. "Depends on the ship." He tapped a foot on the deck, then chucked his chin at the stack of containers. "The *Pacific Eagle* had over eight hundred shipping containers on her when it joined us. Tons and tons of made-in-China crap."

"Sounds like a lucky break for you," said Barry.

The sunburned man shrugged. "Eighty percent of it was useless shit. Electronics, car parts, toys, games. Stuff like that."

"At least all the kids had a couple good Christmases," said St. George.

Peel smiled. A real smile. "My kid got fifteen Transformers that first year."

"That was a good year for Transformers," agreed Barry. "They did some really sweet G1 rereleases."

The guard frowned.

"Never mind," sighed Barry.

"Past that, we got a bunch of clothes. Some extra cookware. And a bunch of gardening tools."

St. George nodded. "Lucky."

"Yeah."

"No offense," said Barry, "but, uh, why aren't you wearing any of the clothes?"

"We are," said Peel. He tugged at his shirt. "Almost six hundred people, almost five years. Clothes don't last forever. We've gone through all five containers worth, plus everything we could find here on the *Queen*."

Little Devon took the girl's empty bowl, stacked it in his own, and held them out between the cage bars for the guard. The boy leaned in, grabbed the two bowls by Barry, and pushed those out, too. "I'll leave you the canteen," the guard said. "It's gonna get pretty hot out here around noon."

St. George wiggled one of his fingers to point up at the cage's top. "Can you talk to someone about throwing a blanket or a sheet over this?"

Peel's mouth twisted into another sad smile. "Don't think they'll go for giving you privacy."

"Not privacy," said St. George, "just some shade for the kids so they're not out in the sun all day."

The guard looked over at the girl and Little Devon, and his face shifted.

"If it helps, you can even put it all on that side so I don't get any shade. That'll score you points, right?"

"Yeah," he said. "It will. Sorry."

"It's not your fault."

The sunburned guard stood up with the bowls and swung his tray under one arm. He looked at the two prisoners. "Are you really him? The Mighty Dragon?"

St. George nodded. "I am."

"He is," agreed Barry.

The guard glanced over at Mitchel again, then crouched back down. "How'd you survive the bomb? Where were you?"

"There was no bomb," said St. George.

"So what destroyed LA then?"

"Nothing. Los Angeles is there, in one piece. It's got a ton of exes, but there's over twenty thousand survivors, too."

"Twenty thousand," echoed Peel. He whistled.

"Ryan," yelled Mitchel. "Give 'em their food and then leave 'em the fuck alone!"

"I'm getting the bowls," the peeling guard—Ryan—shouted over his shoulder.

"How long's it take you to pick up a fucking bowl? Get out of there." The cowboy marched across the deck and used his shotgun to wave sunburned Ryan away from the cage.

The guard gave St. George a thoughtful look, then walked away.

x x x

Barry twisted his head around. "You know what?"

"What?" St. George stretched his fingers again, brushing them against the handcuff chains.

"I think this is the longest I've been human in about four years."

Little Devon's eyes got wide.

"What?"

Barry shrugged, and the chain hopped away from St. George's fingertips. "Well, I mean, I'm in the electric chair so much of the time, doing the power thing. I'm out for eight or nine hours at the most, and I usually spend that asleep."

"Is it everything you remember?"

"Being human? Not really, no."

"You're not human?" asked Little Devon.

Barry smiled. "No, I'm human. I can change, though. Kind of like Nautilus does."

"You turn into fire." This from the little girl. St. George realized he still didn't know her name.

"Yeah, sort of," said Barry.

Little Devon looked at him. "Does it hurt?"

"A little bit. The change stings for a second or two. But once it happens . . . it's great."

A guard walked up. The Asian man with the tattoos. He looked to the kids and fired off a few quick syllables. Little Devon answered back in the same language.

The guard set his shotgun down away from the cage and pulled some folded blue fabric out from under his arm. He shook it out, and St. George realized it was a tablecloth. The guard flicked it across the cage, like he was making a bed, and shade fell across Barry and the kids.

"Thank you," said St. George.

Little Devon said something else. The guard glanced at St. George and grunted. He picked up his shotgun and walked away.

"Dude," Barry smiled at the boy, "what was all that?"

"What?"

"What were you speaking?"

"Oh," said Little Devon, "it's Chinese. A bunch of people are from Chinese boats, so a lot of us learned it."

St. George turned his head. "You can speak Chinese? That's amazing."

Little Devon blushed under his red cap. "A lot of people can. I'm not very good."

St. George leaned back and lowered his voice. "Have you noticed their guns?"

Barry nodded. "All the shotguns? Yeah."

"Not just shotguns. I'm no expert, but I think they're all the same model. I think all the people with pistols have the same make and holster, too."

"So, about twenty, twenty-five matching weapons. Sounds like an armory to me."

"Me, too."

"Or maybe your basic starship replicator unit."

"I'm going to stick with armory for now," said St. George.

He drummed his fingers on the deck. "Thing is, I didn't think cruise ships were allowed to have armories. Nothing bigger than a basic weapons locker."

"They're not?"

"I don't think so. I seem to remember reading it somewhere before, back when all the Somali pirate stuff was happening."

"Huh," said Barry. "Could be from this ship or the tanker."

"Why so many, then? These ships are big, but I'm pretty sure they have small crews for their size. Just off what we've seen, that's more guns than crew members."

"Maybe there aren't that many. Maybe they're just passing them off to each other so we always see people with big guns."

"Maybe," St. George said. "I don't think so, though. There were a lot when we first landed, and at that whole trial-meeting get-together."

"Yeah, good point."

"I'm hungry," said the girl.

"Me, too, kiddo," Barry said. He turned his head back toward St. George. "What about one of those bigger yachts? Not too hard to believe some billionaire'd load up their boat with an arsenal to prepare for the end of the world."

"Yeah, for all the good it did," said St. George. "Still seems like too many of the same thing, though. Would someone like that have an arsenal or a collection?"

"Hmmmmm. I'd go for the collection, personally. But maybe that's just me."

St. George turned to look out at the sea. The sunlight pinged and sparked off the slow waves. "Do you think there've been any other ships here? Like, ships they looted or got people off of, but then they got rid of the ship?"

"I don't know." Barry looked at the kids. "Did you guys ever hear about anything like that? Did a boat ever just stop by for a while and not stay?"

The girl shrugged twice. Little Devon shook his head. "Everyone stays."

Barry straightened up a bit. "Hey, what about . . . No, forget it."

"What?"

"I was going to say what if it was smugglers. Gunrunners, whatever you'd call 'em. Maybe somebody on one of the ships had a side business. But shotguns seem kind of low-end for that."

"Yeah. You'd expect M-16s or AK-47s or something like that."

"Exactly. Oh, frak me."

"What?"

"Do you think there are zombie Somali pirates out there somewhere? That would be so awesome."

x x x

Little Devon's real name was Ash, which Barry found very entertaining but wouldn't say why. The little girl was Lily. Ash remembered living on land and having a dog. Lily had been born on the ships.

Leather-skinned Alice brought lunch. It was more stew, chunkier this time. She replaced the canteen, ignored their questions while they ate, and walked away with the empty bowls.

The gardeners continued to stare as they worked the huge beds. Their expressions ranged from fear to anger. An older man with a broad face gazed at St. George with disgust. Two or three of them looked hopeful.

St. George studied them back. Some of them picked beans or peas. Others just seemed to be maintaining the beds themselves, pushing and adjusting the wobbly plastic liner that held the soil in place. He wondered what it had been intended for before necessity took over.

A new figure came around the corner of one of the distant

containers and walked toward them along the raised garden beds. It was the Middle Eastern man St. George had seen a few times before. Mitchel moved to intercept him. They talked, and their voices went up as they talked some more. The tall man stepped past Mitchel, and the guard yelled after him, "Nobody's supposed to talk to them."

"I will talk to them, and I will do it without you hanging over my shoulder."

"You're not allowed."

"On whose orders?" asked the Middle Eastern man without looking back. His words were tight and precise, the dialect of English as a second language

Mitchel took a few quick steps to keep up. "You know whose."

"You heard this directly from Nautilus?"

"From Eliza."

He stopped short, and Mitchel almost ran into him. "Eliza is a mate, just like me," said the Middle Eastern man. "My orders carry as much weight as hers."

The mustached man snorted. "You wish."

"Are you challenging my authority? Do you want me to bring up your insubordination to Nautilus during our next meeting?"

"You know what? You go ahead and shoot your mouth off. I'm sending a runner."

The Middle Eastern man waved him off and headed toward the cage. "Do that, if it makes you feel better."

Mitchel fumed for a moment, his fingers flexing along his shotgun. Then he bellowed, "Fuck you, towelhead," and marched to the other end of the raised bed. One of the farmers got in his way, and Mitchel swung the shotgun at the woman.

"Man," said Barry, "he is such a nice guy. I really need to spend more time with him."

The Middle Eastern man walked up to the cage. He

glanced at St. George and Barry, then crouched in a spot where they could both see him. "We do not have much time," he said. "Ten minutes at best. He will send a runner, and there is a good chance Nautilus himself will come to see what is happening. His hearing is exceptional. He will hear us talking from a hundred yards away."

"Makes sense," said Barry. "Got to have good hearing underwater. Especially if he's got sonar or something."

The man looked at them through the cage bars. "My name is Hussein Haddad."

"Good to meet you, Hussein," St. George said. "I'd shake your hand, but . . ." He shook the handcuffs binding him to Barry.

Hussein bowed his head. "I apologize to you both for your treatment. Many of us here feel this is not right, but we are not the majority and have no say in things."

"You seemed to have a bit of say with our cruise director back there," said Barry.

Hussein glanced over his shoulder. "Mitchel is a petty man, a backstabber with no real backbone. He always has been. If he cannot have power of his own, he clings to those who do have it. Or cringes from them."

"Like you," said St. George. "You're a . . . mate?"

"Like first mate," said Hussein. "There are several of us below Nautilus. We are each in charge of an area. A ship. I am the mate of the *Jonah III*, the fishing vessel off the port side of the *Hannah*."

St. George turned the other way, toward the cruise ship. "That's the oil tanker, yes?"

He nodded.

"Shouldn't that be first officer?" asked Barry.

"It was agreed we should not use the word officer," he said. "It makes it sound like we . . ."

"Like you have some authority?" said St. George.

Hussein shuffled a bit closer to the cage. "There is only one authority here," he said, lowering his voice, "and everything is set up so he remains the only one. Any other title is more about bearing responsibility than wielding any sort of power."

"Hussein," barked a voice. The wrinkle-faced old man who'd looked at the heroes with disgust. "You heard Mitchel. Leave them be."

"Mind your own business, Malachi," shouted Hussein.

"Malachi," repeated St. George.

"He was the head chef on the *Queen*," said Hussein with a nod at the big cruise ship. "His training made him the best choice for raising plants."

"Malachi working in the corn," murmured Barry. "Nothing to worry about there." He cleared his throat. "So, what brings you out here, Hussein? Sunset view? You're early for dinner, but I've heard a rumor it's going to be the fish stew tonight. It's worth waiting for, believe me."

"I wanted to tell you not everyone here is like this," he said.

"And you're telling us this because . . ."

Hussein bit his lip. "Because when the fight began, you both put yourselves at risk to protect the children. The children we put in harm's way to hinder you."

"Not the first time you've done it, from what we hear," Barry said.

"It is not. And it sickens many of us every time it happens." He inched closer to the cage bars. "Are you the Mighty Dragon?"

"Yeah. Most people go with St. George now. Or just George."

"Or lovable idiot," added Barry.

Hussein smirked.

"You believe us?"

"I do not know if you are . . . were . . . the Mighty Dragon," said Hussein, "but you are definitely not Marduk. Back before the ex-humans, I saw him twice in person when I visited family in Baghdad."

"I'll take what I can get," said St. George.

Hussein nodded. "Everyone is so convinced you are not from California they ignore the fact you must be from somewhere. Somewhere where people are alive and well."

"We're from California," said Barry. "Honest."

"We have a safe zone," said St. George. "Two now. It's not fantastic, but people have homes and they feel safe."

"Safe," said Hussein. He looked at both of them, glanced over his shoulder, then studied their faces again. "You have room for others?"

"Others . . . other people?" St. George nodded. "Like I've been saying, that's the whole reason we came out here. To see if any of you needed help."

"There are many who feel like I do. We would leave Lemuria, but we have few supplies, and many believe there is nowhere else to go." He set a hand on the bars of the cage and nodded at the children shackled to Barry. "If we help you escape, will you help us leave?"

St. George nodded. "If people don't want to be here, of course. Like we keep saying, that's why we're—"

"Company," said Barry, coughing into his hand. Hussein turned his head, and St. George tried to twist his neck enough to see.

Four figures marched down the deck along the garden beds. Hussein stood up out of his crouch and waited for them. Little Ash perked up.

Even with his bad viewpoint, St. George could see Nautilus in the lead. His skin was sky blue and glossy. Three people followed close behind him. As they got closer, St. George recognized Mitchel, Eliza, and Devon. Barry hummed something familiar, and it took St. George a minute to realize it was the Darth Vader music from *Star Wars*.

The quartet stopped almost behind Hussein. Devon took a few more steps, but stopped a few feet from the cage. A few expressions and lip-read words passed between him and Ash, confirming what St. George suspected.

"Hussein," rumbled the merman.

He dipped his head. "Nautilus."

"What are you doing here?"

Hussein turned and waved a casual hand at St. George. "I was trying to get them to talk. The stick had not worked. I attempted the carrot. I wanted to see if they would slip up and reveal who they were."

"I see," said Nautilus. "So you're saying ... I'm the bad cop."

"The what?"

The shark smile spread across his face. "I'm joking, friend." He set a webbed hand on Hussein's shoulder. "Did they tell you anything useful?"

"Nothing. They still insist their story is true."

Nautilus stared down at the heroes with his ink-black eyes. "I see."

Hussein cleared his throat. "Is there ... is there any chance they're telling the truth?"

Eliza's eyebrows went up.

"What?" The merman looked at him. "Of course not. Why would you think that?"

"It's just ... They're so adamant about their story. It may be a lie, but I think they believe it is the truth."

"You're too trusting," said Nautilus. "They're not who they say they are. They can't be."

"We are," said St. George.

The merman took another step toward the cage. Hussein stepped away and cleared a path. "I'm going to make you an offer," Nautilus said. "Stop talking about Los Angeles, stop calling yourself the Mighty Dragon, and we'll let you out of the cage. I can't have you confusing people."

"Can I call myself the Mighty Dragon?" asked Barry. "Because, to be honest, it'd be a lot easier. He's not using it anymore, and everybody spells Zzzap wrong."

Eliza scowled at him. "You still think this is a joke?"

"Yeah," said St. George, "I do. I'm just trying to figure out the punchline."

"Oh, that was good," said Barry.

"Thanks."

"The 'punchline,'" Nautilus said, "is I'm willing to do anything to keep these people safe. I'm not going to give them false hope and see them get hurt." His voice shifted tone and pitch as he talked, and he became the politician and showman who'd spoken the other day in the courtyard.

"Except this isn't false hope," said St. George. A wisp of smoke slipped from his lips as he shook his head. "Seriously, what happened out here that made you all so paranoid?"

"We've seen schemes like this before," said the merman.

"Pirates and raiders stumble across us out here," said Eliza. "They see what we've got, and they try all sorts of things to get it. They try to turn us against each other. Divide and conquer, right?"

"What you've got?" echoed St. George. He looked out at the rusty ship and foul-smelling garden beds.

"And now you're here," said Nautilus, "telling us blatant lies about who you are and where you're from. Trying to convince us you've got some amazing film studio fortress in Los Angeles where everyone can be safe and live like they used to. What would you think, in our position?"

"I'd at least give people the choice of finding out," Barry said.

Nautilus shook his head. "We're living on the edge out here," he said, waving his tattooed arm at the garden and the workers. "Not even a week's worth of supplies to fall back on. We can't have people daydreaming about a world that doesn't exist anymore and abandoning their jobs. We depend on each other. All of us. If even a dozen people decided to leave, to see if you were telling the truth, so much of this would collapse."

"So the needs of the many outweigh the needs of the few," said Barry.

"Of course they do," Nautilus said. "They always have."

St. George opened his mouth . . . and paused. He closed his lips. Trails of smoke streamed from his nostrils. It struck him that this was what Stealth felt like all the time. Being two steps ahead.

"You're soooo missing the point of that quote," Barry said. "Spock would be very upset with you right now."

Nautilus shook his head. "Do you accept my offer," he said, "or are you going to make us keep you in the cage? Make us keep these children in the cage?"

St. George stared at him.

"Well?"

"We never said the Mount used to be a film studio."

The expression on Nautilus's mouth froze, but his eyes widened. Just a bit. His words died on his lips.

The silence spread out across the deck.

"Yes, you did," he said.

"No," St. George said. "No, we didn't."

"Frak me," said Barry. "You've known all along."

The silence was replaced by low murmurs.

Nautilus took a breath, and his eyes calmed. "It came up during the examination. One of you mentioned it, and someone repeated it to me."

"I didn't mention it," said Barry.

"Neither did I," said St. George.

"Your pet ex, then."

"You mean Madelyn, the girl you ripped in half?"

"She was a monster."

"She was a teenager," said St. George. "And I don't think she was in a very talkative mood during her 'examination.'" He let his eyes drift off Nautilus to settle on Mitchel.

Nautilus turned to stare at the man.

"What?" said the mustached man. "It's not like I touched her or anything. Alice was in there, and so was—"

Nautilus smacked him.

Mitchel dropped like a sandbag. His shotgun clanged on the deck an instant before his shoulder and his head. He didn't stop breathing, but he didn't get back up, either.

"I apologize," said Nautilus. "That should not have happened. We have laws out here. He'll be punished for his—"

"You ripped her in half, but you're upset some pervert watched her undress," said St. George. "Very noble of you."

"Noble attempt to change the subject," muttered Barry.

"Did you know?" Hussein asked the merman.

"What?"

"Have you known all along that we could go to land? That there was shelter?"

"They're lying," said Nautilus. "That's all they've done since they got here."

"So you say. But then how did you know about their base?"

"Shut up, Hussein," Eliza growled.

"They're lying about it," the merman said. "They're trying to divide us."

"A moment ago it was part of their story that slipped out," said Hussein. "Now it's a lie?"

"Their whole story is a lie!" roared Nautilus.

"Who are they?" Hussein demanded. "Where are they from? The man has all the powers of the Mighty Dragon. His friend has the powers of the electrical man, Zap."

"Zzzap," said Barry. "Let the Z buzz on your teeth for a second."

St. George elbowed him.

The merman rolled his shoulders. "Are you telling me I wouldn't know the Mighty Dragon if I saw him?"

"No," said Hussein, "but I am beginning to wonder if he would know you."

The murmurs had grown into whispers, in a range of tones. Some echoed with awe and disbelief. Others were sharp and heated.

Nautilus glared down at the Middle Eastern man. "How dare you . . ."

"You told everyone at the meeting you knew St. George was a fake because he could fly," interrupted Barry.

The merman refocused his glare. "What of it?"

"So how'd you two hang out?" asked Barry. "He was in LA, you were in Hawaii, right? He couldn't fly, so did you just swim back and forth all the time?"

Eliza's snarl faded. Her stare lost some of its certainty as it shifted over to Nautilus.

"No one has ever seen the mainland except you," said Hussein. "No one has seen any signs of the bombs except you. No one alive, anyway."

The words hung in the air.

"We've seen it," said St. George.

"I've seen most of the planet," said Barry. "There's only been one nuclear detonation. Honolulu. Christmas Eve 2009. That's it. Which is kind of amazing, really, when you think about it."

Nautilus looked at Hussein, then Devon, and his eyes settled on Eliza. "You all know what it's like out there."

"No," Hussein said. "None of us do. We know what you tell us it is like. For years you have asked us to have blind faith that you are telling us the truth." He took a deep breath. "Why don't we just go look?"

The merman took a deep breath of his own. His barrel chest swelled up, then eased down. "Hussein," he said, "I understand your frustration. I do. But we cannot risk lives going to shore. The journey will take days. The radiation will be dangerous."

"But it'd be the truth," said Devon. "We'd all know for sure."

Nautilus looked at each of them again, then at Barry and St. George. His shoulders slumped. "Then we'll do it," he sighed. "If you need the assurance that badly, we'll go to the mainland. To Los Angeles."

Hussein breathed a sigh of relief. "Really?"

"Of course," said Nautilus. He took another breath. "If it's what needs to happen for you to trust me again, to believe in Lemuria, then that's what we'll do. We could take the *Sushi Express*. It's still solid, yes?"

Eliza nodded. "It is. But how will we power it?"

"I can push," said Nautilus. "It wouldn't be hard."

"The *Sushi Express*?" murmured St. George.

"I think it's one of the smaller yachts," said Barry. "I remember it from one of the flybys I did."

"We can take as many people as you want, although . . ." The merman paused. His tight smile faded. "We should warn them of the risk. Perhaps people with families should not come."

"No," said Devon. "I'm asking the question. It's only fair I go." He looked at Ash in the cage. "I want to do this for my son."

St. George cleared his throat. "And what about us?" he said. "Maybe we should go back, too?"

Nautilus ignored him. "Each mate should pick a few people to come," the merman said. "If our goal's to assure as many people as possible, to calm as many doubts, we should have a larger pool of witnesses. Eliza, you could pick two or three other guards."

The doubt that had lingered on the big woman's face was gone. She nodded and shifted her weight, leaning closer to Nautilus.

"Seriously," said Barry, "I would love to leave."

"There's only one favor in return, Hussein," said the merman.

"Yes?"

"The imaginary radiation doesn't scare me at all," Barry added.

"Trust me for now," said Nautilus. "If I'm right, if what I've told you all these years is true, these two men are liars. Liars who brought an ex onto our home. Don't help them escape until you're sure you know the truth."

Hussein's eyes went wide. "I would never . . ."

Nautilus tapped his ears. "I heard you," he said. "I hear everything. You know that."

"You don't hear everything," murmured Barry, "or you would've smacked me a couple times now."

"I was not—," Hussein began.

"You've done nothing but talk," said Nautilus. "I don't blame you for wanting to know the truth. I never considered how hard it is for all of you. I . . . I'm sorry." He reached out a hand, hesitated, then set it down on the Middle Eastern man's shoulder.

Hussein nodded and let out a breath. "You have kept us safe this long," he said. "I have my doubts, but I can trust you until I see Los Angeles with my own eyes."

"Thank you. Once you're all convinced, we can figure out what to do with these two."

On the deck, Mitchel groaned and shifted his arms.

"That's it?" St. George said. "Fifteen minutes ago he was a dictator, now you're listening to him?"

"He has heard our concerns," said Hussein, "and he is going to address them." The Middle Eastern man winked at St. George.

"He's got your kid locked in a cage," Barry said to Devon.

"Just to keep you in," said the bald man. "He's tough. He can take it. Right, Ash?"

Ash didn't look as sure, but he nodded.

"Eliza," said Nautilus with a glance at the groaning man, "make sure the guards continue to keep a close eye on them. The cage system is still in effect. Mitchel can stay on guard duty for now, but we'll be discussing his indiscretions in the very near future. Make sure he understands."

"Of course."

Hussein and Devon headed back the way they'd come as Mitchel pushed himself to his knees. Eliza slapped the man on the back of the head, a move that reminded St. George of Billie Carter, and dragged him to his feet. She prodded him back to his post.

Nautilus waited by the cage until they were gone. Then he stepped closer and looked at St. George and Barry through the cage bars. "I want you to remember," he said, "I gave you a way out. I'm sorry it came to this. I truly am. I never wanted to do it. But I can't risk everything we have out here because of you."

The merman turned and walked away.

Opportunity Rocks

THEN

MITCHEL KIRBY WITH one *l* knows a good thing when I see it. I'm not stupid.

My pop told me that he and Mom argued for two weeks about my name. She didn't want to use the regular spelling, Mitchell. She said I was special so I needed a special name. Pop tried to tell her he was all for that, but why not just give me a special name rather than messing up a perfectly good one? I'd just spend most of my life telling people how to spell my name. Plus, what was so special about knocking one letter off it? Why not add something to it?

But Mom won. She always won. And then she claimed "abuse" and left Hawaii. Took off with some businessman or banker or something, moved to Las Vegas. Crushed Pop, but he tried to be a man about it.

You want to know what abuse is? Abuse is getting stuck with some stupid-spelled name you've got to explain every time you open your mouth. Every. Single. Time.

Fucking good thing I'm rock solid, or I would've snapped years ago.

You want to know what *was* awesome? The end of the world. One day I'm doing delivery runs. Next day my boss tells me to take the day off. I think it's 'cause I caught Mrs. Slattery sunbathing with her tits out again, but before I can say anything he tells me everyone's sick and there's no work. First bit of good luck, and it just went up from there. Fucking zombie plague spreads everywhere, and suddenly names don't matter no more.

I'm not stupid. When things got bad I waited inside, ate

up all the food in my apartment. After a couple of days I banged on Nikki's door across the hall. Little drug-dealer skank wasn't home—maybe she was already dead. But she had some more food and a sweet Sig pistol. Even had seven bullets for it.

Stole a car and headed for the marina. Killed three zombies on the way. Used up all my bullets, but found two dead cops and got their guns and stuff, so I was good.

I wasn't surprised a lot of the boats were gone. Figured I wouldn't be the first person to realize zombies couldn't swim. Lots of dead people on the docks and walkways. Had to shoot a couple of them, but then I had my boat.

I knew a little bit about boats. Crewed one or two tourist things when I was in my twenties. It's a lot easier when you don't care about scraping some paint off or bumping into something. By the time I was out of the marina, I could handle it okay.

I always knew rich people liked boats, but I never really got it until then. Go anywhere. Do anything. It's an awesome feeling, knowing you can do anything.

I found a couple others a little farther out. Most of 'em were abandoned, or filled with dead people. No problem for super-sniper kill-shot-maker Mitchel Kirby with one *l*. For the next couple months, I just circled around the islands again and again. Whenever I needed food or fuel or booze, I'd just find another boat.

You want to know stupid? Fucking zombie apocalypse is going on, and you know how many times I just waved somebody down and they'd come right to me? Then pow-pow, bang-bang, I got a new boat for a couple of weeks. Maybe a new lady friend, too. That happened two or three times.

Yeah, I killed some people. So what? Zombie apocalypse, anything goes, right? We all did some stuff we normally wouldn't've.

Okay, honest. June 2009 to March 2010, best almost-year

of my life. I did it all. Y'know that thing, the one where you know the end's coming and you're gonna die, so you just do all that stuff you always thought about trying but were too chickenshit to do any of 'em? The fuck-it list? I crossed a lot of stuff off my fuck-it list that year.

I think I killed about two dozen people altogether. I was keeping count for a while, but then there was this one drunken binge around Christmas and I lost track. I was sure I killed three, but there were only two bodies on the boat when I sobered up.

Watched Oahu burn somewhere in there during the binge. Was twenty or thirty miles off of Kahuku, I think, and I heard this big noise. Like thunder and a wave crashing at the same time and echoing off the mountains. Headed in and everything was on fire. The whole island.

I burned up a boat a little bit after that. Poured gasoline all over the deck, shot it with a flare gun, and moved over to my new yacht. Sat there with the old owner's girlfriend tied to the railing and watched it burn all night. Spring bonfire.

She was named Nikki, too. Just like my old neighbor. She was really into me for a while. Wild chick. Let me do anything to her. Then she kind of snapped. Had to shoot her when she tried to kill me. She was number fourteen out of the about two dozen.

Then I had to kill her again when she got back up. Fucking zombies.

Had a teenaged boy, too. All those stories about rich businessmen flying to Hong Kong or Singapore or whatever to have sex with boys, there had to be something to it, right? But there wasn't. Bunch of weirdo pervs, all those rich guys.

I let the kid jump overboard when I was done. Tossed him a life preserver and pointed him toward land. It was only twenty-something miles. He probably made it. I could've.

Tried eating human flesh. Heard lots of people talk about it. Cooked up part of a leg and had a few mouthfuls, just enough to be sure I wasn't really missing out on something. Tastes like chicken, just like everyone says, but it feels a little more like fatty pork in the mouth, y'know? Then I thought it might be infected. I know cooking's supposed to take care of that, but maybe I hadn't heated it enough. So I puked all that up.

Necrophilia wasn't really my thing. Still isn't. Only some really fucked-up people would be into that. But I'd had a couple drinks one night and the woman wasn't too ugly. Still pretty fresh, too. Don't need to ever do it again, but kind of proud that I did it, y'know? Another one of those things everybody thinks about.

A couple weeks after that, though, had a chance to do it with an ex. Nikki again, just for a couple of minutes. Held her down with my foot on her chest, took one last look at her sweet tits and ass. But one dead chick was enough for me. It's not like I'm some weirdo or something. So I shot her twice in the head.

Over the course of the almost-year, I crossed a lot of shit off my fuck-it list.

I got pretty bored, though. I liked to tell myself I was some pirate king of zombie Hawaii, but I was just bored as hell. I had one bullet left in one of my pistols. Not the cop guns. Those were long gone. This was some rich prick's big chrome revolver. Something like Dirty Harry or the Lone Ranger would use.

Anyway, I'd saved one bullet. I'd told myself it was for if I got bit or something, so I wouldn't have to change. I could go out on my own terms, like Pop did. Honest, though, I knew the right day was going to roll around and I'd just suck the big hard one. I mean, that's the whole point of the fuck-it list, right? When you've done everything, it's time to check out.

And then he showed up.

I heard all this water dripping, and the boat rocked a bit.

Just enough to feel it. It was a pretty good-sized yacht, but he's pretty fucking big.

I saw him standing there by the back ladder. Seven feet tall, five across, and blue as a goddamn Smurf. It was like some kind of man-shark crawled up out of the ocean to get me. A were-shark.

Nautilus. The hero of Hawaii. I'd seen him on the news a couple of times. Rescuing lost boats or swimmers. One time he fought off a shark, and another time he caught a couple drug smugglers using a sailboat.

You want to know scared? I'd spent a year doing everything I could think of off my fuck-it list—some stuff you know can't be excused, normally—and a superhero shows up.

He had the teeth and the skin. Could he smell blood in the water like a shark, too? I'd cleaned up the business guy and his wife a couple of days ago, before I even touched their liquor cabinet. Even mopped up and threw the sheets overboard with the bodies. Real burial at sea, which is probably more than they deserved. Maybe that was how he found me?

I remember wondering if I could pull the gun and get it in my mouth before he stopped me. I didn't want to go through zombie apocalypse justice. Whatever it might be.

We stood there looking at each other for a minute. Then he waved at the pistol and told me I wouldn't need it. He was here to help. Something like that. I was kind of hungover.

Anyway, he asked if I was doing okay. If I needed help. Said he'd been rescuing people lost at sea for months now and had pretty much given up on finding anyone else. Then he asked if I'd seen what happened to Oahu. I told him sorta, and he said that was good, too.

And the whole time his nose was twitching. Sniffing the air. Maybe he smelled the blood. Maybe it was just me. I was on the fourth or fifth day with that shirt. Hadn't had a shower since dumping the old folks overboard.

But he never said anything. I think he understood. We all had to do things to survive. Nobody was judging.

He gave me a sales pitch about this safe place he'd been helping to build. A fleet or an island or something. Again, hungover at the time. It makes sense now, looking back, but I wasn't really sure what he was saying then.

Still, whatever he was offering had to be better than blowing my own head off out of boredom. So I said yes. And he said good.

Which was how I ended up out at Lemuria. Stupid fucking name, but it was weird to see so many people at once.

First thing I did was run. They had this big long oil tanker, and it was the first time I'd had more than a hundred feet to walk in a straight line. I ran the whole thing. Got sick as a dog. Threw up. I'm not built for speed. More of an endurance guy. The ladies like that more, anyway.

And Nautilus made me one of his top people. 'Cause I think he did know. He knew Mitchel Kirby with one *l* is a guy who'll get things done. I'm a guy who's not afraid to get my hands dirty if I need to.

We had a good thing going out here. I had all the power and perks, but not a lot of responsibility. More than enough women were willing to get me off at night for a few extra mouthfuls of food. Hell, I think I'd fucked half the women on the island in the first two years. Life was good. Maybe not pirate-king-year good, but better than I ever had things before the dead started to rise.

And then the rest of the superheroes showed up.

TWENTY-TWO

NOW

"WITH ALL DUE respect," said Gibbs, "you really stink."

"Shut up," Danielle told him without looking up from the weapon. She'd pulled the housing off and was tightening one of the springs.

He leaned back and looked around the workshop space. "I mean, I've slept in a barracks and you reek."

"I changed my shirt, okay? I don't have much up here for clothes."

"Forgive me for being blunt," Gibbs said with a smirk, "but I think you need a couple buckets of water and some soap."

"Look, will you just say 'I told you so' and get it over with? We've got work to do."

He nodded once. "Considering all the other work the Mark Two needs, it's going to be a miracle if we can get range and accuracy out of this thing in less than a month." He rapped the hybrid crossbow with his knuckles. "I think three months is more likely, and even that's a minimum."

Danielle looked at the weapon, then glanced out at the battlesuit. It stood in the courtyard where Cesar had left it, sucking up electricity.

She sighed and turned her attention back to the crossbow. Gibbs was right. Bringing the weapon up to Eden for a week of work had been a waste of space. "Yeah, I know getting it to work perfectly is a long . . ." She smiled. "It's a long shot."

"I said that, more or less."

"No." She set her hand on the housing. "This. It's a Longshot. That's what we're calling it."

His brow furrowed. Then he smirked. "Nice. I like it."

"One thing done, then."

"We should still prioritize a bit." He looked out at the battlesuit. "You want to get back in it, right?"

"Yeah," she said. "Yeah, I do. I think it'd be good for me."

"So weapons should drop down the list. Armor's the priority."

"Right." She tapped the blueprints spread out between them. "This might seem backward, but I think we should do the arms and legs first."

Hector de la Vega came in through the courtyard door. His scavenger chain mail hung over his shoulders. A black grocery bag hung from his hand, stretched tight with weight. He stood and waited.

"Can we help you with something?" asked Gibbs.

He looked at the lieutenant, then Danielle. "Got these for you while we were out." He held out the bag. "What you were looking for?"

She took the bag and pulled out a laptop. Then another. Then a third and fourth. "Oh, these look great." she said. "Do they work?"

Hector shrugged. "Beats me. Were all just sitting out on desks and tables and stuff."

Danielle flipped the first one over and took a screwdriver to its case. A minute later she was studying the insides. "This is great," she said. "Yeah, I can use this. Thank you."

"Welcome."

Hector stood there while she opened the second one. And the third.

She looked up from the laptops. "There something else?"

"Yeah," said Hector.

Another long minute stretched out between them.

"Any day now," she said.

He looked over at the lieutenant again, then back to Danielle. "Can we talk? Like, in private?"

Danielle glanced at Gibbs. He shrugged. "I'll go see what Cesar's up to."

Hector gestured at the far wall. "He was talking with Desi outside the pantry when I walked in."

Gibbs nodded, looked at Danielle again, and left. Hector turned to watch him leave, then waited until he heard the steel toes scraping in the gravel outside. He turned back to Danielle.

"You have a problem with Gibbs?" asked Danielle.

"Maybe," said Hector. "You're still, like, a hero, right?"

"What do you mean?"

"You know. Superhero, fighting for the good guys, all that shit."

She smirked at him. "You saying you're one of the good guys now?"

Hector didn't smile back. "Soldiers are up to something," he said.

Her lips flattened out. "What do you mean?"

He looked out the side door Gibbs had exited, then back toward the one he'd entered through. The sounds and voices of soldiers on the weight bench echoed in through the courtyard. "Couple of 'em went out scavenging with us," Hector said. "Pierce. Taylor. Hancock."

"And?"

"They took a bunch of stuff for themselves."

"How so?"

"Third house we hit had this big mother lode of stuff. Was like some health nut lived there. Big jars of protein powder, vitamins, shake mixes—all that shit. The stuff we love to find on scavenging runs. All just sitting there with no bodies or exes or nothing."

She nodded. "Okay."

"We bring the first load out, and Pierce starts downplaying it. Tells Al there's not much there. When I point out there's a whole closet of it, fucker talks over me, and then Taylor joins in."

Danielle set one hand down by the Longshot. "Just to be clear," she said, "are you sure there really was a lot."

"Fuck yeah," he said. "Next trip it was pretty much all they brought out. Six bags of it. Got stuck with two flats of bottled water. And I handed my stuff off to Al. They gave all theirs straight to Hancock, so Al never saw any of it." Hector set his own hands on the worktable and leaned forward. "So I've been over in the pantry since we got back, helping Al sort stuff. Guess what?"

"What?"

"Almost none of it's there. They turned in one jar of the powder, two cans of shake mix. Nothing else."

"You're sure?"

Hector raised an eyebrow at her.

"Hey, I've got to ask."

"Yeah, I'm sure. Been in there with Al for an hour, and the damned pantry's not that big. Even went out to the Hot Zone and double-checked *Mean Green*. Went through the cab, the jockey boxes, everything. Guys kept a ton of stuff for themselves. Six or seven bags worth."

She glanced past him toward the courtyard. The clang of barbells echoed in from the canopy area. She heard a few voices and picked out Wilson. And Taylor. And Kennedy.

"Somethin' else, too."

She looked at him again.

"You heard about the other day, the gate popping open?"

"Yeah." Her eyes dropped to his bare arms. Hector never had a problem with showing off his gang tattoos, even years after leaving the Seventeens. "You weren't hurt, right?"

"No," he said, "no thanks to them. They were screwing off and just watched those things come after me."

She shook her head. "Gibbs and Cesar both told me they helped out."

"Yeah, they helped," said Hector. "In the end. Cesar took out most of them with your suit."

Danielle glanced at the shadow of the battlesuit in the courtyard. "Cerberus is a hell of a lot stronger than any of them, and even unarmored like this it's more damage-resistant. It makes sense he could—"

"They were all maybe forty feet away from me," Hector said. "Cesar got to me first. Hell, he got most of the exes back outside and the gate closed before those guys did much of anything."

She'd seen the super-soldiers in action. Most of them were three or four times stronger than a regular person and could run a three-minute mile. Hell, a lot of them could jump almost thirty feet. Even with just sidearms, two of them should've cleaned up half a dozen exes before the battlesuit crossed the parking lot.

"You're sure about this?"

Hector crossed his arms. "I'm here talking to you, right?"

The distant sounds of weights and exercise slipped through her workshop.

She turned her head to the side door. "Gibbs!"

They heard the scrape of metal on stone, and he walked into view. Cesar followed close behind. "Did you just yell?"

"Yeah."

"I have a walkie."

She waved the words away. "Who sent you out here?"

"What?"

"Simple question. Who sent you out here?"

He looked at her, then at Hector. "No one. I volunteered." He glanced over his shoulder. "You and Cesar were both there, remember? With Stealth and St. George."

"Who's your boss?"

"What's this about."

"Just answer the question, man," said Hector.

"You don't give me orders."

"So who does?" asked Danielle.

The lieutenant crossed his arms over his chest. "Captain Freedom's the only officer in the Mount who outranks me," he said, "but I thought I'd been pretty clear you're the boss as far as I'm concerned."

She relaxed. "Good."

"So I pass?"

Hector grunted. "You just going to take his word for it?"

"Yeah, I am," Danielle said.

"Thanks," said Gibbs. "My word for what?"

Danielle looked around the room. Another clank and rattle echoed in from the weight bench outside. "A couple things have been nagging me about the Unbreakables since we got out here," she said, dropping her voice a bit. "Hector just came to me with something he noticed, too."

Cesar's eyes got big. Gibbs furrowed his brow. "What kind of things?" asked the lieutenant.

She glanced out toward the courtyard. "Have you noticed how much drilling they've been doing? The runs? The exercise? It all feels . . . more intense. Like they're preparing for something."

"That's half the reason they're out here," said Gibbs. "Kennedy was running them all through the basics again, whipping them back in shape."

"And they're hoarding supplies," said Hector. "Keeping stuff from the scavenging runs for themselves."

"Are you sure?" Gibbs asked.

"Yes, I'm fucking sure," said Hector. "We already had this talk."

"Have either of you noticed anything?" Danielle asked.

The lieutenant stuck his hands in his pockets. "Yeah," he said. "Yeah, I've seen a couple things."

"Like what?"

"The soldiers have taken charge of all the weapons," he said. "It's supposed to be an armory for all the guards and scavengers up here at Eden, but Kennedy's in full control of the weapons and the ammunition."

"They're letting the guards have rifles," Danielle said.

"Yeah, but the Unbreakables are checking them all in and out. I didn't think of it until you said it, but . . . well, nobody gets a weapon without their permission."

"What's the other thing?" asked Hector.

"They're not watching the exes," Gibbs said. "Not as much as they should be."

She raised an eyebrow. "What?"

"Something I noticed the other day, when Cesar and I were walking the fence." The lieutenant pointed a finger up at the roof. "I saw Johnson in the sniper nest up there, and he wasn't paying attention to the fence. He was watching the people in the garden."

"Hey, yeah," said Cesar. "I remember that."

"I seen it, too," said Hector. "Remember on the first day here, seein' that guy up there watching me and the others while we were working."

Cesar looked at Danielle. "Is Javi right? Are we, like, prisoners up here?"

"You're not," said Hector. "Not that sure about me."

"That doesn't make any sense," Danielle said. "Even if this was supposed to be some kind of prison work camp for the Mount—which it isn't—they'd still need to maintain the fence lines. If the exes get in, they're not going to be selective about who they kill."

"Unless that's the point," said Hector. "They get in, kill most of us, and that's a bunch less people to feed."

"Not enough," said Gibbs. When Hector snarled he raised a hand. "I just mean killing off fifty people isn't going to change the food situation. It's about one fourth of one percent of the population."

"And if that was it," asked Danielle, "why are we here? They don't want to lose us or the suit. Or Eden."

Cesar glanced out at the battlesuit. "First Sergeant Kennedy," he said, "she's been, like, real friendly with you lately, right? Like she's trying to get you on their side."

Danielle opened her mouth to dismiss the idea, but it took root. The Unbreakables had been part of the Mount for years. How many conversations had she ever had with Kennedy before coming to Eden? They'd exchanged a few words and polite greetings, but other than that . . . ?

"Oh, hell," Gibbs said. "I don't think you're prisoners. I think we might have it backward. Focused on the wrong things."

"How so?"

"I don't think the Mount has anything to do with this. Not directly." He looked out toward the courtyard, toward the soldiers and their supplies and their gym equipment. "I think the Unbreakables might be getting ready to stage a coup."

TWENTY-THREE

NOW

"**WHAT DO YOU** think he's up to?" Barry asked.

St. George stretched his fingers out and brushed at the chain. The sun was touching the western horizon, and shadows covered their cage again. "I have an ugly idea."

"What?"

"I don't think that boat will ever come back. I think they're all going to go to shore and then die from 'radiation' before they can get back."

"Frak me," said Barry. He glanced at the kids, then leaned back and lowered his voice. "You think he's going to kill them?"

St. George shrugged. "I don't know. I want to believe he's just been confused somehow, there was so much chaos for a while. But he knows about the Mount. He's been lying to these people for who knows how long." He organized his thoughts. His head had been buzzing since the merman had appeared. "Hussein said he was in charge of his fishing boat, right?"

"Yeah?"

"Why isn't the captain in charge?"

"Maybe he died? Turned?"

"I don't think anyone here used to be a captain. Or any kind of officer. Remember the whole bit about not wanting authority figures?"

Barry turned his head. "Yeah. And we haven't met any, have we?"

"Nope. Don't you think somebody would've been introduced as a former captain or something?"

"There's a lot of people we haven't been introduced to yet."

"But I think we've met a good chunk of Nautilus's command structure. And there doesn't seem to be a single former officer in the bunch, does there?"

"No," said Barry. He jerked his head out at the gardens. "Hell, I think Malachi-of-the-corn out there is the first staff member we've even heard of."

"So, consider that, add in his whole 'sorry it came to this, can't risk anything' speech he gave us . . ."

"Yeah. A little ominous. But still . . . He's taking some of his people, too. They'll know."

"Going off how fast he belted Mitchel, I don't think that's going to slow him down," St. George said. "Hell, if some of his people die, too, it just makes the story more believable, doesn't it?"

"I don't know. It seems a little wonky to me. And risky. If the boat doesn't come back, won't it make any doubters left out here doubt him even more?"

"I don't know. How many do you think there are?"

"Beats me. But I mean, it sounds like more than a dozen, the way Hussein was talking."

"People are going to die?" whispered Ash.

Barry shook his head. "Not if we can help it, buddy."

St. George looked up at the red-and-gray-streaked sky, then at the garden beds. Most of the workers had left about an hour ago, but a last six or seven were inspecting the plants. "I'd say we've got maybe ten or fifteen minutes until sunset, then another half hour until full dark. We do it then."

"You sure?"

"Not really, no. But we can't just sit here while he takes everyone over the horizon and drowns them. We'll move fast, try to save all the kids. The darkness should give us better odds. And then we can deal with Nautilus."

Barry jerked his head a few times. "This'd be a perfect time for our ace in the hole, Corpse Girl, to show up and take out a guard or two. It'd really shift things in our favor."

"I don't think we can gamble on that," said St. George. "We still don't know for sure if she's woken up, or what kind of shape she'd be in if she did."

"Well," said Barry, "I'm looking right at her and she looks fine. I think everything's coming up Milhouse."

"What?" St. George twisted around.

Madelyn loped along one of the cargo containers, as far from the garden plots as she could get. Her jacket was tucked under her arm, and a bright blue baseball cap was perched on her head. The orange sunlight masked her white skin. One or two of the garden workers glanced at her, but it seemed keeping their heads down and quiet won out over reporting someone they didn't recognize.

Or maybe Hussein was right about how many people wanted off the island.

Madelyn stepped into the gap between one of the big containers and the next one. Her pale skin almost glowed in the shadows. She leaned her head out to watch one of the far guards, the Asian man, and then slipped back out. A few quick steps took her to the next opening. It was barely a crack, ten feet from the cage, but she crouched against it.

St. George could see where her wet suit had been ripped apart. Where *she*'d been ripped apart. A swath of translucent skin stood out across her midriff, brilliant against the black wet suit. "Hey," she stage-whispered, "what the hell is all this?"

St. George cast his eyes down at her exposed stomach. "Are you okay?"

She smiled. "How many times do I have to tell you? Being dead is my superpower."

"See?" murmured Barry.

Madelyn started to move forward, but St. George gestured

her back. She wiggled her fingers at the cage struts. "So what gives? This thing can't actually be holding you, can it?"

"They've got hostages all over the island," said St. George. "Kids. If we try to get out, the guards give a signal and the hostages die."

The Corpse Girl shook her head. "Man, I hate this place."

St. George turned his head to gaze at Mitchel, a few dozen yards away. The man was half turned from them. He had a long knife out and was sharpening it against a metal rod. "There's him and two others. One over there between the gardens, and another one facing Barry."

She nodded. "I snuck past him coming over here."

"Think you can get all three? Fast and quiet?"

"Dead quiet," she whispered with a smile.

"No joking around," he said. "If one of them yells out, the kids are going to drown."

Madelyn's smile faded. "Got it," she said. She straightened up, walked along the storage container, and vanished into the next gap.

St. George twisted his head back to Barry. "Lean forward a little more."

The kids shifted away, and Barry stretched toward his knees.

St. George stretched his fingers to the shackle on Barry's far wrist. He fumbled, gripped the chain between his fingertips, and squeezed. There was a faint squeal, a sharp ping, and a broken link clattered on the deck.

"Lord almighty, free at last," Barry drawled.

"Almost," said St. George. He put his free hand close to the other and snapped the cuff, then did the same with the other wrist. "Keep your arms in place until she's got the guards."

x x x

Mitchel Kirby with one *l* was hating life.

He dragged his bowie knife along the sharpening rod.

It was really some kind of big kitchen knife, not an actual bowie knife. Malachi had told him the name of it once, when he'd showed Mitchel how to sharpen it without wrecking the edge.

Normally the sound of the knife on the rod made him feel tough, but now the slight vibration from it traveled up his arm to his nose, like the little tremor before a sneeze. And the tremor felt like broken glass in his nostrils.

He was pretty sure Nautilus had broken his nose, and positive he'd broken a tooth. His first square one, top back left. Mitchel'd touched his nose once, and it felt like being stabbed with a red-hot knife. He'd wiped his mouth five or six times, and there was still blood in his mustache. The side of his face was swelling, too. He could feel it.

The boss had just turned on him for looking at some dead girl's cooch and little apple titties. What was the big deal? It's not like he'd touched her or anything. Well, sure, he'd touched her when he'd dumped her body in the Hole. But she was for-real dead then, so who cared?

The top of the sun dropped under the horizon. The sky was still bright, but it wouldn't last long. Have to light the fires soon. And maybe goddamned Hong would come relieve him so he could get someone to check out his nose. Could a broken nose get infected?

Who cared about the dead girl at all? She was a fucking ex. Why was he getting his nose broken and his tooth knocked out over her? It's not like he killed her. Or infected her.

He was getting thrown under the bus was what it was. The boss was losing hold, and Mitchel was the sacrificial lamb. Nautilus needed to look fair and tough and all that shit, so Mitchel had to take the fall.

If the damned fish man tried something like that again, though, Mitchel would gut him like a fish. Yeah the boss was strong and tough, but a sharp knife would still go through his skin and open him up. If nothing else, he needed to remember Mitchel was one of the chosen. He knew where the bodies were buried, so to speak.

Mitchel wasn't stupid. Every job he'd ever had, he figured out how he could rob the place. The Walgreens in Kailua. The Jack in the Box at King and McCully. The beach sandwich shack. Even that secondhand DVD store in Honolulu, and he'd only worked there for twelve days. He could've robbed any one of them blind and gotten away with it, because he planned ahead.

He always knew there was a chance his past would come back to haunt him. Maybe one of the girls would start talking and make herself out to be some kind of victim. Or maybe one day the big guy would come back from a swim with one of the people he'd let live, and they'd point the finger at him. Nautilus liked having loyal people, but Mitch knew sometimes examples had to be made. And in one or two of these hypothetical cases, he'd be prime example material.

So he had a plan ready. He called it plan B, because everybody in the movies ended up going to plan B anyway and it always worked. So he figured he'd just start with that one. He was smart that way.

Something moved in the corner of his eye and knocked him out of the shallow depths of his thoughts. He brought one hand up to protect himself while the other hand fumbled with the knife, but it was just a girl. One of the older ones, walking toward him. She was wearing a tight black sweatshirt that left her smooth belly exposed, and it was zipped low, too, so he got a glimpse of the cleavage between her firm little apple tit—

Mitchel's gaze went up to her face, and as she stepped forward he saw the dead white eyes under the brim of her baseball cap.

He glanced down, just for a second, looking for his shotgun, and when he looked back up her fist was coming at his face. He lashed out with the knife and the little fist hit him right in his broken no—

He didn't black out so much as white out. His whole brain just turned to light and roaring and then he came out of it and SWEETHOLYSHITTHEPAIN!! A fucking Fourth of July Roman candle was going off in his head. His jaw locked up so his breathless scream just came out as a long hiss. He couldn't even open his left eye and his right eye was watering and there was blood in his mouth and holy fuck the little dead girl was back and she was going to kill him because his nose hurt so much.

His hands were empty. He'd dropped his knife. He still didn't know where the shotgun was. He was on his knees in front of the dead girl. He put his hands up to protect his nose, and her fist slammed into the side of his head. Not hard enough to knock him out, but it shook his nose again and made his eyes spasm.

Her foot sank into his gut, air shot out of his mouth, and it whistled over the empty socket of his tooth like a fucking razor blade. He tried to suck some air back in. One scream. One scream and the brats died and it was all her fault. Her and the fucking super—

She punched one of his protective hands right in the palm. He tried to grab her fist, but the back of his own hand smacked into his broken noOHFUCKINGHOLYJESUS-THEPAIN. The white sound faded, and he opened his eyes in time to see the deck rushing up at him. He tried to twist out of the way, and the metal plates hit him in the forehead and shook his broken nose.

This time he did black out.

x x x

Freedom had taught Madelyn to always go for the weak spots, and the cowboy's bruised and swollen nose had made a great target. She leaned in, ready to throw another punch, but the guard with the cowboy mustache was out cold. She kicked him twice in the leg to be sure, and thought about kicking him in the nads to be *really* sure, but she didn't want to risk waking him up.

The man's nose and mouth were bleeding a lot, and she felt good about that. Having him stare at her chest, even for just a few seconds, had made her skin crawl for some reason. She was pretty sure the guy was a creeper, whoever he was.

His knife had cut right across her boob. Through the wet suit and sports bra into her skin. The zipper had stopped it from going farther across her chest. She poked at the wound, just to be sure her body and her clothes were going to hold together.

She took the cowboy's shotgun and knife with her. Circling around the large garden patch took her a few minutes. She tried to move casually, but with a purpose. Act like you belong there and nobody will look too close. She'd heard that somewhere. Or read it.

When she reached the second guard, he was watching the last few inches of the sun vanish behind the horizon. It was pretty, with all the reds and orange and even some purple striped back and forth. But he had his back to the cage, which Madelyn thought was sloppy for a guard.

He heard her footsteps and started to look back over his shoulder, but he was way too relaxed. She just walked up and hit him in the back of the head with the butt of the shotgun. Both hands, jerked it forward, hit him right in his mess of dreadlocks. His body spasmed, his own weapon slipped from his fingers, and then he crumbled.

She watched his body for a moment to make sure he was still breathing. These guards all needed to be knocked out, but she didn't want to kill anyone. Not even creeper-cowboy guy.

There was a big metal barrel near the guard that looked

and smelled like it was used for fires sometimes. She dropped both shotguns and the knife in it. One guard left.

Madelyn crouched by another storage container and peered over at the last man. He was looking in the direction of the cage, just like he'd been when she worked her way around him a little while ago. Clear view in front of him, but she could probably walk right up behind him.

She found a gap between one of the storage containers and the ship's railing. It wasn't even a foot, but it was enough to squeeze in sideways and shuffle down to the far end of the ship. It was like inching along a ledge with the ocean shifting back and forth forty or fifty feet below. She couldn't remember ever having a fear of heights. Good thing.

Seven minutes of shuffling later, the ledge opened up into a wide space near the front of the ship. No more containers, just some hatches and little pillars and other ship-things she didn't recognize. She slipped to the edge of the big steel box and eased her head out to look around. She wasn't quite behind the guard, but she was close. At his eight o'clock, if she was using the term right.

How good was his peripheral vision? He hadn't noticed her sneaking up to the cage. Or maybe he had seen her and just hadn't said anything because she hadn't tried to break the other heroes out. Maybe a lot of teenaged St. George groupies had been stopping by the cage in the time she'd been healing and climbing out of the oil tanker's ex-filled hold.

If she walked back a little bit, she could curve around and come up right behind him. It was already pretty dark, and she'd just be a shadow to him if he did catch a glimpse of her. She just had to move fast and not hesitate. She wasn't sure how much longer the other two guards would be out.

Madelyn started walking. Slow, easy steps at first, just in case he caught a glimpse of her. Then faster as she got behind him, out of his field of vision. She took long strides on her toes, not quite running so her boots wouldn't make noise on the deck. The guard was thirty feet away. Twenty. Ten.

Her foot scuffed as she put it down. A bit of dried dirt and rust. Not a loud sound, but a different one. It stood out. The guard's shoulders shifted. His chin came around and gave her a glimpse of Asian features.

She lunged and tackled him. They tumbled down, and her hand slapped over his mouth. He tried to yell, and she pushed her fingers between his teeth. His tongue twitched against her fingertips. He looked at her and screamed, but it was a stuttering, muffled screech around her knuckles. Then his mouth was opening wide, his tongue pulling back, and he almost gagged trying not to touch her cold skin.

Madelyn pulled herself up on top of him and slammed her forehead down against his. It was a clumsy head butt. She knew there was a certain way to do it, but didn't know what it was. So she just smacked their skulls together again and hoped the blow would connect right.

He twisted under her and got an arm against her throat to hold her head back. He wrenched his head around. Her fingers slipped from his mouth, he took in a sharp breath and—

The cage exploded.

x x x

"She's got the last guy," said Barry. "Let's do it."

"He's out?"

"He's down. Time to go no matter what."

St. George turned and grabbed the shackle holding Ash to Barry's thigh. He snapped it with a quick jerk of his hands, then broke Lily's. "Come on," he told them. "Let's go to the other side of the cage."

Ash looked between the two men. "Now?"

"Yeah, right now. Come on."

Barry shuffled on his hands, turned around, pushed

himself up against the opposite wall. He reached out and grabbed the bars of the cage.

"Hug each other tight," St. George told the kids, "look that way, and keep your eyes closed, okay?" He put his back to Barry, shielding the children with his body, and put his arms up so his hands covered their faces. "Do it."

Light and heat blasted across St. George. Arcs of power cracked up and raced along the struts and beams of the cage. The kids wailed.

The blazing light lasted a few seconds, then vanished. St. George looked over his shoulder. Smoke rippled off his leather jacket.

The far wall of the cage was gone, replaced by a hole almost six feet across. The edges of the bars still glowed dull red. One section fell off and clanged onto the steaming deck.

The sun had come back up, and it raced across the sky.

x x x

Zzzap did two fast circuits around the island and spotted the cages held out over the water. One on the bow of the container ship, closest to where he and St. George had been held. One on a fishing boat. One on the tanker.

Just over three seconds since he changed into his energy form.

He hoped the element of surprise meant he wouldn't have to hurt anyone.

The container ship first. The cage hung three feet out past the ship's railing, held up by a thick length of aircraft cable that ran along a short steel arm. The cable ran back through a series of heavy block and tackles and what looked like a winch. Maybe part of a small crane that had been part of the ship to start with.

The whole thing was mounted on a raised section of deck. The man and woman standing by the manual cranks were closest to the guards Madelyn had taken out. They'd be the first to hear anything if someone shouted. He recognized the woman with the slack face and sun-leathered skin. Alice, very clearly not through the looking glass. She was looking out at the ocean, twisting her head around. Probably still registering his trips around the island and what they meant.

The three children in the cage—two boys and a girl—looked at him with wide eyes as he placed his gleaming hands around the block and tackle. He inched his palms closer, and the heat swirled between them. The block glowed red. Hot enough to fuse, but not to melt the block or the cable.

A thunderclap echoed across the sea as Alice fired her shotgun. The kids screamed. Barry shuddered as the pellets melted inside him. He glanced at the kids to make sure they hadn't caught any of the blast, but didn't see any wounds.

He turned and deformed the barrel of Alice's shotgun with a wave of his hand. He reached out and destroyed the man's, too, just in case they decided to carry out their threat in a more direct way. He let off a growl of light and heat that made the two guards flinch back. Alice leaped off the raised deck and landed rough. She limped away, followed by the man.

The kids were safe for the moment.

Then he was across the island at the back end of the oil tanker. Same setup here, but with a smaller crane, thicker cable, and four kids in the cage. Three girls and a boy. Only one guard, a bearded man in a ragged Hawaiian shirt, also with a shotgun. He dropped the weapon and leaped back as the gleaming wraith appeared above his platform.

Zzzap applied heat and welded the block and tackle into a lump of metal. Two strands of the aircraft cable melted and curled apart. He flinched. No room for mistakes. Fast, but not rushed.

Once he was done, a quick brush of his fingers fused the

shotgun to the tanker's deck. The heat cooked off a round, and the guard flinched away from the thunder. "I never would've hurt 'em," whimpered the man. He dropped to his knees and held up his hands. "I swear, man."

The wraith sliced through the night sky and down to the fishing boat. This cage was on some kind of chain hoist, and an arm made from a steel pipe. Three kids, one of them a boy close to ten or eleven. No sign of a guard. He ran his hand along the links and fused about a yard of chain into a solid rod.

Footsteps came from behind him. A sagging man with a greasy Picard hairline and a thin pelt of chest hair inside his open shirt. He saw the glowing silhouette and fumbled with his weapon.

Zzzap rushed at the man, stopping a few feet away. *QUICK*, he yelled. *Abandon ship before it's too late!*

The man turned and ran for the railing. He stopped himself after a few hasty steps, but when he turned back Zzzap had his hand up, and the air was shimmering with heat. He glanced down at his shotgun.

Just toss it overboard, said Zzzap. *If I have to take care of it, there's always a chance it could just blow up in your hands.*

The man looked at the heat rippling off the wraith, then tossed the weapon over the railing.

Good job. Now go in after it.

The sagging man glanced after his shotgun. "It . . . it's already sunk."

Don't kill the moment with details. Just jump off the boat.

"I can't really. . . . I'm not a good swimmer."

Zzzap flitted out over the water and then back between the guard and the children. *There's a couple of ropes dragging in the water. You'll be able to climb out or you can hold on until someone comes to rescue you.* He pointed at the railing.

The man sighed and swung a thick leg over the railing. He

tottered for a second, then slipped and splashed below. "I'm okay," he yelled up.

Good. Don't think about Jaws *while you're down there.* Zzzap turned to the cage. *Sorry about all that. Hopefully we'll have you out of there soon, okay?*

"What's going on?" asked the boy.

A couple things. I'm sure your parents will explain it all to you when you're older.

× × ×

St. George rolled his shoulders. His back was stiff as hell from sitting on the deck. He took in a deep breath and let it billow out as smoke. Ash watched with wide eyes.

Madelyn ran up to him. "You didn't even wait for me to get the last guy."

"Yeah. We were a little impatient after a day and a half in the cage." His eyes dropped away from hers, down to her chest.

Madelyn stared back, and her brow wrinkled up. Then she blinked and glanced down at the gash in her swimsuit. "Oh!" she said. "I'm fine. Just a flesh wound."

"You sure?"

"Yeah. Didn't even hit bone."

A blur of light shot past them, lighting up the deck.

She watched Zzzap hover over the distant crane tower, and then the gleaming silhouette flitted away. "So what's the plan, boss?"

"Barry's going to keep making sure the kids are okay. That nobody tries to carry out the threat after the fact. If you can keep an eye on Lily and Ash, I'm going to go get the others out of their cages."

"Okay."

Zzzap shot by again. In the flash of light, St. George saw people heading toward them across the deck. It had been too fast to see who. "Maybe I'll stay here for another minute or two, though."

Madelyn raised her head. "Two men and a woman," she said. "About a hundred feet away."

"Do you recognize them?"

"C'mon, boss," she sighed. "It's a miracle I recognize you and Barry."

He managed a tight smile. "Stay with the kids."

Madelyn crouched down, and Lily's wide eyes locked on the Corpse Girl. "Are you a zombie?" the little girl whispered.

"Nooo ..." Madelyn said. "I'm not an ex. I'm ... I'm a ghost."

"Are you a friendly ghost?"

"Of course I am." She smiled at the little girl.

"No you're not," said Ash. He reached out and poked her in the shoulder.

"I am. Do I smell like a dead person?"

"Your clothes do," he said. "You're a zombie."

Madelyn kept her smile up. "Not exactly."

"Ash," called a voice.

"Dad!" The boy ran toward the figures as they marched out of the gloom. Devon scooped him up and hugged him.

"It appears our jailbreak comes a little too late," said Hussein.

"Still nice to see a friendly face. I wasn't sure you were coming. You did kind of an about-face."

The Middle Eastern man nodded. "We have long since learned, when Nautilus talks, it's best just to agree. And I did wink. I thought you saw it."

St. George nodded once and turned his attention to the woman. "I've got to admit, you're one of the last ones I expected to see here."

"I'm not stupid," said Eliza. She brushed her leather jacket back and set her hands on her hips above her holsters. "I owe

Nautilus a lot. I've always trusted him. But you being here brings up a lot of . . . I just want the truth."

"Good enough."

"Thank you," said Devon. He extended one hand out to St. George while he held Ash with the other. "Thanks for watching out for my boy."

"She's a zombie," Ash stage-whispered to his father, pointing at Madelyn, "but she's a pretty one."

"Awwww," said Madelyn.

Eliza stared at the Corpse Girl. "He ripped you in half," she said. "Tore you in half and broke your neck."

Madelyn looked down at her torso. "Did he?"

"You were dead," said Devon. "I helped . . ." He glanced at his son. "I helped clean you up."

"The dead never stay dead," said Madelyn with a confident smile. "Especially not when they're dead sexy like me."

"Stop," said St. George.

The deck brightened, and Zzzap was above them. *There's some people over on the tanker. They say they're there to free the kids. Are they with us?*

Eliza nodded. "They're with us. Should be two or three people at every cage."

So now you're with us, too? Zzzap looked to St. George and got a nod. The silhouette gave a quick salute and zoomed away.

"How many of you are there?" asked St. George.

"A few dozen," said Hussein. "People are nervous about admitting their true feelings. There's us, the people rescuing the children, a few more watching the gangplanks between ships." He gestured behind him. "Huojin was our inside man. He was going to help us take out Mitchel and Russ before they could sound the alarm."

"He was a good guy?" Madelyn looked past them and frowned. "Sorry."

"He knew what might happen," said Eliza.

"So where's Nautilus?" asked St. George. "Aren't you worried he might hear all of this?"

Eliza shook her head. "He's gone fishing."

"What?"

"No, seriously," said Devon. "He's gone off to catch a couple tunas or something. We fish off the boats all the time, but once a week or so he'll go catch a couple huge fish and we all eat well for a night."

"Since we could be gone for several days," Hussein explained, "he thought it would be best to go now, so there is extra food here while we are away."

"That seems . . . thoughtful," said St. George.

"If kind of odd, timing-wise," Madelyn added. She knelt with one hand out, and Lily studied the pale flesh with all the intensity of a focused four-year-old.

"He's gone for now, that's all that matters," said Eliza. "Hussein says you're willing to make sure we can all leave safely."

"Yeah," said St. George.

"We'll need to go see the mainland and come back," she said. People are going to want proof."

"Besides us?" asked Madelyn.

"Yes," said Hussein. "They'll need to hear it from people they know."

St. George nodded. "Of course."

Zzzap flashed through the night sky and lit up the deck. *Kids are all safe,* he said. *Anything cool going on here?*

"Just a little rebellion," St. George said.

Muah-hah-ha, said the brilliant wraith. *This will be a day long remembered. It has seen the end of Kenobi, it will soon see—Hey, y'know, all the good quotes about the Rebellion are very pro-Empire.*

"Hi, Barry," said Ash.

Hey, you found your dad.

"Yup."

"Can I go home now?" Lily asked Madelyn.

"I think so." The Corpse Girl looked up at the others. "Do you know where her parents are?"

"They're in one of the staterooms on board the *Queen*," Hussein said. "People whose children are chosen get the best accommodations."

Gosh, I'm surprised more people aren't up for it, said Zzzap.

The deck shifted under their feet. A low vibration echoed up through the hull, the aftershock of a gong. Every inch of the ship trembled, then settled.

"What the hell was that?" Devon looked back and forth across the deck. His eyes settled on St. George.

The hero put up his hands. "How should I know?"

Madelyn stood up and kept a hand on Lily's shoulder. "Did we hit something?"

"We are in the middle of the Pacific Ocean," said Hussein. "There is precious little for us to hit."

"Another ship?"

"We'd've seen it coming," said Steve.

The deep clang echoed from below again. Madelyn looked over the railing. "We're running into something," she said.

Could the ships be bumping against each other?

"Not in calm water," said Hussein, "and it doesn't sound like that when they do."

Zzzap shot up into the air and made a quick circle around the ships. He zipped back down to them. *I don't see anything,* he said. *It's got to be something underwater.*

"What?" said Devon. "Like Hussein said, we're in the middle of nowhere. It's too deep for reefs."

"Maybe something new?" Madelyn looked over the railing again. "An underwater volcano or something? Or a shipwreck?"

"Still too deep," Hussein said.

The sound echoed up through the hull. This time St.

George saw the cruise ship tremble, too. Either the shock-wave was growing, or it had been hit, too.

It had been hit. The words echoed in his mind. They hadn't hit something, they'd been hit.

"Oh, hell," he said. "I don't think Nautilus went fishing."

TWENTY-FOUR

NOW

"WHY?" SAID DANIELLE. "What would they get out of it?"

"They get to be in charge again," said Cesar. He glanced out at the courtyard. The sounds of exercise went on without pause. "I always said you can't trust the government people."

"Hell, yeah," agreed Hector.

"They're not the government," said Gibbs. "They're the military."

"Same thing," Cesar said.

"Not even close," said Danielle. "But it still leaves me asking why."

"Government paranoia aside, I think Cesar's right," said Gibbs. "Think about it. They've got their own enclave set up here. A safe zone, a decent supply of weapons and ammunition, two big trucks with gasoline. Almost, what, three quarters of the Valley has never been scavenged, so there's even more supplies."

"And they got a whole garden," said Hector, "and people to work it for them."

Danielle ran it through her head again. "I don't know. I'd buy Taylor staging some kind of mutiny, maybe Hancock following him, but not Truman or Pierce. Definitely not Kennedy."

"Pierce was out there scavenging," Hector said with a snort. "He's the one who lied about the supplies."

"I just . . ." She closed her eyes. "If Barry was here, he'd be rattling off some stupid movie rules about the military doing crazy things during a zombie apocalypse. No offense," she said to Gibbs.

"None taken," the lieutenant said. "But we're a ways after the apocalypse now, and this isn't a movie."

They all watched her, waiting for a cue.

"Okay," she said. "Let's go ask them."

Cesar's eyes got wide. "Just like that?"

"I don't want to waste time on this," she said, walking across the room. "It's either something we need to deal with right now or not at all. So let's go find out."

Gibbs came up behind her. "We shouldn't . . ."

"Shouldn't what?"

Gibbs's gaze flitted back to the Longshot. "We shouldn't go out there unarmed. Just in case."

"We won't be," said Danielle. She looked at Cesar. "Get in the suit."

"What?"

"Now. We need muscle backing us up."

"It's still charging," he said. "We'll only have an hour, tops."

She glanced at Gibbs. "One way or another, I don't think this'll take long."

Cesar nodded and tugged off his gloves. He followed her into the courtyard and wrapped his fingers around two of the main struts in the exoskeleton's torso. Electricity climbed across his body. It arced between him and the suit. Three small cracks echoed in the air and he vanished. "Yeah," said the battlesuit. "I'm only at twenty-three percent in here."

Gibbs stepped in and unhooked the power cable. "It'll have to do."

The skeletal titan flexed its fingers.

Danielle walked through the wide door and stepped out under the canopy. She curled her hands into fists as she left the walls behind her. A shudder tried to start in her gut and she clamped down on it. No weakness. Not now.

Most of the Unbreakables were there, working out in the

long, end-of-day shadows. Johnson and Wilson traded places on the weight bench. Hancock held one of the big plates in both hands and was curling it behind his head. Taylor had a dumbbell in each hand and curled them up to his shoulders again and again. A bar settled behind Kennedy's neck just as she locked eyes with Danielle.

Why did all their exercise seem so wrong?

The rack of rifles was behind them. Behind all of them. If Gibbs or Hector had any thoughts of grabbing a weapon, they'd have to fight past every one of the soldiers.

Danielle wondered who was up in the sniper nest, and how good a view they had through the canopy.

Gibbs settled in on one side of her, Hector on the other. She didn't hear the exoskeleton, but sometimes Cesar managed to move damned quiet in it. Better than she ever could. She hoped he was right behind them.

"We need to talk," she told the first sergeant. "Now."

Kennedy heaved the bar up over her head and brought it down in front of her. It paused at her waist before she crouched and let it settle on the ground. "Sure," she said. "What about?"

Danielle pulled her fists up and set them against her hips. "What are you all up to?"

"I'm not sure what you're—"

"No games," said Danielle. "Explain the supplies you're hoarding and why your soldiers aren't exactly killing themselves to help out when things go wrong."

The smile melted off Kennedy's face. Everything drained away until the only thing left was the first sergeant. "I beg your pardon?"

"What happened the other day at the gate?"

Kennedy's face shifted from neutral to aggressive. "That's not your concern."

"Fuck it isn't," spat Hector. He pointed at Wilson. "Exes

got in and this guy took his sweet time doing anything about it."

Taylor's weights hit the ground. Wilson let the barbell clang down onto the stands. He sat up on the bench, opened his mouth, then snapped it shut. He looked at the first sergeant.

"You're lucky he did anything for you, you fucking gang-banger reject," snarled Taylor.

"Shut up, Specialist," said Gibbs.

"Fuck you," Taylor said. "Sir."

Kennedy glared at the soldier. Taylor glared back, then bit his lip. He shuffled a few steps back and muttered something under his breath.

She turned her attention back to Danielle. "It's an internal matter," Kennedy said. "Nothing that concerns you."

"If exes are getting into Eden, it concerns me," said Danielle.

The four other super-soldiers spread out. Not much, but enough to be out of each other's way. All of them stared at Danielle.

The battlesuit crunched in the gravel behind her. She wondered if it was strong enough to take all of them. Two or three, no problem. Five at once, with no armor and no weapons . . .

Past the weight bench and the gun rack and the crates of supplies, a few people stood up in one of the garden lots to find the source of the raised voices. Keri the big scavenger. Javi the loudmouth. Lester. Smith. Like Danielle didn't have enough reasons to be worried about what could happen here.

And then her eyes settled back on the barbell. The damned barbell. What was wrong with it? She looked at the dumbbells Taylor had dropped and tried to find a correlation.

Kennedy was looking her in the eyes. The first sergeant's

face and brows were rigid and stern. Her eyes were . . . sad? Pleading? The look popped in Danielle's mind—the expression of someone hoping desperately you were going to cover for them.

Cover for what?

And then, days late, she did the math.

She looked at the barbell on the stand. And the one at Kennedy's feet. And the dumbbells Taylor had dropped. And the iron plate Hancock had been using.

The pieces lined up in her mind.

A single set of weights, split four ways.

Danielle looked Kennedy in the eyes. "What's happening to you?"

The first sergeant's mouth was tight.

"Tell me," she said. "Tell all of us, or I will."

"It's none of your fucking business," Taylor said.

"Everything that happens up here is my business," said Danielle. She focused on Kennedy again. "You're all getting weaker, aren't you? Weaker and slower."

Gibbs blinked twice. "What?"

"You've all been working out with less weight," said Danielle. "You're running laps around the garden, but not much faster than any of us could."

She looked at the other soldiers. Wilson and Taylor wouldn't meet her gaze. Hancock stared down at the iron plate in the dirt.

The sun dropped below the houses to the west. Danielle crossed her arms. In the corner of her eye, she saw Javi the loudmouth slink off toward the concrete path and other garden plots. Half the crowd drifted away. The rest shamelessly eavesdropped as best they could.

"Well?"

Kennedy sighed. "They're fading."

"What is?" asked Cesar.

"The enhancements Professor Sorensen gave us out at Project Krypton. They've been fading for months. Decreasing. However you want to put it."

Danielle looked at the tall sergeant. "How? I thought he changed you genetically."

Kennedy shook her head. "He warned us this could happen. Over time, our brains could make new pathways, relearn how to play it safe again."

"How to be weak," Taylor muttered. "Fucking science bullshit."

"We just don't do enough," said Gus Hancock. "It all kinda crept up on us."

Gibbs looked at him. "What's that supposed to mean?"

"These were intended to be active combat enhancements," Kennedy explained. "Soldiers would get them and go into a combat zone for eighteen months or two years or whatever their deployment was. Being in-country, being on constant alert, would keep everything going. Our bodies and brains would keep running on the levels he set them at."

"So you're saying . . . what?" Hector crossed his arms. "Zombie apocalypse wasn't active enough for any of you?"

"No," said Kennedy, shaking her head again, "it wasn't. Once we had the Big Wall built, the threat level dropped. Once Legion vanished, it plunged. We've been doing busywork for almost a year now. Every now and then one or two of us might go out on a scavenging run. We can exercise tons, but our day-to-day activity is . . . well, normal. And our bodies have been readjusting."

"But, the other day in the garden," Cesar said, "you jumped, like, thirty feet without even trying."

"I jumped fifteen feet with a running start," corrected Kennedy. "This time two years ago, I could do twenty feet from a standing position." She waved a hand at the weight set. "We all used to be able to press close to half a ton. A few of us could even go higher. Now most of us can barely press five hundred pounds. Franklin can't even do three hundred anymore. At this rate, I figure we've got another six months to a year before we're all, well, human again."

Danielle let her arms drop to her side. "Not exactly something to complain about."

Kennedy gave her a weak smile. "Says the woman desperate to get back into her armored battlesuit."

Hector snorted. Gibbs almost managed to hide his smirk.

The exoskeleton leaned forward. "So you're taking all the protein powder and stuff because . . . ?"

"To try to slow it down," said Gibbs. His eyes passed over the soldiers. "That's it, right? You thought maybe if you kept feeding your muscles they'd last a little longer."

"That was the hope, yeah," Johnson said.

"That's why we're all out here," the first sergeant explained. "It was a chance to start training again, to be more active, to try to halt the degeneration. And to do it with a lot fewer eyes on us."

"Why? Why not just ask for help? Doctor Connolly could've—"

"Because this is a military problem."

Gibbs rolled his eyes.

"Jesus," Danielle said. "When are you going to get it through your heads? There is no more military. No more us and them. We don't have enough people left for us and them."

"These are my soldiers," snapped Kennedy. "My platoon. They're my responsibility."

"What about Freedom?" asked Gibbs. "Is this happening to him, too?"

Wilson snorted. "The captain's unstoppable. We're all the prototypes. He's the next generation. The real deal. He's going to be like that forever."

"Are you sure?"

"Sorensen was sure," said Kennedy, "and he's been right about everything else."

"Does he know what's happening to all of you?" Danielle asked. "The captain?"

"He does," the first officer said. "We debated this action, but in the end he agreed it would be better for morale if we were training out of sight."

"So you both knew you were leaving Eden poorly defended."

"No," said Kennedy with a shake of her head. "We're still the best choice to be up here. We may not be as strong as we were, but all of us are still twice as strong as an average adult."

"But not as strong and capable as you'd led us all to believe," Gibbs said.

Hector pointed a finger up at the roof. "What about your watchtower?"

"What about it?" Kennedy glanced up, then back at Hector.

"Why're they watching the people inside the fence?" asked Danielle.

Kennedy shook her head. "It's a sentry position to watch the exes."

"Is it?"

"Of course it is. What else would it be?" She leaned her head back. "Sergeant Pierce?!"

A call came down through the canopy. "Yeah, First Sergeant?"

"What's in your sights right now?"

Johnson noticed something on his boots and began to study it. Pierce's voice rang down from above. "Dead guy over by the east gate. Ugly bastard with one arm and half his face gone."

Kennedy looked at Hector, then Danielle.

"Sergeant Johnson," said Gibbs, "care to tell us what you were looking at?"

"Sir?"

"You're the one we all saw looking somewhere that wasn't the fence line."

"I don't recall, sir."

"I think the lieutenant just asked you to remember, Sergeant," Kennedy said.

Johnson twisted his lips. "I was checking out the woman," he said.

Danielle almost laughed. "What?"

Johnson straightened up a little more. "It's been warm, ma'am, and Desi, one of the people working the gardens, she's been wearing a lot of shorts and tank tops and . . ." He shot a quick glance at Kennedy. "She's really well-shaped, First Sergeant."

Hector rolled his eyes. "Pig."

"Hey, I mean it," said Johnson.

Kennedy turned back to Danielle. "Happy now?"

"Yeah. I think so."

"Hang on," said Cesar. The battlesuit unfolded a steel finger to point at Kennedy. "Still one question. If this isn't some big plan, why've you been so friendly? Why've you been trying to get Dr. Morris on your side?"

Kennedy shifted her stance. "I don't know what you mean."

"Ahhh," Gibbs said after a moment. "I'm going to guess the first sergeant wasn't trying to get Dr. Morris on 'their' side as much as on 'her' side."

A quick flush of blood washed through Kennedy's cheeks and vanished. She had remarkable self-control. "You have no business talking about it, Lieutenant," she said. "It's my private life. I keep it private."

"I think Dr. Morris made a good point a few minutes

ago," said Gibbs. "There isn't much of a military left. You can safely assume you're not obligated to follow the 'don't ask, don't tell' guidelines anymore."

Danielle blinked. "Oh."

"Fucking dyke bitch," muttered Taylor.

Kennedy spun and slammed her fist into the soldier's gut. It hurled him back through the thin wall of shrubs. He crashed to the ground, rolled over twice in the dirt, and came to rest at the edge of the garden plot. Smith looked at him and smirked.

"Specialist," bellowed Kennedy, "you'd better stay down if you know what's good for you."

"Oh, yeah," Hector said. "Weak as a kitten. No good like this at all."

Taylor coughed a few times, sat up, and shook the dust from his hair. He glared at the first sergeant, but he kept his mouth shut and didn't stand up. He turned his gaze on the people watching, instead. Smith and the others slipped away into the garden.

"So," Danielle said to Kennedy, "I think we need to reconsider how things are going to work up here, with all this new information in mind."

Kennedy took a breath, then nodded.

"We'll want to get Lester in on it, too." She nodded at the head gardener. He'd snuck closer to listen. "And Al. They'll both need to know."

"Right," said Kennedy. "Of course."

"For now, we could burn up some extra power and give the battlesuit an extra patrol each day, but after that we—"

The warning bell rang. They all looked in different directions, at the closest borders of Eden. The main building was in the way for most of it. The chain-link and wooden fences off to their left looked as solid as ever.

"Probably Pierce got his rifle stuck in the cord again," muttered Johnson.

The bell kept ringing.

Lester stepped forward. "Doesn't that mean—?"

"Oh, crap," Danielle said. Her arms pulled in tight against her body.

"Holy hell," shouted Pierce up above. "Half the south fence just went down!"

TWENTY-FIVE

NOW

MITCHEL KNEW HE was screwed. He prided himself on being good at reading the signs. And he knew what the signs were saying right now.

Get. The hell. Out.

As soon as he'd woken up from the dead girl's ambush, he'd crawled away, then run. Every step made his face ache and he bit back howls of pain. But he had to run, because it was time for plan B.

It was all over. No denying it anymore, these guys were the Mighty Dragon and Zzzap. And he was pretty sure the zombie girl was Stealth. Or maybe Banzai. They were here, all good and righteous and truthful, and the boss's time on top was over.

Hell, even if Nautilus wasn't done here, Mitchel's throbbing face was a pretty clear indicator where he was going to be left when things settled. Either the heroes would throw him overboard or Nautilus would. Damned if they do, damned if they don't.

His nose hurt. Like getting jabbed with pins and razors and burning cigarettes all at once. If it hadn't been broken before, the little zombie bitch had done it for sure.

Definitely time for plan B.

One of the yachts, the *MystRunner*, had a spare lifeboat down by its stern. Not one of the big deluxe boats, just an inflatable raft with oars. That's why it had been ignored for so long. Well, that and he'd put a big padlock on the hatch. He'd stashed a few bags inside when he could—some simple tools, bottles of fresh water, dried fish. About two weeks of supplies, if he wasn't greedy. Enough to get him away from Lemuria.

He couldn't get away from Nautilus, though. If the big guy came after the lifeboat, he'd catch it, easy. Mitchel knew he'd need a distraction. Something to keep everyone busy long enough that once they had time to go after him, he'd be halfway back to Hawaii and it just wouldn't be worth the effort.

Which is why he was deep inside the oil tanker. Nobody wanted to see their still-moving wife-husband-kids-parent get tossed overboard, so most of the infected bodies—and almost-bodies—got tossed down into the Hole. Mitchel had just tossed the zombie girl down there the other day. There were almost three hundred exes in the Hole. A damned good-sized distraction.

There was really only one way for the exes to go with all the narrow hallways and stairs. He'd spun the wheel and pulled the latch on the inspection door to the tanker's forward chamber. It slid open, the zombies stumbled out, and then someone hit the side of the ship with a big hammer.

The hallway rang like a gong. The deck plates shook like the vibrating bed in a cheap motel. The tremor made Mitchel's nose jangle with pain, and he stumbled to his knees.

A bunch of the exes fell flat on their faces. One dead woman tipped over, and its forehead hit the raised edge of the hatch with a sound like breaking wood. It slid down into the chamber and out of sight.

He scrambled away from the exes. The one in front, a young blonde with short hair and a cruise ship uniform, reached for him with two mutilated hands. Its snapping teeth echoed in the metal hallway. Behind it was a dead black man with a gore-soaked mustache and a red jacket.

Mitchel got to his feet and ran. He might've been a little hasty setting plan B in motion. If the island had hit something, people'd be distracted enough. He might've set all the exes loose for nothing. Which would suck for them.

He glanced over his shoulder, his one small shred of decency wondering if there was any chance of getting the hatch closed again. But there were already a good twenty or thirty exes in the hallway, with more stumbling out over their fallen numbers. A few of them had wandered in the opposite direction, but most of them were between him and the hatch.

So Mitchel went back to plan B. He led the exes down the narrow hall and to the set of metal stairs. And the dead men, women, and children followed him back up to the deck.

x x x

The impact shook the ship again.

Not good, said Zzzap.

Hussein ran for the railing. "Is he attacking us?"

"He might've already broken through the hull," said Eliza. "He's strong enough."

St. George and Madelyn followed him. "Wouldn't we feel it if the ship was sinking?" she asked.

"Not as fast as you'd think," Devon told her. "There's a lot of different bulkheads that are sealed off from each other. It's more like, by the time we could feel the ship was sinking, it'd be too late to do anything about it."

St. George rolled his shoulders. "I need to get down there."

And do what? Zzzap flitted above the deck. *Almost drown again?*

"I could go," said Madelyn. "I don't need to breathe."

Yeah, but we've seen how the Corpse Girl versus Nautilus fight plays out, said Zzzap.

"If I build up enough speed," said St. George, "I might be able to grab him and drag him out."

What do you mean?

"Straight up, straight down. A high dive."

Devon frowned. "Won't that just, like, crush you?"

"I'm tougher than I look."

He's going to have home court advantage, said Zzzap. *Better sight, better maneuverability. A chunk of your strength is just going to go to fighting water pressure.*

"Yeah, but so will his."

No, said the gleaming wraith, *his body's designed around being underwater. That's why he's so strong on the surface.*

St. George bit his lip. "Do you have a better idea?"

Another tremor shook the man-made island.

"Here," said Devon. "You'll need these." He held out a pair of long, sealed packets. Glow sticks.

St. George tore open the ends and slid the tubes into his hand.

"How long have you been hiding those for?" asked Madelyn.

"Got 'em out of your packs."

St. George flicked his wrist, and the tubes slapped hard against his other palm. He shook them three times and a dim glow appeared. Two more shakes doubled the intensity. "Not sure how far I'll be able to see with these."

Don't worry. I'm sure he'll be able to see you.

"Great."

"Kick his ass," said Madelyn.

St. George focused on the spot between his shoulder blades and shot into the sky.

He sucked in air. He'd read somewhere, ages back, it was more efficient to take lots of short, quick breaths than one long one. He sucked in air again and again and his chest expanded as he arced across the sky, passing over the oil tanker, a smaller yacht, and the tugboat.

Then he kicked his feet up, pointed his hands down, and accelerated toward the water.

Hitting it wasn't as bad this time. He was going faster, but he was prepared, like a high-diver knifing into the water.

Bubbles roared in his ears. Salt pricked at his eyes. The hull of the yacht rushed past him, and then there was the tanker a little farther off.

He spent his momentum arcing back beneath the ships, gliding into the dark. The glow sticks made a hazy ball of light around him. Barely ten feet. He could see the bottoms of the ships, but even those blurred into the nothingness.

He moved forward, crossing under the yacht, amazed at how far his momentum was taking him. Then he spun in the water, looking back at the dim shafts of light beyond the boats. He'd gone almost fifty feet down and another fifty under the island. He hadn't taken a single stroke or kicked his legs once.

The water flowed across his clothes, and his clothes brushed his skin. But he still felt it. The tingle between his shoulder blades.

He was still flying.

He was flying underwater.

St. George managed a brief smile before moving forward.

The water shifted around him, and the whale loomed out of nowhere.

It headed straight for him, a huge black-green dome less than twenty feet away. He couldn't tell if it was deliberate or he just happened to be in the way. It moved with the slow grace of something massive, forcing the ocean out of the way.

The rounded front of it was almost fifty feet across, and the body stretched out behind it into the darkness. There were no flippers. No eyes. The dark skin looked featureless in the weak light.

It drifted up and brushed against the bottom of one of the ships. He saw the sound quiver its way through the water and felt it on his ears. The clang was sharper here. He could hear the scrape, the grit of rust and barnacles and paint.

The not-whale passed him, and he saw twin rows of square panels the size of garage doors along its side. In the dim view the glow sticks gave him, he wasn't sure if the squares were set into the skin or raised above it.

Another shape swelled out of the darkness, heading for him. A lump on the side of the cylinder, as wide as he was tall. Tubes and pipes jutted out from it, like massive pins skewering the lump onto the body.

St. George sailed up to pass over the deformity and saw the swaths of paint, bright green in the light of the glow sticks, and finally realized his mistake. The whole thing was tilted almost on its side. That's why it had confused him. He needed to get back to the surface and warn the others. And tell Zzzap. And he needed air. Being prepared had extended his time, but his chest was getting tight.

He turned and saw teeth. A shark's hungry grin. Nautilus slammed one of his boxing-glove fists into the side of St. George's head.

He sprawled back, and a few bubbles of air spun from his mouth. One of the glow sticks spun away as his fingers shifted. He clutched the other one and surged forward.

St. George didn't waste time with a punch. He launched himself at Nautilus and tackled the merman, driving him back through the water. Elbows landed on the hero's shoulders. Knees slammed into his stomach. Clawed hands clapped against the sides of his head and his ears throbbed.

It was enough for Nautilus to twist loose and slip away through the water.

St. George shot after him, then reconsidered and headed for the surface.

The punch hit him in the back of the head. It was strong enough to spin him in the water a bit, but not to hurt him. He spun around, swept the hair from his eyes, and a pair of thick arms wrapped across his stomach. They jerked hard against his abdomen, squeezed, and then jerked hard. Half his remaining air formed a wobbly silver balloon and whirled away.

St. George grabbed Nautilus's arms and focused on the spot between his shoulder blades. The ocean roared in his ears as the two of them shot up toward the surface. Nautilus tried to let go, but St. George shifted his hands and grabbed the other man's thick wrists.

They broke through the surface and hurtled into the night sky. They went up fifty feet, a hundred, two hundred. St. George spun in the air three times and flung Nautilus away.

Toward the ships. He'd thrown him at one of the smaller ships. Dammit. St. George launched himself after the merman, but Nautilus crashed through the roof of one of the yachts before the hero had closed half the distance between them. Screams of alarm echoed up to him as he dropped feetfirst through the hole into the boat.

There was an empty bar at one end of the room, and couches lined the large windows. Small lamps gave off sputtering light and fishy smoke. A trio of people crouched, all looking back and forth between the cracked floorboards and the hole in the ceiling.

St. George looked at the trio. Two of the people had been working on the plants in the raised gardens. "Which way did he go?"

They said nothing for a moment. Then one of the women raised a hand and pointed to a doorway past the bar.

A few quick steps carried him across the room. The door led to a narrow hallway, but at the end he saw the light of an open hatch. Nautilus had run straight down the hall and up onto the front of the yacht.

One leap carried St. George to the end of the hallway. Another shot him up through the hatch without touching the tall steps. He heard a whoosh of air and ducked fast enough that something sailed past his head rather than striking him. It rushed away through the air.

Nautilus stood on the prow of the boat and growled

through his shark teeth. "I told you, I don't want to do this," yelled the merman. "You've left me no choice."

He had one arm up over his head, moving it in a slow, heavy circle. Moonlight glinted on the spinning length of chain. The big steel shape came at him again. Nautilus leaned into his swing, St. George tried to duck, and the yacht's anchor slammed into his shoulder.

The impact hurled him off the ship. He caught himself before he hit the water and pushed his body back up through the air.

Nautilus whirled the anchor around his head. It had to weigh close to a thousand pounds easy, with another five hundred pounds of chain, and he swung it one-handed like a kid spinning a shoelace. It whooshed through the air like the blades of a massive propeller.

The chain passed and St. George lunged at Nautilus. The merman snapped the chain forward like a whip, smashing the anchor into the hero again. It would've crushed a normal man. Turned his rib cage to powder and pulped his insides. It slammed St. George back into the yacht's bridge. Wood and fiberglass and glass shattered around him. He heard more screams from the people up front, and maybe some more belowdecks.

He pushed himself out of the wreckage just in time for the anchor to rush at him. He got his hands up and caught it, grabbing hold of the shaft. A thousand pounds, easy, with a lot of momentum behind it.

Nautilus jerked on the chain and yanked St. George off his feet. The hero sprawled forward on the yacht's deck, but didn't let go of the anchor. Nautilus snapped the links like a whip, and the big piece of iron thrashed in St. George's hands. Another lash of the chain tore the anchor away.

Then Zzzap shot down out of the sky and lit up the deck like daytime. He held up his hand, and everything went white. Nautilus roared. The anchor and chain crashed to the deck.

St. George blinked the light from his eyes and looked around. "Where'd he go?"

D'you like that? I remembered Deathstroke used the same trick on Aquaman once, because his eyes were made for—

"Barry, where did he go?"

What? He dove off the side. Launched himself right over the fishing boat and hit the water.

"Crap. Can you see him?"

The wraith flitted a few yards up into the sky. Zzzap's head swiveled back and forth across the ocean. *No,* he said. *The water makes things tough, especially with his body temperature being on the low side. He was heading away from the island, but I—*

"Dammit."

What's the big deal? We've got him on the run.

"He's got a submarine!"

Zzzap froze in the air. *What did you say?!*

"He's had a Navy submarine hidden under all the ships, and I'm pretty sure it's got a bunch of silos across the top. He was dragging it out from under the boats when I grabbed him." St. George looked out at the water. "I think he's going to nuke Los Angeles to prove he's been telling the truth."

TWENTY-SIX

NOW

SCREAMS DANCED BACK and forth across Eden as the sky darkened. Danielle looked around. The sound of clicking teeth echoed around the building. How had it gotten so loud so fast? The exes couldn't be here already, could they?

"Let's go," shouted Kennedy. She snatched up a rifle and lunged down the path toward the southern fence. Wilson, Taylor, Hancock, and Johnson were right behind her.

Gunshots echoed down from the roof as Pierce slowed the undead advance.

The exoskeleton looked down at Danielle. "What do I do?"

She looked at the door into the courtyard, a panel of expanded steel that could latch shut. The tremor she'd been fighting to control got loose in her gut and churned her stomach.

"Come on," Gibbs told Cesar. "This is what you're here for." He grabbed a rifle from the rack, shoved a spare magazine in his pocket, and headed after the Unbreakables as fast as his mechanical foot would allow.

The battlesuit looked at Danielle again. She set her jaw and managed to nod without making it look like some kind of spasm. "Go."

He followed after Gibbs with long, loping strides.

"Goddamn," said Hector.

"You, too," Danielle said. "They need fighters. People with experience."

"You got more experience fighting them than me."

She shook her head. "Not like this. I'm no good like this." She gestured at the courtyard. "Get everyone back here. This is the safest place. If they can't make it here, get on a watch-tower or climb a tree or find one of the garden plots that still has a fence around it."

He glanced at Lester, then looked at her. "What about you? You don't look so hot."

"I'm fine," she snapped. "Stop wasting time, go."

Hector looked at the rack of weapons, snatched up a pistol, and shoved it into the waistband of his jeans. He gave her a last look, then headed into the garden. He turned a corner and vanished behind a tall cluster of okra plants.

Another gunshot echoed from above Danielle. And another. Was there a ladder up to the roof, or did the Unbreakables just jump? Even in their weakened state, they could probably jump.

The roof was safe.

She stared down the path after Hector. Then she turned and looked after Cesar. After her battlesuit.

The bell stopped ringing. Whoever had sounded the alarm was focused on other things now.

"Oh my God," said Lester. "They're inside. They're inside the fences."

The clicking teeth sounded so close.

Danielle grabbed Lester by the arm, dragged him into the courtyard, and pulled the gate shut behind her. She made a fist and stopped her hand from flipping the latch. Other people would be coming. They'd need to get in. She couldn't lock them out.

She moved into the main room, pushing Lester ahead of her.

x x x

Kennedy ran along the concrete path. To her right, past the double rows of tomatoes and beans and squash, she could see what was left of the southern fence line. Pierce hadn't been exaggerating—it had collapsed.

No, she realized, even *collapsed* was too small a word. It had pretty much vanished. Almost forty feet of barrier was flat on the ground. This was pretty much the definition of catastrophic failure.

The exes were stumbling into Eden. Over two hundred of them, easy. The only saving grace right now was that they were too mindless to run. They staggered in with halting, uneven steps, propelled by lack of resistance more than any conscious motivation.

Kennedy dropped to one knee, swung her rifle up, and squeezed off a burst. The three rounds caught a dead man in the throat, jaw, and forehead. The ex's head exploded and it crumpled to the ground. She thumbed the rifle's selector and put a single shot through a zombie's nose, then another one into a dead woman's eye. Three exes down in less than a minute.

A wall of exes shambled toward them. The other Unbreakables opened fire around her. Some of the undead dropped. Others tripped over the fallen. But it was such a small fraction of the horde. Barely a tenth. They needed something big to shift the odds.

And then, right on cue, something big appeared.

# # #

The titan charged into the crowd of exes. An icon warned Cesar how much power the charge was burning up, but he swept it aside. He needed his mind and his vision clear.

The exoskeleton stomped forward and slammed one of its pile-driver arms into a withered dead man. The zombie exploded, spraying dried meat and bones across the pavement. Cesar punched another one, rocketing the ex's shattered body back into the horde. He swung one of the battlesuit's arms around and clotheslined two dead people at once. They dropped, and he stomped down on one, crushing its chest beneath steel toes.

He looked around, and the targeting system highlighted dozens of figures. There were exes everywhere. Some of them swarmed around him. Others headed after the soldiers.

The battlesuit's microphones picked up the crack of bullets splitting the air, and one of the exes near him twitched and fell over. Another one spun and dropped. A third jerked its head to the side and stumbled forward, the right side of its head a mess of twisted tissue and clotted blood. A round pinged off one of the pistons in his arm and came close to crippling the exoskeleton. "Hey," he shouted over his shoulder.

"Sorry," yelled Hancock.

Cesar turned back to the fence and swept his arm around. Three exes were hurled back toward the street, one with a crushed skull. He swung his foot forward and shattered the knees of a dead housewife, dropping the dead woman to the pavement.

A dead man with a crooked hairpiece grabbed the battlesuit's other arm. A gray-skinned woman with hollow cheeks wrapped withered arms around the exoskeleton's waist. A gore-covered child tried to gnaw through the cables in the left calf. Another ex closed its bony fingers on a support strut.

Cesar thrashed at the undead and shifted his hips. Some fell away from the battlesuit. Others lost fingers and teeth as they clung to the titan. He brushed the last few away, then slammed his fists into some others closing in on him.

Something metal clanked under one of the suit's toes. He glanced down and saw a crescent wrench on the pavement. It was clean and new, not rusted.

Another gunshot echoed through the suit's external microphone systems. A pale-skinned man with bloody teeth and a gore-covered sweatshirt tumbled back as a black crater opened up above its right eye. The body was limp before it hit the pavement, and another ex stumbled over it and pitched forward.

In the suit's rear camera he saw the Unbreakables form a line. Gibbs appeared on the path. His toes sparked on the concrete as he ran. He took a few steps toward the soldiers, then dropped and brought his own rifle up.

They didn't have any cover. The parking lot was just a big open space. It didn't even have the concrete bumpers in the spaces that exes could trip over. The kind of place he used to skid around and pull donuts in back when he was possessing sports cars.

What would St. George do?

No. What would the Driver do?

He'd get right in there and spin donuts through the crowd.

Cesar waded deeper into the horde. The current of exes drifted after him, and even flowed backward at a few points. Every few seconds one of them would twitch in time with a rifle shot and drop to the ground. Many of them stayed down, but some of them kept crawling after the exoskeleton. A few were spun around by the force of the shot and dragged themselves toward the soldiers.

He made his way over to the dumpsters reinforcing the big gate. Both of the bins were filled with assorted trash, scraps, and a few of the split-skull exes the old Gardener had left in piles around Eden. Cesar's steel hands closed on the edge of a dumpster and tugged. It felt like about a ton, altogether, but he hadn't been good at judging weights in the naked exoskeleton. He let the suit's fingers slide down to the corner, then pulled hard.

The dumpster swung away from what was left of the fence. It whipped around, scraping on the pavement, and the metal bin rang with impacts as it battered exes in every direction. Cesar took a step, gave himself some room, and spun it in another wide circle. Bones cracked. The dumpster plowed over some of the zombies and crushed them beneath its squealing wheels, driven on by the battlesuit's muscles.

Cesar spun again, aimed, and let go. Momentum carried

the dumpster across the parking lot, along the fence line. It slammed through the wave of undead bodies and left a path of broken exes behind it. A few went flying, struck the ground, and then were crushed when the rolling dumpster caught up with them.

The green box traveled almost forty feet, two-thirds of the way across the parking lot. By then dozens of collisions had bled away its speed and power. It came to rest a few yards from the big compost pile.

The move had taken out almost fifty exes. Some were down for good. Others tried to crawl on broken limbs. A few flopped on the pavement and snapped their teeth at the air.

Cesar looked out at the street, and the battlesuit's targeting system overloaded in less than a second. Dead men and women staggered toward the fallen fence, drawn by the noises of fighting and gunfire and the overlapping *click-click-click* of hundreds and hundreds of teeth. He'd punched a good-sized hole in the horde, but it was filling up again fast.

He had to get the fence up.

× × ×

Gibbs aimed down the sights, and the rifle kicked against his shoulder. An ex sprayed its brains behind it and toppled over. He re-aimed, fired, and the dead woman stumbled at the last instant. His round tore a wide strip of the ex's scalp away and knocked its head to the side, but it kept plodding forward.

A shriek echoed behind him, and he glanced over his shoulder. Had the exes already gotten past them? Christ, had the fence failed somewhere else? If there were two breaches in the line, they were all pretty much dead.

He saw wide eyes through the leaves in a nearby garden plot.

His rifle was halfway around when he recognized Desi. And then he saw an older tattooed man he'd seen a few times before. And two others he sort of recognized. It was a full work crew.

And Smith. Behind them all was Smith. Of course.

"If you're not fighting," he told them, "you need to clear out. Get back to the main building."

The *click-click-click* of teeth filled the air. The dead woman had staggered forward another two yards. Black fluid oozed from the scalp wound.

At this range, Gibbs barely had to aim. Less than fifteen feet. His first round took a baseball-sized chunk of bone and hair out of the side of the woman's head. The next round caved in the cheek and eye socket of a near-mummified thing in a sky-blue T-shirt shambling behind the dead woman. A third round punched right between the eyes of a teenaged boy coated from nose to crotch with dried blood.

All three exes folded to the pavement.

The three best shots of his life, thought Gibbs. They gave him some breathing room. He glanced back at the people in the garden. "Go," he said. "What are you waiting for?"

"They're on the path," said Desi. "We'd need to go almost all the way to the back fence to get around them."

"Then do it," Gibbs snapped. He looked back the way he'd come and saw clumsy forms moving between him and the distant main building. They were headed for other guards and other gardeners, the ones up by the Hot Zone.

Hell, everywhere was the Hot Zone now.

Gibbs turned back and realized the soldiers had moved on without him. A good twenty feet separated him from the other soldiers, and that space was already filling with exes. The undead didn't slow down at all. Some of the exes staggered right for him, lurching forward on stiff legs.

At the front of the pack towered a huge, top-heavy ex with shaggy hair and filthy overalls. It was slick with the fluids of decay. A chain dragged from its right hand, and Gibbs realized there was a steel animal trap clamped on the dead man's wrist. There was some gore on the trap, but not enough to be a fatal wound.

His mind spun, trying to figure out how a redneck-looking zombie had gotten its hand stuck in an animal trap and then ended up in the middle of a higher-end Los Angeles neighborhood. Some exes had wandered a lot in the years since the dead first rose, but it still seemed odd.

The dead man took a few lumbering steps forward on tree-trunk legs, and Gibbs dismissed the thoughts. The redneck zombie was twenty feet away from him. He put his rifle to his shoulder and lined up the sights on the big ex's broad forehead. It lurched to the side as he squeezed the trigger. The shot tore off the redneck's ear and some hair. The dead man didn't notice. Didn't even break stride. Fifteen feet and closing.

He fired again. The big ex's chalky eye vanished. Another damned lucky shot. He was using them all up today.

The zombie twisted around as it fell, and the animal trap clanged against the pavement.

Gibbs lined up again and blew the head off a gray-skinned woman whose body had withered down to skin and bones. Another shot put down an older man with a black tie and a crooked pair of glasses. He lined up on a little Asian girl with gory lips and a bloodstained school outfit and watched the dead thing's face vanish in a burst of dark colors.

An ex tripped over the redneck's body, kicking the animal trap as it stumbled. It hit the ground a few feet from Gibbs, but its outstretched arms and wrists took a lot of the impact. It crawled forward on broken bones, its jaw gnashing up and down on jagged teeth.

Too close. They were too damned close.

Another barrage of gunfire came from the Unbreakables. A quick glimpse showed they were dealing with fifty or sixty of their own problems. The battlesuit stood in a small horde of exes closer to the fallen fence. It smashed at them with its arms, but the pose of the head told Gibbs that Cesar was listening to something.

He was on his own.

Metal scraped on pavement. The animal trap shifted and slid on the ground. The big ex pushed itself up onto its hands and knees. Its stringy hair hung over its face like the ghost girl from that Japanese movie about the well. The dead man crawled forward and staggered back up onto its tree-trunk legs.

Gibbs had heard of things like this. Exes that took head shots and didn't go down. Just like how some people survived a bullet going into their brain, every now and then an ex did, too.

On his own with a handful of civilians and an unkillable redneck zombie.

He stepped back past the greens. "We have to go," he told them.

Desi took a step back, her eyes flitting from the rifle Gibbs held to the exes. "Go where?"

"That way," he said, pointing back. "Away from them."

The *click-click-click* of teeth was even closer. They could all feel the sound in the air. It drowned out the gunfire from the Unbreakables.

Gibbs herded them back. They moved with him. "We need to move now. We need distance."

The older man with the tattoos looked all around. "But we—"

"Now. Run."

Two of them took off with no further prodding. Desi, Smith, and the tattooed man stood there with him. Gibbs looked over his shoulder. The exes were stumbling a bit on the softer ground of the garden plot, but not much. Their grasping hands were just a few yards away now.

He slung the rifle over his shoulder, grabbed Desi with

one arm and the older man with the other. "Come on," he said. He dragged them through the plot. It took a second for them to stop resisting and march with him. They went across the path on the other side, and into the next plot.

The older man looked back. "What if we run into more of them?"

"We won't," said Gibbs. "The fence only broke there. They'll all be coming from that direction." The lieutenant glanced back at the exes, and then at the clawing footprints his mechanical toes left in the soil. They dragged in the dirt like a rake. He tried to lift his foot higher.

They ran.

x x x

Danielle paced back and forth, trying to control her breathing. She shot quick glances out the window toward the fence. Just over the tops of the pea trellises and sunflowers and corn, she could see the battlesuit. Its arms went up and back down. Gunshots echoed from the parking lot, punctuated now and then by louder ones from above.

Lester slumped in the corner, his arms wrapped around himself. He muttered quietly while his eyes went back and forth between the two doors and the window. Danielle had seen people react this way before.

Jesus, she thought, is this what I look like to everyone?

She tried to blot out the distant sound of teeth and her own breathing and the cold sweat running down her front and back. She needed to calm down before the tension made her freak out. If they were all going to get through this, they needed her to be . . .

Tension.

She pictured the fence lines in her mind, the ones Lester had shown off that first day. The ones she'd seen in her pathetic attempts to walk around the garden. None of the fences had a solid top rail. The chain-link just hung off a long, heavy tension cable, clamped in place by a trio of wire rope clips.

They were all idiots.

Her included.

She turned away from the window and pushed down the waves of nausea running up and down her body. A quartet of walkie-talkies sat in a charging station on the table. She snatched one up, flicked it on, and spun the dial. "Cesar?"

"What?" His voice echoed up out of the walkie. "Oh, hey. Cool."

"I don't think the fence is broken."

"Yeah, it is," he said. "I'm right next to it."

"The fence went down," she said, "but I don't think it actually broke. I think the support cable slipped loose. All you need to do is pull it tight again."

"Whoa, what? What do I need to do?"

"There's supposed to be a thick wire rope, a big cable, across the top of the fence. Everything's hanging off it."

"Like curtains?" asked the walkie.

"Yeah," she said, "like curtains. You need to find the end and pull it tight. It'll make the fence come right back up."

"Yeah?"

"Yeah, but be careful. It's going to weigh a lot and it's going to have some exes standing on it. You've got to pull hard enough to raise the fence but not enough to snap the cable."

"What happens if it snaps?"

Danielle closed her eyes and took a breath. The clicking of teeth seemed even louder. "If it breaks for real, the fence is ruined and I'm pretty sure we'll all get eaten by exes."

"Okay, then," said Cesar. "Not breaking the cable."

"Good idea."

"You think it was Legion?"

"I don't know. I didn't get a good look at it, but it looked solid when I saw it the other day. If it was rigged right, it shouldn't have slipped."

"I saw a wrench in the parking lot. You think maybe— Hang on a sec," said Cesar. The exoskeleton swung its shoulders in the distance. "Sorry, had to sweep a bunch of 'em away, y'know. So you think maybe somebody did this?"

"We can worry about it later. First, get the fence back up."

"Okay. I think I see the post where it came apart. Lemme try this."

"Be careful. Not too hard."

"Yeah, that's not what you were saying—"

"Jesus, Cesar," she said, "not right now."

"Right, sorry. I'll let you know when I got it."

She set the walkie down and watched the titan crouch down. It vanished behind the rows of plants.

God, the clicking teeth were so loud. It almost sounded like they were in the . . .

Something shuffled near the side door. Lester shrieked. Panic struck Danielle in the chest and she turned.

It had been a man. A short man, dressed in the semicasual look that seemed so popular in Los Angeles. Jeans, T-shirt, dark blazer. A trim beard, spotted with filth, covered its jaw.

The zombie stumbled off the walkway and into the workshop. Its chalk eyes stared at her without blinking. Its teeth cracked together. One of the top front teeth was gone, and in its place was a steel implant post.

Cold fear spread out from her heart. It crawled down her legs and arms. It wrapped around her shoulders and throat and sent threads into her head.

The ex lurched toward her, and the *click-click-click* of its teeth filled the workshop.

THAT'S CRAZY TALK, said Zzzap.

"It makes sense," said St. George, pushing himself off the yacht's smashed deck and into the air. "If he takes a hundred people back to shore and they find LA's been nuked, no one's ever going to question him again."

Yeah, but it'll be freshly nuked, not five years nuked.

"Who'd be able to tell the difference?" St. George flew back to the cargo ship. The gleaming wraith followed. "To most people, ruined buildings and radiation means a bomb site. I don't think there'll be any elaborate tests to confirm when it happened."

But there'll be a blast. Light, heat, all sorts of stuff.

"If anyone even sees it, it'll be a light on the horizon. You think after years of this he won't be able to brush it off as a thunderstorm or something? Hell, half these people believe him now without any evidence."

Besides, he can't just launch the missiles. He'd need special keys and codes and a computer named Joshua and—

"He's had years to figure this out," said St. George. "Hell, for all we know he was on the crew."

Madelyn waved to them from below. They dropped down to the deck. St. George explained what he'd seen below the ships to her and the Lemurians.

"You are sure?" asked Hussein. "It was not a trick of the light or a distortion in the water?"

St. George shook his head. "I was less than ten feet from it at one point," he said. "I could see the rivets and the writing on the periscope-tower thing."

Eliza shook her head. "No," she said. "That's just nuts. Maleko might be . . . controlling, but he's not . . . he's not going to kill a couple thousand people just to back up his story. He's not a maniac."

Devon's lips twisted. He set his son down and whispered some instructions. The boy took Lily by the hand, and they ran off into the night.

"What do you think he's up to, then?" asked St. George. "He offers to take you all to see the nuclear wasteland that we know doesn't exist, tells us how much he 'didn't want to have to do this,' and then just before you go he decides to drag his secret submarine out and . . . what? Please, give me another way to look at this."

Eliza bit her lip.

"I don't know why he's doing it," St. George said. "Maybe he thinks he's protecting you from something? Maybe . . ."

"Maybe he's just nuts," said Madelyn.

"Not helping."

"Hey? Torn in half, remember?"

"That's just because you're an ex," said Devon.

She glared at him. "No, I'm not."

"I'd rather be wrong about it than sorry," St. George told Eliza.

She shook her head one last time. "If there's a sub," she said, "shouldn't there be a crew?"

"Perhaps they are on the sub?" Hussein offered.

Devon frowned. "Would it still be running after all these years?"

Nuclear subs can run for decades if they're maintained, said Zzzap, *but the crew would still need food and air. I don't think their filters would last that long.*

"They could be dead," said Hussein. "It is possible Nautilus merely found the vessel somewhere and stowed it beneath the island."

"Ummmm . . ." said Madelyn, "what do people on submarines wear?"

They looked at her. "What?" asked St. George.

Is this a riddle? I'm not good with riddles.

"Do they wear a sort of blue jumpsuit thing?" She waved her hands up and down her body. "Y'know, kind of like a janitor?"

"Yeah," said Devon. A few of them looked at him and he shrugged. "I had a cousin who was in the Navy."

"There's a bunch of exes dressed like that down in the place they dumped me," Madelyn said. She pointed across the cruise ship toward the tanker. "Maybe thirty or forty of them."

Devon tapped the side of his chest and let his fingers bounce on either side of his neck. "Did they have names here? And badges here?"

"Maybe," she said. "I saw names on some of them, but a lot of the uniforms were torn up and bloody. Lots of gore around the mouths, you know? There could've been stuff there. I was more interested in getting out."

Eliza's face was grim.

St. George saw the expression grow. "What's wrong?"

"When we first started the island," she said, "we were cleaning out the ships, getting all the exes away from everyone. I thought . . ."

"What?"

"I thought the Hole was filling up kind of fast. Maleko told me not to worry about it. I was just stressed and counting wrong."

"What's the Hole?" asked St. George.

"If someone had the virus, if they turned, they went into the forward tank. The Hole. It was empty and made for a good holding pen."

"Been there," said Madelyn, flexing her arm. "Broke out of that."

"So," said St. George, "I'm guessing you thought the Hole was filling up fast right around the time Nautilus showed up with a bunch of new shotguns and pistols for you to defend yourselves with."

The Lemurians glanced at each other. "It was maybe a month after we'd cleaned out the big ships," said Devon. "We just figured they came from one of them."

Seriously?

"Well they had to come from somewhere," he said. "Why would we think they came from a submarine hidden under the—"

A scream echoed down from the cruise ship.

You hear that?

St. George and Eliza nodded.

Zzzap launched himself up into the air, looked around, and dropped back down to the small group. *There are exes on the tanker. At least sixty or seventy right now, but it looks like a lot more of them are coming up from belowdecks.*

Hussein muttered something angry in Arabic. "Someone's opened the Hole," he said.

Devon looked across the deck. "Jesus," he said. He took off after his son without another word.

St. George looked up at Zzzap. "Do you think you can find the sub and stop it?"

The wraith shrugged. *It's going to be Predator-level invisible at night and in the ocean, even to me. And that's not considering how deep it is.*

"You've got to find it. We don't know how far he's going to go before he launches one of the missiles. Madelyn and I will help contain the exes here."

Mekka-lekka-hi, said Zzzap. *The wish is granted.* He shot up into the sky.

St. George turned to Eliza. "Do your guards have any experience with exes?"

"We . . ." She looked over at the cruise ship and the tanker beyond it. "Not enough. None of us have dealt with large numbers of them since before we formed Lemuria."

"Get your people off the tanker, if you can. Tell them to keep the exes off the walkways. Better yet, cut the walkways loose and let them drop."

"We can't do that. We don't have a way to replace them."

"You don't have a way to replace the people, either, do you?"

Eliza bit her lip again.

"Right. We'll try to keep the exes contained to the tanker and rescue anyone still there." He looked at Madelyn and held out his hand. "You and me, then."

"Sweet." She reached out, grabbed his wrist, and his fingers closed around hers.

St. George launched himself into the air and dragged the Corpse Girl along with him. He swung around to the cruise ship and flew over its tall hull. Another shriek rang up to them, then a gunshot, and then more screams.

Then the sound of teeth.

Once they passed the *Queen*'s smokestacks he could see at least a dozen exes. They'd already made their way up the long gangplanks and onto the cruise ship, lured by the sights and sounds of prey. Three of them were crouched and using their jaws to tear mouthfuls of flesh out of a figure. The light was bad, but St. George was pretty sure he glimpsed dreadlocks when one of the exes rocked to the side.

More exes spread out across the tanker's low deck. Some of them staggered through the gardens. Others headed for the lower ends of the walkways.

A few figures moved faster, but they were almost all heading in the wrong direction. Some ran toward the front of the tanker. One had a shotgun, but a few of them tried to fight the exes with garden tools. Several of them screamed.

"I'll save the people down there," said St. George. "Can

you hold that first gangplank on your own? The one closest to the hatch they're coming out of?"

"Yeah," she said.

"You sure?"

She smiled up at him. "Dead certain."

"Please stop that."

"Never!"

St. George swung his arm, loosened his grip, and Madelyn dropped to the upper deck of the cruise ship near one of the stairwells. She put her hands on the railings and slid down the first flight of stairs. A few running steps put her at the next landing and she leaped down that flight, guiding herself along the rails.

The sound of teeth echoed up to her.

She jumped down one more staircase and landed in front of the long gangplank that led down onto the tanker. A man and woman pushed themselves flat against the wall opposite it. The walkway was covered by a white awning with the dolphin logo printed all over it.

A dead man lumbered off the gangplank and onto the cruise ship's deck. The bony ex had a ring of white hair around a circle of bald. Half the skin of its jaw was gone, showing off yellowed teeth and bone streaked with dark red.

The zombie ignored her. Its dead eyes turned to the couple. Its teeth slammed together again and again, louder for the lack of skin covering them.

Madelyn slammed into the ex, driving her shoulder into its chest. It tumbled back, and its head slammed against one of the metal guide rails of the walkway. Not hard enough to stop it, though. It fell at the feet of another ex and pawed at the ground.

"Go," she yelled over her shoulder. "Get away."

The man and woman stared at her with wide eyes. They were scared of her, too. They just saw another zombie.

The second ex stepped forward. Its nose was a bloody, broken mess. This one was wearing one of the blue Navy coveralls. Its name had been LOWE. Now that she knew what to look for, she could see the white eagles on the collars, blurred by gore. A large chunk with charred edges was missing from Lowe's shoulder, like someone had tried to blow the dead man's head off with a shotgun and just taken part of the collarbone.

She caught it in the gut with a solid kick. The dead man staggered and tipped back into the sloped walkway. It landed on two exes behind it, a pair of women, and the three of them formed a wobbly undead tripod.

She grabbed the railings on either side of the gangplank, swung her legs up, and drove both feet into Lowe's chest.

It was enough to make the tripod collapse. The exes knocked down one more as they fell, but there were more shuffling up the ramp. The angle was low enough for them to stagger and crawl without risk of tipping.

She glanced back. The couple had vanished. She wasn't sure if they'd run up the stairs or down the hall deeper into the ship.

She took a moment to tug at her wet suit. Ripped into two pieces, the top half was riding up and the bottom half kept sliding down. It was still tight enough to stay on, she just felt like she was on the verge of a wardrobe malfunction, even wearing her jacket and shorts.

The white-haired ex pushed itself up onto its hands and knees. She reached out with her foot and tugged the dead man's arm out from under it. It collapsed back to the ground, and its head hit the deck with a loud thunk.

On the walkway, the four exes she'd knocked down crawled forward. A dead woman in a swimsuit clawed its way past Lowe, even as Lowe dragged itself forward on bruised arms. More of the dead behind them tried to walk over the fallen ones. They slipped and wobbled and had trouble keeping their balance, but they were working their way back up the long ramp.

There were at least a dozen of them farther down the covered walkway. Exes as far as she could see. If it got too packed, she wouldn't be able to knock them over again. Their own numbers would keep them standing, even on the ramp. And then they'd make it up to the *Queen*.

A few yards down, a thin chain dangled on the side of the gangplank. A small clip almost touched the ground. A matching chain hung on the other side. At some point it had probably held a sign warning people about wet floors or closed doorways.

The closest ex on its feet—a black man in one of the blue coveralls—was just passing the chain.

She ran down the ramp, stepped on Lowe's back and swimsuit woman's shoulder, and shoved the dead man as hard as she could. It outweighed her two to one, but the run gave her momentum. The big ex stumbled back, but the massed undead kept it from falling, just like she'd feared.

Madelyn grabbed the chains on either side and pulled them together. The clip slipped through one link and hung just below her waist. She stepped back and stumbled on the legs of the other dead woman, the heavy one in shorts and an oversized T-shirt.

The big ex—the name on the coverall said BERNARD— lumbered up the ramp again and the chain tightened against its thighs. It didn't notice and kept shifting its feet. Another ex shuffled past, a dead girl a few years younger than Madelyn, and the chain caught it across the waist.

The railings trembled a bit, but they seemed to be holding for now.

She turned to the other half of her problem. The crawling exes kept moving forward. Five of them, if she counted the white-haired man near the top of the walkway.

She grabbed swimsuit woman by the ankles and shuddered. The ex's skin was puffy and moist. All the fluids had settled low inside it, and it had been on its feet for years. It crawled forward and stumbled over its own hands when its legs didn't move.

Madelyn heaved and dragged the dead woman back down the ramp. It left streaks on the walkway floor. She dropped its legs, grabbed Lowe by the cuffs of the blue coverall, and hauled the dead man back, too.

It wasn't a great solution, but she figured it would let her hold the walkway until more help arrived. If she was quick, she could run and maybe do the same thing on the next gangplank.

Then, with a snap and the jingle of loose links, the chain snapped behind her.

× × ×

St. George soared over the tanker. Down on the deck, a man with a shotgun put down another ex before his weapon racked empty. He pumped it two more times as St. George dove toward him, and at the last minute spun it around and slammed the butt into a zombie's jaw. He hit it again and ignored the two other exes coming up alongside him.

St. George grabbed the man under the arms and carried him into the air. The shotgun plunged to the deck. The man screamed bloody hell until St. George dropped him onto the crane. He grabbed the railings and glared up at the hero.

"You'll be safe up here until we get things under control," St. George told him. He took off before the man could say anything.

He swatted three exes away from a pair of women and pointed them up onto the low catwalk running the length of the tanker.

A dead man had a woman pinned down on the deck next to one of the garden plots. She pushed and kicked until St.

George grabbed the ex by the neck and hurled it across the deck. It bounced once, slammed into the far railing, and fell in a heap.

He helped the woman up and tried not to look at the bites and scrapes on her arms. "Thank you," she cried. "Thank you. You saved me."

He threw himself back into the air.

Most of the exes seemed to be coming out of a door beneath the ship's bridge. The sooner he cut them off, the better. More than a hundred dead people already roamed the deck, and maybe a third of them were headed toward the gangplanks.

He landed by the door. A dozen pairs of zombie eyes turned to him. The closest was a thin, grandmotherly woman with thin gray-white hair and matching skin. It wore a gore-splattered sweatshirt with the cruise line logo. The dead grandmother reached for St. George with stubby, chewed-off fingers. A stout ex in a wifebeater and flannel shirt shuffled at him from the other direction. A gaunt thing in a stained T-shirt grabbed at him with its one good arm. The other one was pinned to its chest with what looked like a steel rod, and St. George realized the ex had been shot with a speargun. The *click-click-click* of their teeth seemed louder as it echoed off all the metal surfaces.

A quick flick of his wrist broke Grandma's neck, and the ex collapsed with its jaw still gnashing up and down. His fist came around and struck the flannel shirt zombie, knocking it off its feet and a few yards down the deck. The speared ex clawed at his arm and bent its head to chew on his flesh. He swatted its skull like a mosquito, crushing it. Teeth and bone and damp meat pattered onto the deck.

He glanced over his shoulder just as an ex stumbled through the doorway. Its chest was a mass of dried blood, shredded fabric, and knotted tissue. A shotgun wound that had dried in the air—St. George had seen it before. He slammed his palm into what was left of the zombie's breast-bone and sent it flying back through the door. It struck the far inside wall and left a smear as it slipped to the floor.

He slammed the steel door behind it and yanked down the latch. A person could open it. To the dead, it might as well be a steel wall.

Another ex, a teenaged blonde in a cruise ship uniform, staggered toward him with arms up. St. George grabbed one of the dead thing's arms and swung the body into the air. Its feet knocked down two more zombies as he brought the dead woman around in a circle and . . .

His hand tightened on the gray wrist before it slipped away from him. There were other boats down below the tanker's railing. He wasn't sure where they were, and the last thing he wanted to do was drop an ex on top of some family as they were turning in for the night. Strong as he was, he didn't think he could throw the dead woman and be absolutely sure it'd gone past all the ships.

The ex hung at the end of his arm, teeth clacking together. It reached up and clawed at his wrist with its free hand. He swung the woman's body again, low this time, and knocked down three more of the walking dead. Then he let go and momentum sent the dead blonde tumbling and thumping across the deck.

Screams echoed across the deck. In the distance, some of the farmers backed up to the far rail. A cluster of exes had blocked them from the walkways leading up to the cruise ship. The farmers pushed them back with rakes and hoes.

St. George launched himself into the air. He skimmed across the deck, spread his arms wide, and plowed through the crowd of zombies. At least seven of them were dragged away, and when he stopped they went tumbling across the deck. Two of them twisted their necks and stayed down. The others stumbled back to their feet with limp arms and jaws.

He marched back and grabbed two of the remaining exes

by the necks and slammed their heads together. A crack of bone echoed up from the impact, and both zombies sagged in his grip. He let them drop and punched another one in the back of the neck, turning its spine to gravel.

He recognized Malachi in the group of farmers. The bitter-faced old man had hit the last ex in the chest with his hoe. It pressed in and tried to reach past the tool for the older man. They leaned into each other, an inside-out game of tug-of-war.

St. George grabbed the ex by the neck, set his hand on its head, and twisted the skull around so it faced him. The body sagged beneath his hand, and he noticed the constant motion of the teeth and jaws had worn furrows into the dead man's lips. He turned and tossed the body at the exes he'd bowled over with his charge. Three of them went down again. The others would be in reach in a minute or so.

He looked at the group. "Everyone okay? No bites or scratches?"

The farmers nodded. Malachi's mouth was a tight line. "We tried to get to the *Queen*," said one of the others, a woman with scars under her thin hair, "but they're everywhere."

He glanced back at the crowd of exes. Some were milling about as the undead did when they didn't have a target. Another dozen were heading toward him.

"They're going to kill us all," muttered one of the others, a man about St. George's age. "All dead. All of us."

"Shut up, Claude," snapped an older woman.

The hero stepped past them and looked down. A few yards back, a rope ladder led down to one of the fishing boats. "There," he said, pointing. "Let's just walk back over there. You can get down to that boat and you'll be safe."

"But they'll know where we are," Claude whined.

Just like Eliza had told St. George, most of the people had never dealt with a full-scale outbreak of the undead. They'd had isolated individuals, but never mass numbers. Never a horde. They'd been living in fear of something none of them had ever experienced or understood.

"They won't be able to follow you," St. George said. "They can't climb a ladder, and the railing's too high for most of them to fall over it by accident."

"But—"

"You'll be safe," he said. "Trust me."

He walked back and grabbed one of the approaching exes, a thin man with a wispy beard. His hand closed on its throat, and its jaw beat down on his knuckles. He wrenched its neck and tossed the limp body at a dead woman in a long sundress. They crashed down on the deck together.

St. George looked out at the deck as he wiped his hands on his pants. More screams reached his ears. He hoped the guards were better at fighting exes than the farmers.

They moved twenty feet down the deck to the ladder. There was a small gate in the railing. Malachi pushed the older woman out of the way so he could climb down first. St. George rolled his eyes. Claude, for all his whining and doomsaying, held his arms out and let the woman go next.

Another ex stumbled toward them. It wore moldy jeans and a denim shirt missing one sleeve. The exposed arm had three clear bites on it. One of them was still half covered by some dangling bandages. The dead man's teeth were muffled by bits of dried material jammed between them. St. George tried not to think about what the material could've been.

It reached for him. He batted its hands away and drove a punch into its cheek. The side of the ex's face collapsed even as the impact snapped its head back. It crashed to the deck, twitched twice, and went limp. Even its teeth stopped.

Maybe a dozen down, another hundred or so to go.

He hoped things were going better for Barry.

TWENTY-EIGHT

NOW

THERE WAS A clump of bone jammed in the left elbow joint. Cesar thought it might be part of a jawbone. The servos strained against it, and it limited his range of movement. He thought about folding the exoskeleton's arm up and trying to crush it, but worried he'd blow out the motors altogether and leave himself with a crippled arm.

He could still swing it like a club for now.

The power levels worried him more than the arm. The fighting and his stunt with the dumpster had burned off a chunk of the batteries' charge. He was down to seventeen percent—maybe twenty-five or thirty minutes under great conditions.

And these really weren't great conditions.

There were still more exes in front of him than the battle-suit's targeting systems could handle. Sixteen of them were on a direct path between him and the fence's closest point. Another forty-two between him and the farthest point of collapse.

The exoskeleton pivoted at the waist so Cesar could look over his shoulder at the soldiers behind him. He'd lost Gibbs somewhere. The lieutenant had vanished, along with the gardeners who'd been working in one of the nearby plots.

"I'm gonna try to pull the fence up," he called back. "Can you hold 'em for a few minutes?"

"Make it fast," Kennedy yelled over the sound of teeth and bullets. Her head settled back to her rifle sights and she fired again. One of Cesar's sixteen exes twitched and sprayed black blood out of the back of its skull. It collapsed.

Cesar stomped forward and brought his fists down to crush two skulls. He scooped up another ex, a woman with white-blond hair and jogging clothes, and hurled it out past the fence. The hand came back down as a fist and shattered a dead man's neck and shoulders. The battlesuit's other arm, the stiff one, hurled a zombie away, but it got more height than distance. It dropped hard out on the street and splattered across the pavement. The fist came down like a hammer even as the other hand grabbed an ex by the arm and flung it away.

The system cleaned a path to the fence, even if all the movement attracted more exes. Better him than the soldiers, though. Even as he thought it, a dead man with dark hair and a withered blade of a nose tried to grab the exoskeleton's arm. The zombie cracked teeth on one of the pistons before Cesar swatted it away.

The fence sagged for about forty feet before righting itself at a distant post. At least a dozen exes stood on the fallen section as they staggered into the garden. He shoved an ex away and crouched to grab the end closest to him. The battlesuit's steel fingers slid through the chain-link.

Just like Danielle had said, a stiff cable threaded through the top of the chain-link. The frayed end had a sharp loop in it, like it had been curved so long or so tight the curve had just become part of the cable. Just inside the curve hung three little things like padlocks held together with hex nuts. The little locks hung loose, but the cable was crimped on the side of the loop across from them where they'd bound the wire rope tight against itself.

He tugged on the fence, and a double handful of zombies wobbled as it shifted beneath their feet. Another pull gave him a sense of the weight and made a dead woman topple over. He straightened the battlesuit's legs and hauled the fence back up into position. Exes tumbled on both sides. One bent over backward, and its spine made a sound like a branch breaking. He stepped back, pulled the chain-link back to the post, and it stretched tight and solid.

The barrier was back up.

"Okay," he called back to the soldiers. "I got it!"

As soon as he spoke, he realized he was trapped.

The moment he let go of the chain-link, the fence would drop again. He could see at least twice as many exes in the street outside, with more shambling closer. There was no way the suit's oversized fingers could work the hex nuts on the little clips, and he wasn't sure how they went on, anyway. There wasn't enough of the cable to tie it around the post.

There were still more exes inside the fence line than the targeters could count. Maybe eighty or ninety. Some of them were still trying to gnaw on the exoskeleton, but most of them were closing in on the small group of soldiers. Rifles were dropping them, but not fast enough.

And they were running out of ammo.

# # #

Javi stumbled through the dark garden. He'd headed for the main building and figured he could lock himself in the pantry or the bathroom or the toolshed or something. Somewhere safe.

He hadn't expected the cable to slip so fast.

When he'd seen Cerberus and the soldiers and the robofoot guy all arguing, Javi knew what way things were going. He saw the writing on the wall and knew it was time to add a few tags of his own. He'd already snuck a wrench out to the fence once or twice over the past few days and just given the connectors a little quarter-turn. Enough so he could loosen them fast when he needed to. It was supposed to be a fail-safe protection thing. A weapon of last resort. When the guards all made their move, tried to kill all the Seventeens, he'd be able to take them all with him. Or die knowing they were going to get theirs as soon as the cable went.

But then he got down to the parking lot and there were so many damned exes there. Hundreds of them, all pressing up against the fence and banging their teeth. He couldn't even get near the nuts he'd been loosening, not without putting his hand right in some zombie's mouth.

Made sense. All the new people in Eden had attracted the exes. That's what happened—they saw people and tried to eat them. Probably what all the soldiers and guards had planned all along.

And then the cable had made this metal-scraping noise and the fence had fallen down. Ten feet away from him. If he'd been any closer the exes just would've had him, but he'd thrown the wrench at one and run back into the garden.

And now there were exes in Eden. They'd already drunk-walked in through some of the front plots and passed the whole firefight up front. Three staggered between him and the main building, and there were a couple more wandering through Lester's goddamned precious peas.

Javi ran down another path between two overgrown garden plots. He remembered the safety rules. If exes couldn't see you, they forgot you. All he had to do was find a spot to hide deep in the garden.

The assholes at the Mount may have sent him and the others up here to die, but he wasn't going to go easy.

He turned a corner, tripped over a big plastic bucket, and went facedown in the path. Lester was always nagging people to put stuff away, and Javi blew him off most of the time, but why was everyone else so fucking lazy? They were going to get him killed.

Something rustled nearby and he froze. Dammit, the exes followed noise, too. He'd just been running and panting and tripping over goddamned fucking buckets without thinking about noise. He held his breath and listened.

There was a faint, whispery sound. Not the chattering of

teeth. Almost like quick, scared breaths. It came from just ahead of him. The next row.

A little foot slid out from behind a fence of dried wood. It wore a ballet shoe. Pink with polka dots. Javi stared at it as another foot joined it. Two little feet in polka dot ballet shoes, skinny legs in white tights. The polka dots went up the tights, too, where they became long ovals and streaks.

The world slowed down. Even as his eyes went up, he knew those weren't polka dots on the shoes. Or the tights. Or the frilly tutu that looked like it had old mud splattered on the front, like the clumps dried to its tiny fingers.

Except for a raw gouge on its shoulder, the dead girl's skin was just a shade darker than the sun-bleached white of the leotard and tights. The ex's mouth was a gaping hole in its face. The broken jaw hung in three or four pieces, making a ring of teeth inside the stretched-out lips. Muscles tugged the sagging jaw up and down like a gasping fish. It pushed air in and out and made the whispering noise.

The ballerina dropped to its knees and fell on him. Javi threw up an arm to protect himself, and the weight of the ex's whole body came down on the top teeth as they struck. The broken jaw flapped against the bottom of his forearm as the dead girl tried to chew. Tiny fingers closed on his wrist and elbow.

Javi could feel its teeth scraping on his arm. Not ripping or biting, just dry edges of enamel going back and forth. Every third or fourth flap one of the bottom teeth would hit just right and jab his arm.

A scratch could do it. Just one. All they had to do was break the skin. Fever started in seven or eight hours, dead in a day or two. Desi'd tried to tell him once there was more to it than that, but he understood the basics.

He started to yank his arm away, and his flesh went tight against the little ballerina's teeth. His heart pounded as he brought his fist around. It cracked into the little girl's ear and knocked the tiara loose. Another punch twisted the ex's head back, away from his arm, and he wrenched it away. The little fingers slipped off him, and he scrambled back.

The dead girl crawled after him.

Javi drove his foot into the ex's face. Its button nose and front teeth crunched under his heel. He kicked again, and little teeth pattered onto the wood-chip path.

The tiny fingers grabbed at his shoe and tried to draw it into the ruined mouth. He pulled away and scampered a few yards back down the path. Once he had distance, he hopped back to his feet.

The ballerina dragged itself after him. Its face was a blackened mess of gore and teeth now. The ruin of its mouth twitched up and down. It stumbled on its knees once, twice, and it was back up on its feet and reaching for him.

He turned and ran. It took him a moment to realize he was heading back the way he'd come, back toward the gate. Toward the sound of clicking teeth.

An ex stepped out in front of him. Its stubbly hair and beard were extra-white against its gray skin. One of its arms was nothing but gore, fingers to shoulder, but the rest of it was clean. The ex displayed a collection of yellow teeth that gnashed at the air.

Javi skidded to a stop and changed direction again. He crashed through a trellis covered with layers of bean vines and ran deeper into the garden. He was pretty sure he was heading for the north fence now, the one by the freeway. There were the tall trees, and the . . .

He stumbled to a stop, his heart thudding inside his rib cage. His left arm had swung into view, and it just hit him what he'd seen. He held it up in the moonlight. "No," he muttered.

Muck from the dead girl's mouth was smeared on the arm. Between the dark streaks Javi could see a jagged scrape an inch long. Just deep enough for a few bright red spots of blood to swell out and mix with the dark filth on his skin.

"No, no, fucking NO!!"

x x x

Danielle took a few quick, stumbling steps to the right and put a worktable between herself and the ex. The dead man turned as she did, shuffling to intercept. Its feet dragged on the carpet. It filled the air with the sound of teeth on teeth. The implant post glinted in the front of its mouth whenever its jaw opened wide. She could see a crust on the steel that could've been old mortar or dried meat.

Cold sweat drenched her clothes. She tried to breathe, but the fear had wrapped around her chest and bound it tight. Her heart was smashing against her ribs, fighting to be free of her chest so it could get away, so it could escape.

The ex's hands stretched out across the table. Its thighs bumped the edge. It took another awkward step and swayed as the table refused to get out of its way. Another step made the table legs scratch against the industrial carpet, shifting a quarter of an inch before settling back down.

She flinched back and ran into the tool chest. A thin mouthful of air wheezed into her nostrils. Her fists slammed back against the metal drawers.

Lester whimpered. He'd pressed himself against the wall. He chanted something, and it took a second for her brain to realize it was just "no no no no no no" again and again.

Gray hands stretched across the table for her, swinging back and forth through the air. A good five feet separated them from her. The fingertips barely reached past the width of the table.

A thimble of air squeezed between her lips. She focused, pushed, willed herself to take another breath. A deeper one. It filled her chest and put some space between her violent heart and the ribs it had been pounding against. She stopped banging on the tool chest and forced her fists to un-roll, her fingers to straighten. She pressed them flat against the drawers.

The ex's teeth snapped together again and again. *Click-click-click-click*. It bumped against the table edge again. The impact jarred a few strands loose from its comb-over, and they draped down to hang across one of its milky eyes.

More gunfire echoed from outside. A few shouts and screams. And the sound of even more teeth.

No one was coming to help her. Not anytime soon. Maybe never.

Maybe Cesar hadn't gotten the fence back up. Maybe he broke the cable. Maybe . . .

She pushed the thoughts away. They weren't helping. She needed to breathe. Breathe and stop shaking and deal with this ex, or she and Lester were going to die.

The dead man took another lurching step against the table. The front legs lifted up off the floor, then settled back down. The ex's gray hands groped the air.

She leaned to the side, grabbed the whimpering man's shoulder, and pulled him closer to the tool chest. A bit closer to the ex, too, but solidly behind the table now.

Her eyes flitted to the left. The door to the courtyard was about fifteen feet away. Less for Lester and the ex. And she'd closed the gate out of the courtyard to the canopy area, where all the weapons were. They could run for it, but the ex would be close behind them. It might catch her.

To the right was a wall of low windows with a view of the still-standing sections of the south fence. She could try to dive through one of the windows, but she knew she wouldn't make it. By the time she wrestled her way through the frame, the dead man would've taken a bite or three out of her calves, maybe even her thighs.

And that didn't even consider Lester being almost catatonic with fear. So much worse than her. There was no way she'd get him moving fast enough to avoid a zombie.

Left and right were out. A wall behind her. The ex in front of her. She'd done an amazing job of cornering herself behind the table.

Why the hell hadn't she grabbed a pistol off the rack? Kennedy and Gibbs and Hector and half the Unbreakables did it right in front of her. What had she been thinking, running inside without grabbing something to protect herself?

She hadn't been thinking. She'd been running scared. She'd been trying to hide.

Now the ex was in here with her and Lester. And Lester was useless. No more hiding. Now she had to fight.

She was Cerberus, damn it. Not the suit. Her.

Click-click-click-click.

The tool chest behind her held electronic tools and components. Nothing useful unless she wanted to try stabbing the dead man with a soldering iron. The big wrenches and hammers were all in the smaller chest across the room, which made the odds of getting away from the ex seem a lot . . .

Danielle mentally kicked herself and barked out a single laugh. She'd been so focused on the dead man in the ratty blazer she'd been overlooking the best weapon she had. Literally, looking right over it.

The Longshot sat on the worktable between her and the ex, pointed at the zombie's hip. The housing was off, but the magazine was still loaded with more hex nuts. The weapon just needed to be cocked.

And fired. The trigger was in the front. Within easy reach of the ex's hands. And mouth.

First things first. The manual lever was under the dead man's elbow. The same arm with the ragged cuff.

She took a breath, set her palms against the tool chest,

and pushed herself off. Her right foot slid forward. Then her left. Her heart threw a few punches at her sternum, but calmed down. She took another step closer. And another.

The gray fingertips went back and forth in front of her face, stretching and grabbing. One hand swiped at her shoulders. The other almost brushed her nose. Small cracks ran through the yellowed fingernails. One of the thumbs didn't have a nail at all. The ex swung its arms again and again, like a machine.

Danielle understood machines.

Both arms out. Lean left. Lean right. Every three passes some neuron would go off and the left arm would drop down low. Then it would overcompensate and go high, and then return to normal for three passes. A cycle of five. She watched it happen six times, enough to convince her it was a pattern.

On the seventh, as it started to go high, she reached forward and grabbed the lever.

The ex *lunged* for her.

Lester shrieked. Danielle threw herself back and hit the tool chest again. One of the drawers caught her right on the spine, just below the ribs. The panic twisted around her and squeezed. Her heart slammed back and forth, determined to get free this time.

Her hand was okay. She held it up, forced it open, looked at the back, looked at the palm. Nothing. Not even a faint scratch. The ex hadn't touched her. She was okay.

The dead man lifted itself off the table. Its remaining front tooth had broken on the Longshot's exposed framework. Now it had a jagged fang next to the steel post. The better to bite with.

Its blazer lifted away from the weapon. The lever sat back and cocked. Armed and ready. She'd pulled it back. She didn't even remember getting her hand on it.

She released the knot of muscle in her gut and took a deep

breath. A calming breath. Her mind and heart were racing, but she was pretty sure it had just been two or three minutes since the ex had wandered in through the side door. No more than four.

It hadn't lunged. It wasn't smart enough to lunge. She'd gotten under it, and when it went after her gravity had taken over and given it speed. It had fallen on the table, not lunged.

Danielle forced herself to breathe slowly and studied the ex. Its build, its jeans, where its shoulders sat. She took a small step to the right. The dead man leaned after her. It bumped the table again. The gray hands stretched for her and fell short by almost two yards.

The ex's stomach pressed against the Longshot's muzzle. A hex nut at this range would tear through the dead man's gut and shatter the spine. It would still be able to crawl, but not fast enough to stop her from running out, grabbing a pistol, and blowing its head off.

The Longshot's trigger sat on the front left. If she moved around, the ex would follow and spoil the shot. She might get it in the hip, but she wasn't sure that would do enough damage to cripple the dead man. Was there a way to make it crouch and put its head in front of the muzzle? Probably not.

She'd have to reach across the weapon again to fire the Longshot. Or figure out a way to release it from behind. But that would take time she didn't have. The side door was still open, and other exes were out there.

The dead man's teeth slammed together, and she heard a harder *click* when the jagged front tooth struck the enamel below it. The steel post and broken tooth could rip through her shirt sleeve. And the contact suit. And her arm.

The impact of the shot would knock it away. Even with gravity on its side, it wouldn't be able to reach her before she reached the trigger. It couldn't.

Danielle glanced over at Lester. The man had slid the rest

of the way down the wall and into a crouch. He pushed himself back into the corner of the wall and tool chest, his arms still over his head.

She shook her hands at her sides and squared her jaw. Sucked in a breath. Tried to ignore the trickles of cold sweat crawling through her clothes.

The table rocked as the ex tried to shamble through it again. The dead man's gray fingers grabbed at the air in front of her. The chattering of its teeth seemed to grow louder in anticipation.

Danielle reached for the trigger.

The ex dropped toward her arm, jaws spread open.

# # #

Gibbs was slowing the gardeners down.

He knew it. He was pretty sure they knew it, too. Cutting across the soft earth of the gardens was just too much work with the mechanical foot. And slogging through thirty feet of soil clogged up the joints. The gears in his ankle and toes were stiff, his limp was even worse, and it was slowing him down.

It wasn't by much in the big scheme of things. But it was enough that the huge ex with the trap and the others with it kept up with movie-monster efficiency. They lurched and staggered and managed to stay about twenty feet behind his group.

He needed more space. Enough time to stop, line up his rifle, and drop all of them. If his math was right, he had nine rounds left in the magazine.

They stumbled onto another path. He recognized it. There was a display of birdhouses with peeling paint and a grove of tall cactus plants. He stopped and waved them down the path. "This way," he snapped. "Back to the main building."

Desi and the rest of the work crew ran past him. Gibbs herded them along and picked up the rear. The path was hard dirt with patches of wood chips. Much faster. His mechanical foot hit the ground, and he felt it give a bit as the impact shook some soil out of his joints.

They ran to the end of the path, where it opened up onto a small lawn. Up ahead he could see the toolshed and the greenhouse lit up in the stark floodlights of the main building. Danielle had the side door open and waiting for them, a bright rectangle in the dark. There were two exes between the group and safety. Easy to dodge.

He stopped and swung up the rifle. The ex-redneck was just under thirty feet away. Not a great lead, but enough of one. The zombie's single white eye made a great target in the low light. Gibbs lined up, breathed out, and squeezed the trigger.

The eye vanished. The redneck dropped. The animal trap pinged against a rock as it hit the ground.

Gibbs shifted his aim onto the next ex, a dead man with thinning hair and a baggy brown suit. His first shot missed. He growled, re-aimed, and the ex lurched just as he fired.

A gray-skinned woman in a lab coat tripped over the fallen redneck and tumbled onto the path.

Gibbs fired a third shot, and the dead man in the brown suit twitched once and collapsed. He tracked it down as it fell, then panned the rifle over and put a round through the top of Lab Coat's head. Six shots, three dead.

More exes came up the path behind him. More than he'd thought. At least five or six. He lined up on the next one, realized he didn't have enough ammunition, and took a few steps back.

His foot—his real foot—slipped on a patch of wood chips and loose dirt at the edge of the lawn. There was plastic under them, some kind of anti-erosion thing Lester had talked about over dinner the other night. Gibbs went down hard. The impact rang in his tailbone and jarred the rifle from his hands. The strap tangled around his arm, and he fumbled to get the weapon back in his grip. His metal foot kicked at the path, but the spike-heel just plowed through the dirt.

The exes shambled closer. The *click-click-click* of their teeth broke the air into small, jagged bits. At the front of the horde was a gray-skinned girl with long pigtails and a gore-stained dress. The dead girl's left arm ended just past the shoulder in a dried, messy stump. The ex's remaining hand reached for him.

He let the rifle drop and pushed at the walkway with his hands and feet. It moved him back, but not enough. As slow as they were, the exes moved faster. The dead girl crouched, her gnashing teeth dipped toward his leg, and—

Warm fingers brushed his neck. His collar and shirt yanked up, and he was dragged away from the undead. His steel foot carved a furrow across the lawn. His savior huffed and grunted and hauled him five-ten-fifteen feet away from the horde before letting go of his collar. Gibbs scrambled to his feet and turned to give a quick thanks to—

Smith panted and glowered at him. She stepped past him, put both hands on the haft of the shovel she'd been carrying in her claw-hand, and smashed it across the dead girl's jaw. The ex spun in a full circle and dropped to the ground. The dead man behind it, a workman or groundskeeper in simple clothes, tripped and fell forward onto the path. She brought the shovel down on the dead man's head.

Smith turned back to Gibbs. Anger and regret and disgust fought for dominance on the woman's face. She jerked her thumb once at the main building and then took off. She didn't look to see if he followed.

The dead girl clawed at the dirt path and pushed itself up on its one good arm. It flopped over twice before it managed to push itself to its feet. Its head sat crooked on its neck, but not enough to put it down.

Gibbs followed after Smith. His metal toes dug at the lawn but didn't slow him down. He threw his legs forward and caught up with the Asian woman halfway down the path.

The exes followed.

× × ×

The sound of gunfire by the fence dropped. "I'm out," shouted Taylor. He let his rifle drop and pulled the home-made brass knuckles from his pockets.

Kennedy did a quick head count and came up with about seventy exes left in the parking area. Sixty-nine as Wilson dropped another one. Hancock's rifle bucked against his shoulder, and he lowered it with a scowl when none of the zombies fell. "Same!" he yelled.

Between Wilson and herself, they had maybe a dozen rounds left between them. Even if every one dropped an ex, it left them on the wrong side of an eleven-to-one fight. Tight odds even if they were all still in peak condition.

Across the parking lot, a baker's dozen of zombies pawed and grabbed at the exoskeleton. Its movements weren't as fluid as usual, as if it had been damaged. Or wounded, with Cesar running it. The battlesuit grabbed them one by one with its free hand and flung them away. The other hand stayed clamped to the fence pole with the links threaded between its fingers.

"Cesar," she yelled. "Support!"

"I can't leave the fence," he called back. "I'm holding it up."

Kennedy lined up on a bald ex with what looked like a saw blade stuck in its head. "Figure something out."

"I need some rope or chain or something."

"Figure it out!" She squeezed the trigger, and the round pinged off the goddamned saw blade. A second round punched into the dead man's forehead and it collapsed.

Her rifle was empty. She swung it around to use like a club. "Falling back, heading east," she told the squad. "We'll try to lure them away from the main building."

The closest ex was four yards from them. Its jaw snapped shut with a *clack*, and Wilson blew its teeth out through the back of its skull. It tipped back into the horde behind it.

"Who's going to lure them the fuck away from us?" growled Taylor.

The Unbreakables dropped back a few feet and shuffled to the left. The zombies shifted and staggered after them.

"We get them heading that way," said Kennedy, "swing around the back fence and double-time it back to the main building. We reload and regroup there."

They each took a few steps and leaped. Their muscles were still strong enough to carry them a few yards—enough to make the exes pivot and stumble. Some of the exes fell. A few others tripped over the fallen.

The path on this side was a dirt service road between two small boulders. A good chokepoint. They jogged a few yards down the road, and Wilson turned with his rifle. "I've got about five or six rounds left, First Sergeant," he said. "I can slow 'em down a bit."

"Stay together."

"Noise'll keep 'em coming this way, too," he pointed out. "We don't want to lose 'em in the dark."

"He's right," said Hancock. "We need to keep their attention."

Kennedy nodded. "Don't be brave," she told Wilson. "They get close, you catch up to us."

"No worries there, top."

The Unbreakables ran deeper into the garden. Wilson looked at the approaching zombie horde and raised his rifle to look down the sights. Right in front was the dead teen-age girl he and Franklin had tossed over the fence the other day. Its left shoulder and arm hung low, even while the hand at the end twitched. Part of the dead girl's cheek had been torn loose against the pavement when it'd hit the road, and it hung in a loose flap against its face.

"It's always the cute ones," he muttered, and squeezed the trigger.

× × ×

Cesar watched the soldiers vanish between the two boulders. He heard a shot, then another one. Most of the exes stumbled down the tree-shaded path after the Unbreakables. A few stragglers lurched off into the garden plots, more or less in the direction Gibbs had run with the garden people. A couple zombies in the far back of the horde shifted around and wandered back toward him.

He swung his stiff arm and slammed it into two exes, catching each of them in the skull. The dead people collapsed. He grabbed a one-armed woman with a skinless face and flung the zombie over the fence.

Another gunshot from the path.

He could do this. He could deal with all of them. He just needed to figure out how to get away from the fence.

There was a stubby chain on one of the dumpsters, something to lock it shut, but it was barely long enough to go around the post, and he didn't have a way to fasten it. There were a few lengths of old twine and thin rope inside the big bin, things that had been cleared out of garden plots, but he could tell they were all too brittle and rotted to be any good. If he had both hands free, he was strong enough to tear the dumpster apart and make strips of metal . . . but he didn't have both hands free.

Another gunshot echoed to the battlesuit's microphones. A moment later, over the clicking of hundreds of teeth, he picked out the hard *clack* of a gun locking open. Whoever was shooting had just run out of ammunition.

He looked around for a trash can or a garden stake or a

signpost. Something he could use to tie the fence in place. Something metal and solid.

And then he had an idea. It wasn't a great idea, or a safe one, but he knew it would work. And he didn't have anything else.

He shifted his bulk around and traded hands so the stiff arm was holding the chain-link. He squeezed it a little tighter, pulling the fence right up to the steel post. A few more exes tried to gnaw on him, and he backhanded them away. The blow knocked the head off a dead man and sent it spinning into a garden plot. The plot with the white-and-orange birdhouse. He'd have to remember it and make sure everyone was careful there until they found it.

He looked at the battlesuit's left arm and wondered if he was going to have some more killer scars or something a lot worse.

Cesar's steel fingers reached into the superstructure of the crippled arm and tore out one of the support struts. He screamed, and the suit's speakers turned it into a roar. His vision fogged with white and gray static. His legs trembled. He focused on his hand, on keeping the fence tight and near the post.

The camera view cleared. A few lines of text across his vision warned him of possible structural damage. Oh, Jesus, his arm was on fire.

A bunch of the exes had turned back. Looked like his screams sounded better than gunshots. Good thing.

Then he reached over and ripped another strut loose. Another scream echoed off the trees and houses. He felt his knees shift. The battlesuit staggered, and he caught himself before it tipped over. He willed the static out of his vision.

The left arm wobbled. Two of five supports gone. The wrist felt weird, like it was sitting wrong. But the hand was still holding the fence up.

His free hand bent one of the supports against the post.

Then he looped it around the steel pole and threaded it through the chain-link. He squeezed the ends together and bent them over each other twice like a giant twist tie.

He smacked a few more exes away and bent the other support. This one went under the hand holding the fence. It took a little longer to get this one around the post and through the fence, but then he knotted it in place.

It took him a moment to wiggle his fingers free of the chain-link. The fence squealed a bit as exes piled against it, but it held. It'd hold for a little while, at least.

Cesar stepped back. An ex grabbed his damaged arm, and he flung it away. One of the fingers trembled when he made a fist, and the wrist was tweaked. An ache throbbed deep inside it. But it worked.

He swung the fist around, and an ex's skull exploded on impact. He grabbed one in each hand and hurled them back over the fence. A dead woman tried to wrap its arms around his waist, and he crushed its shoulder and neck between his fingers.

The throb in his arm faded a little.

He set the battlesuit's speakers to PA mode, max volume, and his power level tipped from thirteen percent to twelve. "Hey," he shouted. He flung the dead woman away, swept his arms out, and smashed half a dozen exes to the ground. "Zombie folks! Get back over here. Got a little something special for you."

The horde turned and came to see what he had to offer.

TWENTY-NINE

NOW

SLOW WASN'T IN Zzzap's nature in the energy form. His speed tended to fall into either "ambling" or "supersonic" categories. There wasn't much in between.

But as he circled the island for the fourth time, he tried to move slowly and study everything below him.

Truth was, he couldn't see a damned thing. He didn't use the visible spectrum, but it wouldn't have helped him. A black submarine, underwater, at night, was going to be pretty much invisible to regular vision.

In his eyes—well, if the energy form had actual eyes—the ocean was a riot of temperature swirls and electromagnetic currents. Every wave and ripple sent out dozens more across the wide spectrum he could see. Plus it reflected some of his own energy back at him. It was swirling paint and clouds in coffee and lines of force and a dozen other things all at once. He'd tried to explain to people that sometimes he was almost blinded by the sheer, overwhelming excess of it all.

And that was all just on the top. If he looked beneath the surface of the water, it became layers and layers of patterns. So much movement and energy.

Zzzap swung around for his fifth circuit, expanding his range a little wider. He was almost half a mile out from the island now. More area to cover, better chance he might miss something.

He wondered if the sub might've already made it past him. If Nautilus was as fast and strong in the water as everyone said—and two fistfights with St. George seemed to back that up—maybe the sub was already a mile away. Or maybe it was still in his range and he'd skimmed right past it.

He wondered if Nautilus would really launch nukes at Los Angeles. And how far he'd be from the island when he did it. And if he didn't find it soon enough, what were the odds he could catch and disable an ICBM in midflight without setting it off? Or getting dumped in the ocean like Captain America?

He couldn't see the submarine anywhere.

x x x

Madelyn grabbed the ex by its outstretched wrist and tugged it forward. The dead man didn't resist, barely registered her touch. It leaned toward her, toppled, and dropped onto the pile.

When the chain snapped, she'd realized the one thing she had to make a barrier out of was the exes themselves. She tripped, pulled, and shoved them together. Then the next wave tripped over the fallen ones, and then she yanked more dead people on top of that layer.

The bodies were five deep, a wall across the walkway. Random arms reached out and grabbed at the air. Bodies shifted as they tried to get back to their feet. Their gnashing teeth got caught on each other's clothes and hair.

More of the undead hit the pile from behind. The whole thing shifted forward as the exes crawled over one another, but they were too slow and too mindless to untangle themselves. It'd take them at least twenty minutes to make it to the top of the ramp.

"Score one for the Corpse Girl," Madelyn said. And even as she said it she realized she had to make it to the next gangplank before the exes stumbled across it. Assuming they hadn't already.

A *thump* came from behind her and the walkway shuddered. An ex behind the pile tipped over and vanished. Madelyn turned around just as another impact shook the ramp.

Two men stood at the head of the walkway, about fifteen feet away. And the over-tanned woman, Alice. They had big tools, and they were hammering and prying at the edge of the ramp. Trying to knock it loose, the Corpse Girl realized. If they'd already made it to this walkway, things were looking good for the cruise ship.

"It's okay," she called up to them. She sucked in some air and raised her voice over the chattering teeth. "They're down for a couple of minutes. You don't need to rush."

One of the men glanced up at her, then hit the end of the gangplank again. The planks shifted, and the left side of the ramp sagged. The ropes tying the ramp to the cruise ship went tight. Madelyn stumbled against the guide rail. The pile of exes rocked to one side, and one of the precarious ones on the top, a dead man in a ragged wifebeater, flopped down near her feet.

"Hey," Madelyn called out, "wait a minute." She put her foot on the dead man's ribs and pushed it over onto its side. It flopped on top of two outstretched arms, each one from a different ex.

A gunshot went off up on the *Queen*. A big one, like a shotgun. There was some shouting. The sound of clicking teeth suddenly had an echo.

The people attacked the other side of the ramp. Crowbar and sledgehammer. The men grunted and hissed. The ramp shifted, dropped, bounced. Madelyn heard the creak of the ropes and felt the gangplank rock side to side.

One of the men had a knife and was sawing at the rope closest to him. Alice lifted a bright red axe above her shoulder.

"WAIT!" Madelyn took three long strides toward them. One of the men looked terrified. All he saw was an ex with its arms reaching for him.

The fire axe slammed down through the ropes. The floor dropped away from Madelyn's feet. The dolphin-covered ceiling came down, the walkway spun, the pile of exes dissolved into a swarm of bodies.

They fell.

x x x

St. George brought his fist around and hammered the side of an ex's head. The skull and spine cracked, and the impact sent it sprawling into one of the supports for the catwalk. The steel rang with the impact, and the dead woman's head became a shapeless blob. He reversed the swing and backhanded another ex in the face. Its nose, jaw, and right cheekbone collapsed. It stumbled back, fell over, and flailed until he reached down and twisted its head around.

Two people had been killed on the tanker, plus the woman who'd been bitten but wasn't dead yet. She still had a slim chance, provided they had any medicine left on the ships. Not a great chance, but it was better than none.

He'd put down at least thirty zombies. The people trapped on the tanker with him had put down another ten, maybe, before he got each of them to safety. Maybe a third of the undead on the tanker accounted for. Hussein's teams had managed to take down two of the walkways connecting the tanker to the rest of Lemuria.

St. George thought there was a chance the exes had been contained.

A crack and a loud scrape echoed from behind him, and he turned in time to see the third gangplank slide fifteen feet down the hull of the cruise ship and hit the tanker's deck. The cloth cover swept up like a parachute, then settled back down over the wreckage. He caught a glimpse of at least two dozen zombies.

And one dead girl.

He leaped across to the fallen gangplank and tore the loose canvas away.

Madelyn leaned on the railing. Exes crawled and twisted in the broken wreckage at her feet. Broken bones jutted out from gray limbs.

A few of the zombies turned their heads toward him and tapped cracked teeth together. Some flapped broken or dislocated jaws. They reached for him with snapped fingers and tried to drag themselves out of the press of bodies.

"What a bunch of jerks," muttered the Corpse Girl. She limped over to St. George. He tore the other railing off, let it clatter on the deck, and lifted her out of the wreckage of the gangplank.

Her left leg twisted at the knee. Her foot pointed almost straight to the left. "You okay?"

"I don't think anything's broken," she said. She looked up at the trio standing in the open doorway of the cruise ship. "No thanks to you!"

Alice stared down at them. She didn't look upset.

St. George helped Madelyn over to a heavy pipe she could rest against. "Give me a minute, okay?"

"Yeah, sure."

He stepped back to the wreckage and knelt near the huddle of exes. They pawed at his arms, and their weak fingers grabbed at his sleeves. He reached out and twisted their necks one by one. Ten minutes later the teeth were still clicking, but the arms and legs were still.

He wiped his hands on the canvas cover and walked back to Madelyn. She tugged on the fingers of her left hand. Each one popped back into place. "Hey," she said, shaking the hand loose, "can you stand on my foot?" She swung her hips and put the twisted leg in front of him.

"You sure?"

"Yeah."

He pressed his boot down on hers. "Good?"

"A little harder. Make sure you've got it pinned."

"It's pretty sol—"

The Corpse Girl wrenched her hips back, and the leg cracked three times. She yelped. St. George yanked his foot away and she stumbled. "Okay," she said, "that tingled a little more than I thought it would." She rubbed her stomach, then took a few cautious steps. "Don't think I tore anything, though."

A rumble and crash echoed across the water—the sound of a wave breaking on the shore. The crash faded into an ongoing hiss. Even some of the remaining exes turned, attracted to the sound.

A wall of gray clouds rolled across the ocean toward Lemuria.

x x x

By his seventh pass, Zzzap was almost three-quarters of a mile out. Two circles back he'd decided to focus on the eastern side of Lemuria, the side closest to the mainland. It made sense Nautilus would head in that direction.

He still hadn't found the sub.

He shot higher into the air and tried to see something—anything—in the mess of signals and waves and patterns of the ocean. Some clue to where the sub might be or where it might've been. A trail of heat. A series of ripples that went against a current. Anything.

Back on the island he could see people running. And dying. Even from a few thousand feet away, they were bright yellow-and-orange outlines against the cool blue of the tanker's deck. Electromagnetic auras crackled around them.

One of them gleamed like a star as it rushed across the ship. St. George in flight. The distant outline stopped, reversed, and lifted two of the glowing outlines up above the deck.

One of the orange outlines at the other end of the tanker

flared and began to cool down. Its aura flickered and faded. The figure dropped, and a rippling wave passed over it. An ex, moving in to feed.

Back during the Zombocalypse, when the virus first swept across the planet, Zzzap had had a lot of trouble spotting the exes. They didn't give off any heat, barely had an electromagnetic aura, and sometimes they wouldn't bang their teeth together. He saw the entire electromagnetic spectrum, but they only registered in a small fraction of it.

It had taken him almost three months to figure out he needed to change how he looked for exes. He was used to looking for the pile of signals and wavelengths living things gave off. But exes weren't explosions of heat and color. They were cold and dull. They blended in. He had to know to look for them, like trying to spot the Predator. They were the monster that was in plain sight until it moved, and even then they could be tough to pick out.

Son of a bitch. If he'd had a mouth in the energy form, he would've smiled. Or kicked himself if he'd been physical.

His gaze swung back to the ocean. He'd been searching all the currents and patterns for another boat, looking for one of them to stand out like a copper penny in a pile of silver dimes. He changed his focus.

He looked for the quarter in the pile of dimes.

A sub was going to be subtle. It'd be insulated to keep in heat so nobody froze. And it'd be shielded from radiation. No point having a nuclear sub loaded with missiles if the enemy could just find you with a Geiger counter. Plus the crew wouldn't have anywhere to go, so all possible radiation sources would be shielded for them, too.

Just ahead of him and off to his left, in the middle of the spraying lines and spinning circles, there was a dull spot. Just enough to register. Long and thin, like a gigantic cigar. It was about a mile past the island and picking up speed.

Now that he knew where to look, he could also pick out the wiggling, kicking form at the end of it. Nautilus was actually pushing the sub. It weighed a hundred tons or so, and he was pushing it through the ocean like a guy trying to push start his car.

Maybe he was the strongest man in the world when he was in the water.

Zzzap swooped down and flitted along the surface. If Nautilus was still outside the submarine, there wasn't any danger of him launching a missile at the last minute. So once it went down, the threat should be done.

And even as he thought this, the kicking figure stopped pushing and slid up the length of the ship. Heading for a hatch. Nautilus had spotted him, and apparently the merman was a big fan of Operation: Spoilsport.

Zzzap knew the basics of nuclear bombs. Enough to know there was a small chance he could set off a warhead if he passed through it. So no burning a hole through the front of the sub.

He wasn't sure where the reactor was located, but he was willing to bet it was toward the back, closer to the propellers and the actual engine. Logically, from the back, it'd be propellers, engine, then the reactor. So if he punched a hole or two through the back fifth of the sub, he felt pretty sure he wouldn't cause a major radiation leak or an explosion.

Well, not an additional explosion, anyway.

He steeled himself, lined up, and knifed down into the water.

The ocean boiled at his touch. Only a thin sheaf of it, barely half an inch from the energy form, turned to vapor as his energy bled off into the surrounding water. But it kept bleeding, like a gunshot wound to the gut. He hemorrhaged heat as more and more water poured in to fill the envelope of steam around him.

Zzzap willed himself even hotter, easing back on the mental hold he kept around himself. He cut through the submarine's hull. Water bubbled around him as it flooded into the ship and hissed into steam on the molten edges. A few tubes melted, a steel shaft, and he was out the other side, his phantom skin crawling at the physical contact.

He looped down through the ocean and shot back up through the sub. This time he went straight through the engine, a huge block of hardened steel. It turned to slag at his touch, and he blasted out the top of the hull. More water seethed around him, and then he was back in the air.

The ocean roared and churned below him. A last few air bubbles erupted from the sub and scattered the patch of boiling water. Steam rose up off the cooling water. Lots of steam. Ten seconds in the ocean had created a dense fogbank, and it was spreading out across the water.

Zzzap shuddered in the sky. On a guess, he'd just used up about a quarter of his energy. Maybe more. He didn't want to think about what that meant when he changed back to human form. It wasn't like he had a lot of excess weight to burn.

Below him, the water bubbled and spat into the air. He could just see the long shadow, the cool lack of radiation, as its tail end sank down. The nose tilted up and brushed the surface. Then the sub let out a last burst of air, rippled the water one more time, and headed down to the ocean floor.

Zzzap hoped he hadn't just cooked the last six blue whales. He couldn't see anything floating on the surface. Nothing the size of a whale, anyway. Or even a dolphin.

Or a person.

He wondered if Nautilus had made it inside the sub. Or, if he hadn't, if he'd been scalded by the water. Neither was a pleasant way to go.

Then he thought of the children hanging in cages, waiting to be drowned, and found he didn't care.

x x x

The wave of warm steam rushed across the island. Condensation coated everything. St. George wiped water and sweat from his brow.

"Wow," said Madelyn. "I thought that was a bomb going off."

"Me, too," he said. He glanced up at the cruise ship. People lined the higher railings. "Everyone okay up there?"

The Lemurians waved and called back.

"They're still a bunch of jerks," muttered Madelyn.

"Try to remember they've been under different conditions than us," said St. George.

"Yeah," she said, "sometimes people are in bad conditions, but sometimes they're just jerks. Maybe they weren't all jerks to start with, but I think a lot of them are jerks now."

"At least you're just calling them jerks."

"I'm being polite."

The fog brightened around them. It wasn't daylight. More like a full moon had come out from behind the clouds. He looked up and saw the glowing figure above them.

"Whoa." Madelyn looked up at the wraith. "Are you okay?"

Maybe. Not sure. Zzzap's light was dim, not much more than a hazy glow in the mist.

"How bad are you?" asked St. George. "We can try to get some of our supplies back. Maybe get you a couple sweet potatoes from their—"

Zzzap waved his arm. *I'm past the really hungry phase,* he said. *I don't think . . . I think I shouldn't change back until we're somewhere with, y'know, better medical facilities.*

"Yeah?"

Yeah. I'm . . . I'm feeling a little light-headed.

"Do you need to go now?"

I'll be okay. Just . . . don't ask me to kill any more submarines.

The wraith shook its head. *Besides, how would you two find your way home without me?*

Madelyn peered out at the ocean through the mist. "So that was the sub?"

Yeah. It's about half a mile down by now.

"Nautilus?" asked St. George.

Zzzap shrugged. *No idea.*

"Did he go down on the sub?"

Madelyn snickered.

Zzzap buzzed out a chuckle. *Honestly, I don't know. I think he saw me coming and went to launch his missiles, but then I lost track of him when I boiled the ocean.*

"So what happens now?" asked Madelyn.

St. George looked back up at the cruise ship, then down the length of the tanker. All four gangplanks had been knocked down onto the tanker's deck. "I think all the exes are trapped on this ship now," he said, "but we need to make sure none of them got onto the *Queen*. Once we know, we can—"

Something heavy and metal rattled behind him. Madelyn's eyes got wide. Zzzap brought his arms up, fingers spread. St. George turned and—

The anchor knocked him across the deck. The chain trailed after it, then whipped back into the mist. The links clinked in the fog, and the huge piece of steel came rocketing out at him again.

St. George lunged into it, grabbed the anchor, and yanked hard. The ripple shot up the chain, and Nautilus came flying out of the mist. It was like a shark rushing in to feed.

St. George swung the anchor up and struck the merman across the face with it, smashing him to the deck.

Nautilus rolled, spat out some blood and a triangular tooth, and threw himself at St. George. The shell shoulder plates slammed into the hero's chest, and the impact flung them both down the length of the ship. They landed on an ex and crushed its hips to gravel. The merman twisted around and pinned St. George to the deck.

Blisters dotted Nautilus's arms. In places his blue skin had sloughed off to show tender, raw flesh beneath it. Heat radiated off his body. He glared down at St. George.

"Why?" he growled. "Why couldn't you just leave us alone?" His punch slammed St. George's head back against the metal deck. The boxing-glove fist came down again and again.

St. George pushed down against gravity and threw the merman off him. Nautilus spun in the air and landed in a crouch. He took a step forward, and the tanker deck brightened.

Hey, Jabberjaws, said the wraith. *Back off.* He held up a hand that popped and sparked in the mist.

"Save it," said St. George. "I've got this."

You sure?

St. George nodded, and Nautilus slammed into him again. They slid through one of the garden plots, spraying plants and dark soil across the deck. St. George smacked the merman in the chest with a palm and sent him flying.

As soon as he landed, he charged forward again. St. George batted away the first punch, and the second. The third caught him across the jaw but left Nautilus open for a gut punch that bounced him into the air and dropped him to his knees.

"Not so good without a bunch of children covering for you," St. George said.

Nautilus roared, lunged, and swung one of his boxing-glove fists around again.

St. George grabbed the wrist, twisted, and got it behind the merman's back. Nautilus snarled and brought his other fist around, but the hero was already too far behind him. He threw another punch anyway, and when his fist swung back St. George slipped his arm under the shell-armored shoulder and grabbed the other man's bull neck.

Nautilus roared. His shark teeth snapped in the air. It was a thin, sharp sound. "You can't hold me forever," he growled.

"Not planning on it."

St. George focused on the spot between his shoulder blades and launched them up into the night sky.

The merman's head slammed back and cracked into St. George's forehead. The hero shook it off. The arm in the half-nelson jabbed back, but it couldn't reach.

They flew faster, higher into the air, and the mist fell away. The wind shrieked in their ears. St. George glanced down and saw a flicker of light on the deck of the tanker. Zzzap, taking out the last of the exes.

"Barry pointed out why you're so tough," he said to the merman. "When you're like this, your body's designed to survive deep underwater. Tougher, stronger, more resilient. That's why you're so strong on the surface."

Nautilus brought his legs up and swung them back in a kick. It only grazed St. George's knees, but it made the two men sway in the air. The merman wheezed out a breath and twisted his shoulders again. St. George tightened his half-nelson and willed them to go higher.

"But it hit me a few minutes ago," said St. George, "that if you're built for those super-high undersea pressures, really low pressure must be brutal on you. Like those stories about deep-sea fish that explode when you bring them to the surface."

His breath, always hot from his fires, steamed in the cold air. It bit through his jacket and his wet suit and nipped at his ears and nose. He looked down and guessed the ocean was almost three miles below them.

He sucked in a mouthful of thin air and went even higher.

Nautilus threw his elbow at St. George's head again. It didn't come anywhere close. The veins bulged on the arm.

"As I see it, you've got two choices. You can stay like this and we'll see if we both freeze before I hit deep space or if you explode like a fish."

Nautilus turned to St. George and hissed. The sound rattled in his barrel chest. His teeth gnashed together like an ex.

"The other option is you change back to your human form. The high altitude will still mess you up, but I think your odds of survival will be much better. And we go back down and talk and figure out what to do with you."

"Why?" hissed the merman.

St. George slowed their ascent. "Because those people down there trusted you. You owe them answers." He took in another breath of thin air.

"Why are you so greedy?" asked Nautilus. The arm in the half-nelson sagged. The fist behind his back flopped open.

"What?"

"All I wanted was what you have," the merman whispered. Dark blood was trickling from his nostrils, and veins bulged across his chest and face. "What they've always given you. Admiration . . . respect . . . Why did you have to take it all away?"

St. George took a few breaths. "You held them prisoner and demanded it from them. You forced it out of them. I didn't take it," he said. "You never really had it."

Nautilus sighed and sagged in the hero's grip. St. George hung in the air. The ships were tiny models far below, the little Matchbox boats he'd had as a kid.

Then the merman twisted around and slammed a punch into the hero's side. It was hard and sudden enough to break St. George's concentration. They dropped a few feet before he focused again.

Nautilus threw his arm up, slid free of the half-nelson, and kept dropping.

St. George lunged after him.

The merman fell like a skydiver, angling his body into the wind. He picked up speed, dropping as fast as St. George could fly after him. His clothes rippled and snapped in the wind as he cut through the sky, passed over mist-shrouded Lemuria, and rocketed toward the ocean.

St. George willed himself faster. They were halfway down. He shrank the distance between them to twenty-five feet. Twenty. Fifteen.

They hit the fogbank and the horizon vanished. Clouds and water filled his view in every direction. He could see individual waves.

His fingers brushed webbed toes. He put on a last burst of speed and grabbed at the foot. Nautilus kicked him away. St. George reached and grabbed again. The ankle was small enough that he could get his fingers around it.

The merman spun and lashed out and howled. His gnashing teeth were small and square. White showed around desperate, dark eyes.

St. George tried to slow them down, tried to bleed off a little bit of their momentum. Nautilus slammed his other heel down on the hero's hand. He kicked again and again, but there was only normal human strength in the tanned leg, and St. George's fingers were like stone.

St. George pushed back against gravity. Inertia tried to tear the other man from his grip, and he fought that, too, grabbing hold of the ankle with both hands. The downward plunge became a slant. And then an arc.

They swung across the ocean. Nautilus stretched down, and his fingers brushed the surface of the water. Then St. George lifted them up into the air and brought them around in a wide circle. The ships of Lemuria were dark shapes in the mist, but they were enough for him to get his bearings.

Nautilus—Maleko—stopped fighting and let himself hang from the hero's grip. His oversized clothes sagged on his small body. Frustration squeezed his eyes shut.

"Sorry," said St. George. "You don't get to take the easy way out." He paused as they flew through the air. "I don't know what went wrong, why you did all this, but it's over. You're going to explain yourself, and then you're probably going to have to answer to all these people."

A light cut through the fog and stopped in the air in front of them. *Holy frak,* said Zzzap, *that was amazing. Like,* Reign of Fire *archangel amazing.*

"Is everything good back there?"

The glowing wraith looked over his shoulder. *Yeah, all under control. Maddy's keeping the last few exes down, and some of Eliza's people are dealing with them.* Zzzap looked down at Maleko. *What about him?*

"He's done," said St. George. "They know the truth now."

THIRTY

NOW

CESAR LOOKED UP at the battlesuit. The big, empty lenses looked down at him. It didn't look too angry he'd messed it up.

Metal edges curled up out of the forearm. One of them looked like the jagged edge of a steak knife. From this angle, outside of the exoskeleton, he could see how one of the remaining supports had been torqued out of line. He'd been lucky the whole hand hadn't snapped off while he fought the horde.

At least it could be rebuilt.

Wilson had died buying time for his squad. The exes had spread wider than expected and he'd been cut off. Going off the bodies, he'd put down half a dozen using his rifle like a club, then four more with his bare hands when they were too tight around him to swing the weapon. There wasn't enough left of him to reanimate.

One of the scavengers, Paul, had died that morning while they cleaned the last of the exes out of Eden. No one was sure how. One minute he'd been searching the garden plots with two other sweepers, the next minute they found a dead ballerina gnawing on him, its frilly dress soaked in blood. Kennedy put it down with a quick knife to the base of the skull.

Lester lost three gardeners. One of them wasn't dead yet. Javi's temperature hovered around 101, and he'd been throwing up a lot. They'd tied him to a tree in case he died and reanimated when no one was looking. The plan was to take him back to the Mount and see if Doc Connolly could do anything for him.

Lester himself was still a wreck, although now it was shame rather than panic. It had taken him half an hour to stop crying. He barely remembered Danielle saving him.

In the big scheme of things, Cesar knew he'd got off easy.

He walked into the big room. It was still a mess of tools and components that needed to be repacked. He tapped his fingers on the Longshot. "So," he said, "are we calling this done now?"

Danielle looked up from the worktable and shook her head. Her ponytail slid back and forth across her shoulders. "Hardly."

"Gibbs says you fought off an ex with it. Saved Lester."

She snorted. "I shot an ex at point-blank range. Doesn't mean it works." She waved a hand at the dark stain on the carpet.

He smirked. "You just don't want to give me any guns."

She rolled her eyes and turned her attention back to the motherboard she'd freed from a laptop.

Cesar watched her for a moment. "You okay?"

She didn't look up. "Fine."

"No," he said. "I mean . . . y'know. Are you okay after having one of them in here with you?"

Danielle sighed.

"I just . . . I know you have problems, sometimes, with the exes. We don't talk about it, and I know you don't want to talk about it, but I just—"

"I'm fine," she said.

"Yeah?"

"Yeah." She looked him in the eyes. "I think it might've done me some good. Made me think about how I've been wasting a lot of time hiding like this." She waved her hand at the room and the worktables. "I've got a lot of stuff to get done. I can't let being scared slow me down anymore."

Cesar smiled. "That's good," he said.

"Yeah. But you're deflecting a bit, aren't you?"

"What?"

Danielle gestured at his left arm. "How are you?"

"I'm good."

"I've seen the suit. I know you're not good."

He shrugged. "Is what it is, y'know? God's will, that's what my mom would say."

"Let me see it," said Danielle.

He sighed and tugged up his sleeve. Once it was past his elbow he held the arm out to her. She leaned in to study it.

His forearm sagged across the top. The loose skin sunk down and formed a shallow trench from the inside of his elbow to his wrist. There were a few long scabs at either end of the gouge. Two or three of them were going to leave scars.

"Did it bleed a lot?"

Cesar nodded. "Not, like, tons, but enough to freak everybody out when I got out of Cerbe—out of the battlesuit."

"You can call it Cerberus," said Danielle. "I think you've earned it."

"Really?"

"Yeah."

His lips curled into a smile. "So, anyway, d'you know Megan?"

"The scavenger? Yeah, I met her back at the Mount. I think she was an EMT or something like that."

"Paramedic, yeah. Near as she can tell, I ripped out one of my arm bones. The radials."

"Radius."

"Yeah, that one. And some tendons, maybe. They won't be sure what until I get it X-rayed, maybe CAT-scanned."

"But you're okay?"

"Feels a little weird, but yeah." His hand flopped back and forth. Palm up, palm down. Palm up, palm down. The valley of flesh rippled, filled in, and then sunk back into his arm. "Think it gets me out of any heavy work for a while."

"At least until we can get the supports back in."

He blinked.

Danielle gestured out at the courtyard. At the wounded exoskeleton. "Once they get the fence reinforced," she said, "we can get the supports back, straighten them out, and put them back into—"

Cesar shook his head. "Nah," he said. "I don't think it works that way."

"You don't know that."

"No," he agreed, "but it doesn't feel right, y'know? I think when part of me, of whatever I'm in, is gone, it's just ... y'know, gone."

He flexed the arm again, twisting the hand back and forth.

"I'll see if I can come up with some kind of brace for you," Danielle said. "Something to reinforce your wrist. I mean, if Doc Connolly doesn't have a good one back at the Mount."

"Nah, you don't have to."

"Yeah," she said, "I do." She looked at him. "I'm glad you're on the team, Cesar. That you're part of Cerberus. You're going to do great things with the battlesuit."

"Thanks."

Danielle cleared her throat and waited for him to say something else. When he didn't, she bent her head back to the motherboard on the worktable.

"So," he said. "The first sergeant, huh?"

"Kennedy? What about her?"

"She's kinda got the hots for you."

She shrugged and didn't look up. "Sounds like it."

"Does she even have a first name?"

Danielle stopped and thought about it. "I mean, she does, yeah, but I don't think I know what it is."

"And you?"

She raised an eyebrow at him. "You know my first name."

"No, not that."

"What?"

"I don't know." Cesar made a point of studying something outside the window. "I didn't know if you were into, y'know, girls."

"Never thought about it."

"No?"

Danielle shrugged again.

"I mean, it's cool with me."

"Gee," she said, raising an eyebrow, "thanks."

"No, I didn't mean it like that, I just meant, y'know, if it makes you happy, that's cool."

She smirked and shook her head.

"Way I see it, you like girls, I like girls, just gives us something new to talk about, right?"

She hid her chuckle behind a cough, or maybe it was just lucky timing. "Cesar," she said, "if anything happened between me and First Sergeant Kennedy—and it's not going to—I wouldn't talk about it with anyone."

"I'm just saying, y'know, I'm here for you."

"Great. Since you're here, grab my soldering kit, would you?"

He chuckled and pulled open a drawer in the tool chest. He pulled out the leather bundle and tossed it to Danielle. She grabbed it with both hands and winced.

"You okay?"

"Yeah, it's nothing." She put the kit on the table and pulled her sleeve back down to her wrist.

"Hey," he said, "you're not wearing the contact suit. I been trying to figure out why you looked different."

"My braid's not tucked in."

"Yeah, that too, but I think the only time I've ever seen you not wearing it was when we—"

"Hey," she said, coughing out the word. "We don't talk about it anymore."

"Sorry."

"Like I said, after the whole thing with Lester and the ex, I just . . . I didn't see any point in being scared anymore."

Cesar smiled. "Good. 'Bout time we got you out there to kick some ass."

She reached over to brush her other sleeve down, and he saw the edges of white tape and gauze peeking out. "Hey," he said. "What happened to your arm?"

Danielle glanced down as if she hadn't noticed the bandage before. "Oh, it's nothing." She gestured at the Longshot on the worktable. "It wasn't mounted on anything and didn't have the housing on, so when I fired it the whole thing jumped up in the air. I cut myself on one of the interior struts."

"Is it okay?"

She tugged the sleeve down over the bandage and managed a tight smile. "Yeah, of course. It's nothing to worry about."

THEN

MY COSTUME WAS junk at this point. Gone. The suit and cape were both ruined. I'd lost one of the gloves—it fell out of my pocket while I was helping to clean out the studio. I'm guessing the Mighty Dragon mask was still up on the roof at Hollywood and Highland, but I'd been busy and hadn't seen a point to going back for it.

It took some work to find the right jacket. Stealth was right. I needed something more durable to wear, especially if we were going to keep heading out into the city. About ninety percent of the jackets I found were heavy, black biker things, though. Lots of snaps and straps and . . . well, black. Much more her style. Or Gorgon's.

The brown flight jacket suited me better. It was a little easier on the eyes, not quite so harsh. The leather was a bit softer, too, so I'd be patching it more. But it was worth it to not look like some kind of super-SWAT cop or motorcycle gang member.

Plus, yeah, it's a little Indiana Jones. Not a bad thing for anyone.

So, the costume was gone. The closest thing I had to it was the red Henley I had on under the leather jacket. I was hoping the splash of bright color would help remind people who I'd been.

I stood near the examination tents and wondered if I looked inspiring or reassuring at all.

I'd been there for about half an hour. Some people looked at me like I was a nut. Some recognized me from rescuing them and thanked me again. I'd like to think the positives were in the lead.

And just as I was thinking this, a shout came from the Melrose Gate. Then another one. I could see people moving there. Someone had come through the gate, and the guards were jumping into action.

I leaped into the air. I could get up about thirty or thirty-five feet and glide about three hundred if the wind was right. It was enough to carry me to the gate. I could look down and see a lot of it before I landed.

Three people. Man, woman, girl in her teens. The women helped the man stay on his feet. He was in the middle of a coughing fit and had one arm close to his body. The guards at the gate all had their guns trained on him.

"It's okay," the woman was saying. The man tried to say something, but she talked over him. Pretty much yelled over him. "He's okay. Just leave him alone."

I hit the cobblestones and heads turned. Costume or no, somebody dropping out of the sky commands attention. "What's going on?"

One of the guards, Derek, made a little wave at the man with his rifle. "Infected."

"He's not infected," said the woman.

"He's not that bad," added the teenager. She looked enough like both of them I felt safe calling her their daughter.

"Once it's cleaned up, you'll see," said the woman. "It's nothing." She was edging toward hysterical. Maybe three good steps away from it.

The man . . . the father coughed again and looked at me. His family might've been in denial, but he wasn't. He'd been expecting this. He'd accepted it.

That'd make this easier.

"Let's put the guns down," I said. I stepped forward and

put myself between the family and as many guards as I could. "We're not trying to scare anyone."

Another guard, a black man with dreadlocks, glanced past me at the father. "Yeah, but he's defin—"

"I've got this," I told him.

His eyes opened a little wider, and his chin went up just a bit. Understanding and relief, all at once. He nodded, let his rifle swing down to the pavement, and turned away just enough from the man to make it clear he wasn't considered a threat anymore.

I waited until they'd all aimed their rifles somewhere else before I turned to the father. "Hi," I said. "I'm George." I held out my hand.

The father smiled a little. His shoulders relaxed. "Bryan," he said. "With a *y*." He reached out and shook my hand. His palm was warm and clammy. I saw the spots of blood on his other sleeve that the guards had seen. We'd all seen it a bunch of times over the past few months. Blood seeping up from underneath and into the fabric. A bite someone was trying to hide.

I let go of his hand. "Can you and I talk for a couple of minutes?"

"Yeah," he said. "We probably should."

"No," hissed the woman. She put a hand on his good arm, and I saw a glint of gold on her finger. Husband and wife with their daughter. "Don't let them—"

"We're just going to talk," he told her. His voice caught, like he was holding back another cough. He looked at me. "Just talking, right?"

I nodded. "Just talking. I promise."

His wife swallowed and took her hand off his arm. He wobbled, then glanced at me. "Could I get a little help?"

"Do you need to lean on me?"

"That'd be good."

I slung his arm up around my neck and did the same to

him. Two old friends. Heat rolled off him. If he wasn't so pale, I'd think his whole body was sunburned. This close I could smell it on him. A bit of stomach acid from throwing up, and under that was the hot, dark smell of someone who was really sick.

We walked away from the gatehouse, past the parking lot, and stopped by one of the big planters. I eased him down so he could lean against it. "Okay?"

"Yeah," Bryan said. "Thanks."

"You sure?"

He let out a long breath. His shoulders slumped. "I just . . . Jesus, I didn't think . . . I didn't want them to gun me down in front of my family."

"They wouldn't've," I told him. "They were just nervous, that's all."

He nodded and coughed. This time it was a deep, rattling cough. When he took his hand away from his mouth, there were splatters of blood on his palm.

"How long ago?" I asked him.

He sighed and pushed his sleeve up. There were three big cloth Band-Aids stretched across his forearm. They were all wet and dark. "Yesterday morning," he said. "I stepped outside and the neighbor's kid got me." He shook his head, chuckled, and it turned into a cough. "I was stupid. Should've been more careful. I just saw him by the garage and I thought he . . ." The words turned into a bout of sharp hacking.

"You're strong," I said. "Most people are bedridden by ten or twelve hours, tops."

He swung his head back at his wife and daughter. "I was out of it for a little bit," he said, "but I had to get them here. Get them safe. That was all that mattered."

"You did it," I told him. "They'll be safe here."

"You promise?"

As of this morning, we'd brought almost two thousand

people inside our urban fortress. Odds were we were going to double that in the next month. We'd already attracted about a hundred exes to every gate inside. None of us were sure if this was going to work or not.

"I'll do the best I can to keep them safe," I told him. "Them and everyone else here. I promise."

Some worry flowed out of his neck and shoulders. He sagged against the planter. "Thank you."

I shook my head. "I wish we'd gotten to you sooner. You might've . . ."

He raised a hand. "There's a lot of people in Los Angeles. You're saving everyone you can, I'm sure."

"You're really calm about this."

"You have anyone special?"

I thought about it. "Not really, I guess."

His mouth twitched into a smile. "My wife and little girl are safe," he told me. "That's all that matters to me."

He took in a breath, and it sputtered out of his lungs.

"So," he said, "what happens now?"

I'd had to do this eleven times now. All of them fought and screamed. I'd kept hoping for someone reasonable who'd understand and accept it.

Turned out it didn't make it any better.

I kicked at the ground. "You can't stay inside," I told him. "Zero tolerance for the infected. I can take you outside, drop you someplace . . . safe. Somewhere you won't be attacked."

He sighed. Something gleamed on his cheek. He was crying, but trying to keep it hidden.

"I'm sorry," I told him. It sounded weak and stupid.

He shook his head. "They're safe. That's the important thing," he repeated. "Can I say good-bye?"

"Yeah," I told him. "Of course."

He hooked his arm over my shoulders, and we walked back to the gatehouse. Most of the guards tried hard to make it look like they weren't watching. They all knew what was coming. I think they were freaked out by how calm he was, too.

I don't know what Bryan said to his wife and daughter. I'm glad I don't have some kind of super-hearing or something. They cried. They hugged. He kissed them both on the forehead. They helped him back over to me, and then they backed away.

His wife and daughter looked at me. They were devastated and pleading and holding back tears. There was no anger or hate, at Bryan or at me.

He hooked his arm around my neck again. I held him by the waist, kicked off, and we sailed up to the top of the Melrose Gate. Both of us pretended not to hear the wails and crying behind us, but I think he did a better job than me.

Another leap sent us over the street and above the studio next door. It was awkward gliding with another person, but I was getting better at it. At least he wasn't fighting me.

I kicked off the roof of a studio stage and got us higher in the air. We sailed past the studio, over a few houses, crossed another intersection, most of another block, and came down on the roof of an apartment building almost half a mile from the Mount.

The roof had a few potted plants, three wooden deck chairs, and one of those big shade umbrellas. It had been a great place to hang out once. If it wasn't for the sound of clicking teeth from the street below, it'd be peaceful.

I let go of Bryan. He looked fine now. If I hadn't seen the red on his sleeve, I wouldn't've guessed he was sick.

Then he let out a deep, hacking cough and sprayed blood on the concrete roof. His knees buckled, and he dropped onto one of the chairs. He hung his head between his legs and shook for almost a full minute.

Then he pushed himself up and looked at me. There were

spots of red on his lips and chin. "I've been holding it together so long," he said. "Feels like my body's catching up for lost time."

I pulled one of the plastic bags out of my pocket. I'd been carrying two or three of them at a time for the past week or so. In my head I called them survival packs. I was pretty sure if Stealth had caught me with them she'd've given me a lecture about wasting resources. I liked to tell myself she knew I was doing it and just wasn't saying anything until she had to.

I handed the bag to Bryan. "Here," I said.

He looked at the collection of pills and lozenges. "What's all this?"

"The round ones are aspirin," I said. "Those are cough drops. The square ones are gum. Y'know just to make your mouth feel clean. It'll help with hunger, too."

"Okay," he said. He sifted through the bag's contents as I named them, then stopped on another pill. Blue and oval. "What are these?"

"Those," I said. "Those are sleeping pills. Y'know, for if you can't sleep."

He smirked and then coughed again.

"It's not a suicide thing," I told him. "There aren't enough of them. It's just . . . if you'd rather be asleep."

"I get it." He nodded. "Thank you."

"There's some bottled water over there." I pointed in the corner of the railing. Half of it was gone, used one way or another by other people I'd brought to this rooftop. "The door leads down into the building, but there might be . . . well, exes down there."

"Right." He dropped the bag on the roof next to the chair.

"And you get a nice sunset view."

He choked down another cough. "Never been much of a sunset person."

"Sorry."

His head hung on his shoulders for a minute. "Will you really keep an eye on them? Jen and Lynne?"

I crouched next to him. "I will."

"Jen's my wife. Lynne's my daughter."

I nodded.

"And can you . . ." He took a deep breath, and it rattled in his chest. "Can you make sure they . . . that they don't run into me again? That they never see me like that?"

"If that's what you want?"

His head went up and down three times, quick. Then he turned away and coughed. He kept coughing. Some liquid streamed out of his mouth and hit the roof near the plastic bag. It was clear with streaks of red.

He hacked up a bit more. Then he rolled back onto the chair. "I think you should go," he said. "Thanks for everything. For all of this."

"I didn't do anything."

"I thought they were going to shoot me at the gate. You let me say good-bye to my family." His foot scuffed the roof near the bag. "You're giving me the option to die in peace. Thank you."

"I . . . You're welcome."

He settled his body and closed his eyes. "Just keep them safe," he said. "Please. Just keep them safe."

"I will."

I stood there for another minute and watched his breath go in and out. Each one rattled in his chest and shook its way out of his lips. Once it sputtered, and I saw two drops of red spit out.

Another minute passed, and I realized he was done with me. No more looking or talking. I couldn't blame him. Exile sucked, even if you understood why it was happening.

I found the spot between my shoulder blades, took a few steps, and launched myself off the roof.

Epilogue
NOW

MADELYN SAT ON the top of the water tower and looked down at the Mount. There was a tiny lip around the edge of the tower. Just enough to brace your heels on. She thought about crawling up to the peak and standing by the needle, but she liked sitting down.

It was a nice night. Warm. No clouds. The lights across the Mount made it look warm and friendly in the middle of the dark city.

She'd woken up two hours ago in her room. There'd been a wet suit by her bed somebody had ripped in half, some clothes that smelled like brine, and a note to be on top of the water tower by nine o'clock. It was her own handwriting, including the upside-down ampersand she drew in the corner sometimes to prove a message was really from herself.

She skimmed her journals and read about a mission out to an island, a night in a life raft, an island made of ships, some creep watching her undress, and fish stew. Then the entries jumped two days ahead and talked about Nautilus, exes, being torn in half, most of the people on the ship-island being jerks, Barry almost killing himself to save Los Angeles from a submarine that was going to launch a nuclear missile, and spending the night on an old yacht in the middle of the ocean on the way home while Barry went on ahead.

There was a full-length mirror on her closet door. Madelyn stood in front of it and looked at the smooth, unmarked skin of her stomach. No wounds. No scars. Not even scabs or stretch marks.

She'd pulled some clothes on while she read the journal entries again. There were enough of her tics and shortcuts to know she'd been trying to cover a lot in very little time.

And now she sat alone, watching people wander around below the water tower and wondering why she'd told herself to climb up to the top of the water tower.

"He should be here shortly," said a voice behind her.

"Ahhh!" She bounced and almost slipped over the lip.

Stealth stood at the tower's peak. Her cloak swirled around her in the breeze without making a sound. Beneath her hood, her masked face seemed to look at the Corpse Girl.

"Hi," said Madelyn.

"Good evening."

"You scared me for a second there."

Stealth said nothing.

"He who?"

"St. George. He left this afternoon on an errand. I expect him back in the next four minutes."

Madelyn smiled. "Four exactly?"

"Assuming he keeps a constant speed and does not alter his course, yes."

She thought about questioning that, but shrugged it off. "So where'd he go?"

Stealth turned her head and looked off toward the hills and the distant mountains. "He did not say. But judging from his trajectory, I believe I have an idea."

"Where?"

"That is for him to say."

Stealth was a statue at the top of the water tower. Madelyn thought about climbing up the slope to join her, then decided against it.

"Is Barry okay?"

"He is in intensive care," said the cloaked woman, "two floors above your room. He weighed ninety-seven pounds when he reverted to human form. He has lost significant muscle mass, all of his hair, and his finger- and toenails. He displayed several symptoms of imminent myocardial infarction, but Doctor Connolly has managed to control these."

"Is he going to be okay?"

Stealth crossed her arms under her cloak. Madelyn wondered how the woman was standing so straight and still on the sloped surface while a breeze tugged at her cape.

"He may not be able to transform into Zzzap for some time without putting himself at risk," Stealth said. "Once his condition stabilizes, he will need to regain much of the mass he has lost."

"Oh." She tapped her fingers on the top of the water tower. It echoed like a big drum.

Two uncomfortably silent minutes later, St. George came soaring out of the night sky.

Madelyn laughed and looked up at Stealth. "How did you do that?"

St. George pushed his goggles up onto his forehead and looked at her. "Do what?"

Stealth said nothing.

He hung in the air in front of Madelyn. "I've got something for you," he said. "If I'd known, I would've gotten them sooner."

"Gotten what?"

He unzipped his brown leather flight jacket and pulled out a manila envelope. It bulged a bit in the middle. He held it out, and Madelyn leaned forward to take it.

The envelope was filled with photographs. Thirty or forty of them in different sizes. She pulled a few out and angled them to catch the moonlight. The top one in her hand showed a dark-haired, brown-skinned woman in her thirties sitting at a desk in front of a laptop.

"Who's this?" Madelyn shuffled the picture to the back. The next one was the same woman smiling, caught in the moment just after a laugh. The photo after that showed a man with a beard and glasses holding a baby in his arms.

Then there were two ten-year-old girls doing homework together at the table. One of them had dark hair and eyes like the woman in the other photos. The other girl was blond, with a ponytail that ran out of frame.

"Is that me?" Madelyn held the picture up to the light. "Is that me when I was alive?"

"Captain Freedom told me that your father kept lots of pictures of you in his office out at Project Krypton," said St. George. "I think I got all of them. There's a bunch of you, your dad, a couple with friends. A lot with your mom."

"My mom?" She flipped through the next few photos and found herself back at the front of her small handful. The woman at the desk. The woman smiling.

"There's a couple of the two of you together, too. And some of the whole family."

Madelyn slid the pictures back into the envelope and stood up. Then she threw herself off the water tower and wrapped her arms around St. George's neck. He grabbed her by the waist and floated back to the top of the tower. "Easy."

"Thank you," she whispered. "Thank you so much." She pulled back and smiled at him. A tear slid away from her chalk eyes.

"You're welcome," he said.

She stood there, smiling, and then glanced up at the cloaked woman. "I should go and let you two talk or ... whatever."

"Be careful on the way down," he said. "No more sudden jumps."

"Sorry." She swung her legs onto the ladder. "Thank you."

He smiled at her and nodded.

Madelyn vanished down the ladder. The sound of her boots on the rungs faded to distant vibrations. Then those were gone, too.

"You have a new coat," Stealth said.

"Yeah." He tugged at the lapels of the flight jacket and smelled saltwater. "A goodwill exchange with Eliza, the woman who's running Lemuria now. She's about my size, and we each liked the other's coat better."

"Are you confident they have Nautilus confined?"

"I don't think he wants to escape," said St. George. "Having everything collapse on him all at once like that, having the truth all come out, I think it kind of broke him. Last I saw him, he was just sitting in the *Queen*'s brig in his human form. Wouldn't even look at me. Eliza's got him on suicide watch."

St. George stared across Los Angeles toward the Pacific.

"You are worried about them?"

"Not them," he said. "Well, a little bit them, but I think they'll be okay once they're all ferried back to here or San Diego and better fed."

Stealth dipped her chin. "The submarine?"

"Yeah." He let his boots settle on the top of the tower near her. The breeze wrapped him in her cloak. "Nautilus had nuclear missiles. He just stumbled across a sub, and he had the power to wipe us out, just like that. If he'd fired them when he found it, we never even would've known what hit us."

"And you worry someone else may do the same."

He nodded. "There's a ton of this stuff lying around out there. We've been worrying about rifles and helmets, and for all we know there's a survivalist militia out in Colorado with a dozen Minuteman missiles or something."

"Doubtful," said Stealth. "Most Minuteman silos are located in either Montana, North Dakota, or Wyoming."

"The point is, we've been thinking the exes are our big problem, and there's tons of big problems out there. All the old ones, just waiting for someone to find them. Or, hell, just waiting for a natural disaster. What if an earthquake hits a missile silo? Or a tornado hits some CDC laboratory?"

"The world has never been a safe place," she said. "The ex-virus did not make it more so."

"I know," he said. "It's just . . . scary. Just a reminder how fast we could still lose everything."

She took his hand. "Then we shall make sure we do not," she told him.

"You sound pretty confident."

"Of course. I have the Mighty Dragon on my side."

He chuckled. "Thanks."

"That was a good thing, what you did for Madelyn."

"I should've done it ages ago. I knew she had memory problems. I knew the pictures were out there. I just didn't think how much better it would make things for her." He looked down at the Mount. "I was thinking, while I flew home, I should do this for all the Krypton soldiers. I could fly back, fill two or three duffel bags with personal belongings they left behind. Photos. Clothes. Books. Whatever they want me to grab."

She wrapped her arms around him and lowered her head to his shoulder.

"Really, we should do it for anyone we can. How many people would love to get an old wedding album or a year-book, or just some photos off their wall? Something to remember the past."

"It would be a large undertaking."

"It'd be worth it, though." The breeze filled her cloak out, then pulled it tight on them again. Beneath it, he wrapped his arms around her waist.

"You are a good man, George."

"I'm trying."

Acknowledgments

Well, I'm never doing a book like this again.

Allow me to explain.

Last year I finished up a book called *The Fold* that a lot of you have read and enjoyed. As I mentioned in its acknowledgments, it took some extra work to get that book as polished as it was. Said extra work took time. And said time cut into the schedule for writing this book, the one you're holding and reading right now.

I needed to be able to write *Ex-Isle* fast and clean with no hesitations or wrong turns. Knowing this, I made a decision. I would do something I hadn't done in years, something I swore never to do again. I would outline the book.

Now, to explain, outlines and I . . . we don't have a great history together. There were some fun flings back during our shared school years—a little dabbling, you might say—but in the end we figured out that we really weren't right for each other. If I get involved with an outline . . . well, I end up blindly following it. No matter what. Even when it's really clear that things should be going another way, I keep following the outline. It's a bad habit I've never been able to break.

It took me a while to figure out I'm much more of a pantser, as some folks like to call it. I do much better with loose guidelines and general directions than a solid map. It's a method that has done very, very well for me, overall, and some of my most popular books have had the least amount of planning behind them. If someone else happens to work well with outlines, that's fantastic. They're not for me, though. Nowadays, if an outline and I see each other at a party, we make excuses to never cross the room so we can keep the illusion of civility.

But I figured these were desperate times. And I think many of us here have gone back and done things we know we shouldn't during desperate times. I just figured this time I'd know what I was in for. I would outline the hell out of the book—every chapter, every beat, every character moment. But I'd also remember that I had a say in it and watch out for the traps and blind alleys that I was following for no reason. Everything would be fine this time.

It didn't work out that way. Shocking, I know.

Oh, sure, it was fun and easy at first, but after a few weeks the outline and I were butting heads. Things slowed down and by the two-month mark we were being very passive-aggressive toward each other. And, as always happens in these cases, it's the book that gets stuck in the middle, wondering what it did wrong.

I ended up trashing about a third of what I'd done with the outline, starting over, begging my editor for more time . . . and, well, you're holding the result.

Moral of this story—if you've got a system that works for you, don't go revisiting one you know doesn't.

Especially not when you're on a deadline.

All that being said, there are a few folks who deserve some thanks for all of their help.

Mary answered questions about scurvy, nutrition, and other medical things. Also, double that thanks retroactively to her and Tansey, who both helped me with the original science behind Project Krypton's super-soldiers.

Thom gave me so much information about submarines I felt guilty not using more of it. Marcus answered random questions about military terminology at all hours.

The Eden garden is loosely based off the Sepulveda Garden Center just north of Los Angeles. I spent many hours walking back and forth through the garden plots, occasionally asking questions of different folks, and getting answers that ranged from enthusiastic to mildly horrified. There were also a few odd looks as I bounced myself against the back fence again and again.

Any mistakes or flaws are entirely my own, some deliberate for narrative reasons and some because I wasn't clever enough to understand what was being explained to me.

David and John both looked at an early draft and caught a lot of things that my outline-scarred eyes could no longer see.

My agent, David, set things up so I could continue the Ex series with a little break to write *The Fold*.

My editor, Julian, is clearly the most patient man in the publishing industry. He forced his way through a barely-over-the-outline-breakup draft of this book, then gave me a chance to turn it into the (hopefully) much more entertaining book you're holding.

Finally, many thanks to my lovely lady, Colleen, who reads early drafts, indulges my long rants with absolutely no references, puts up with my whining and anxiety, makes sure I don't forget anything, and somehow sees all of this as some kind of a positive in her life. No, I don't know how, either. But I'm very thankful and happy for it.

—P.C.
Los Angeles, October 21, 2015
(*Back to the Future* Day!)

ALSO BY
PETER CLINES

"The Avengers meets *The Walking Dead,*
with a large order of epic served on the side."

—Ernest Cline, *New York Times* bestselling author
of *Armada* and *Ready Player One*

B \ D \ W \ Y

Available wherever books are sold